THE CYBORG TINKERER

THE CURIOUS CASE OF THE CYBORG CIRCUS
BOOK ONE

MEG LaTORRE

To Kevin, the man who convinced me dreams don't have to wait.

PRAISE FOR THE CYBORG TINKERER

"The Cyborg Tinkerer puts the 'steam' in steampunk and subverts romantic tropes in the most refreshing and unexpected way possible."

– Jenna Moreci, Bestselling Author of *The Savior's Champion*

"The Cyborg Tinkerer is an epic sci-fi, steampunk mash-up of intergalactic proportions. Full of love, lust, battles, and seduction. It will keep you turning the pages all night long."

– Sacha Black, Bestselling Fantasy and Nonfiction Author and Podcaster

"A twisty thrill-ride crackling with sexual tension and macabre secrets. Combining a high-stakes competition, steampunk spacefaring, and an undercurrent of dark fairy tales, this is an adventure you don't want to miss!"

– Claire Winn, Author of *City of Shattered Light*

"In *The Cyborg Tinkerer*, Cinder [*The Lunar Chronicles*] is all grown up and finds herself in the middle of a Hunger Games-esque, steampunk, action-packed adventure."

– Elliot Brooks, Author of *Peace and Turmoil* and BookTuber

"Meg LaTorre is a writer to watch."

– Michael Mammay, Author of *Planetside*

TRIGGER WARNINGS

This novel contains graphic violence, sexual content, profanity, and references to eating disorders. Reader discretion is advised.

CHAPTER 1

Sometimes, death required a change of scenery.

Gwendolyn Grimm marched up the warped, wooden steps of the *Crusty Tulip*. As she shouldered her pack, a single thought formed in her mind.

Good fucking riddance.

She wouldn't miss being the ship tinkerer on this creaking bucket of soured engines and deflated tits for sails.

Men scurried about the partially open deck of the ship, dashing up rope ladders to tend to the rigging. The sails bloomed with the force of the solar winds ushering them to their next destination, Anchorage. The small, manufacturing moon belched a welcoming plume of smog out toward space, which bounced off the moon's artificial gravity field—and back toward its residents.

A woman appeared beside Gwen on the main deck, carrying her own pack.

"Why didn't you come to my cot last night?" Alberta cooed, her red lips parted and cracked from too many days on low water rations.

It was tradition to find a partner below deck before

coming to port, but Gwen hadn't exactly been in the mood. "I'm kind of busy dying."

According to the asinine doctor on the last planet they'd ported on, she had a few months left to live.

Alberta crossed her arms. "Isn't that more reason to enjoy your final days?"

Although Alberta's tone was playful, Gwen could feel the heat behind it.

Quit being a pussy, her erstwhile bedmate seemed to say. *It's only a brain tumor.*

This was precisely why Gwen wasn't big on making friends in the workplace—and why she hadn't bothered to get to know anyone on the ship. It was also why she would soon be dying... alone.

"You sure this is where you want to hop off?" Alberta asked with uncharacteristic concern. "Why not head home to your family?"

Gwen shook her head. "I'd be dead before I made it back to Orthodocks."

She didn't have enough time to journey to her home planet on the opposite side of the Crescent Star System. The *Crusty Tulip* wouldn't be setting a course that way for another six months. Let her family think she was off adventuring in the galaxy somewhere.

All that was left to do was find a place where she could afford a room for a few months. Anchorage was as good a place as any.

A pang of loneliness bolted through her, but she shook it off.

It wasn't time for regrets just yet. First, she had some living to do. Maybe she would find someone to fuck the time away with. Perhaps she just needed a palate cleanser to get her in the mood again. It'd been months since she'd bedded a man. At the very least, there had to be decent underground gambling on this skanky-as-fuck moon.

The captain's first mate appeared, giving Gwen her final pay. "Nice working with you, Ms. Grimm."

Was that pity in his eyes? It couldn't be. Gwen hadn't told anyone except Alberta why she was leaving, and Alberta wasn't a gossip.

Frowning, Gwen nodded her head in return.

Around them, the *Crusty Tulip*'s gravitational and oxygen fields shimmered before falling when they entered Anchorage's artificial gravity. The wooden docks stuck straight out from the moon, and the sailors threw out lines, which the crew on the docks caught, securing the ship.

And a good fucking life to you, Gwen thought as she pulled goggles over her eyes and a scarf over her mouth and nose. She disembarked with a nod of farewell to Alberta and the life she'd known before. The crew wouldn't stay more than a night before moving on to their next destination.

Wondering what the hell one does on a manufacturing moon with mere months left to live, Gwen headed for her customary cheap inn near the docks. As she paid off the greasy innkeeper, he hissed under his breath. "Did you hear? Cirque du Borge is in town."

Gwen raised an eyebrow, unbelieving. "I thought the cyborg circus had been run out of the Crescent Star System."

Ten years ago, Cirque du Borge had been the most famous of all circuses. They had traveled from planet to planet, unannounced. Every show sold out, every person eager to see the performances beyond the capability of man alone—to see what was possible with both man and machine.

That had been before the thirteen planets of the Crescent Star System formed the Union and the emperor created the Cyborg Prohibition Law. This law made the creation of new cyborgs, the use of surgical implants, and the use of robots for surgery *very* illegal.

It didn't make existing cyborgs illegal, just the social equivalent of having machine fleas. No one was eager to hire cyborgs for work—or entertainment, for that matter—and all manufacturing of cyborg implants had been shut down.

This law was the very same reason Gwen had no way of addressing the oversized resident in her skull. Without the funds to travel outside of the Crescent Star System *and* pay for a pricey surgery, she now knew what she intended to do with her final pay.

The innkeeper shrugged, pocketing Gwen's payment. "They're set up deep in the storage yard."

"Good to know." Gwen passed another mark to the man.

"Best be keeping quiet." The man grabbed a soiled rag, wiping the counter. "Wouldn't want the feds hearing about it. Anyone caught at that circus will spend time behind bars. Mark my words."

Indeed, the feds never messed around when it came to the "cyborg threat."

Nodding, Gwen left to deposit her belongings in her room.

Although Anchorage wasn't nearly as cold as deep space, Gwen didn't bother to change out of her usual trousers, leather jacket, and magnetic boots. She washed her face, then combed her long brown hair and put it in a respectable bun.

As always, her fingers felt for the tumor beneath her skull, though she knew she'd find nothing. A sudden pang of envy clapped against Gwen's consciousness—envy that no one else had an internal clock turning ever closer to eternal midnight.

Within months, she would pass out of existence.

Would anyone remember her?

It had been years since Gwen had communicated with her family, and she had no close friends to speak of—courtesy of taking tinkering jobs on new ships nearly every year.

A nameless anger surged inside her like a raging solar storm. She removed her homemade and questionably legal skimmer from her bag, assembling it in moments. Then she kicked the engine on in her second-story room at the inn, smoke billowing all around her, before leaping out the window and riding into the night.

For the thousandth time that day, she reminded herself there would be time for regrets later.

Now it was time to see if the cyborg circus was as spectacular as rumors claimed.

She soared low over the town, careful to keep out of sight of the main thoroughfare—and the feds. Only Union-grade hover boards were permitted within this galaxy, and only government employees were to ride them, naturally. But racers, like Gwen, were known to create their own boards that could be broken down and hidden in a bag to transport without detection.

The storage yard where the circus was located was a short ride on the skimmer from the inn.

As she weaved between stacks of rusted storage crates, the sound of bells and lyres rose above the smoggy air. Turning a corner, a massive tent of silver and white appeared before her.

Gwen gaped.

Even with the tears in the fabric, it was easy to see it had once been made for extravagance. The sections of the tent not covered in streaks of atmospheric grime or stark slashes bore an unmistakable shimmer as though the fabric contained traces of silver and crushed pearl.

Several smaller tents branched off the massive one. Strange-looking guards in top hats and masks were stationed outside every entrance.

Gwen dismounted and stashed her skimmer behind one of the storage crates before joining the line waiting to enter the center tent.

Dozens of lowlife sailors, dockworkers, barmaids, wenches, and other friendly types talked excitedly amongst themselves. With the exception of the cyborgs, of course, who stood quietly at the back of the line.

Poor bastards aren't even welcome at a cyborg circus.

In front of her, a man spoke excitedly to his comrade. "I've heard rumors of the ringleader who can bend cyborg beasts to his will, magicians who can pluck your soul straight from your chest, firebreathers who need no torch, and acrobats who tumble skillfully beneath the sheets."

Gwen rolled her eyes as the men elbowed each other. Had she not received her unfortunate diagnosis, she would have done just about anything to see if the latter was true.

She might still. She had a few months to kill, so perhaps the mood would strike her.

Eventually, she stood before the tent flap and passed money to a masked guard. The mute soldier gestured for her to enter.

As she strode inside, her breath whooshed out.

Dozens of miniature stages were set up across the tent. All shimmered as brightly as polished brass or were covered in glitter.

On the center stage, what must be the entire cast moved in a group number, their cyborg limbs and other implants flashing brightly in the spotlights. They moved with an otherworldly grace, flipping and spinning through the air. They didn't shy away from what made them different. They were both man and machine.

And fucking proud of it.

Realizing her mouth hung open, Gwen snapped it shut.

She watched in mute wonder as the performers completed the number before separating and striding to the individual stages throughout the room. Following the audience weaving in the spaces between the stages, she lingered in front of one performance and then the next, eager to see everything. Above it all, musicians trilled a quick melody.

Every stage bore more extravagance, more daring performances than the last.

On one stage, a cyborg juggled wooden batons larger than himself. On another stage, a contortionist with a cyborg foot encased herself in a small box. Far above the stages, two acrobats moved through a trapeze performance. As she watched, the woman released the rope and flew freely through the air for an impossibly long time before the man caught her and the two swung toward the opposite platform.

In here, it was almost possible to forget she was dying. Almost.

As she neared another stage, she blinked before nodding in appreciation.

An arctic bear, a tiger, and an albino wolf prowled in circles around a man garbed in a black suit with white pinstripes and a matching top hat. The ringleader seemed rather disinclined to reflect upon his mortal state as the wolf snorted and shook its head, revealing massive metal canines.

Each performance she saw was a beautiful ode to death— or perhaps in defiance of it.

How poetic.

Eventually, she ended up before a small stage with a slackline set up between two poles secured onto either side of the stage.

When she looked up, her eyes fell upon the most beautiful creature she'd seen yet in Cirque du Borge's tent of wonders.

A woman perched atop one of the posts at one end of the slackline. Slowly, she raised her arms to either side of her. As she did, the lights caught the curve of her full hips, the warmth of her light brown skin, and the glint of mischief in her dark eyes.

Without warning, the acrobat launched forward, catching the slackline in one human and one cyborg hand before flipping neatly onto the opposite post.

Nicely fucking done.

As though sensing her, the woman's gaze turned and fell directly on Gwen.

Hot damn. Those cheekbones could cut out a woman's heart.

As Gwen's mouth dried, a woman appeared beside her, lingering in front of the slackline stage. By the look of her grease-stained trousers, she probably worked in the manufacturing district.

"What brings you here, beautiful?"

"Death," Gwen muttered softly. In a louder voice, she said, "Just looking to pass the time."

The woman nodded, closing the distance between them. Slowly, she wrapped one arm around Gwen's waist. "I know one way we could pass the time."

Gwen's stomach turned even as the flesh between her legs awoke. Desire swam through her. She didn't fight as the nameless woman's lips pressed to hers.

I'm more than a corpse. I'm not dead yet.

The woman's lips tasted of cheap ale and smoke. Bringing her arm up, Gwen wrapped it casually around her neck as she parted eager lips with her tongue.

"Come with me." The woman took Gwen's hand, leading her to a secluded spot outside of the tent.

They didn't take long to pick up where they left off.

Within moments, they were gasping.

Gwen pulled the woman's blouse free from her trousers, slipping her hand up to cup small breasts. Nipples hardened beneath her touch. She traced a line of kisses down the woman's neck, nibbling salty flesh.

Hands loosened Gwen's belt, fingers running along her waist. Then the fingers slipped beneath her pants, teasing slowly at her entrance. The next moment, they were inside her, plunging in and out, a thumb caressing Gwen's clit in slow circles.

Even as she felt herself growing wet from desire, hips moving in rhythm with the woman's fingers, Gwen's mind retreated.

What the fuck is wrong with you? You have a very willing woman in front of you. The Grim Reaper can wait.

But Gwen couldn't focus on the beautiful woman or what she was offering. All she could think about was her inevitable end and the worms—rather than fingers or cocks—about to fill her vagina. And no quick finger fuck in a questionably discreet public area would change that.

Suddenly, a sharp whistle blew.

Fuck, Gwen thought. *Already?*

A hush descended and a moment of tense silence passed. Then voices in the tent behind them shouted in unison.

"Feds!"

The woman ripped her hand free of Gwen's pants. Without a word of farewell, she turned and ran for the storage yard.

Hordes of people swelled from the circus's main entrance, scrambling over each other in their rush to get away.

Gwen quickly belted her pants and bolted toward the storage crate where she'd stashed her skimmer. Her head swam as nausea and bile rose up her throat in tandem. Shaking it off as best she could, she pushed through the swell of bodies. Eventually, she made it to where she'd stashed the skimmer.

Kicking the engine to life, she took to the sky.

Streaks of another rising moon revealed a copper city beyond the loading docks and storage fields, pocketed with alleys and massive generators with clicking gears.

As suspected, the feds shouted at her, demanding she disembark her vehicle, but she didn't listen. Flying low between stacks of storage crates, she tried to lose the feds flying on Union-grade hoverboards.

At the edges of her sight, she caught a flash of movement and heard the humming of engines.

Beyond the storage yard, plumes of inky smoke puffed into the air above brick towers and turning wheels and mills. Smoke bounced off the gravitational field and skirted back toward the moon's surface. If she could get to that smoke, she would be home free. There was no way the feds could keep track of her in there. Gwen pressed her goggles snugly against her eyes and tightened her neck scarf over her mouth.

Before she could clear the storage yard, inky blackness crept down over her vision.

Panic surged through her veins.

Not now.

Of all times to have an episode from her illness, why *now*?

A wave of dizziness washed over her. Her body felt strangely light, and she tilted sideways. Eyelids heavy, she fought as they fluttered closed.

It was a fight she knew she'd lose.

Her grip on the board loosened, and she fell into open air.

For a moment, she thought she'd float endlessly, as weightless as open space.

Too soon, the jagged edges of the crates scraped against her leather jacket as she bounced atop several more. She skidded to a stop on the ground. Nearby, her board's engine had clicked off as it slammed somewhere in the storage yard.

Gwen tried to lift her head but couldn't. Pain thrummed behind her eyes, and her heartbeat slammed in her ears. But the pain didn't drown out the protests of men and women as louder voices infused with authority read out rights, demanded permits, and shot pistols.

The throbbing in Gwen's head drummed in time with the growing chaos.

Get the fuck up or you'll be next.

It was no use. Her arms and legs were trembling noodles, and a headache glanced between her temples, blurring her vision. She was in no condition to run, let alone fly.

Fear bolted through her at the thought of spending her final days being interrogated—to die from poor treatment and not her brain tumor.

A squad of feds on hoverboards appeared above her, and they weren't alone.

More feds escorted countless cyborg laborers on foot. Their faces were bruised and bloodied. Interestingly, there were far fewer of their human counterparts—none of whom seemed nearly as roughed up as the cyborgs.

But all were cuffed. All would be deposited into cells.

Sighing, Gwen nodded to the nearest feds, ignoring the fear squeezing her chest. "Hello, officers."

Without further preamble, she blacked out.

CHAPTER 2

Gwen kicked the railing of her bed with her white prison-grade sneakers. "Shut up!"

Head pounding, she wasn't sure if she was well enough to get up from the metal bunk bed. But she *was* well enough to hear her cellmate snoring loud enough to wake the dead—or the dying, in Gwen's case.

The top bunk creaked as a massive body rolled over in sleep. The frame shook, and for a moment, Gwen wondered if the entire thing would collapse on top of her.

When the feds dumped her into this cell, they had declared she would get the formerly occupied bottom bed due to her illness. Doctors examined her on the way into Anchorage's prison, declaring what she already knew: she had a fatal brain tumor. As such, she was prone to bouts of nausea, dizziness, and death.

Her neighborly cellmate had done her the courtesy of pissing herself in the bottom bunk before vacating.

But the generosity didn't stop there.

The feds notified Gwen of her posted bail—fifty thousand marks. A bail only the wealthiest merchant or high lords could afford. Associating with cyborgs without permits was one of the Union's highest offenses. As such, the feds intended to make an example of the schlepps who were too slow or too busy dying to get away. It was either pay the bail or wait it out in prison for one year.

At least paying for a room at the inn was no longer an issue.

Gwen's stomach twisted as she thought of the family she'd never see again.

She might have taken an apprenticeship on a departing merchant vessel five years ago—leaving Orthodocks and her family behind—but it didn't mean she didn't care about her parents or siblings. Country life suited them, but she hadn't been made for a quiet life on the most conservative planet in the Union. So, she'd left, and she hadn't seen them since.

Thankfully, they had parted on good terms. Her parents and siblings had wished her well and made her promise to write. She had only done so sparingly, though, courtesy of never being on a single planet or moon for long—and never long enough to receive mail.

A deep sorrow swelled in Gwen's chest, and she struggled to take a deep breath.

Footsteps pattered down the hallway.

Gwen looked up. With the single light bulb in her shared cell, she could see the empty hallway through the barred window in the cell door. The guard on duty wasn't due to walk down their hallway for some time yet, if their previous rotations were any indication.

A strange clicking accompanied the soft pattering of footsteps. Step, step-*click*. Step, step-*click*. That was followed by the familiar shuffle of the guard's heavy steps and clinking of keys.

The sound drew nearer until it stopped. A guard's face appeared beyond the barred door. Hinges creaked as her cell door was unlocked from the outside. The light of bare bulbs from the hallway fell harshly on two men in the doorway, the latter a tall gentleman dressed in formal dinner attire. He wore black dress pants and a vest with faint white pinstripes, a white button-up shirt, a red tie, and a top hat. Over his arm was a black jacket with matching pinstripes and countless pockets and gears. In his hand he held a black cane covered in intricate patterns and topped with a bright red gemstone at the end of a curved handle.

That explained the clicking.

Gwen didn't bother to get up from where she lay on her bottom bunk. Not that she could, anyway. The nausea and persistent headaches had yet to go away since the feds had brought her in.

"Do you need anything else, my lord?" the guard asked, hand already on the cell door.

A what now?

What was a lord doing in a dank dungeon cell on Anchorage? No one of importance came to this moon.

"No," the lordly man said. "That will be all."

"Not sure why you'd want to see this dreadful lot, sir, but call if you need anything." The guard spoke with unusual politeness before leaving and locking the door behind him.

Slowly, the man turned, surveying the room.

The light bulb's eerie luminescence revealed sharp features —shortly cropped black hair, olive skin, and dark eyes— hidden beneath the shadows of his hat. Despite the fancy-as-fuck clothes, he reminded her of a wild animal.

In a single movement, his eyes swept over the room: a set of bunks, one toilet, one sink, one desk, and one stool. Nothing his type was likely accustomed to. Seeing as the only other options for a seat were to either cozy up on the bottom bunk next to Gwen or the floor, the man lowered himself onto the stool without a word.

What would a man dressed in formal cocktail attire want with Gwen or her roommate in the middle of the night? Her thoughts stopped as she swallowed back bile, waiting for the room to settle as another wave of dizziness washed over her.

"If you're here to glean end-of-life wisdom, you might as well leave now," Gwen said into the silence. "I have no message from the Reaper to share with you."

Speaking was more effort than she cared to think about, leaving her nauseous.

The man sniffed but didn't immediately reply. Instead, he pulled a small scroll from his pocket. Unfurling it, he read: "Gwendolyn Grimm of Orthodocks. The Union's lead ship tinkerer and only twenty-five. Got your first job as an apprentice and have since traveled to eight of the Union's thirteen planets."

The hair on Gwen's arms prickled. She hadn't told the feds her name when they had arrested her to keep her family from learning the truth. There should be no way he could know any of this.

"Diagnosed with a brain tumor, late stage. According to the fools running this prison, you have a few weeks left to live."

Gwen pulled herself to a seated position on her bunk, nearly puking on the bleached floor from her effort. She looked the man in the eye, surprised by the barely restrained power in his gaze. "I don't believe we've been formally introduced."

Beneath the shadows of his top hat, the man was unflinching under her glare. "Do you want to live, Ms. Grimm?"

Gwen flinched as though slapped.

She was dying. Advanced surgery could save her, but no one would risk the wrath of the emperor and Union. It would mean certain death or very uncomfortable life sentences in prison for all involved.

"No sane person wants to die," she replied.

He leaned forward on the stool, casually resting his wrists

atop his cane. "What if I told you there was a way to heal you from your sickness?" The man paused for a heartbeat before adding, "How much are your memories worth to you?"

Gwen sighed heavily. It would seem the only way to die in peace and quiet around here was to indulge this man. "All right, mister...?"

"Kabir," he said. "My name is Bastian Kabir."

Gwen stiffened, growing suddenly still.

Sitting before her was the ringleader of Cirque du Borge.

Every time she'd heard whisperings of the circus in the past decade, his name was paired with it. Yet looking at him, he couldn't be much older than she was. She wondered if cyborgs aged differently.

How had this bastard escaped the feds and impersonated a lord? Moreover, why bother? The circus should be long gone from Anchorage by now. And they would have had to pay a hefty bail of their own.

Seeing the recognition in her eyes, Bastian smiled. "Good. You've heard of me."

But it was more than that. She'd *seen* this man before.

His black suit with pinstripes and matching top hat were strangely familiar.

He was the idiot on stage with the cyborg animals. The man surrounded by the arctic bear, albino wolf, and tiger.

Standing, Bastian walked over to the bunk. For a moment, she thought he neared her to speak. Instead, he poked her cellmate with the end of his cane. Her snoring caught for a moment before resuming once more.

"We are looking for someone with your particular set of skills, Ms. Grimm. As you can imagine, all machines require tinkering over time."

Gwen blinked, her mind reeling. Was he offering her a *job*? She was dying, for stars' sake. She felt tempted to lie back down on her scented bunk and close her eyes, pretending the Reaper had come. It seemed like the only way she could rid herself of Mr. Kabir and die in relative peace.

"All our employees are required to sign a thirteen-year contract," he continued. "For the duration of your contract, you will be a full-time employee and provided with food, lodging, and compensation. You will be granted free time to spend as you wish, though this will vary depending on the time of our performances."

Bastian strode back to the stool and reseated himself. Despite the shadows marring his face, fervor lurked behind his gaze. "During your contracted time at Cirque du Borge, you are prohibited from contacting your family or friends, and you may never share any information regarding the circus and its operations."

Exhaling heavily, Gwen rubbed the bridge of her nose. "I'm dying, Mr. Kabir, as you so kindly pointed out. A tinkerer on a deadline such as mine isn't the most reliable employee."

Bastian waved a hand in dismissal before removing black leather gloves from his pocket and pulling them on. "We can remove the brain mass, and we have medications that can assure it will never grow back. With our lead scientists, we'll have you good as new. But you'll be different at the end of it." He looked up from his gloves. "You'll be one of us. As a cyborg, you will lose your human memories over time."

Gwen couldn't help it. She laughed. She laughed so fucking hard she got hiccups and then vomited on the floor.

Wiping her mouth, she looked up at the revered Bastian Kabir, whose nose scrunched in distaste.

"If I didn't know any better, I'd say you're eager to share my cell, Mr. Kabir. You know as well as I do that advanced surgeries were outlawed years ago."

Bastian sniffed. "I didn't think you particularly cared for Union laws. Not after the venture that led to your current predicament."

"Laws are far less applicable when you're dying."

"What's the difference now?"

She hesitated.

What was the difference? Only minutes ago, she'd thought she'd spend her last days in a prison cell infused with the smell of urine and in the company of a short-tempered cellmate. She'd thought her life was over, and she'd never work as a tinkerer again. Now, when a second chance waltzed into her cell in crisp black leather boots and a pinstripe suit, she hesitated.

One thing she knew for certain—she loved working as a tinkerer, and she was fucking fabulous at it. Solving challenges were her bread and butter. Could she leave her life and reputation as Gwendolyn Grimm, the best ship tinkerer in the Union, behind?

The authorities knew her name, so they would be aware of her condition. They'd never hire her on again. What did that mean for the years after her contract was up? No one would want to hire a cyborg, regardless of her skills. That is, if the feds or other local authorities didn't discover her true identity and sentence her to death for breaking the Cyborg Prohibition Law.

Beyond that, what would becoming a cyborg do to her? Would it change her mind or how she thought? Perhaps she'd simply forget her past life and go on as she always had. But how could you be the same person without your memories?

If what Bastian proposed was true, he offered a way to evade death. It was either join the circus and maybe create a new life for herself afterward or die in this cell.

There was no choice for her.

"What—" Gwen cleared her throat and tried again. "What happens at the end of the thirteen years?"

The light bulb's harsh light glinted off Bastian's square, white teeth.

That smile said one thing: He had her, and he knew it.

"You are free to do as you please. Most performers and

circus staff choose to stay on at Cirque du Borge, but that's entirely up to you." He stood then, extending a hand to her. "I'll offer this once, and only once. Would you like to join Cirque du Borge, Ms. Grimm?"

With a sigh, Gwen took his hand. "I hope you have fifty thousand marks to pay my bail. Because I sure as hell don't."

Gwen leaned heavily on Bastian's arm as they exited the prison.

Lord Bartholomew Blight had paid Clara Cabbell's bail, as they were old acquaintances and he'd been passing through Anchorage when he'd heard of his friend's predicament. Or that's the story they'd told the jailer.

It felt good to have her own clothes on again. One of Bastian's associates with a mechanical arm—that was barely concealed by an oversized trench coat—carried Gwen's skimmer as they walked out the front doors of the detention center and into the dark street.

How had he convinced the jailers to return her illegal skimmer to her, and with the engine still attached, no less?

It was hard to believe she'd lived rent-free for less than one day.

Occupied with watching her steps and remaining upright, Gwen didn't notice the carriage until the door swung open in front of her. Like Bastian's cane, the horse-drawn carriage was covered in intricate carvings on the outside. Inside, there were cushioned red seats. Though nothing marked the outdated vehicle as Cirque du Borge's property.

She hadn't been in an actual carriage with horses since the remembrance festivals on Orthodocks. Most travel was by train, steam-powered cars, one's own feet, or by ship when journeying between planets.

The closer she looked... she could have sworn the horses had metal teeth and gleaming steel horseshoes.

She looked at the ringleader. "How... charming."

"Only the best for our new cyborg tinkerer."

Skidding to a halt, she resisted Bastian's arm as he tried to usher her inside. "What do you mean *cyborg* tinkerer? I'm a ship tinkerer. Those are two very different things. Cyborg tinkerers supposedly studied as doctors, and I'm no doctor. And I don't know a damn thing about biology."

"You'll learn on the job."

A hand unceremoniously shoved her into the carriage before Bastian took a seat beside her.

They rode in silence. Gwen's mind reeled, her thoughts processing slowly through the fog of pain.

Suddenly, her unbound hair floated toward the ceiling. Glancing out her window, she realized they were at the docks at the edge of Anchorage's gravitational field.

The carriage slowed to a stop, and the door opened.

"We're leaving?"

Bastian nodded. "You didn't think we'd perform surgery in Union territory, did you? That would be illegal."

Her mouth hung ajar.

Those sly bastards.

The Cyborg Prohibition Law prohibited advanced surgeries or the creation of new cyborgs within the Union's territory—*on* one of the thirteen planets. The law said nothing about the space between those planets. Not that the argument would hold much weight during a trial.

With Bastian's help, she stepped out of the carriage. Sweat beaded on her temples, and her stomach churned, nauseous from the bumpy ride. Before her, the docks seemed to stretch endlessly toward space.

Not long ago, she'd exited the *Crusty Tulip*, ready to spend her final days on Anchorage. Now, she was leaving the manufacturing moon and about to start a new life—as a cyborg.

At the end of the ridiculously long dock was a massive warship with white sails.

She swallowed reflexively.

What the hell was she thinking? Did she really want to become one of the Union's most hated people? Cyborgs who couldn't find work were forced to live in the slums of cities— alley sweepers, garbage collectors, or just straight-up beggars. This Bastian might whisper pretty words in her ear now, but who would want a tinkerer when her thirteen years were through? Could she wait that long to have her freedom again?

Stopping, she watched as a cyborg carried the last thing she had to her name—a skimming board—onto the ship.

By the time she reached the gangway, her heart pounded and sweat poured off her. She knew she was dying, yet the thought of becoming a cyborg somehow seemed worse.

Bastian extended a hand toward the ship. The gesture was theatrical, sweeping to encompass a ship three times the size of the *Crusty Tulip* and dotted with dozens of small, round windows. "Welcome to *Obedient*, one of Cirque du Borge's finest vessels."

"While this is sweet and all," Gwen managed, panting and vision blurring. "If we don't find me a place to sit, I might vomit on your pretty shoes."

Bastian's eyes skirted from the ship to his black boots, which were polished to a shine.

Suddenly, everything seemed darker. She started, blinking. Was the moon at its darkest tonight? From her left, everything had gone black. Realization hit her, and sheer terror seized her veins. "I can't see. My left eye—everything's black."

Bastian's voice filled with fear. "We have less time than I thought. Hurry."

Ushering her across the gangway, Bastian held on to both of her shoulders. He marched straight across the deck, not acknowledging the saluting crew as they prepared the ship for immediate takeoff. When they reached the stairs, he scooped her off her feet and hurried down.

Voices shouted above the hum of the starting engine.

Gwen closed her eyes and must have passed out. The next thing she knew, she lay on her stomach atop a metal table in a large, open room. Several light bulbs illuminated the cabin. Coarse fabric scratched her skin, and she looked down, realizing she wore a white gown and her skin was scrubbed clean. Around her, four people in surgeon's garb and masks cleaned instruments, which they placed on another table beside her. But she didn't have eyes for any of it. All she saw were the gears, plates, chips, and a massive battery.

Cyborg implants.

Now that they were no longer manufactured, cyborg implants were easily worth millions of marks. Where had they gotten such rare technology?

Panic tightened her chest as she realized her vision in her left eye was completely gone. Not even shadows. Tears pricked her eyes.

Bastian hovered in the corner of the room like an angry storm cloud with his arms crossed. In the artificial light, his dark, almost animalistic grace hadn't faded, but instead seemed more prominent. Intelligence marked thoughtful brown eyes, but his olive skin seemed to stretch over the landscape of his body, hollowing at his cheeks.

He looked like a man who hadn't eaten in days.

The door to the room opened, and a woman with bright red hair strode through, wearing authority like a birthright.

"Mistress." Bastian bowed his head as several of the surgeons assisted her in pulling on clean surgeon's clothes.

"This had better be worth it." Her voice was clipped. "I was in the middle of a surgery with one of our lions."

"I assure you, Ms. Beckett, it will be." Turning to Gwen, Bastian said, "It's time. The surgeons will first remove the tumor and address any remnants of your illness before installing your cyborg mainframe—a chip at the base of your skull. Next, they will install the implant. It usually takes a few weeks until you are fully recovered, but it can take longer for new cyborgs to fully acclimate to their implants. Do you have any questions?"

As he spoke, two surgeons stood at either end of the table, pulling up long strands of fabric, which they fastened around her ankles, wrists, and over her back, pressing her tightly against the table.

Gwen immediately began sweating. "Why am I being tied down?" Her good eye flickered from the surgeons to Bastian. "More importantly, why am I still awake?"

His lips drew into a thin line. "Anesthesia interferes with the implantation of the chip. Your mind needs to be fully alert and unaltered to receive the mainframe—even if you pass out. If you're still awake after, we will sedate you."

"And you've waited until *now* to tell me?" She pulled at her restraints. "I think I prefer to die."

"Stop being dramatic. All cyborgs must go through the procedure, and most make it through."

"*Most?*"

A timely wave of nausea overtook her, and she was forced to swallow both further complaints and bile.

"Although the technology to turn men into cyborgs is advanced, it can be barbaric—at first." Bastian nodded to Ms. Beckett and then to the other surgeons. "Begin when you're ready."

I can do this. If I survived this long, I'm sure as hell not going to die now.

But as one surgeon shaved the left side of her head and cleaned the area with a disinfectant, she found herself pulling at the bonds. After a moment, a strap was placed over her head and pulled tight. Her cheek pressed into the cool, metal table.

One surgeon appeared before her, extending a leather strap. "You'll want to bite on this."

Reluctantly, she opened her mouth as her entire body trembled. The man placed the leather between her teeth.

"We will begin on three," Ms. Beckett said somewhere beyond Gwen's line of sight.

From where she was strapped down, Gwen could see the door to the cabin, which bore the intricate words: Cirque du Borge.

The circus of cyborgs.

"One, two, three—"

CHAPTER 3

Balancing atop the railing on the main deck of *Obedient*, Rora strode past the performers waiting in line to depart down the gangway.

"Get in line, bitch," a man called.

Rora spared a glance over her shoulder. Her least favorite archer scowled in her direction. "Good morning, Abrecan. I see you didn't die in your sleep." She flipped forward atop the railing and landed neatly on the gangway. "I'll just have to pray harder."

"*Fucking acrobats*. Walking around like they own the place."

His further obscenities were lost in the noise of the crowd.

Performers with rolling leather bags and packed satchels crowded the deck of the ship and the connecting series of docks, eager to return to a home they hadn't seen in months.

A home no one had expected to see for many more months.

Why were they back?

Unlike that miserable moon, Anchorage, Grandstand had its own natural gravity and fresh air that didn't smell like deep-fried roadkill.

Here, ships docked on open waters like the Ancients—

when travel was limited to sailing over the seas. The notion seemed terribly romantic.

"Rora! Slow down!" a woman called from farther back on the docks. The sound was accompanied by the loud, rhythmic thump of a rolling wardrobe.

Smiling, Rora rolled her eyes.

She knew the sound of those ungreased wheels anywhere.

Turning around, Rora spotted Marzanna and Akio trundling down the docks. As they moved, one of the wooden boards bowed from the weight, nearly dumping them into the icy waters of the bay as one of the wardrobe's wheels caught on it. With Marzanna pushing from behind and Akio pulling from the front, they yanked it free, earning disgruntled shouts from the dockworkers and sailors who'd had to jump out of their way as the wardrobe—and its two protectors—lumbered down the docks.

Rora stepped to the side, allowing other performers to pass her. As her friends approached, she said, "You do realize there are employees whose job it is to carry our larger luggage, right?"

Sweat streaked down the sides of Marzanna's face as she raised an eyebrow. "And trust our latest batch of ragamuffins with my things? I think not."

With a grunt, Marzanna and Akio heaved the rolling wardrobe forward, following the milling crowds headed toward the shore.

Eyeing the cyborg animals as their cages were unloaded from the ship, Marzanna shook her head. "Why are we back?"

Akio shrugged. "Hell if I know. Weren't we supposed to perform on Botany next?"

Marzanna sniffed. "Bastian promised us pay after that performance. They owe me for at least two months of work."

Akio chuckled. "Yeah, two months of gambling marks."

Leaning toward him as though to slap him, Marzanna narrowed her eyes but kept her hands on the rolling wardrobe. Marzanna had once been a man named Jared. But her gender and sexuality were as fluid as the waters beneath them. Over time, she'd taken on a new name.

Akio, Marzanna's partner in their trapeze performances only, was a short man with broad shoulders, near-black hair, and narrow eyes.

Despite their separate acts in the circus, the three of them had bonded over cheap ale in a lousy pub in the city of Apparatus and had been inseparable since.

At the end of the docks, a line of watchmen awaited the performers.

As ever, the paid mercenaries wore their usual dark pants and buttoned shirts along with two pistols strapped to their backs, a sword sheathed at one hip and a wooden baton at the other, and a top hat with a mask.

Not for the first time, Rora wondered why they never showed their faces. Perhaps they didn't want to be seen associating with cyborgs.

"All performers are to report to the main theater at once." Even though the words were muffled behind the watchman's mask, there was a noticeable lack of emotion as the man shouted to be heard above the noise.

What in the galaxy? They'd never been called to the theater like this before.

"Why?" someone behind Rora called.

"The Mistress has requested an audience with the entire cast immediately upon arrival." Again, the mercenary's words lacked any emotion at all.

Eyes narrowed, Rora followed the line of performers leaving the docks, shoving down a rising feeling of dread she couldn't quite explain.

They walked past storefronts to the massive castle at the center of the city. Apparatus lacked the organization of traditional Union cities, as this one centered around the needs of Cirque du Borge. Tailors, wigmakers, launderers, and makeup artists set up shops closest to the palace, with the usual bakers, butchers, blacksmiths, and the like having storefronts nearby.

Wisps of smoke lingered above sections of the city.

Had there been another dragon attack recently?

Similar to cyborgs, dragons were among the Union's undesirables. Cyborgs, dragons, and the other outcasts of society found their way to the planet of Grandstand—or were deposited onto it, in the case of the dragons.

Most dragons had been hunted down and killed over the past few centuries. But the humanitarians and wildlife specialists had fought against the extinction of dragons after the emperor's rise to power. Thus, the cyborgs had the pleasure of their company and frequent raids into the cities for food.

Looking at yet more sections of the city ravished by dragon flame, Rora wondered what they'd been thinking.

Men and women shuffled through the main gate of the palace and into the theater's open doors, which had been rolled up with a crank lever to let the performers enter more swiftly. Yet another oddity. Why not have the performers enter through the theater's main doors inside the palace?

Ropes, ladders, hoops, silks, swings, and other contraptions hung from the ceiling. Some were neatly draped over hooks on the walls while others swung freely in the open air. Boxes, trampolines, tightropes, wheels, and hollow metal balls were stacked to the side of the circular stage.

Rora and her friends took their place among the performers gathering around the main stage. Dozens more performers filed in behind them. They looked strange dressed in brightly colored civilian clothing rather than their usual performance garb.

Amongst the performers, a flash of dark leather caught

Rora's eye, and she turned. Entering the theater was a tall, lean form silhouetted by the sunlight. Even shadowed as it was, the woman's gaze seemed to mask a deeper darkness.

As the newcomer entered the theater, Rora could see she wore the clothes of a tinkerer—a leather jacket with sewn elbow patches, matching leather pants, tall boots, and a toolbelt with an assortment of tools, including welding goggles.

A new recruit.

Rora had never seen this woman before. Stars, she would have remembered that tall, sinewy figure anywhere.

Still silhouetted by the sun behind her, the woman glanced briefly at the crowd of performers—all of whom were eyeing her with barely masked interest. But she took little note of them or the ringleader trailing her as she walked into the theater with her head held high. Despite what appeared to be a dark purple circle around her right eye, the woman had flawless skin. Midnight black hair hung loose over her right shoulder.

As if sensing Rora's gaze, the tinkerer turned, revealing what type of cyborg implant she'd received.

The tinkerer's left eye was a first-grade implant that twisted and flashed as her gaze settled on Rora. Half of her head had been shaved to the scalp, and there were faint outlines where stitches must have recently dissolved.

A *very* new recruit. That scar couldn't be more than a few weeks old.

A shiver crept up Rora's spine as she remembered just what her implantation surgery had been like. More than once, she'd wished for death, despite having sought out Cirque du Borge. But she'd been determined to secure patronage as a performer—even if it meant giving up a few things.

Rora held the stranger's gaze, allowing a faint smile to touch her lips as she nodded her head in greeting.

The woman's human eye narrowed, her face devoid of expression.

And my, was it a lovely face—with or without her cyborg eye.

Again, Rora sensed a deeper darkness in the tinkerer's hardened gaze, and she couldn't help but wonder just what hardships those eyes had seen.

Bastian leaned in, whispering into her ear. Blinking, the tinkerer turned toward him. Just like that, their connection was broken. He guided the woman away, leading her to some other part of the theater, and they were both lost in the crowd.

An idea stirred in the back of Rora's mind, just beyond her conscious grasp. More than that, something else stirred. Desire tingled between her legs, so strongly she breathed in sharply. It had been years since she'd felt so carnally attracted to another person, and it had never been this immediate.

How very interesting.

Rora mulled on the encounter for the remaining time it took for all three hundred performers to enter the theater. Though her eyes roamed the crowd, her body was restless. Beside her, her friends chatted companionably.

As the last performer entered the theater, the doors rolled shut behind them, snuffing out the sunlight. Gasps echoed around the room. Heads turned toward the watchmen, who locked the doors. Before Rora could think upon the implications, a single spotlight clicked on, and she turned her gaze back toward the stage.

Celeste Beckett, Mistress of Cirque du Borge and Keeper of Beasts, stood proudly in the artificial light. Garbed in a floor-length red gown as bright as her hair, she stood at the center of the stage, shadows forming beneath sharp cheekbones. Hands clasped before her, she nodded in greeting to the room.

"Welcome home." Celeste's voice was as rich as the velvet

gown she wore. "As you may be aware, we had a change of plans in our performances, but we appreciate your flexibility."

Shadows spotted the edges of the room as dozens of watchmen stationed themselves at every exit.

What the hell was going on? Was the Mistress trying to prevent people from leaving? Rora glanced around, but the other performers only had eyes for Celeste.

With no other choice, she turned her attention back to the stage. Bastian and the entire show management team stood at attention behind the Mistress.

"We have received word from our most treasured emperor," the Mistress continued. "He will be hosting a gala and has invited Cirque du Borge to attend."

Rather than cheers from poor circus performers desperate for opportunities, the room fell utterly silent.

The emperor invited Cirque du Borge? Was this some kind of joke?

Why would the emperor seek the company of the people he so openly despised? Didn't he know how it would look? He would be seen as a hypocrite at best and a traitor to the Union's ideals at worst—ideals *he* created.

Emperor Titus Valerius had capitalized on humankind's fears, securing his place ten years ago as the leader of what had once been the warring planets of the Crescent Star System. Under his charismatic rule, they had united against their new enemy: cyborgs.

Cyborgs are modern day's greatest threat to the safety of society. These creatures are more machine than human. They are nothing but super soldiers that can be controlled by terrorists and used against the good people of the Union.

Bogus propaganda.

She'd seen the headlines from countless journalists and knew them for the garbage they were. No one could control her mind any more than they could control the mind of a human. The chip in a cyborg's brain was good only for the control of their cyborg implants and nothing more.

Not only did the emperor scare all cyborg tinkerers and experts out of the Crescent Star System, but he'd also been involved in the elimination of the original creators of cyborgs, the Bellemore family. After the emperor's rise to power, the feds went to arrest Javier and Emmeline Bellemore, the two scientists who'd created and mass manufactured cyborg technology. However, an unexplained fire destroyed the cyborg implant manufacturing facilities, laboratories, and the entire Bellemore estate and also took the life of the Bellemores.

Thus, the cyborg circus had to deal with their declining popularity and resources ever since—and lack of invitations to elite places such as the capital.

Despite her skepticism, Rora couldn't suppress the flicker of hope surging in her veins. Could this be her second chance to secure the emperor's patronage? It seemed too good to be true.

"It seems the emperor has intentions to change the Cyborg Prohibition Law," the Mistress continued. "According to his invitation, his once conservative Union Council now has new members who are... more open-minded toward cyborgs. He hopes that the circus's attendance will help to convince the governors and governesses to change the law and legalize implant production again—and heavily tax it."

The entire room broke out into excited whispers.

Rora blinked, not believing her ears.

Was it possible? Could what happened during the emperor's rise to power all be from his inner circle, who had eventually become the Union Council? Was she going to finally be accepted in the Union as a cyborg?

Rora couldn't even imagine what her life might be like after her contract was over if the law was changed. The possibilities made her mind spin.

"Not everyone will be invited to attend the emperor, however," the Mistress said over the whispers, which quickly died down as everyone was eager to hear her next words. "In the coming weeks, all performers will compete for the opportunity to travel to Covenant in three months. Ten acts will be chosen to attend His Imperial Highness. Our show management team will oversee the competition and select the winners. The competition will begin in a few days, along with a ball to kick things off."

First the emperor might change the law, and now a *ball?*

Immediately, Rora's thoughts turned to the gowns in her closet that hadn't been worn since she became a cyborg. Cirque du Borge hadn't hosted a ball in the two years since Rora had joined the circus. She could picture it now—Akio, Marzanna, and herself dressed up for no one but themselves, dominating the dance floor as they would the stage. Then darkness descended over her thoughts, blood rushing to her cheeks.

If Bastian secured additional funds, why not pay us?

The Mistress spared a condescending smile for the whispering crowd of performers. "You must all be tired after the journey. Go to your rooms, rest, and prepare yourselves for the exciting weeks ahead."

With a final nod, the Mistress descended the stage, the spotlight snapping off.

"That's it?" Rora blurted.

But her words were drowned in the buzz of conversation. Uneasy hope hovered over the room like the smog above Anchorage.

The watchmen moved aside from the exits, opening doors and allowing the performers to exit. As though they hadn't been guarding the exits the whole time.

Marzanna grabbed Rora's elbow, ushering her toward the door. Akio grabbed the handle of the rolling wardrobe, pulling it after them.

As they filed out of the theater and down the palace's long

halls toward the dormitories, her friends discussed improvements they could make to their trapeze act.

As they walked, Rora clung to hope. This was her second chance, and she wasn't about to miss out. She would make it into the top ten acts and fulfill her dream of securing patronage. But how?

Absently, she looked at her outdated robotic installation from her elbow to her right hand. If she had any hope of winning this competition, her hand would need updating. Or better yet, a complete replacement—something that was against circus rules.

Slowly, an idea crystallized in her mind.

An idea surrounding the beautiful new tinkerer.

CHAPTER 4

G wen blinked, the motion sending a wave of pain
through her left temple. Ignoring it, she pulled as
hard as she could. The man grunted beneath her.

Sweat beading her brow, she eyed the cyborg juggler
sitting on her worktable station, waiting for her to fix his damn
finger.

She wasn't a cyborg tinkerer, and Bastian had known. He
had fucking *known*. Yet here she was… poking at things best
left to far more capable hands. Better yet, a doctor who was
also an engineer—even that would be a better qualification
than a ship tinkerer.

As a tinkerer, she knew about revving the engines before
takeoff and how a ripped sail could easily be compensated
during flight by mechanical oars that paddled along solar
winds. She knew the creaking sounds signifying a virus in the
mainframe. But she didn't know how machines and bodies
interacted.

But damn it if she wasn't going to learn to be the best
fucking cyborg tinkerer in the Crescent Star System. If she
could become the best ship tinkerer in the Union in less than
five years, she could learn how to fix a few broken implants.

Implants that were easily worth more than Gwen's family's entire estate on Orthodocks.

"How much longer is this going to take?" The juggler eyed her with something less than enthusiasm. His large stomach hung over his belt, and he had arms the size of small cannons.

What had the idiot been trying to juggle? Lead balls? This circus took stunts to the next level of crazy. With the new competition, it seemed all common sense had been left on the ship.

She sighed heavily. They'd been at this for an hour. He'd managed to jam his robotic thumb deep into the joint while practicing his act. And she'd only managed to jam it farther.

"Did you hear me?" He pointed a meaty, non-robotic finger at her. "How much longer?"

Gwen's new eye whirred as she thought.

Through her left eye, she could see the man's robotic hand as though through an X-ray, with all the gears, screws, and plating. Anything with a trace of metal shone brightly. Through her right, she saw the man's stiff posture and scowl.

Pinching her lips together, she swallowed back nausea, still unaccustomed to the double vision. Paired with the pain in her head from the surgery, she was constantly forcing back dizziness.

She made a snap decision. Running her fingers over his wrist where the robotic arm connected to flesh—which she could quickly identify thanks to her cyborg eye—she pulled a few levers, disengaging the machine and shutting off the battery powering the implant. When the hand fell limp, she removed the thumb joint entirely.

"Hey!" the juggler said. "What do you think you're doing?"

"My job," she replied flatly before turning his implant back on. "Come back tomorrow, and I'll have your thumb ready to be reinstalled."

He stood, looming head and shoulders above her. "What the hell am I supposed to do until then?"

"I recommend strength training." The juggler's eyes bulged as she spoke. "Squats and lunges, especially. I can fix your prosthetic thumb, but you're just going to break it again if you keep relying on your cyborg hand to compensate for the heavy weight." As she walked over to the shelves in her new office, looking for a tool kit, she said, "And stop juggling lead balls. Do something interesting in your performance, not stupid."

For a moment, she thought he might hit her. With all the built-up tension she had since the procedure, she wanted him to. She could use a good fight. Or a good fuck.

"What the fuck do you know?" he spat before striding back into the main theater.

Her new office was attached to the theater and had a rolling door for privacy. From where she stood, she could see dozens of performers practicing their various acts.

Slapping the useless thumb onto the table, she eyed the contents in her office.

Surrounded by shelves of crap—scrap metal, wires, batteries, pieces of prosthetic limbs that were twenty years outdated—along with a few tinctures, books, bandages, oil, polish, and some other unnamable items, she had quite the spacious workstation. Compared to her tiny office on the *Crusty Tulip*, she practically had an office with a window.

With the table at the center, she felt like a doctor, which she most certainly was not. And she was too underqualified to be tinkering with illegal cyborg implants.

At last, she found a tool kit behind what could only be the remains of a robotic shoulder. Pulling out a screwdriver, she tinkered with the thumb joint, praying it would be an easy fix.

Sounds faded into the distance as the joint's mechanics blossomed before her. The cyborg eye revealed the layers beneath the thumb joint. With those layers overlapping on top of each other, she couldn't quite tell where the obstruction was. She tried to will her cyborg eye to stack the layers visually in front of her mind's eye, like she would using a hologram on a ship's mainframe.

Nothing.

Something that wasn't quite nausea twisted her stomach, and she found herself longing for the woman she'd been. For the human she'd been. Now, she was one of them—a cyborg.

A roar from the theater ripped Gwen from her thoughts. She blinked, wondering if one of the tigers had been stabbed with a strip pole. Looking up, she realized it was quite the opposite.

Bastian Kabir stomped around the theater as though he led a stampede, barking orders at each of the acts. Although the man hadn't exactly been the pleasant type when they'd met, he'd certainly seemed far more moderate in temperament than this. Apparently, he took his role as ringleader *very* seriously.

"What are you doing?" he called to a man on a unicycle, who was struggling to balance on a tightrope no thicker than floss. "Are you calling your grandma or riding a unicycle? Put your hands out to the sides and not up against your face."

To Gwen's surprise, the man rallied and did as instructed. The bike stopped wavering at the center of the tightrope, and he pedaled to the other side.

Even from where she stood, Gwen could see the trembling in the man's arms. But he graciously tipped his top hat to Bastian, who was already barking orders at other performers —this time, a man and woman practicing on the trapeze. After telling them to quit "fondling each other's thighs" and "actually perform," he turned his glare on Gwen.

It was only then she realized she'd been staring.

Clearing her throat, she turned her gaze back down to the cursed thumb joint and continued tinkering with it, but it was too late. The table vibrated from the stomps of Bastian's heavy footsteps, which was followed by the clicking of his cane as he approached her office.

"Enjoying the view?"

His voice seemed somehow rougher than before, deep and ragged. What the hell did he mean by that? She was certainly not ogling Bastian Kabir. When she looked up from her work, she noticed dark smudges under his eyes and how his pristine jacket with coattails hung more loosely on him, despite the journey from Anchorage only taking a few weeks.

Like Gwen, the ringleader was tall, standing head and shoulders above most people. Despite his wiry build, he had broad shoulders and a strong jawline. Definitely not the type you'd kick out of bed for farting.

"The view is fine enough," she replied, "but the *racket...*"

Bastian raised a disinterested brow. "Have you been practicing that all morning?"

"Nah." She placed the thumb on the table beside where she sat and leaned forward. "But I could if you think it would help, Mr. Ringleader. I imagine my comedic timing could be improved. Or grander gestures?"

Brows dropping, he stared at her through narrowed eyes. "Are you quite finished?"

With a shrug, she ignored the urge to scratch the back of her neck. "I'm here all day... all week... all thirteen years of this ridiculously long contract."

Something flashed behind the ringleader's eyes. Could it be anger? Fear?

When he spoke, his voice was so low she nearly missed it. "Best you not say such things if you wish to remain employed." He nodded to the thumb on the table beside her. The giant pink cyborg elephant in the room. "Adjusting to your new role well, I see. You are aware not all cyborg implants can be detached?"

Gwen cleared her throat. "What's a life-or-death career change with zero experience? Piece of cake."

Turning, Bastian headed back toward the theater. "Make yourself useful to the circus, Ms. Grimm. The Mistress has been known to employ the contract's fine print."

Just what did *that* mean?

What fine print? She couldn't read the blasted thing by the time Bastian shoved it and a fountain pen in her face in the prison cell. Her vision had been nearly gone.

As Bastian yelled at another group of performers, Gwen slammed her fist down on the table. Two of her knuckles popped, and she withdrew her hand, shaking off the zing of pain. It paled in comparison to the headache zipping between her temples and her throbbing eye socket. But injuring one of the hands she needed to do her job wasn't exactly advisable. Still… it had cooled her anger somewhat even though anxiety still churned in her stomach.

Stomping over to the overstuffed shelves, she found a worn book with a broken spine. The title on the cover read "Cyborg Basics." Taking a seat on the table and crossing her legs underneath her, she scanned through the book. The information was twenty years outdated and didn't have anything about chip implantations—a discovery made in the past ten years. No literature had been published about cyborgs since the forming of the Union. This book even referenced cyborg implants controlled by handheld remotes.

After flipping to the end, she tossed the book back onto a random shelf and picked up another, which was even more worn than the first. She was about to toss this book as well after reading about the toxic oils recommended for maintaining mobility of cyborg implants when a man cleared his throat.

The juggler was back *already?*

"I told you, your thumb won't be ready until tomorrow," she said without looking up.

"I'm not sure what I would do with a mechanical thumb."

The voice was young, male. Not the harsh voice of the juggler or the booming voice of Bastian.

Glancing up, Gwen was surprised to see a handsome, smiling face in her office doorway.

The man leaning against the doorframe wore tight black pants, hunting boots, and a leather jacket crossed with sheaths. Ringed fingers disappeared into his jacket, returning in a flash of scarlet. The smile never left his face as he approached, extending a red rose toward her.

"Thanks." Uncertain what else to do, Gwen accepted the rose, not bothering to stand from the table at the center of the room. "My apologies. I thought you were—"

"No need to apologize," the man said smoothly. "Thaniel can be a little rough around the edges." His words were sickeningly sweet as though he'd swallowed too much nectar. "I should apologize on behalf of my friend. We're all a little… excitable after the Mistress's announcement."

"And you are…?"

"How rude of me." The man took a step back from the table. Unlike the juggler, Thaniel, this man had corded muscles in his arms and shoulders and a trim waist. He was so tall, his head nearly smacked into the top of the doorframe. "My name is Abrecan Karlight, the circus archer and knife thrower."

That explained the sheaths.

"What can I help you with, Mr. Karlight?"

Unlike most of the performers she'd seen, he didn't have any visible cyborg parts.

"Please, call me Abrecan." The words dripped with such overt sweetness, she wanted to pass him a handkerchief.

Placing the flower on the table beside her, she stood. "What can I do for you?"

"It's not what you can do for me, but what I can do for you." Abrecan returned to his place against the doorframe. Looking at him now, the position seemed far too casual.

She'd met men like Abrecan before—the bold, assuming type. But she was no damsel in distress ready to swoon for the first person to offer her friendship or more even though she was still recovering from an unanesthetized brain surgery. Returning the book she'd been reading to the shelf, she was careful not to turn her back on the archer.

"It's good to know your craft, but words on a page will only get you so far," he continued, unperturbed by her lack of response.

Suddenly, pain shot through her temples. She hadn't had many episodes since her surgery. The surgeons had said it would take a few weeks for her body to adjust to the implant. Even so, the pain blinded her. For a moment, she thought she was still dying. Staggering forward, she slapped her knuckles against one of the shelves.

Abrecan appeared beside her, catching her around the waist. Blinking, she tried to see more than the silhouette of the archer's dark hair. Her cyborg eye whirred as vision returned to her implanted eye first. Through her new X-ray vision, she saw beyond the tight jacket to the metal plating beneath his right shoulder.

"Friends are an important asset in Cirque du Borge." His words were a whispering caress in her ear. The sweet smell of peppermint plumed into her nostrils. "With the right friends to help you succeed, I think you could do very well here."

When the vision in her right eye returned, she locked her knees and pulled herself to her feet, extricating herself from Abrecan's hold. "While I appreciate the help and the welcome committee, I'm not—"

Abrecan raised a hand, the light of the theater's artificial lights catching on his rings' gemstones. "Think carefully before you pick your friends." Reaching out, he pushed her hair behind her ear. With a snap of his fingers, the red rose reappeared in his hand.

Glancing behind, she saw the rose she'd placed on the table was gone.

"It'd be a shame to be on opposing sides when we could have been more. Much, much more." Placing the rose into her hand and wrapping her fingers around it, Abrecan turned on his heel and left her office—returning to excited shouts from the other performers in the theater beyond.

His own personal army.

She added avoiding the wannabe magician to her growing to-do list.

It would seem Cirque du Borge was even less of a friendly place than she'd thought.

What the fuck have I gotten myself into?

CHAPTER 5

Rora moved through her usual routine atop the slackline. As she did, her cyborg hand droned its mechanical melancholy.

Lunging forward, she caught the rope with her hands and flipped herself back to her feet. Before she could complete the flip, her hand sparked. A bolt of electricity shot up her arm and into her shoulder.

Pain pulsed through her so sharply, her head swam.

Gasping, she lost her grip on the wire, elbows slapping the mat on the ground below.

The room twisted under her gaze before settling. A strange smell like burning hair and sulfur filled the air. It took her another moment to realize her cyborg wrist was smoking.

"Shit!"

Grabbing a sweat towel, Rora clapped the fabric over the growing smoke.

Marzanna, who had been rehearsing nearby, dashed over and hauled her to her feet. "Come on! It's time you see the new tinkerer about that hand."

Despite Rora's plan, she hesitated, feeling suddenly very small and very nervous.

Marzanna pulled her along toward the tinkerer's office, knocking briskly on the doorframe before marching in with Rora in tow.

"Tinkerer," Marzanna said as a way of greeting. "We require your immediate attention. Ms. Lockwood's arm is smoking."

Hunched over several books and sitting cross-legged on the patient table, the tinkerer looked up and blinked as though lost in thought. Cyborg eye settling on them, she jumped to her feet, shoving the books off the table and indicating for Rora to sit.

Rora's cheeks heated.

This hadn't been what she'd had in mind about *seducing* this woman.

Suppressing a groan, Rora sat on the table and removed the towel, which had blackened in a patch from her smoking hand.

Grabbing tools and parts from the shelves, the tinkerer shuffled over and placed the equipment beside Rora on the table. Turning to Marzanna, the tinkerer said, "If you don't mind, I'd ask you to return to your activities while I care for…"

She looked at Rora, eyebrows raised.

"Rora Lockwood," Rora blurted.

"Right, for Ms. Lockwood," she said. "My name is Gwendolyn Grimm."

Marzanna opened her mouth to object, but Rora held up a hand. "I'm fine, really. Thanks for your help."

Nodding, Marzanna returned to the theater.

Feeling as though she'd just swallowed a lump of nut butter, Rora cleared her throat. But Gwendolyn paid her no mind, donning rubber gloves and tracing the wiring and metal gears near where the smoking had started. Rora felt cheated on by her own hand.

I'd like some of her attention as well, thank you.

Plucking up a screwdriver, Gwendolyn sat beside her and unscrewed the top metal plating, which opened with a click, revealing the machinery underneath. When smoke spewed up, the tinkerer cursed, fingers rummaging through the technology.

It felt like someone had pulled up Rora's dress to look at her undergarments. Blood rushed to her cheeks.

This is not *how this seduction was supposed to go.*

Yesterday, Rora had concocted a plan to get the new hand she so desperately needed. And the plan was simple—to seduce the tinkerer.

At Cirque du Borge, one rule was sacred: cyborgs only received new or refurbished implants upon entering the circus.

After the Cyborg Prohibition Law was put into place and the manufacturing of implants illegalized, implants, replaceable parts, and the rechargeable batteries powering them became scarce, and, therefore, incredibly valuable. Even the base implants were worth millions of marks. Should anything unexpectedly malfunction before its time, like Rora's hand, the cyborg was out of luck. If the malfunctioning implant impacted performances and audience engagement, the performer could be subject to contract termination, which could mean expulsion from the circus or worse.

Tinkerers were prohibited from using the circus' resources to purchase additional parts or to construct a new cyborg hand.

Unfortunately for Rora, the last tinkerer had been a following-the-rules kind of gent. He'd disappeared mysteriously a few months before his thirteen-year contract was up. But this tinkerer would be different.

Gwendolyn Grimm would be so smitten that she'd do anything for Rora—even make her a new hand. With a new hand, Rora could perform even more incredible stunts. In so doing, she'd secure one of the top ten spots to perform for the emperor.

Finally, she'd prove she was good enough.

"What's wrong with it?" Rora asked, foregoing all her carefully planned conversations.

Gwendolyn didn't respond as she worked.

"Ms. Grimm?"

"What?" She looked up as though noticing Rora for the first time. "Oh... It's just Gwen."

Progress?

"Something is wrong with the unit, and perhaps the mainframe as well," Gwen continued. "The original unit is at least ten years old, so it's hard to tell which went first." She bit her tongue between her teeth as she worked. "What were you doing out there anyway?"

"Practicing. I was doing a flip when my hand went haywire."

Gwen nodded absently. "Did you experience any shocks or bolts of electricity from the implant?"

"Yes."

Releasing Rora's hand, Gwen scratched the back of her head. "On a ship, if that sort of thing happened, I'd take the whole machine apart to see where the malfunctioning originated..." She trailed off. Finally, she shook her head before resuming her work. "I'm hoping if I can replace a few wires that your hand will return to its previous functionality."

Which wasn't very good to begin with.

Patience.

"I trust you," Rora said.

Gwen stiffened but didn't look up from her work.

Turning, Gwen shifted her grip on Rora's arm. As she did, her fingers traced lightly over the skin on her elbow, sending gooseflesh up her arms.

Rora wanted to rub her arm, to hide what this woman's touch did to her, but she forced herself to remain motionless.

"I've met a bunch of crybabies all morning," Gwen finally

said. "You're the first person who hasn't complained about the lack of instantaneous success."

Rora laughed. "For once, I don't have decent competition? Excellent."

Abruptly, Gwen screwed the metal plating back into place and stood. "I'm hoping that should do it. You're all set, Ms. Lockwood."

Rora's eyes connected with Gwen's. For a moment, she forgot how to move. Dark lashes framed an iris as infinite as the stars. Her cyborg eye emitted a golden glow from the light where her iris and pupil would have been.

Just what can she see with that cyborg eye?

Recalling her plan, Rora leaned forward on the table until her face was only inches from Gwen's. It was then she noticed how tall Gwen was. But with Rora sitting on the table, her lips were mere inches lower than Gwen's.

"Call me Rora."

Gwen licked her lips, her chest rising and falling visibly.

"Will you be going to the ball?" Rora put on her sweetest, shyest smile.

Gwen cleared her throat, but she didn't step back. "Not if I can help it."

"Although attendance is mandatory…" Rora dared to lean close enough that she whispered the next words into the tinkerer's ear. "I hope I can persuade you to come." Slowly, she pulled herself away and slid off the table. She walked toward the door with a performer's saunter. "We performers can be a dramatic bunch, but we do know how to throw one hell of a party."

A lie, but the tinkerer didn't need to know that.

"If you'd like a good time, Gwen, I'd be happy to show you."

Rora paused long enough to smile mischievously up at Gwen, whose dark eye was rimmed with *possibility*—a single eyebrow raised in unspoken question.

Those eyes narrowed as she considered. "Mandatory attendance, you say?" With a chuckle, she placed the screwdriver on one of the shelves, giving Rora a great view of an ass the sun would orbit.

Rora's gaze swept up to the tinkerer's full hips and narrow waist.

When Gwen turned around, a small smile was on her lips. "So, are you going to ask me, or what?"

Well, she certainly doesn't mess around.

Or does she?

Butterflies fluttered through Rora's stomach.

Smiling, she tried to keep her face smooth. It wouldn't do to show how much Gwen affected her—not if she was going to have this girl wrapped around her finger. Still, she could play along.

"Would you like to go to the ball with me?"

"Do you care if your date wears… informal attire?" Gwen gestured to her tinkerer's clothes. "I'm afraid everything else I own is back on Anchorage."

That's where Bastian picked her up.

Closing the distance between them, she grabbed Gwen's hand. "Don't worry. I have just the thing."

Linking her fingers through Gwen's, Rora led her out of the theater. To her surprise, Gwen clasped Rora's hand in return.

Excited to spend time alone with Gwen, she didn't notice the drone had returned to her cyborg hand.

CHAPTER 6

G wen tried not to look over the short stall to where the lovely, dark acrobat showered next to her.

As she washed herself, she couldn't help as her fingers lingered between her legs. The wetness there had nothing to do with the shower.

What the fuck are you doing? You're supposed to be learning how to be a passable cyborg tinkerer, not getting cozy with the staff.

But damn it if she could refuse Rora.

Seeing the slackliner up close in her office hours before, Gwen recognized Rora at once as the performer she'd watched on Anchorage—before the woman from the manufacturing district had led her away. Gwen had felt an immediate attraction to Rora then. And she sure as hell felt one now.

Even without the makeup and fancy clothes, Rora was breathtaking.

Turning the water colder, Gwen washed off before returning to Rora's room.

Once dressed in underthings, Rora said, "Would you like me to fix your hair?"

Gwen opened her mouth and closed it. Her protests died

on her tongue as Rora placed her hand on the small of Gwen's back and guided her to the stool before a vanity station.

Even the lingering pain on her scalp seemed a distant memory at the feel of Rora's nimble fingers combing out her hair with a fine ivory comb.

After wrapping Gwen's hair in large, hideous rollers—the type women used to give curl to their hair—Rora gently squeezed her shoulders. "Come, let's find you something to wear."

Gwen followed Rora to the closet at the back of her room, the hair rollers bobbing as she walked. Rora's room contained a bed, side tables with electric lanterns, a vanity station beside a large window, a folding screen, over which various discarded dresses hung, one set of dresser drawers, a closet, and an attached washroom. Gwen's room, on the other hand, also had space for a workbench with countless tools and parts scattered atop its shelves.

Pulling back the closet doors, which slid on a slim track, Rora fingered through the left-most side of her closet, which housed countless floor-length gowns of every color.

It looked like a unicorn had thrown up in her closet.

Gwen swallowed thickly.

Please no tassels. Please no tassels.

The other side of Rora's closet was comprised of the acrobat's typical performance garb—tight pants of varying shades and patterns along with matching tops.

"Aha!" Rora pulled a gown out of the closet.

As someone who'd worn only tinkerer's leathers for the past five years, the sight of any gown intended for Gwen was startling enough by itself. Let alone a bright fucking yellow gown.

Forgetting diplomacy, she eyed the dress dubiously.

"I think it will look great on you," Gwen said carefully.

Truthfully, the dress was gold, rather than yellow. And the

color *would* look stunning against Rora's light brown skin. It also had lace sleeves that came off the shoulders and an elaborate corset that would highlight her trim waist.

Rora smiled, rolling her eyes dramatically. "It's not for me. It's for you!" She pushed the dress into Gwen's hands, and Gwen nearly toppled over from the weight. It had to weigh more than two skimmers. How was she supposed to move around in it? She'd start sweating from shouldering the dress's weight alone.

Fine. But she wouldn't give up her boots.

"I purchased this dress off the shelf months ago, but I haven't had a chance to have it tailored to my height. It's much too long for me right now," Rora said. "I think it will be perfect for you."

Gwen hadn't thought about their height difference or that Rora barely came up to her shoulders. Hesitantly, she accepted the weighty offering and trudged over behind the folding screen, which sectioned off a corner of the room so she could change in private.

It took her an ungodly amount of time to figure out how to get into the dress, and even more time to maneuver the tulle skirts with her boots on.

"Need any help?" Rora called over the folding screen.

Gwen grunted. "I may have lost one of your hair rollers in the dress."

When Rora laughed, the sound reminded Gwen of tinkling bells.

"I have more. But I can look for it when you're out and make sure it's not clinging to the hem of the gown."

For a moment, Gwen hesitated as she pulled up the lace sleeves.

Why is she being so nice to me? I couldn't even fix her hand properly.

Her thoughts strayed to the very large pile of joints and other cyborg pieces requiring her attention back in her office. Thus far, she'd only had a chance to fix Thaniel's thumb.

Shaking herself—and setting another hair roller free to roam the wastelands of Rora's room—Gwen promptly pulled up both sleeves and attempted to zipper the dress closed. After the fourth try, sweat dripped between her breasts and beaded on her brow. Though she couldn't tell whether that was from the sheer mass of the dress or the struggle to get into it.

"Um," Gwen began articulately, "I think I'm stuck."

"Oh, dear." Rora's voice drew closer. "Mind if I come around?"

"Sure."

When Rora walked around the changing screen, instead of rushing to Gwen's rescue, she stopped, eyes growing wide.

Gwen sighed. "I knew it. Fun isn't my color. We should get it off—"

"You look radiant." Rora's dark eyes rounded, looking at Gwen, unblinking. "Truly."

Gwen cleared her throat. "I'm wearing hair rollers."

Closing the distance between them, Rora thumped Gwen playfully on the arm with her cyborg hand. The machine hummed, behind which was a faint, unfriendly noise. "I can see the beautiful woman behind the rollers. Besides, I'm wearing them, too."

Unable to acknowledge the hefty compliment and annoyed that the woman could make hair rollers appear a choice accessory, Gwen motioned to the back of her dress. "The zipper?"

"Right!" Rora zipped, buttoned, and then tied the dress's elaborate corset. It felt like Gwen was being suited up for travel in deep space. After she finished, Rora's hands lingered for a moment too long on Gwen's back before she strode back around to face her. "Let's finish that hair."

When Gwen resumed her place on the stool before the mirror, Rora eyed her boots. "I have plenty of jeweled slippers that would go perfectly with—"

"No," Gwen said quickly. "Thank you. These are fine."

Lines formed between Rora's brows, but she didn't say anything further. Within minutes, she'd unraveled Gwen's hair from the rollers, pinned a small, beaded brooch with a fishnet veil to her head, sprayed her curls into place, and found the rogue rollers.

"All right. Time for me to get into my dress." With that, Rora disappeared behind the screen with a pink gown.

It was then Gwen began to wonder if she'd chosen her date terribly wrong.

Date? Is that what this is?

She shook her head. No, it was her giving in to temptation and losing all sense of self-control around a pretty face. She'd go through the motions at the dance tonight, but once the ball was over, they would go their separate ways. Gwen would throw everything she had into figuring out how to be a fanfucking-tastic cyborg tinkerer. Then once her contract was through, she'd leave and never see this circus—or Rora—again.

Still, thirteen years was a long time. And it wouldn't hurt to find another way to pass the time…

From where Gwen sat on the stool, she could see flashes of the massive pink gown as Rora dressed. As she was about to turn her head to give Rora privacy, she glimpsed a bare shoulder and the beginning curve of one breast as the acrobat pulled her dress up. Heart pattering, she swallowed, forcing herself to look away.

There was a rustle of skirts as Rora re-emerged from behind the changing screen.

"Would you help me with the corset?" Rora asked, her voice soft. "I can't reach the ties."

Taking a deep breath, Gwen turned to face the acrobat.

Rora's bright pink gown had an intricate maroon beading woven into it. The patterns swirled along the hem of the dress, bleeding upward and expanding into the vague form of flowers. The neckline arched around the curves of Rora's breasts, leaving her neck and collarbones utterly bare.

Stars, Gwen wanted to trail her lips along that neck.

Making her way behind Rora, Gwen struggled briefly but eventually laced up her gown.

From where Rora stood before the full mirror beside the vanity station, body sideways, Gwen spotted glances of her gown. Like Rora's dress, beading lined the hem and skirts, though it was a dark gold and covered most of the gown. She had to admit the garment was stunning—made for a princess of another galaxy, not for a cyborg tinkerer.

"You're all set," Gwen said after she'd finished tying the corset.

"Thank you!" Rora hurried over to the vanity station, placing herself on the stool and removing the rollers. In a few minutes, she wove her hair into a looser bun than she normally wore, raveling strands of hair into an elaborate style at the nape of her neck. She plucked up a hat, far too small to cover her whole head, and pinned it into her hair. The hat was tilted to the side, uncentered, and positively charming.

Somewhere in the distance, a bell tolled eight times.

"Oh, shoot. We're late." Rora stood, far more radiant than Gwen could ever hope to be. With a smile, she extended an arm. "Shall we?"

They strode past the theater and dining hall, to a far section of the palace Gwen had yet to visit. Countless hallways and stairways led to the upper levels. She hadn't yet figured out what was off-limits to performers and the regular circus staff, but she guessed somewhere beyond here were the kitchens and servants' quarters.

The first thing she heard was the clinking of glass, closely followed by the echoes of laughter. It had been years since she'd been forced to accompany her parents and siblings to the local balls. The idea of having to ask the ladies about their hat tailors and button makers and fawn over the clean, polished nails at the end of soft hands was nauseating.

As they rounded a corner, they were met with crowds of performers lingering in a hallway and dressed in finery. Many of the women wore top hats with netting over their eyes and gowns with elaborate corsets and puffy laced sleeves. Some even wore mechanical wings and other theatrical accessories. Stockinged kneecaps and calves peeked out of dresses that were scandalously short in the front, despite their full-length skirt in the back. The men sported canes in gloved hands as well as long jackets with coattails.

All eyes turned to them as they strode down the hallway, powdered eyebrows rising in interest.

"Don't mind them," Rora whispered into Gwen's ear. "Some of the performers linger in the hallway in the hopes of being announced last. They think it's an honor or some such nonsense. If you ask me, it's a waste of perfectly good time on the dance floor."

As they weaved their way through the crowd, a warm yellow light emerged, leaking out of a nearby doorway.

"Announced?" Gwen's arm was still hooked through Rora's. She suddenly felt rather inclined to make her way back to her chambers. Could they enter the ball through the back? Maybe there was a garden entrance.

Before Rora could reply, they were in the doorway before two massive staircases set across from each other and lined with scarlet carpet. The staircases met at a center platform, which opened to the final set of stairs leading down to a dance floor the size of two warships. The railings appeared to be made of gold or fucking painted with it. As did the herald, who wore a golden jacket and pants, and whose face and hands were covered in what appeared to be golden, glittery paint.

The man bowed to them, and Gwen took a step back as glitter spewed to the floor.

The herpes of décor.

Rora said something to the man that Gwen couldn't hear. Nodding, he picked up his staff and slammed it into the ground three times.

Turning to face Gwen, she whispered in her ear. "He'll announce me first. At the bottom of the stairs, there's a basket of masks. Grab one, and I'll meet you on the dance floor."

Gwen could feel herself paling. "Doesn't announcing us defeat the whole purpose of a masquerade ball?"

Past the stairs, hundreds of dancers wearing masks of every hue and design filled the dance floor and lined the walls. Strangely, there didn't appear to be any food tables.

What kind of party was this?

"Lady Rora Lockwood!" the herald yelled as the room and music temporarily quieted.

Gwen's mouth dropped.

Rora was a *lady*? That particular title was reserved for only upper-ranking nobles, which were rare since the forming of the Union. The nobles who hadn't been in support of the emperor's armies had lost all lands and titles. Gwen's family had been one of the latter.

As though being in front of hundreds of eyes was an everyday occurrence—well, perhaps it was as a performer of Cirque du Borge—Rora inclined her head toward the herald and then to the onlookers far below before descending the stairs. She spared a smile over her shoulder for Gwen.

Something in Gwen softened.

Even still, holding her gaze was like staring into the sun.

Sidling up to the herald as all eyes fastened on Rora, Gwen whispered, "If you don't mind, I'll just follow her—"

"All attendees must be announced." The herald nodded to the scribe beside him, who hurriedly scratched names into a leather-bound notebook. He shook the quill, twisting the gears at one end. For a moment, Gwen's cyborg eye whirred, zooming in on the ink bubbling on the tip of the quill, which was pressed onto the page as he fashioned Rora's name from the now-drying ink.

"That really isn't necessary."

"The Mistress requires it."

Gwen scowled at him, though the gesture felt half-assed with only one human eye to narrow.

"Name, madam?"

"Gwen."

The man raised an eyebrow covered in glitter. "Gwen…?"

Screw delicacy.

"Gwendolyn Fucking Grimm."

The scribe hesitated, looking at the herald. The golden man tilted his head to the side, shoulders rising as if to say, "*Your funeral.*"

Again, he pounded his massive golden staff into the ground three times. The music and conversation stopped again. "Ms. Gwendolyn Fucking Grimm."

Gwen gave her most functional curtsy to him—a masculine swagger of hips—before descending the stairs. Snickers rippled up from the crowd, and the music slowly resumed.

Two of the trapeze performers, Marzanna and Akio, met Rora at the base of the staircase. Despite their masks, they were easy enough to identify.

To Gwen's surprise, they looked at her with smiles. Akio even nodded in what appeared to be appreciation. But she had eyes for none of it. As she walked down the first set of stairs, all she could see was the wide smile spreading across Rora's face.

As Gwen's boots touched the platform before the final set of stairs, the edges of her massive skirts brushed none too delicately against…

Bastian Kabir.

"Ms. Grimm." Although the words were in his usual bass

monotone, they seemed to hold a hint of accusation. "Making a grand entrance, I see."

"Mr. Kabir." Gwen nearly crossed her arms, but the corset was too tight, so she pursed her lips instead. "Why weren't you announced?"

"It's my job to welcome the performers as they enter."

"Everyone likes to see a smiling face before drowning themselves in spiked punch." Gwen turned to walk past him.

As she looked around the room, there didn't appear to be any alcohol either.

Moving to her side, Bastian surprised her by extending an elbow. It was then she noticed he'd replaced his normally formal attire with *more* formal attire. He wore a midnight black jacket and pants lined with golden glittering pinstripes. The jacket ended in a coattail, and his vest was lined with gears of polished brass. He wore a matching black hat with a golden ribbon, though his staff was the same one he always had with him.

It looked as though they'd coordinated outfits. The gold in his jacket and pants perfectly matched the gold of her gown's beading.

"Would you honor me with a dance, Ms. Grimm?"

Hesitating, she looked down the stairs at Rora and her friends. Lines formed between Rora's brows. Forcing herself to look away, Gwen did her best to ignore the hundreds of eyes on the dance floor, which were still trained on her.

Could she deny the ringleader a dance? She didn't know much about Cirque du Borge's politics, but she did know Bastian cozied up to the show management team. And they pulled all the strings around here. If she was going to get anywhere in her new line of work, she'd need to avoid making enemies with those in charge.

Still, Bastian hadn't been forthcoming with her about what becoming a cyborg entailed or the job she'd been hired to perform. And she was feeling less than charitable toward the man asking for a dance.

She tried another tactic. "I thought you were supposed to be greeting everyone."

"Indeed." He extended his elbow toward her. "Though I think a brief respite is in order."

Sighing, she looped her arm through his. "Only if you stop calling me Ms. Grimm."

They strode down the stairs, past the basket of masks, and onto the dance floor to widening eyes.

Gwen mouthed to Rora, *I'm sorry. Be right back.* Confusion bleached Rora's features, but she nodded.

"Would you prefer Ms. Fucking Grimm?" Bastian offered, the crowd on the dance floor parting before him.

Stars. Why did I say yes to go to a ball?

Turning her head, she looked up at Bastian. His stony mask seemed to crack as one corner of his mouth crept upward.

"Yes," she replied as her boots squeaked against the polished wood of the dance floor. "You may either call me Ms. Fucking Grimm or Gwen. Your choice."

Once at the center of the dance floor, Bastian turned to her. The crowd closed back in around them. Tapping his cane on the floor, he bowed to her. A new song fluted to them, the musicians changing tune from the upbeat rhythm of before to a slower melody. With a resigned sigh, she repeated the swaggering curtsy she'd given the herald and took Bastian's extended hand.

Wrapping a hand around her waist, he pulled her into a dance. She managed to step on his feet three times within the first minute. Only one was an accident.

"Did I mention I'm a terrible dancer?"

A smile stiff as a book's spine was plastered across his face, and he didn't deign to reply.

Bastian held her waist tightly to him. The heat radiating

off his body had her wondering what exactly stoked his internal furnace. She could feel the domesticated flames bubbling beneath the surface.

As the music grew louder in volume, he pressed his cheek against hers. "Everything isn't as it seems."

Gwen tried to pull away from him, but he held her tight. The coarse stubbles of his cheeks caught on her curls as his lips neared her ear. "You have an important job ahead this evening. Prepare yourself."

She eyed the dozens of watchmen lining the walls. "What are you talking about?"

Bastian spun her out in some ridiculously dramatic dance move. Boots squeaking on the floor, Gwen managed to remain on her feet even as the ringleader pulled, sending her spinning back toward him. Despite the moderate tune of the song, they never remained still for long like *normal* dancers. The turning steps Bastian led her in felt like a challenge, a test of wills.

The music changed tunes to what she thought was the song's chorus or bridge.

"I offer this warning as a courtesy for someone new to the circus. Prepare yourself, and stay close to me this evening. I will protect you."

Unable to stop herself, she rolled her eyes.

Why do men always think women want their protection?

Panting, she felt sweat drip down her back and between her breasts beneath the heavy gown. "This isn't how normal people go about asking for a date. In fact, I already have one. And I don't need—or want—your protection."

Bastian clenched his teeth, though to anyone looking nearby, it would appear a stiff smile. "This isn't the time for squabbling, Ms. Grimm—"

"That's Ms. *Fucking* Grimm to you."

He looked at her then, eyes flashing with irritation. "I'm trying to warn you."

"Just as you warned me about the clauses in the contract I

couldn't read while I was *dying?*" The song ended, and the dancers separated after bowing and curtsying to each other. She pulled away and swaggered into another curtsy. "I've had enough of your help. Now, if you don't mind, I'm going to find my date."

Even as she strode off the dance floor in a flurry of skirts and squeaking boots, she couldn't help but think of the strange tone his voice had held.

What could possibly scare the great Bastian Kabir?

CHAPTER 7

Pushing through the crowd, Gwen emerged on the other side of the sea of dancing hormonal adults in glittering masks.

Where was Rora?

Turning, she strode toward the staircase where she'd seen Rora last, trying to shake off Bastian's words. But it was as easy as shaking off grease from a ship's engine. What had he meant? What did he want to protect her from?

Bastian was being ridiculous, of course. There was nothing dangerous about a ball. Besides dying from boredom, of course.

A crowd had gathered at the base of the stairs where newcomers lingered. When she squeezed through the crowd, the cage of her dress pressed in as she shimmied between bodies. Neither Rora nor her friends were anywhere in sight.

After several more announcements of performers entering, the song ended. Musicians shuffled through papers on music stands, preparing for the next song.

It was then Gwen realized Rora was calling her name.

"There you are." Rora sounded somewhat breathless as

she appeared beside Gwen. "I've been looking all over for you. I couldn't find you after…"

Her voice trailed off.

After I danced with Bastian Kabir.

Gwen started to run a hand over her head. Remembering the lengths Rora had gone to in styling her hair, she returned her hand to her side. "Sorry about that. He was rather persistent."

Nodding, Rora's eyes scanned the room, her gaze lingering on the empty buffet tables and absence of decorations. "I know the circus is poor, but no food or wine? Weirdest ball ever." She shook her head. "From what I heard, they used to have so many balls back before… Well, you know." She extended a hand to Gwen. "May I have this dance?"

For a moment, Gwen hesitated, thinking of how she'd stepped on Bastian's feet earlier and how Rora's slippers were far less sturdy than the ringleader's dress shoes.

Maybe I should've taken her offer of footwear, after all. If only for her feet's sake.

But she wasn't about to pass up a dance with a pretty woman, regardless of her lack of dancing skills. Gwen took Rora's hand. "I must warn you, I'm no graceful acrobat."

Rora walked backward onto the dance floor, somehow managing not to bump into the dancers, who curtsied or bowed to partners before the start of the next dance. "Lucky for you, I am."

The music started, a harmonic cadence of the flute and harp. The tune was quiet with a quick beat. Dancers immediately raised their arms and extended palms to their partner. As they circled their partners, their hands never touched, and the dancers changed directions, extending their opposite hands as they repeated the motion.

Hurriedly doing likewise, Gwen kept one eye on her feet and the other on the dancers around the room. Her mechanical eye whirred, giving her a nauseating vertigo as it displayed layered black-and-white images of the dancers across her vision, revealing every cyborg implant, steel-toed boot, every decorative gear, and even a few knives and pistols sheathed inside jackets or on leg holsters.

Swallowing back both the nausea and surprise, she narrowly avoided stepping on Rora's slippers as she belatedly turned into the next part of the dance.

The only dances Gwen participated in with any regularity were more of rowdy jigs atop bar tables and counters with a pint of ale in her hand. Well, not since she'd left home. And as far as she could see, the dances on this side of the Crescent Star System bore no similarities to the ones on her home planet.

After the second chorus, Rora's gloved cyborg hand made its way to Gwen's shoulder. That wasn't part of the dance. She knew because she'd been watching the other dancers.

"While your effort is commendable..." Rora wrapped an arm around Gwen's waist and pulled her into the next movement. "You don't have to try so hard."

"Who says I'm trying hard?" Gwen said, eyes trained on the floor.

Rora swept Gwen in a circle. "Trust me."

Hesitating, she thought of all the implications those two small words possessed. Trusting someone with her hair and dress led to trusting them in a dance, which could then lead to a tryst beneath the sheets.

But what could it hurt? It was only a dance, after all.

Releasing some of the tension in her shoulders, she allowed Rora to move them through the dance—their hands and bodies scandalously touching, unlike the other dancers on the floor.

After several minutes, Gwen was surprised to find that dancing wasn't an entirely unpleasant experience. Though it was nothing like the strange battle of wills dancing with Bastian had been.

"Is it everything you expected?" Rora asked. "The circus, I mean."

"I had no expectations," Gwen said, carefully.

Rora's brows furrowed. "Not even from the rumors?" She smiled, her eyes growing distant. "When I joined, I was convinced costumes and props were implanted along with cyborg parts."

"So, you're saying you don't have a retractable slackline up your sleeve?" Gwen sighed. "I must say, I'm disappointed."

"No, but I have something far better."

"What's that?"

"You'll just have to wait to find out."

Despite herself, Gwen smiled. "I'd heard little of Cirque du Borge before I started working as a ship tinkerer."

As the next song began, Rora gently pulled Gwen into the dance steps with her cyborg hand—steps that were far less complicated than the previous song. Thank her lucky stars.

"The people who spoke of the circus always seemed to be the kind you wouldn't want to take home to your mother— smugglers, thieves, swords for hire," Gwen began. "They whispered of cyborgs the size of mountains who could spin planets atop their robotic fingertips."

Rora made a face as though she'd bitten into a lemon.

"I never believed such things," Gwen continued. "But I did hear of the infamous ringleader who could bend cyborg beasts to his will, magicians who could pluck your soul straight from your chest, firebreathers who need no torch." She looked straight into Rora's brown eyes then. "Acrobats who could tumble into your heart."

According to the manufacturer from the line to get into the circus on Anchorage, the rumor had actually been about tumbling between the sheets. But Rora didn't need to know that.

It worked like a charm.

Smiling brightly, Rora pulled Gwen close enough that her

breasts pressed against Gwen's waist as they moved across the dance floor.

I've still got it.

When the announcement of several more groups of performers entering the hall interrupted the music, throngs of people seeming to enter all at once, Gwen and Rora slowed to a stop and stood side by side.

Leaning toward Rora, Gwen said, "What brought you to the circus?"

"The same reason as most." Rora's eyes fixed on the performers descending the stairs in a flurry of bright skirts and flashing gears. "Desperation."

Gwen raised an eyebrow. "Were you an illegal recruit, too? Or was I the rare exception to lawbreaking, given my unfortunate intimacy with the Reaper?"

Rora eyed the performers around them. Although the music had stopped as the announcer chimed name after name of people descending the stairs, couples spoke in hushed tones amongst themselves, filling the room with a whispered chatter. No one was close enough to hear them. "So far as I can count, there have been less than ten recruits since the Cyborg Prohibition Law was put in place."

Breaking the law was punishable by a lifetime sentence in prison or a swift execution for both the surgeon and patient— depending on the mood of the judge. How had a circus known for flaunting its cyborg performers gone unnoticed after making ten new cyborgs?

"I joined the circus two years ago," Rora said, confirming Gwen's suspicions. "After the law had been in place."

"What made you want to join?"

"I..." Rora faltered, her voice wavering. Until this moment, the woman had never seemed unsure of anything— least of all, herself. "I didn't learn how to perform at Cirque du Borge, like many of the performers. I was a gymnast for Redwood Conservatory."

Unable to help herself, Gwen blanched.

Not only was Rora a fucking *lady*, but she'd also attended one of the Union's best all-girls boarding schools?

Well, shit.

Had they not met at the circus, Gwen's and Rora's circles would never have intersected. Rora far outranked Gwen in every sense of the definition.

Rora didn't seem to notice Gwen swaying like a drunkard in a privy, still in shock over the discovery of her schooling, because she kept speaking in a low tone.

"I'd made it onto the school's elite gymnastics team a few years before graduation. That year, there was a competition to perform for the emperor. And it's my dream, you see, to perform for him and secure patronage.

"My team was selected along with several other groups of performers. A few weeks before the performance for the emperor, there was an event for school board members and wealthy donors, which was meant to raise funds for the school. I performed the very same routine with my gymnastics team, and… I broke my wrist. The bone snapped in two. With the limitations on surgery, the doctors said I'd never have full function again, and I could no longer perform." Her eyes darkened, growing distant. "My parents spent so many years paying for me to go to the top schools with the best athletics. I couldn't bear the look in their eyes, knowing that had been my last performance."

"I'm sure they would understand," Gwen began, thinking of her parents who, despite living on a conservative planet, had encouraged her to try new things—even try a line of work that meant leaving her family and home behind.

Rora laughed humorlessly. "You don't know my parents. Without my wrist, I was worthless to them. They had made preparations for a quiet marriage to a lord in the country. To marry off their disgraced daughter who wasn't strong enough to compete." When she shook her head, strands of hair fell loose from her bun. "Sometimes, I'm thankful I can't remember." When she sighed, the sound filled with something akin to regret. "I wish the hurt and anger would go away along with the memories, but it doesn't. Somehow, I can still hold on to a grudge, but I can't remember the color of their eyes."

The Forgetting.

Having been so preoccupied with learning her new role, Gwen had all but forgotten the cyborg curse.

Her heart thumped against her ribs. How soon would she start losing her memories?

Swallowing back the fear tightening her chest, she reached out, taking hold of Rora's hand. "I'm sorry. I shouldn't have assumed." She squeezed Rora's hand in what she hoped was reassurance. When she was about to let go, Rora's eyes found hers, and she closed her fingers around Gwen's.

"There's no way you could have known." Rora bit her lip. "I wasn't ready to stop performing. It was all I'd known. My studies were a joke—a simple education in etiquette with signed documents saying I'd taken my writing, mathematics, and homemaking courses, when all I'd ever done was rehearse endlessly. I wasn't about to go quietly to the country and have some man I'd met once at a gala fill my belly with his seed. So, I joined the circus. As each day passes, I can remember less and less of the woman I was before. But hearing about the competition to perform for the emperor... it feels like the stars have realigned to give me a second chance to get a patron after all."

"If anyone can secure one of the top spots to perform for the emperor, you will." Gwen knew nothing of judging performances or how different acts could be compared against one another. Having been so busy tinkering, she hadn't actually seen Rora rehearse. And she'd only seen her perform the once. But the woman's eyes held passion, mingling with a fiery determination.

"Thank you," Rora said. "So… what was your family like?"

"My parents and siblings live on Orthodocks," Gwen said. "They run the House of Timber. It's a woodworking business."

For a long moment, she thought about leaving it there and not telling Rora the truth about her family's history. But she'd already raised a royal middle finger to the emperor and Union by becoming a cyborg. What was the point of hiding her past now? Not to mention, Rora had just opened up to Gwen.

"My family didn't support the emperor," Gwen admitted. "And we lost everything in the process—lands, titles, social standing. Everything but the ability to start again."

Ten years ago, when the emperor emerged with his armies, the Grimm family was given a choice—support the charismatic emperor's rise to power or risk his wrath if he gained control over the Crescent Star System. When the emperor's armies returned after he'd been inaugurated, every noble family who hadn't supported him was stripped of power and their entire staff executed. Gwen and her family had been forced to watch as servants, butlers, and the people they had grown up with and thought as family were gutted like animals.

Then they had been thrown out onto the street with nothing.

Homeless, friendless, and disgraced, Gwen's parents had found a way to protect her and her siblings. More than that, they'd found a way to rebuild.

"I'm sorry for what happened to your family," Rora said. "I heard the emperor's soldiers weren't merciful to many noble families."

No, they weren't.

"But maybe it wasn't his fault," Rora continued. "According to the emperor's letter to the Mistress, it was the Union Council who pushed for the Cyborg Prohibition Law, and maybe it was the Council who'd pushed for such harsh

measures against noble families. Now, the circus has—we have
—the chance to change the Union for the better. We can show
the emperor and the Union Council there is nothing to fear.
Cyborgs aren't mindless super soldiers, but people with gifts.
Gifts that can contribute to society."

Memories of her family's staff being murdered in the
muddy street filled Gwen's mind. Clenching her fist, she willed
the flames of her anger to cool. Everyone was capable of
change and human decency, weren't they? Perhaps the
emperor and the Union Council did want to make the Union
a more accepting place.

She sure as fuck hoped so for the day when her contract
with the circus was up.

Taking a breath, she swallowed back her skepticism as she
watched childlike hope fill Rora's eyes. "If anyone can change
a politician's heart, it's you."

Rora's gaze was a glimmer of moonlight at the bottom of
a deep well, and Gwen could feel her heart reaching
toward it.

The music picked up again after droves of people had
been announced. Slowly, they started to dance again. As they
moved, they were so close that Gwen could feel the quickening
of Rora's breath as her breasts heaved against her corset.
Gradually, they slowed to a sway at the center of the dance
floor beneath the massive chandelier.

Couples moved around them in dances far more graceful
than theirs. But Gwen couldn't see them anymore.

All she saw were lips the color of a deep red rose, and hair
the color of ebony wood. Though it was far, far softer than
anything Gwen had touched in her parents' woodworking
shop. Slowly, she reached up to tuck a loose strand of hair
behind Rora's ear.

Rora's gaze slid from Gwen's eyes to her lips. The
gymnast's body shifted against hers as she stood on toes, her
breasts pressing beneath Gwen's. Desire filled Gwen, making

her dizzy. She wanted to slip her hands down Rora's dress and run her fingers over her nipples until they peaked.

Abandoning caution, Gwen leaned her head down. As she did, she was met with the scent of roses.

Before their lips met, the doors to the room slammed shut. They paused, looking up.

At the top of the stairs, the golden announcer had been pushed to the side as watchmen stationed themselves in front of all the doors and windows. Dozens of them lined the room, covering every inch of the walls.

The music teetered to a stop as the musicians looked up, irritation plain on their faces. Watchmen rounded up servants, ushering them through guarded exits. Musicians called loudly, insisting their instruments couldn't be left behind as they, too, were towed from the room. Then the watchmen barred the doors.

It was then Gwen recalled Bastian's words.

Everything isn't as it seems.

"What's going on?" Rora whispered, a sharp fear in her voice.

The performers lingering in the corners or alcoves of the room were ushered onto the dance floor. Soon, Gwen's arms rubbed against Rora's and many other people around her. If not for her ridiculous skirt, she would have been pressed by bodies on all sides as the crowd shuffled inward.

As she looked around the room, above the heads and top hats of those around her, she noticed the look of bewilderment in the faces of all the performers—all except Bastian. Standing on the stage the musicians had occupied not long ago, he stood beside the Mistress and show management team, his face devoid of emotion.

More watchmen stood at attention in front of the stage, creating a barrier between it and the performers.

"Good evening," the Mistress began in a velvety voice. "Thank you all for coming out tonight."

The hushed whispers tapered off as the Mistress spoke, and the room seemed to reverberate with tense silence.

"At Cirque du Borge, we pride ourselves not only in our dedication, but our style, and we are excited for tonight's events." The Mistress stopped, assessing the hundreds of performers crammed onto the dance floor. When her eyes fell on Gwen, the look was cold enough to make a wolf shiver. "Before we have our announcement, will our circus staff in attendance please join me on stage?"

Everyone around craned their necks to look at Gwen.

Rora squeezed Gwen's hand before letting go.

She thought of all the things she could say to reassure Rora, but no words came. Only Bastian's warning held weight in her mind.

You have an important job ahead this evening. Prepare yourself.

Was this what he'd been warning her about? What did he know? What exactly was going on here?

Slowly, Gwen nodded to Rora in farewell and made her way forward. The crowd did their best to shuffle aside and make a pathway for her, but the cage of her dress bent dangerously in, near to snapping, as she walked. Nearby, there was more shuffling.

Several other circus staff appeared and walked up the stairs, standing behind Bastian and the Mistress. Gwen did likewise, following them up and forming a line.

As the Mistress spoke of the history of the circus, Gwen tried to ignore the weight of the performers' eyes as they studied her and the other staff.

"We are excited to kick off the competition," the Mistress said, jerking Gwen's attention back to the present. "As you know, the circus has hit hard times since the Prohibition Law ten years ago. Gradually, the planets that once welcomed us with open arms—hosting our entire circus at their expense—have closed their doors to our show. As a result, Cirque du Borge will no longer host its large cast and will be eliminating performances that don't meet our standards."

Gwen's mind reeled. Was she firing people at a *ball*?

The Mistress continued over the murmurs of the crowd. "The emperor has invited the circus to Allegiant, and invitations from His Imperial Highness aren't optional. So, not only will you compete to claim one of the top ten acts to attend the emperor, but you will be competing to remain as part of our renowned circus. Those who don't make the cut will have their contracts terminated."

Gasps echoed throughout the ballroom.

The word "terminated" held a weight behind it that Gwen didn't understand. Celeste didn't mean she'd kill the cyborgs, did she? By the looks of horror on every performer's face, Gwen couldn't think of what else it would imply.

"Circus staff and management are exempt from the competition and will remain as part of Cirque du Borge—so long as they abide by our rules." The Mistress gestured first to Bastian, then to Gwen and the line of men and women behind her, the long sleeves of her gown brushing the stage floor.

"There will be three contests before we journey to the emperor's planet, Covenant. These contests will test your agility, determination, and skill.

"Know the path won't be easy. You will be tested like never before. I cannot guarantee everyone who participates will still have breath in their lungs at the completion of each competition."

Gwen blinked.

What the actual fuck?

"For those who complete the competition but do not make it into the top ten acts, I personally guarantee work and passage off Grandstand," the Mistress continued. "One performer from each act must participate, and you may choose a different representative for each competition if your act is a group number. But know—the entire act will share their fate."

"You can't do this!" someone yelled from the dance floor. "We signed a contract for thirteen years."

Several performers rushed toward the stage, shouting over one another. But the watchmen were ready.

Gwen wasn't a stranger to death. As a tinkerer on trading vessels, she had seen plenty of people die between the stars as pirates attempted to board their ship. Countless times, she'd had to fight for her own life.

But as a watchman swung his wooden baton, bashing in the head of a man pushing toward the stage, Gwen's eyes fixed on the trail of blood. The scarlet drops hung in the air for an impossibly long moment before splattering the stage and the circus staff on it.

The hall was so quiet, you could hear the gasping breaths of the performers. Those rushing toward the stage stopped before slowly retreating.

The message was clear.

The Mistress was untouchable, and the cyborgs were expendable.

What could Celeste possibly hope to gain by hosting some life-or-death competition? It was madness.

"One more thing," the Mistress said. "If you refuse to compete, your contract will be terminated on the spot. Break a leg."

The watchmen ushered the crowd toward a set of double doors at the back of the room. Folding her hands in front of her, the Mistress watched as the performers dressed in all their finery were ushered toward where the first contest must be taking place.

Gwen scanned the crowd for Rora, hoping to catch sight of her dark hair. Toward the back of the crowd, she spotted her. Dark eyes met Gwen's. Instead of the fear she'd expected to see laced through Rora's gaze, there was only betrayal.

"You knew," she seemed to say.

Shaking her head, Gwen moved forward. She wasn't sure what she planned to do. It wasn't like she could push through the wall of watchmen and make her way through the crowd to Rora. Not before those massive doors slammed shut.

But she had to do *something*. She had to explain she didn't have a hand in any of this.

Before she'd taken two steps, a hand caught her elbow.

"Don't." Bastian's voice was dangerously low as he stared ahead. "It's too late."

Pulling her arm free of Bastian's grip, she glared at the side of his head as he watched the procession.

That's why there was no alcohol, Gwen realized. *They knew the competition was about to begin. And the herald recorded every person who walked through the door to make sure all of the performers were here.*

The watchmen forced every last performer through the door and slammed it shut behind them.

Turning from the closed doors, Bastian looked at her, his brown eyes as emotionless as his stony expression. In a voice loud enough that the Mistress could overhear, he said, "Ms. Grimm, you will be assisting in the extraction after the competition tonight."

Realization dawned on her as fear sliced through her chest.

A terminated contract didn't mean death, not exactly. It meant the circus would reclaim its property: the cyborg implants.

And Gwen was the person who would do it.

CHAPTER 8

Someone stepped on the hem of Rora's pink gown.
Lurching forward, she tried to catch herself. A man's elbow to her cheekbone broke her fall. Fumbling, she grabbed his coat sleeve as pain glanced through her nose and teeth. Before she could right herself, more bodies pressed into her, the tidal wave moving ever forward—toward the open doorway and whatever lay beyond.

All of Cirque du Borge's cyborgs knew what was at stake.

They were now fighting for their lives in this competition.

In the fine print of every contract, there was a clause saying the circus could terminate a contract at any time for any reason. In other words, the circus could reclaim their property without explanation. Losing their implants was a gamble every cyborg in the circus had to make.

And Gwen had *known*. She'd known about this competition and hadn't told Rora.

The betrayal stung like an electric bolt from her cyborg hand.

So much for being a seductress. You're the one who's been played.

Was that why Gwen didn't want to go to the ball tonight? Had she known about the competition all along?

Then why did she try to kiss me?

Bitterness took root in Rora's chest.

While she was about to compete for her life, Gwen and Bastian were kicking their feet up and sipping champagne.

As Rora passed through the doorway into a darkened room, Marzanna and Akio appeared beside her. Together, they continued toward whatever awaited them in the darkness.

"I know the electricity sucks in this building, but why haven't they turned on any lights?" Marzanna whispered.

"Surprise," Rora said. "They don't want us seeing what's in store until we begin."

The crowd in front of them slowed. Rora hadn't noticed the man in front of her had stopped moving until she bumped into him.

A single spotlight flicked on, revealing the set designer, Matthieu Eaves. Despite years of creating everything and anything—from the stage itself to the massive ladders, balance beams, and supporting structures—Matthieu was a man devoid of muscles, good humor, and eyebrows. The spotlight cast shadows below his eyes and hollow cheekbones.

There was a loud snap as several more lights in the room flickered on. In front of Rora was a massive wooden wall with a single rope dangling in front of it. Beyond the wall, the room stretched endlessly. From what she could recall, this was one of the convertible amphitheaters.

What have you created, Mr. Eaves? What's beyond that wall?

"Good evening, performers," Matthieu said. "As the Mistress stated before, one performer from each act must participate. You may pick different people for each competition. But know that they compete alone. There are no teams in this contest, and the only thing you will share is the fate of the performer competing on behalf of group acts. If you are a part of a solo act, then you must compete in every competition. To win, you must beat those around you from different acts.

"There will be three competitions in total. Tonight is the first competition. Your agility will be tested. Brute strength will do you no good here, nor will wit or a slightness of hand. You must be nimble and quick."

Matthieu pointed at an upper-story window above the amphitheater, where dark figures loomed in the shadows. "Our show management team is present to witness the feats of Cirque du Borge and determine your worthiness to continue.

"Tonight, fourteen acts will be leaving our circus. Therefore, the first thirty-six performers to reach the finish line will go on to participate in the second contest. Every performer will be timed individually, and ten performers will participate in this competition at a time. Those who come in last and their entire acts will be terminated.

"As you know, the final ten acts who survive all three competitions will go on to attend the emperor in hopes of convincing the Union Council to change the Cyborg Prohibition Law. Afterward, those performers will continue as part of Cirque du Borge. Only the best and most determined performers will remain.

"You have one hour to prepare yourselves. Nominate your representatives wisely."

For several long moments, Rora forgot to breathe.

Fourteen acts would be eliminated *tonight*? If one of the trapeze acts or stuntmen were eliminated, that could mean dozens of people per act would leave this building without their cyborg parts.

Then, it clicked.

If there were fifty acts at Cirque du Borge currently and only ten of them would perform for the emperor, that meant forty acts would be leaving the circus in the coming months.

Rora glared at her fickle cyborg hand.

Unlike some of the cyborgs, she could live without her hand—if it was removed properly. But could she live with taking the place of a cyborg who *couldn't* live without their implants?

From what she'd seen during rehearsals, most of the performers had visible implants, such as robotic limbs, feet, or hands. How many cyborgs depended on their implants to live?

Finding an open space on the floor, she sat, and her friends joined her.

Marzanna had a cyborg foot and could live without her implant. But finding work in the Union would be hard without all of their limbs, no matter what the Mistress promised to those who survived the competition and lost.

Akio's feet and ankles were reinforced with a cyborg implant that wasn't visible, so far as Rora knew. He could live without those as well, but he'd have a limp and be in pain when on his feet for the rest of his life.

Even with all of this, there was still the fact that Rora would never be able to achieve her dream of patronage or performing for the emperor without securing one of the top ten spots.

She forced the guilt filling her empty stomach back down.

Years ago, she'd approached the circus to escape life as a wife to a lord. She had given up something very important to get here, and she wasn't about to go running home now. There was no choice for her.

Eyeing the wall and then her skirts, Rora made a decision. She stepped out of her slippers and strode to Marzanna. "Unlace me."

Marzanna's eyes lit with recognition. "Good thinking. Akio, start unlacing my dress, too."

Akio cursed under his breath. "I'd hoped you'd say that to me under different circumstances."

"Anyone else thinking what I'm thinking?" Marzanna said in a low tone as she loosened the laces of Rora's dress.

"Reading minds isn't one of my superpowers," Rora replied dryly.

"This whole competition is nuts," Marzanna whispered. "What is the Mistress thinking?"

Rora shook her head. "All I know is we have no choice but to play her game."

Around them, other performers shared similar feelings in their harsh whispers.

None of this made any sense. Why have the competitions? Why not simply choose the top ten acts?

Her eyes skirted up to the figures looming behind the windows several stories above.

Because they want us to put on a show.

"There's something bigger at play here," Rora said as though speaking to herself. "I just don't know what."

There wasn't time to speculate more now. She had to keep her mind focused on one thing—winning.

Soon, Rora and Marzanna had removed their massive ball gowns and were in their undergarments.

Grabbing the hem of her dress, Rora pulled until the fabric tore. Creating long slices of fabric, she passed some to Marzanna, who wrapped them around the pads of her feet and hands. They didn't know what would be out there, and while bare feet might work best for that wall, for all they know, there could be hot coals or a bed of needles on the other side. The fabric was thin protection against such things, but it was better than nothing.

Most of the men wore shoes and trousers, lucky for them. But when they spotted Rora and Marzanna undressing, they removed vests and jackets.

Once finished removing their extra garments, Akio and Marzanna moved off to the side, speaking animatedly. It was clear from the way they spoke that Akio had elected himself to participate in this first competition.

When the hour was up, the watchmen ushered the fifty performers who were competing on behalf of their acts into ten lines. The remaining performers were escorted to the back of the room.

It was then Rora realized they would be timed in groups. That meant, even if she won in her group, she wouldn't know if she'd actually made it to the second contest until the final tally—unless she came in one of the top spots. It also meant that, if she performed beside her friends, she could potentially be the reason for them coming in last place.

Rather than remaining in the line of performers beside Akio, Rora turned to him and said, "Good luck. I better see your sorry face on the other side."

Then she pushed her way to the front line where none of her friends were. She wouldn't compete beside them.

Abrecan appeared beside her. "Hello, dyke. So eager to start your new life as a human?"

Rora didn't bother explaining to him, yet again, that she had no gender preference for her partners. The moment she'd turned down his offer of "friendship" after she'd joined the circus, he'd decided she wasn't into men. It wasn't worth the time or energy to explain it was *his* cock she found undesirable. Not others.

"I was looking for an easy win," she said instead. "Didn't feel like actually breaking a sweat tonight."

"You little cunt," Abrecan hissed, but before he could raise a hand, one of the watchmen walked by, and the archer stood dangerously still in the line. "One way or another, you'll leave this circus."

"Don't be bitter because Ms. Grimm chose me over you," she said, eyes ahead.

She could practically feel him seething next to her.

"I saw your little stunt in her office." Turning, she looked him up and down. "You did the same thing to me when I first joined the circus. And it would appear she's not interested in your cock either."

Rora didn't trust Gwendolyn, not after tonight. But

Abrecan didn't need to know that. All that mattered was getting him off his game—and beating him.

Veins bulged in his neck and jaw, but he didn't have time to reply.

One of the watchmen whistled, drawing all eyes to him. "You'll proceed through the course in five groups, ten performers in each. All of you will be timed. Proceed on my mark."

The watchmen stood in two lines, forming a path toward the wooden wall and holding stopwatches on copper chains. Others took posts around the room and at the exits, preventing anyone from leaving.

Clenching her fists, Rora tried to force blood to muscles she hadn't stretched or warmed up. With nothing else to do, she took her position, squatting low, preparing to run toward the single rope dangling before the massive wooden wall. The section of the former stage was flat and lacked handholds. It spanned the length of ten doors across with a steep drop-off on the floor at the end of either side of it. Below must be the basement floor.

The rope was the only way up, and ten people needed to get there first. She had to get there before Abrecan.

The watchman standing before them raised his hand into the air. Rora held her breath and crouched low. A moment later, his arm swung down.

The competition for their lives had begun.

Rora dashed forward before any of the other performers had left the starting line, throwing her weight into each stride. She willed her short legs to run faster. Close behind, Abrecan gained on her. The rope was nearly within reach when he passed her, grabbed it, and pulled himself up.

No!

Several times, she tried to start climbing, but performers shoved her aside or pulled her down. Stumbling backward, she fell to the very back of the line.

"Come on, Rora!" Akio's voice was distant above the roaring frustration of her thoughts. She couldn't think of her friends now.

As the last person ascended the rope, Rora followed, climbing up until she was close enough to swing to the wall.

There was no platform atop the wall, so she swung herself over, letting go of the rope and landing atop the narrow wall. Crouching, she had her first look at the course. Because that's what it was—an obstacle course.

Only, it clearly wasn't one most of the cyborgs were supposed to survive.

Below Rora was a pit of water with shards of ice. The icy pit extended for a short distance before it was cut off by another wooden wall. As she watched, two of the cyborgs— one who had an implanted shoulder and another with no visible cyborg part—plunged beneath the water where the wall was, visibly trembling.

Rora gaped.

Older implants couldn't be fully submerged underwater. It would blow the mainframe or short-circuit the implant, especially if the battery was an older model. At best, submersion would leave dated implants immobile. At worst, it would kill the host from a series of electric shocks.

Newer implants could be submerged underwater... but there was no way of knowing how old Rora's refurbished implant was. She'd never dared test it before.

Hesitating, Rora stared down at the pit of ice.

Where in the galaxy had the Mistress gotten ice on such a low budget? The nearby mountains, perhaps. By the look of the two walls, it was clear she was recycling old circus sets and props for the competition.

It looked like the only way to get past the second wall beyond the pit of icy water was to swim beneath it, which meant her muscles would be stiff and cold for what lay on the other side. If she didn't short-circuit or die before then. The most she could hope for was to get in and out of the pit of ice as quickly as possible.

Slowly, she rose to her feet atop the narrow wooden wall, just as she would for her balancing beam act atop the wire.

This is going to suck.

Then she launched herself off the wall and into the pit far below.

CHAPTER 9

I cy shards bit into her flesh.

Rora spewed out some of the air she'd been holding. To her surprise, her feet never touched the bottom. She waited for it, perhaps too long, before kicking her way to the surface. Her arms and legs grew stiff from the cold, and she trembled violently.

Cold bled into her implant. Her hand stiffened almost to the point of immobility, but there were no electric bolts.

Relief washed over her as she kicked. Her implant wasn't a complete piece of junk, after all.

Breaking the surface of the water, she gasped. Ice tumbled out of her hair, and her entire body trembled. Clenching her jaw, she forced her legs to kick. One, then the other. As she neared the next wall, her feet touched the ground beneath the water's surface.

Some kind of platform the wall was anchored to?

Taking a deep breath, she eyed the wall and plunged beneath the surface a second time, kicking with all her might and praying her muscles wouldn't seize up from the cold. As she swam, she opened her eyes, trying to see in the murky ice water. But it was too dark, so she held a hand up, feeling along the wall above her as she swam. When the wall stopped, she pushed herself to the surface.

Her teeth chattered so hard against each other that she thought they'd crack. But this wasn't the other side of the wall. She was in the center. A bike ramp from one of their old shows had been flipped upside down and converted somehow. Where she stood was large enough for five men to huddle closely together. Only, she wasn't surrounded by men.

For a moment, she didn't feel the cold as she stared at them.

Three dead cyborgs.

A scream tore through her throat, and she clapped a hand over her mouth as her body trembled harder. Only, this time, it wasn't from the cold.

Asa, the tightrope walker with a cyborg foot, a gymnast whose name Rora had never known, and Charles the stilt walker. They floated, bodies limp. Smoke didn't trail from their bodies, but she could see blackened flesh from where their cyborg implants must have sparked.

Rubbing away the tears from her cheeks, she accidentally scraped her skin with her cyborg hand. The pain brought her out of her foggy chill, her thoughts forming too slowly.

Gwen's face appeared in Rora's mind—how radiant she'd looked in the golden gown, and how, if those had been her last moments of freedom, she would have loved to kiss the tinkerer. Even if whatever hovered between them was a lie.

We are all liars at Cirque du Borge.

Rora plunged back into madness.

Feeling along the wall, she eventually made it to the other side. When she kicked up to the surface and brushed the water from her eyes, she saw three massive tubes with one end in the water and the other sticking straight up. They were attached to some platform far above.

Heart racing, she trudged through the icy waters toward the three tubes. Her body shook violently, and it took every ounce of self-control not to stop and give in to the cold seeping into her bones.

Keep going. If you stop, you'll lose your hand.

A warmth settled in her chest, and she clung to a deep-rooted determination and flicker of hope. If she was going to perform for the emperor, she had to win. She'd already lost her chance once, and she wasn't going to do so again.

When she neared the tubes, she noticed the faint outlines of bodies in all three of the tunnels. In the left- and right-most tunnels, the performer in each moved steadily upward. In the center tunnel, the shadow didn't move but remained at the top.

She couldn't stall her climb until they finished. Icy shock stiffened her limbs, and her entire body was wracked with chills. When she moved to the left-most tunnel, she found herself hesitating, looking back toward the center tunnel.

Where the body still hadn't moved.

For a moment, she thought of her dreams of getting a patron, how she had to come in the top thirty-six acts to get past this round in the competition. But her mind immediately retreated to the images of Asa, Charles, and the third cyborg dead in the icy water. She couldn't let another person die. Not if she could help it.

Diving under the water, she came up at the base of the center tunnel. The tube was slick with water and lacked any handholds beyond the ribbed texture of the tunnel itself. Like the bike ramp, she recognized these tunnels from an old set.

Looking up, she saw the performer at the top of the tunnel tremble, body and limbs twisted. Even though most of what she could see was the performer's backend, she knew perfectly well who it was.

Thaniel Chors.

One of Abrecan's closest comrades was stuck at the top of the tunnel.

She shook her head. It *had* to be him. But she didn't dare go back now. She'd made her decision.

"I'm coming up," she called.

Pressing her palms on opposite sides of the tube-like structure, she slowly made her way up the tunnel. When her cyborg hand kept slipping from the wall, water dripping between her robotic fingers, she pressed her back to one side of the tunnel and her feet to the other, shimmying up the tube slowly and pushing beneath her with her hands.

"G-go back," Thaniel said. "There's n-no way I'm getting out of this f-fucking tunnel."

"It's nice you're—" She bit back a chill threatening to send her body into spasms. "Concerned for my safety f-for once."

"F-fuck you." His words didn't hold his usual bravado but were quiet and resigned.

Eventually, she was only a few feet from Thaniel. His trembling had subsided, and her breath caught. Was he about to pass out and bring her down to the bottom of the tunnel with his unconscious body?

"Is that how you treat your rescuer?" Locking her knees, she pressed her back against the wall, icy water dripping from her undergarments. She tried to determine where his body started and where it ended. Like Abrecan, Thaniel was a large man, both in height and stature. "I'm going to try to give you a boost."

"G-go away now, or we'll b-both d-die," he rasped, his body going dangerously still.

Moved by impulse, she slammed her fisted cyborg hand into his back.

"Hey!" he cried, his usual obstinacy returning to his voice.

"Quit being lazy and do something for once."

"You sound like my lovers," he mumbled.

"You're despicable."

Still, he was talking again, which seemed like a good sign.

Eyeing him, she positioned herself below his shoulders,

where his head and neck were wedged. "I'm going to push your shoulders up. Try to move on my count. Ready?" She didn't bother waiting. "One, two, three!"

Stretching her arms up, she heaved, pushing with all her might. Thaniel remained where he was, hardly moving. Hands slipping, she skidded down the tunnel, barely managing to catch herself. He was just too big, and she was far too small.

"It's n-no use."

"Again," she called as she climbed back up beneath him. "One, two, three!"

When he still didn't move, his body only managing to slide back down toward the frigid water, she shimmied up even farther. In a most ladylike manner, she shoved her head and shoulder into his back and pushed, pressing her hands and feet to either side of the tunnel.

Something slipped, and Thaniel shifted up. The sudden lack of pressure had her skidding back down the tunnel. Before she'd slipped far, a hand gripped her human one.

Above her, Thaniel was upright in the tube with one hand holding her wrist. He nodded to her, releasing her once she got her footing. They both made their way up to the top of the tunnel. When she climbed out, the juggler was waiting for her.

"This doesn't make us friends."

"Stars, I hope not," she replied. "I plan on beating you tonight."

The corner of his lips twitched. Not a smile, exactly, but it was more than they'd ever shared before.

Thaniel turned from her without a word, moving to their next obstacle. Rora followed.

The two performers who had been in the other tubes were crossing the next obstacle now.

Rows and rows of small gymnastic rings hung suspended over a pit of icy water. Unlike the first rope they had climbed up, here there were enough rings that they wouldn't have to take turns swinging across.

The man on the left struggled to keep his hold. His hands slipped more and more as he swung from one hoop to the next.

Rora looked down at her own hands, both dripping wet.

The man lost his grip, falling two stories to the water below with an icy splash. Moments later, his head broke the surface, and he swam backward—toward the three tunnels.

Rora gaped.

If they fell, they'd have to climb back up those awful tunnels and risk getting submerged in the icy waters again.

Still trembling from the cold, she wasn't sure she'd survive another plunge.

Thaniel wiped his palms on his wet shirt before extending a hand out to the nearest hoop at the edge of the platform they stood on. Without further preamble, he swung forward, moving from ring to ring. Rora expected him to struggle with his massive gut, but he moved with ease.

Taking a deep breath, she followed suit. Though, she had to jump up to reach the first hoop. She caught it with her human hand. Short as she was, she had to swing her legs to get enough momentum to swing to the next hoop. Halfway through the course, her arms shook, and she struggled to keep her grip. Not only were her hands wet, but so were nearly all of the hoops—from six other wet performers using them.

Suddenly, her hand slipped and she threw up her cyborg one. Catching the hoop, she latched her fingers onto the wet wood. As she did, Thaniel's feet thudded onto the opposite platform. Gritting her teeth, she swung forward.

She would *not* lose to Thaniel. Not after saving his sorry ass.

Eventually, she reached the other side, passing the woman who'd been climbing up the tube earlier. Like the man who'd fallen, she struggled to keep her hold.

Fifth place, she realized, with three performers dead and two behind her. *I need to do better.*

Adrenaline surged in her veins.

I can do this. I will *make it to one of the top ten spots.*

Rora moved in a fog through several more obstacles, all of which were recycled pieces or props from former shows. Some of them she'd been in, while other sets were unfamiliar to her.

Throughout, she never once saw Abrecan. Slowly, she passed three other performers until she was in second place. But Abrecan was nowhere to be seen.

Until now.

At the final obstacle, with the remaining performers at her heels, she finally spotted him.

Above her were two parallel obstacles.

Two sets of walls were set several feet off the ground. Once again, there were no handholds, and the two walls of each were wide enough apart that most performers would have to put their backs to one side and their feet on the other to shimmy up.

Abrecan was a quarter of the way up on the left one. Since he was so tall, he was able to have one foot and one hand on each wall as he slowly pushed himself up toward the finish line where there were watchmen with timers.

Thank the stars the man wasn't skilled at climbing, or he'd have beaten her by now.

Sprinting, she leaped upward. She slowly inched her way up, but her arms and legs were nearly at their full distance just trying to touch either side. As she climbed, the ground growing distant below her, her sweaty palms and feet kept sliding back down.

"I must say," Abrecan's voice called. Was that a hint of fatigue she detected? "I'm surprised you made it this far. I thought you'd be as dead as Asa. Though I wish I could have assisted in the process."

Rora's knees locked, and she froze in place. "You killed

Asa?" She could have sworn she'd seen the blackened flesh and metal, a sign she'd short-circuited.

"She made a little tumble off the first wall," Abrecan grunted. "Hit her implant on the way down, poor thing. She short-circuited during the swim shortly after. Must have busted her implant somehow in the fall. Really too bad. But if we're being honest, she didn't stand a chance."

Unlocking her knees, Rora forced herself to keep moving.

He's trying to distract me because he knows I'm gaining on him. He's big, and for once, it's not an advantage. That means he's slow.

Sweat beaded on her brow, and her arms and legs shook, utterly exhausted from the competition. Despite years of training and having a mechanical advantage to regular humans, her muscles were stiff and fatigued. She had to finish and soon, or she'd run out of energy.

More importantly, she had to beat Abrecan.

She threw every ounce of energy she had left into her muscles, pushing toward the top, rotating hands, then feet, then hands, then feet. Her arms shook, and she breathed in ragged gasps.

Soon, she was close enough to the top to see the color of a watchman's blue eyes behind the mask.

When she threw a hand over the edge, her fingers landed on a platform. Gripping it, she pulled herself up as another body tumbled beside her.

Several watchmen stood above her, looking down at a clipboard.

"We have our winner."

Gasping, she nearly vomited as she sucked in air, her head swimming.

Turning, she saw the truth in Abrecan's eyes. He rose to his feet, but she didn't have the strength to get up.

With a snicker, Abrecan brushed his hands together. "You lose, dyke."

CHAPTER 10

G wen paced in front of the door where the performers met their fates.

How much longer?

Heeled shoes clicked against the floor, and she spun around at the sound. "Piss off."

"Keep your voice down." Bastian's eyes flicked to where the watchmen were stationed every few paces and at each exit.

Were they waiting for something?

Rora could be dying right now, she thought, cursing her inability to do a damn thing.

Looking around, she saw that the Mistress still hadn't returned. Celeste had disappeared with the show management team down a hallway near where the performers had vanished what felt like hours ago.

Gwen didn't bother hiding her glare as she strode past Bastian and sat down on a nearby windowsill.

You knew. You knew, and you let this happen.

Begrudgingly, he joined her. His silence sent spikes of anger shooting through her.

Against her better judgment, she turned to face him. "Why?"

Bastian raised an eyebrow.

"Why warn me and not them?"

Veins in his jaw bulged, and he hesitated before saying, "I don't know."

Gwen shook her head. "Isn't this violating the contract? Don't performers have thirteen years before their contracts are through? The Mistress can't—"

"The Mistress can do as she pleases. Never forget that." The warning in his voice faded as he sighed. "There is a clause in the contract that states the circus can terminate a contract at any time and for any reason."

Standing, Bastian straightened his coat.

"I tried to warn you, Ms. *Fucking* Grimm. Try to remember that tonight."

The Mistress and show management team strode through the room and onto the stage. Moments later, the watchmen opened the doors at the opposite end of the room.

A relieved laugh escaped Gwen's lips as Rora and Abrecan stepped into the ballroom. Both had towels draped around them and shook visibly. Was that *ice* in their hair?

Before they'd gotten far, Rora stumbled over to a potted plant against the wall and vomited for several long moments. She eventually stood, wiping her mouth with the back of an arm.

Abrecan waited beside the watchmen with a tapping foot.

When they resumed walking, Rora didn't look at Gwen, staring straight ahead as several watchmen escorted them across the empty ballroom. Her bare feet slapped against the floor, ribbons of cloth barely clinging to them. Abrecan, on the other hand, seemed completely unfazed by whatever horrors they had just faced.

Before Gwen realized what she was doing, she ran over to Rora. "What happened? Are you hurt?"

Bastian materialized at Gwen's side, and the watchmen

and performers all stopped walking. "Mr. Brower will see to your injuries."

The healer appeared, his head bowed and eyes glued on the floor as he nodded.

"You are needed for another task," Bastian said to Gwen. Turning to Abrecan and Rora, he said, "Ms. Beckett will speak to you now."

Rora's mouth drew into a thin line, but she didn't say anything to Bastian or Gwen.

Looking toward the stage, to where the show management team now stood, Gwen stiffened as she realized Celeste was staring right at them—at her. Gwen looked away and cursed herself for a coward.

"Congratulations on your victories," Celeste said, palms upraised as though in prayer. "You completed the competition with such swiftness that your names won't be placed in the lotteries. Therefore, you will both move on to the next round of the competition. After you see the healer, go to your rooms and rest. You have the morning off."

There was a *lottery system*? The idea of life or death boiling down to a name drawn out of a metaphorical hat was preposterous.

Bastian's fingers encircled Gwen's elbow. "Come with me."

It was an order if she ever heard one.

Gwen thought of objecting or lingering to see if Rora was all right. Instead, she accompanied Bastian to a room off the main ballroom with several watchmen at their heels. For some reason, the room had been set up similar to her office. There was a massive patient table at the center and a tub beside it. On a table on the opposite wall, her cyborg eye fixed on the metal tools. Unlike the tools in her office, there were no screwdrivers, pliers, or other common tinkering tools, but hooked metallic instruments.

Tools for extraction.

Shaking her head, she backed away from the table. Her pulse thumped like an executioner's ax against a stump.

She couldn't—

Again, Bastian caught her elbow. There was an almost imperceptible shake of his head as warning filled his eyes. *Don't,* he seemed to say.

A moment later, a young woman Gwen's age was towed into the room by watchmen who pulled her by the wrists. Tears streamed down her face. "Please," she begged. "Please don't do this. I can be useful. I'll improve my act. I can—"

The Mistress strode into the room after them.

"Ms. Charlotte Laney," Celeste began, her voice as mechanical as the cyborg parts in all of them. "Due to your inability to complete the course, your contract will be henceforth terminated. All properties of Cirque du Borge will be removed, and you will no longer be bound to the circus. Thank you for sharing your talent with us."

When Celeste stopped speaking, she didn't move or even acknowledge the words tumbling from Charlotte's mouth as freely as her tears. The Mistress stood resolutely, hands behind her back, as Charlotte was forced onto the table by the watchmen and strapped down.

Like Rora, Charlotte had a cyborg hand that extended to her elbow.

"Ms. Grimm," the Mistress said, her voice as cold as the ice falling off Charlotte and splattering onto the floor. "You are to extract her cyborg implant. The chips installed into the mainframe in her skull can remain, as those cannot be repurposed."

Not long ago, this seemed like some stupid circus with petty politics she could easily keep a distance from. But now? This wasn't some competition for the emperor—it was a massacre.

Bastian, the Mistress, and the show management team knew Gwen wasn't qualified to safely extract cyborg implants.

Even if she was qualified, she wouldn't do it. She wouldn't help them hurt people.

"No." To Gwen's surprise, her voice didn't tremble. "Her implant is integrated into her muscles and tissues. If I detach it, she could lose the use of her whole arm or worse—she could bleed out and die."

Charlotte wailed louder and pulled against the restraints strapping her to the table. All she managed was to twist her neck around, directing panicked, pleading eyes at Gwen.

A half-smile flicked across the Mistress's face. She nodded to one of the watchmen, who loosened the wooden baton at his hip.

Without warning, the guard strode over to Gwen and swung. The baton connected with her bare shoulder. Pain erupted, coloring her senses in a violent shade of red. She stumbled backward, too surprised to defend herself as the watchman swung a second time. The air was knocked out of her as he struck her stomach.

Gasping, Gwen crumpled to the ground in a pile of golden skirts.

Did that fucker just break one of my ribs?

"I don't think you quite understand the predicament you're in, Ms. Grimm," the Mistress said. "You work for me, for this circus. If you don't obey my instructions, there will be consequences, and those consequences will be severe. Don't fool yourself. I don't need you. Even as a surgeon and scientist, I'm a far better tinkerer than you will ever be. But I don't have time for such trivial matters."

Gwen wheezed, unable to take a deep breath.

How is killing off your performers trivial?

Celeste gestured to the wailing Charlotte. "It's simple. Either do your job, or you will join them." She flicked manicured fingernails as though a thought had just occurred to her. "I'll let this one instance slide since it's your first week. But consider today your one and only warning. If you disobey me a second time, my watchmen will not simply remind you of your place. You will lose the use of your legs. After all, tinkerers do not need their legs to work."

Unable to stop herself, Gwen's eyes slid to the massive sword sheathed at the watchman's hip and then to the two pistols strapped to their back.

"If you disobey me a third time or step out of line in any way—and stars help you if you do—I will remove your new eye. I installed the implant. I can, and will, take it back." A glint of malice she'd never seen before swirled in the Mistress's eyes.

Could Gwen survive without her eye and the plating and technology reinforcing her skull? Perhaps not.

Celeste didn't move from where she stood above Gwen. "Have I made myself clear?"

Gwen thought of every horrible boss she'd ever had working as a ship tinkerer—launderers, rapists, thugs. But never murderers.

She'd been so excited for the challenge of a new position at the circus, of proving herself as a tinkerer in her new life as a cyborg. More than that, she'd been so damn confident in her skills, in her ability to learn a completely different job. But cyborg tinkering was as different from ship tinkering as life and death. At this moment, her skills meant the difference between life as a human for Charlotte and no life at all.

For the first time, she wondered if she should have turned down Bastian's offer.

Slowly, Gwen stood. Her eyes skirted to the table of instruments behind her, which were cleaned to a shine, revealing her reflection in the metal—wide eyes, clenched jaw, brow slick with sweat.

If I don't do this, Charlotte could lose her entire arm or worse. Surely, I'm a far better option than Celeste. At least I have a fucking heart.

"I'll do it," Gwen said, and Charlotte screamed. "Where are your surgeons? I could use their assistance."

"Besides myself, we do not have official cyborg surgeons on staff," the Mistress said. "But Mr. Kabir and these watchmen are at your disposal."

Gwen eyed the watchman who'd struck her twice, the baton still in his fist.

Goody.

Gwen sighed. "What about anesthesia?"

The Mistress shook her head. "No additional anesthesia will be given to performers with terminated contracts."

"But that's…" Gwen began, but stopped.

Looming quietly at the edges of the room, Bastian shook his head, almost imperceptibly. Yet another warning.

Biting her tongue, she turned back to the task at hand. With shaking hands, she smoothed Rora's golden gown before she picked up several tools and a strip of leather and turned to Charlotte. Ignoring Bastian, the Mistress, and the watchmen, she said, "I'll need you to bite on this."

Charlotte froze as Gwen held the piece of leather before her mouth.

"I'll work as fast as I can, but this will hurt. If you want to save your teeth along with your life, I suggest you bite on this."

Slowly, Charlotte opened her mouth, and Gwen slipped the leather strap between her teeth.

Not too long ago, Celeste had done the very same thing before turning Gwen into a cyborg.

To the watchmen, Gwen said, "I need alcohol. As much as you can find."

The Mistress nodded, and two of the guards left the room.

After washing her hands and donning gloves lined with rubber, Gwen popped open the plating to the woman's cyborg hand, revealing the main panel. She turned off the system's magnetic energy and removed the battery, hoping that would prevent any electric shocks to either herself or Charlotte. Next, she used her cyborg eye to locate where the implant met the flesh and bone, wondering just where she could detach it.

For the first time in her life, Gwen wished she'd pursued a profession as a healer and not a tinkerer. She knew precious little of human anatomy. Only what she'd learned while working as a tinkerer, acting as a pseudo healer in deep space when there had been injuries following pirate attacks.

Turning to the Mistress, she dared to meet her eyes. "How many cyborgs are critically dependent on their implants?"

From what Gwen had seen, there were at least three hundred performers employed by Cirque du Borge. Fourteen of the fifty total acts were to be eliminated in a single evening. How many wouldn't leave here alive because they depended on their implants to survive? And how many could have left alive without their implants if only Gwen was more knowledgeable?

The Mistress raised a perfectly plucked eyebrow. "One-eighth of the circus."

Gwen blanched.

If there were three hundred performers in the circus, thirty-eight of them would be sentenced to death if they lost the competition.

Thirty-eight people dead, and for what?

"What do you plan to do with the implants I'm extracting?" Gwen dared the question. She knew Bastian would be writhing under his skin right now. But if she was to harvest these performers and they'd lose their implants, everyone here had a right to know.

The Mistress's heels clicked on the floor as she stepped up to Gwen, close enough that their chests nearly touched as she whispered in Gwen's ear. "I plan to use them."

Brows drawing together, Gwen wasn't sure what the hell that meant and didn't have time to think on it as the Mistress stepped back and positioned herself against a nearby wall.

Piling loads of cloth on the table beside her, Gwen picked up a knife, studied where the metal from Charlotte's implant blossomed in her cyborg eye, and made her first incision, cutting deep enough into the skin to reveal muscle and bone.

Blood pooled from the cut as Gwen widened it. The woman screamed, writhing under the straps that bound her to the table, but they held fast. Blotting up the pooling blood, she pulled the skin back so she could see more clearly. Then she sliced off the edge of the muscle and other flesh where the cyborg implant was attached.

Charlotte's back arched as she screamed louder, thrashing on the table.

Blood filled the cloth that Gwen had lined the edge of the table with. She placed the cyborg implant into the massive tub at the side of the room before returning to Charlotte. Eyeing the table, she realized there wasn't a needle or thread.

The door clacked open. Two watchmen strode in with a glass bottle of what she hoped was alcohol.

"What took you so long?" Gwen snatched the bottle from their hands. "Get me one of the candles from the ballroom." She turned to Bastian. "I also need a needle and thread. Lots of it."

A watchman appeared with a candle, and she ran a knife through the flame.

"If I'm to do this again, I can't sear everyone's skin shut," she said. "It's barbaric and a last resort."

The woman whimpered behind them.

Bastian looked at Charlotte, then to Gwen before nodding and disappearing.

Gwen did her best to clean what remained of Charlotte's arm with the alcohol. Then she held the flaps of skin down, ran her knife through the candle's flame a second time, and pressed down.

The room filled with the smell of roasting flesh.

Finally, Charlotte passed out. Relief flooded Gwen's chest as she finished her work. When she was done, she panted heavily, sweat mingling with the blood and gore soaking her dress. Looking down, she realized her once beautiful golden gown was covered in deep scarlet.

Turning, Gwen looked at the Mistress, not bothering to dampen the heat in her eyes. As expressionless as a piece of parchment, Celeste nodded before turning and leaving the room. As if in approval.

The rest of the night passed in a blur.

The cyborgs were escorted into the room by watchmen—some fighting, others begging for their lives—and then carried out unconscious after Gwen's administrations. Bastian never left her side and helped wherever he could. By the early hours of the morning, fourteen acts no longer had their cyborg implants.

All because one woman couldn't bear to be parted with her property.

But the performers had all left *alive*. So long as they didn't get an infection, most of them should survive. They would be disfigured, but they would be alive.

And human.

Thank the stars none of them had been among the eighth who required their implants to live.

When the last person was escorted out of the makeshift surgical room, Gwen's dress was more scarlet than gold. Bastian's once handsome black jacket and pants were soaked through.

She hated him.

She hated what he and this circus had made her do. But he had also helped her to save lives this evening. How much of this was following orders? He *had* warned her, after all.

Tears streamed down Gwen's cheeks, and she wiped them away with bloodied hands.

She wasn't a stranger to hardship or death. Not as a child growing up on Orthodocks after the emperor's ascension nor as a ship tinkerer fighting pirates boarding her vessel in deep space.

She'd always found something to fight for, whether it was a new life or for her family. Now, she had to protect her new family. Her cyborg family.

Not too long ago, she'd been on death's doorstep and given a second chance at life. These cyborgs deserved the same.

It was time someone took a stand at Cirque du Borge.

Gwen wouldn't be cowed so easily. She'd do everything she could to protect the remaining cyborgs.

Cyborgs like me.

CHAPTER 11

"Get back!" a watchman shouted, a wooden baton in his fist.

A line of watchmen pushed the cyborg performers back as dozens attempted to rush Gwen's office when the theater doors opened for the morning before rehearsals started.

It had been this way for more than a week.

Her office was a cacophony of noises—shouting voices, grinding gears, sparking implants. Sweat poured down the sides of Gwen's cheeks, plopping onto the floor as she worked on Marzanna's foot.

"No new implants will be ordered," one watchman called, his monotone voice raised to be heard over the crowd. "Only the final ten acts will receive new parts for their current implants. In the meantime, we recommend you make time to see the tinkerer for any serious technology glitches prior to the second competition. Refurbished materials can and will be used."

Gritting her teeth, Gwen reached a gloved hand into the inner workings of Marzanna's foot and replaced several faulty wires. The machine sparked as she worked, but she doused it, hurriedly working to secure the wires into the machine.

It would be so convenient if I knew what I was doing.

Unlike Rora's hand, which sparked with overuse due to outdated machinery, Marzanna's foot appeared to have been installed improperly. The response time lagged when she tried to move too quickly, and the foot often flopped as she spun in the air or dragged as she walked. Certain wires and plates connected to her flesh weren't symmetrical all the way around, making her ankle turn in and her one leg longer than the other.

When she finished on Marzanna's foot, Gwen recalled her list of things to address. Turn off the battery, detach and remove faulty wires, check systems for any additional malfunctions, install new wiring, double-check the wiring and color-coding, turn the system back on.

That should do it.

With her lack of new supplies since the second competition, she'd been hard-pressed to find the right wiring for the implants. From the notes she'd taken for herself the night before, she knew she needed at least eight different varieties of wires. If she had the manual of the implant, she'd know for certain. As it was, she had to guess which wires went with which classes based on size and general appearance.

Stars, she prayed she did this right.

Like every day before, she barely managed to get by. Thanks to this ludicrous competition, she not only had no idea how to be a cyborg tinkerer but now she had no time to *learn*. The books in her office were outdated pieces of shit, more useless than the scraps of metal, mismatched screws, and other machinery lying around her office shelves. She needed to get medical textbooks, the kind that would have been outlawed or collected by the Union ten years ago.

Gwen closed the panel on Marzanna's foot. "All set. Thanks for your patience. Hopefully, it shouldn't lag as much.

Truthfully, it looks like the unit wasn't installed properly, but I don't have the tools or the skills to surgically remove it and reinstall it. But if you keep it clean and dry, it should get you through the next few weeks."

"Thanks." Marzanna hopped off the table and tested her foot, slowly shifting her weight from one foot to another. "It's better."

Unable to stop herself, Gwen sighed.

Marzanna nodded to where Rora rehearsed atop the slackline across the theater... without so much as turning her head in Gwen's direction. "You two still not talking?"

Rora had been the only performer who refused to have her cyborg implant inspected since the first competition. When Gwen watched her train, she could tell from the way Rora avoided using the hand that something wasn't working properly.

Gwen ran a hand over the half of her head where she'd never stopped shaving since her implantation surgery. "Is it that obvious?"

Planting one hand on a hip, Marzanna raised an eyebrow. "The sexual tension up in here is so thick, it's distracting. Stop being a little bitch and talk to her."

"That's easier said than done," Gwen grumbled. "She won't listen to me."

Marzanna rolled her eyes, striding back toward the theater. "Make her listen."

Gwen sighed.

Great pep talk.

The watchmen permitted more cyborgs in throughout the day. But in every free moment Gwen had, she pulled out a secret project she'd been working on since the first competition, using every spare part that wasn't garbage and careful not to let anyone spot it. As soon as the bell struck, indicating rehearsals were done for the day, she hurried out of her office and toward the dormitories.

Before she'd gotten far, she hesitated, looking over her shoulder.

Three watchmen followed her.

"Can I help you?"

No one moved or spoke.

Sighing, she said, "Why are you following me?"

The center watchman, a woman, spoke up. "The Mistress has decreed there shall be a guard around the tinkerer at all times for her safety."

She didn't doubt performers from thirty-six acts either wanted her help or wanted her dead. Though she suspected that wasn't the real reason she was being followed.

The Mistress is making sure I don't step out of line again.

Gritting her teeth, she didn't say anything as she turned and strode to the dormitories. She tried to ignore the single question swirling around her thoughts.

Can I survive without my implant?

She knew the Mistress's threat to take out her eye wasn't an idle one, but she'd had the surgery to remove the tumor in her head. The cyborg eye was a bonus. Could she survive without the plating in her skull? How far could she push the Mistress's boundaries?

Most of the performers were cleaning up before the evening meal. Rather than going to her room in a separate wing of the palace, Gwen strode straight to a door at the end of the hall.

Hesitating, she glanced over her shoulder to the three watchmen hovering behind her. With a groan, she swallowed her pride and knocked on the door.

The door opened, revealing Rora, who looked as though she'd just bitten into a lemon.

"Tinkerer, at your service," Gwen began awkwardly before clearing her throat. "I'm here to look at that hand. Since... Well, since you seemed pretty busy at rehearsals today."

Since you've been ignoring me this past week.

Rolling her eyes, Rora moved to shut the door. Expecting as much, Gwen shoved a screwdriver into the door, blocking it before it could click shut.

"Go away," Rora bit out.

"Can we talk?" Gwen gestured to the watchmen lingering in the hallway behind her. "I'm trying to help you here."

Rora held the door, unmoving.

"Please, just give me five minutes," Gwen persisted, not daring to remove the screwdriver. "If you think I'm full of shit by the end of it, I'll leave you alone."

Rora's gaze shifted to the watchmen loitering in the hallway. Performers awkwardly trundled around them, pausing long enough to frown at the watchmen, Gwen, Rora, and the state of the Union before finally moving along.

"Fine." Opening the door, Rora took a step back into her less than immaculate bedroom. "Five minutes."

"Excellent." Gwen bolted into Rora's room before closing the door in one of the watchmen's faces. "You won't regret it."

"Don't be so sure."

How the hell did I fall for a fucking pessimist?

Gwen paused as she removed her toolbelt.

Had she fallen for Rora? That was ludicrous. You couldn't fall for someone you hardly knew. Rora was just... well, she was beautiful. And Gwen wanted to fuck her beautiful, dark, petite body. That was all.

Slowly, she donned her usual rubber gloves after laying out her instruments on the only clean section of the floor she could find. Grabbing several tools, she sat on the edge of Rora's bed, gesturing for the gymnast to join her.

Still not speaking, Rora sat down, the bed squeaking beneath their combined weight.

Slowly, Gwen unscrewed Rora's main panel. Before she could open it, the unit sparked. Electricity flickered out, biting through Gwen's glove.

Hissing, she yanked off the scorched glove and tossed it onto the floor.

"Are you okay——" Rora began. But when Gwen looked up, their eyes meeting for what felt like the first time in weeks, she closed her mouth——as though afraid to show sympathy.

Gwen didn't bother digging around her tool kit for a new glove. Instead, she studied Rora's hand as she held it between her own, one gloved, one bare. Even though it wasn't Rora's flesh——and she likely couldn't process the touch the same as skin to skin——Gwen's stomach fluttered at their nearness. Her mind drifted to the moments when they'd held each other on the dance floor, ignoring the dance and dancers alike as Rora moved Gwen in sweeping steps through the song.

Why didn't I kiss her?

As Gwen peeled back the panel, she thought of her secret project and how Rora was in desperate need of an upgrade or better yet, a replacement. If Gwen had seen machinery on a ship in the shape Rora's arm was in, she would have pulled it out and sold it as scrap metal long ago. The battery was in good condition. In fact, the battery was one of the more recent models——the kind that recharges itself with motion. But the implant had been refurbished too many times and could no longer function at full capacity.

As it was, Gwen could do little to help Rora besides replace a few parts and wires and clean it up.

"Has your hand been malfunctioning or performing strangely since——" Gwen began but was cut off.

"Since you played me like a fool at the ball?" Pursing her lips, Rora studied the wall behind Gwen. "The response time is slower, and the movements are stiffer. But the sparking has remained the same."

Gwen stopped working and looked up at Rora. "What are you talking about? You were the one who asked *me* to go to that ball. Shouldn't I be pissed at you for flirting with me only when you needed a date and then ignoring me?"

"Needed a date?" Rora's eyes snapped to her then, her cheeks flushed. "I've gone to plenty of balls without dates and had a good time with my *friends*. People who wouldn't lie to me."

"How did I lie to you?" Gwen grit her teeth.

"You *knew* the competition was happening," Rora said. "That's why you didn't want to come to the ball. Why didn't you just warn me? I would've worn my performance gear underneath my dress. I could have been better prepared, I..."

When she trailed off, Rora's eyes skirted up to Gwen, who stared at her, slack-jawed.

"You think I knew about that? Bastian only told me what was happening after you were all brought into the other room."

Shifting her shoulders, Rora averted her gaze to the nearby changing screen. "Then why didn't you want to go to the ball? You weren't trying to avoid the competition?"

"I'm a terrible dancer, and I don't play nicely with other children."

Rora sniffed. "What changed your mind?"

Gwen exhaled slowly. "Isn't it obvious? A beautiful woman asked me to go." Finally, Rora's eyes found hers. Although her gaze had softened from its former granite state, it was clear the woman still hadn't put her guard down.

"I want to help you," Gwen continued. "What the show management team is doing to the performers is barbaric. Dissecting cyborgs like they are worthless investments..." She shook her head.

Rora's teeth sank into her rosebud lips. "I heard the performers from the fourteen losing acts all survived with the exception of those who died during the competition. Is that true?"

Gwen nodded.

Rora's gaze slid back to the shelves. "It might have been a mercy to let them die."

"Everyone deserves a chance to live," Gwen said, surprised. "Even if it's a hard life."

Sighing, Rora softened. "I know."

Reaching out, Gwen took Rora's human hand in hers. "I want to help you. I can fix up your hand as best as I can, but until you get a new implant, it's going to be damage control. Let me help you achieve your dream of performing for the emperor. But I can't unless you let me."

Although Rora didn't hold Gwen's hand in return, she hadn't pulled away either.

"You really didn't know?" Rora asked.

Gwen shook her head. "I had no idea the competition was happening that night… or the consequences for the losing performers. If I had, I would have warned you."

Perhaps I could have convinced you to run away with me.

The thought came unbidden. As it faded to the back of Gwen's thoughts, it left a trail of warmth behind.

Rora nodded. "I believe you."

Well, hot dandy. It's about time.

"What do we do now?"

Scratching her head, Gwen studied the mess that was Rora's cyborg hand. "We get you in the best shape we can." She opened her mouth to say more, but closed it.

Plucking up her tools, she went to work, trying to think of Rora's hand like she would a malfunctioning machine on a ship.

As she worked, she sighed.

"What is it?" Rora prodded.

Gwen blew air out between her lips. "While I will do *everything* I can to make sure your hand is functioning, there's another way to make sure you get into the top ten acts."

Rora leaned forward on the bed, head cocked to the side.

"Have you considered joining another act—?" Gwen began, but Rora immediately made a disgusted noise.

"And here I thought you were different, that you believed

in me. But you're just like everyone else." Rora angrily shook her head. "I want to be the best, *and* I want to earn it on my own. How can no one see that?"

Throwing away her sense of self-preservation, Gwen said, "It's not that I don't think you're capable." Rora slapped the panel on her hand shut, pushed past Gwen, and made for the door. "But think about it. If your hand is prone to malfunction, wouldn't it make sense to join another performance where there are other performers who can compete if you can't perform at your full capacity?"

Rora spun on her heel. "I appreciate your overwhelming confidence, Ms. Grimm, but I'm perfectly capable of winning this competition by myself."

Gwen nearly growled in frustration. None of this was coming out the way she'd hoped.

"You are a strong, capable woman. And fucking resilient." Gwen's voice softened as Rora reached for the door. Although she would respect Rora's boundaries, she had to speak these words—even if it killed her pride to do so. "But I know what it's like to lose someone you care about… and even though we've just met, I'm already terrified of losing you." Rora's hand froze in midair. "Three cyborgs *died*. More than fifty people were stripped of their implants and banished from the circus to stars know where. The fact that they lived was a stroke of luck. I'm no cyborg tinkerer. Who's to say that next time… that if you…" Gwen took a breath. "I'm afraid if I have to operate on you, I won't think quick enough or do the right thing. I sure as hell don't have the experience. And you might die because of me."

When Rora turned around, her eyes were wide.

"You wanted me to join another performance because… you're afraid you'll hurt me?"

Swallowing back the lump in her throat, Gwen nodded.

Once, she'd been confident she could learn how to become a cyborg tinkerer. She'd joined the circus, excited for the challenge. Now, she wasn't so sure if she had what it took, if she was smart enough. She'd become the best in her field once, but perhaps that was a stroke of luck.

Shaking her head, Rora closed the distance between them, reaching her human hand out and clasping Gwen's. "I think it's time someone reassured *you* how strong and capable you are. You saved fifty-two people, Gwen. That wasn't just luck. You're smart. And I trust you with my life."

Rora was so close Gwen could smell her perfume—roses and peach blossoms. Heart fluttering, Gwen's breath grew shallow and her mouth went dry. She looked down at the shorter woman, who was far from fragile. Arms corded with lean muscles, she was strong and capable, just as Gwen had said. And she was looking up at Gwen with... could that be desire in her eyes?

Licking her lips, Gwen managed to take a shallow breath. Everything in her screamed to lean down, to kiss this woman she'd grown fond of so quickly. They weren't guaranteed tomorrow. Still, she wanted to do this right. This was more than a quick fling.

Grabbing Rora's human hand, she brought it to her lips.

As she did, she marveled at the warmth of Rora's touch and the loyalty behind those eyes. It reminded her of the way her parents had...

It was gone.

Fear seized her veins, and she tried not to show it on her face to Rora.

When Gwen tried to think of the faces of her parents, she could remember nothing but faint silhouettes with black hair. Did her mother have a kind face? Did her father have a strong jaw or a straight nose?

The Forgetting, she realized. *It's beginning.*

According to what Rora had shared with Gwen at the ball, the acrobat couldn't remember her parents' faces either. But she had been a cyborg for two years. Gwen had been a cyborg for weeks. How were her memories fading already?

I can't forget. I won't forget. But how can I stop it?

But her chances of stopping the Forgetting were as likely as saving all of the cyborgs she would soon be forced to harvest.

Doing the only thing she knew how to do, she fucking compartmentalized and pushed the Forgetting to the back of her mind. She would deal with that later.

As she looked at Rora, a single thought came to mind.

This is my family now. Defending these cyborgs comes first.

"Shall we get to work?" Gwen gestured to Rora's implant.

A smile spread across Rora's lips as she seated herself once more. "One of these days, I'll figure you out, Gwendolyn Grimm."

Gwen smiled in return. "I hope you do."

CHAPTER 12

G wen lingered at the door.

They'd been in Rora's room for hours, and *stars*, she didn't want to leave. But it was late, and they both had responsibilities awaiting them in the morning.

When did I become so fucking sensible?

As she reached for the door handle, Rora spoke softly behind her.

"Don't go."

The words were barely a whisper.

Heart pounding, she turned back toward Rora, as restless as the swirling butterflies in her stomach. The gymnast stood before her, no longer in her performance gear, but wearing red lingerie.

Her eyes roamed hungrily over Rora, taking in her beautiful curves and dark skin. The lace cupped round breasts, dipping almost to her navel. Even from where she stood, Gwen could see Rora had shaved *everything*.

Holy shit. Gwen wanted to touch her *right fucking now*.

They were mere inches apart, but the space felt like a bottomless chasm.

They stared at each other for a long moment before their bodies crashed together.

Rora wrapped her hands on either side of Gwen's face and pulled her down. Gwen came willingly, kissing Rora feverishly. They hadn't gotten far from the door, and they were already gasping.

Their lips met in a frenzy, teeth pulling and tongues flicking. It wasn't enough. Gwen grabbed Rora, pushing her against the door to her room, wood cracking. Her breasts heaved against Gwen's ribs between breathless kisses.

Slowly, Gwen's hands left Rora's face and neck, sliding down until they were over her breasts. She hesitated, waiting for Rora to object. When she didn't, moaning between kisses, leaning into the touch, Gwen gave in. She squeezed, slipping a hand beneath the thin fabric, feeling Rora's nipple harden beneath her calloused palm. Gwen let out a moan of her own.

It was only then she noticed Rora's finger trailing the length of her waist where Gwen's belt held up her trousers. She leaned in, inviting Rora to do more. That was all the encouragement she needed because Rora's hand slowly made its way to her belt, untying it with torturous slowness.

Stars, go faster, Gwen thought, squeezing Rora's breasts as she pushed down the flimsy lace. The faint artificial light of a nearby gas lamp highlighted two dark breasts and darker, hard nipples.

Unfastening her pant button, Rora's hand trailed down Gwen's hip, to her leg, and down to—

Stars.

Her fingers slipped into Gwen easily.

For a moment, Gwen's limbs stopped responding to conscious thought. All she could feel was one finger and then two.

Her entire body wracked with delicious, trembling pleasure.

When she came to herself again, Gwen kissed Rora

harder, gasping. Unable to take more than a shallow breath as she felt Rora go deep inside her.

It wasn't enough. She needed more.

A bang sounded on the door, and Gwen bolted upright in bed.

Looking around at her very own, very empty room, she groaned. It had all been a *dream*?

She turned over in bed, eager to return to what would have been the best part. "Fuck off."

Just as she closed her eyes, the banging came again, louder this time. Still, she didn't move. Peeling one eye open, she glanced at the pocket watch on her bedside table.

Shit. She'd overslept.

After skipping dinner and spending most of the night in Rora's room, it was no wonder. They'd spent the entire time working on Rora's hand. Nothing at all like Gwen's dream.

When the banging became so loud, her whole room shook, she sighed, pushed the sheets back, and headed toward the door.

Hesitating, she grabbed the secret project she'd been working on that was in the middle of the floor and stashed it in her wardrobe. But she didn't bother to don her trousers or put on undergarments. Instead, she walked straight toward the pounding door in nothing but a loose shirt.

When Gwen swung the door inward, she was met with the glaring face of Bastian Kabir. As ever, he wore an immaculate suit and top hat. His finger tapped on his cane in obvious irritation.

"What do you want?" she demanded.

Rather than his usual smart remark, he stiffened as he took in her disheveled clothing and hair. His eyes skirted down to where the shirt's neckline scooped low between her breasts.

"What's the matter with you?" She leaned against the doorframe and crossed her arms. "Never seen tits before?"

Blinking, his eyes returned above sea level. "That's none of your business."

She raised an eyebrow. "Prefer the company of men, then?"

"No."

Sexual frustration poured through her, making her lightheaded. She wasn't sure if it was entirely from the dream, but her thoughts strayed along with her gaze. As she studied Bastian's pinstriped suit and the wiry body beneath it, she wondered just how good Bastian Kabir would be in bed.

It had been quite some time since a cock had filled her.

She didn't move from where she blocked the doorway. "What do you want?"

As Bastian tapped his cane on the floor, she could practically see the steam coming out of his ears. "You're aware you have a job to perform at this circus, correct?"

"I was sick," she lied.

"You don't look sick."

"Why are you looking?"

His mouth drew into a thin line. "Don't change the subject, Ms. Grimm. I'm here to escort you to your appointment with the Mistress."

Fuck. She'd completely forgotten about her mandatory checkup. Not that she was excited to see Mistress Morbid.

Turning back into her room, she didn't bother to close the door. She grabbed a pair of trousers from the floor, yanked them up, and pushed her feet into boots. Locating her pistol, holster, knives, and sheaths, she donned those.

Bastian stood, frozen in the middle of the doorway.

She glanced over her shoulder. "In or out."

The door clicked shut as she pulled her sleeping shirt over her head, tossed it to the floor, and put on a shirt, vest, and her tinkerer's belt.

"Have you no modesty?"

As Gwen turned back to him, he was intently studying the

stone castle wall. By the look of him, there was nothing immodest taking place behind him. He was a man dressed for a dinner party and taking inventory of the room.

Never took him for a prude.

"When you live on a ship for months at a time, often without private sleeping quarters, you quickly realize how pointless modesty is." She gestured to the door. "Lead the way."

They left her room and strode down hallways she'd never gone down before, the now customary watchmen padding softly behind them. Eventually, they made it to the hallway for the show management team's offices. Stopping in front of one of the doors, Bastian knocked softly.

"Enter," a voice called from within.

With a nod to the watchmen, who took up stations farther down the hallway, the ringleader opened the door.

"Mr. Kabir. Ms. Grimm." Celeste Beckett rose from her desk and gestured to two empty chairs at the desk across from her. "Welcome. Please have a seat."

"If you require nothing further, Mistress, I will take my leave." Interestingly, his posture was even stiffer than usual.

"Leaving so soon?" Celeste leaned forward, her manicured red nails pressing against the top of her wooden desk. "I must say, I miss the days when you were my pet. Although you make a fine ringleader, I sometimes wonder if your skills are better put to use elsewhere."

If it was possible, Bastian stiffened further. Despite a thin stature, his grim expression indicated barely refrained violence. It was as though a beast lurked beneath his skin, waiting to get out. In any other person, that look alone would inspire terror. The faint-hearted might be tempted to shit themselves when the great Bastian Kabir leveled *that* gaze on them.

Gwen studied the way his suit hung loosely on him, and it was far looser than the day she'd met him on Anchorage. She couldn't help but to wonder when he'd eaten last. Perhaps the infamous ringleader of the cyborg circus had seen more horrors in his lifetime than the first competition. Everyone had their way of coping, and restriction was a method she'd seen before. Did the poor bastard even realize what he was doing?

"Thank you for your kind words, Mistress," Bastian said. "But I feel my calling is to be a ringleader to our performers."

The Mistress merely nodded. "For now."

Without another word, Bastian turned and closed the door behind him, leaving Gwen with Celeste Beckett. Mistress and murderer of this fine circus.

Trying to slow her breathing, Gwen slipped into a cool wooden chair. As always, her cyborg eye hummed as it darted back and forth, assessing the contents of the room alongside her human eye.

The most notable aspect of Celeste's office was the rows of shelves lining every open wall space with trinkets like books, globes, and a typewriter, along with a series of small devices with screens and keyboards.

"I'd like to formally welcome you to Cirque du Borge." Leaning back in her leather-padded chair, Celeste brushed her mane of red hair over a shoulder. "I can imagine this isn't the easiest time to acclimate to our show, but I hope you know we are very happy to have you join us. Your skills are a valued asset to the circus."

Gwen had to bite her tongue to avoid spewing a remark about the *difficulty* of being forced to butcher cyborgs to pieces and how, not long ago, Celeste had made it very fucking evident how Gwen's skills were a mere convenience for the surgeon.

"Every year, you will have periodic check-ins with myself or another available staff member," Celeste continued. "Today, we will make certain your body is tolerating your new implant and ensure your system is running properly."

Unlike the cyborgs you forced to dunk under icy water. Their systems certainly aren't running properly. I would fucking know.

Standing, Celeste gestured to a door to an adjoining room to her office. Gwen followed her, noting a patient table, not unlike Gwen's, at the center of the room. Rather than tools, screws, plating, and wiring lining the shelves, as there were in Gwen's office, Celeste's office only held a cart on wheels. Atop that cart was a small machine Gwen had never seen before. The machine was small, no more than the width of her chest, with a small screen and what looked like a keyboard beneath it.

Gwen's eyes widened.

"You like it?" Celeste asked. "It's one of the circus's many treasures."

Snapping her mouth shut, Gwen said, "I hear digital technology is expensive. Priceless, perhaps."

As is human life.

Only the wealthiest in the Union could afford to own devices with access to digital technology. Fewer still had devices that actually worked. Most were faulty at best. Often, it wasn't worth the hefty price tag to send a digital message when it wasn't guaranteed to arrive. Paying a carrier to deliver a physical letter was cheaper and far more reliable.

What could the purpose of this little machine be? Not to send letters to family members across the Crescent Star System, certainly.

"It is," Celeste replied.

Slowly, Gwen took a seat on the table. "What is it for?"

"To check that your implant is functioning."

Studying her, Gwen tried to swallow back the fear in her gut as she wondered just what this woman might do to her if she did step out of line. Did she intend to make another show of force?

Moreover, did Gwen dare to ask about the Forgetting? Was there a way to slow the memory loss?

But Celeste willingly helping her—the very same woman running the competition—was about as likely as the emperor removing the Cyborg Prohibition Law. No matter what pretty words he wrote in his invitation.

"Today, I'll need to open the port at the back of your neck and insert your chip into the machine," Celeste continued. "The machine will show all recent communications between your brain and your implant, which are stored on the chip—as well as if there's any disconnect. If there is, we can work to address them at that time."

Exhaling, Gwen nodded.

Nothing like having an evil overlord poking around in your brain.

Slowly, Gwen lay down on her side. Celeste moved behind Gwen to the cart. There was a strange pressure on Gwen's neck before she felt a click as her port opened.

Opening and closing her fists, she did her best to relax.

With the click and release of the chip in her port, the world stilled.

Blinking, she looked around. What had she been so worried about?

In fact, she had a hard time remembering anything at all. She looked around at the empty stone walls and immaculate floor and then to the cold, metal table she lay atop. Where was she?

The itch to know faded and was replaced by a single, overwhelming desire.

To return to the circus.

She didn't know what it meant or where the circus was, only the tugging within her mind, urging her to her feet. The desire overwhelmed her senses until she couldn't think of anything else, only the need to move. Before she could raise herself from the table, a hand pressed her back down, followed by a strap to secure her shoulders and legs.

Several minutes passed like this, and she could only wait.

There was another pressure at the back of her brain and a click.

Gasping, Gwen pulled roughly at the bonds strapping her down to the patient table.

"What the hell was that?" she demanded, reaching a hand down to the knife in the hidden sheath on her pants.

Celeste removed the straps, and Gwen lurched to a seated position, spinning around to face the Mistress of the circus and the Keeper of Beasts.

"I should have warned you," Celeste said, smiling sympathetically. "It can be disorienting the first time your chip is removed."

"That's a nice way to put it," Gwen bit back. "I didn't know my own fucking name. Just..."

She thought of the drive that had consumed her only moments before. A drive to return to the circus. But wasn't she already at the circus? What had that all been, anyway?

"As I said," Celeste continued, "it can be disorienting to have your chip removed. Are you feeling more yourself now?"

Slowly, Gwen mentally checked her extremities and functions. Everything seemed so... normal. Her eye whirred happily, scanning the room. Celeste's skeleton flashed before her eye, the bone a darker hue. Brighter was the table beneath her as well as the rolling cart and the digital machine with the hefty price tag—all of which were made of metal. It seemed her eye had a knack for locating the material.

To her surprise, Celeste's red nails gleamed brightly as well. Did she have *retractable claws*?

"I'm fine." Standing, Gwen gestured to the digital machine. "How was my implant? Any issues?"

Celeste shook her head. "It's functioning at full capacity. You are free to go at your leisure."

She didn't need to be told twice.

All but running out of the room, she already dreaded her

next checkup, which Celeste said would be when the entire cast and crew had their regular annual appointments.

As she hurried toward the theater, a thought occurred to her.

Why was the Mistress performing engineering checkups on cyborg implants?

The masked watchmen's steps clicked closely behind her as she wondered just how she could get more answers—and protect herself and the cyborgs before she lost her memories entirely.

CHAPTER 13

The door to the King of the Damned creaked open as Rora entered.

The moderately clean pub was smack in the middle of the city of Apparatus—and a favorite hangout spot for many of Cirque du Borge's performers.

Rora walked past a bar half as long as her parents' dining room table, which the Lockwood family boasted was the longest piece of oakwood on Starlar. It was also nowhere near as immaculate. Grease stains spotted the bar and tables around the common room. Still, the ale was cheap, the hearth warm, and the musicians a pleasant sort of rowdy.

Glancing around, she spotted Akio and Marzanna, who'd stationed themselves at a corner table along with the firebreather, Gaius, and the head of the equestrian act, Rosalee.

Marzanna had an arm slung over Gaius's shoulders. The two huddled close together, whispering into each other's ears. In the seat next to them, Rosalee straddled Akio—the two unabashedly sucking each other's faces like a couple of hormonal teenagers.

Not for the first time, Rora wondered why Marzanna and

Akio hadn't ever banged each other or done something more permanent like dating. It was clear both of them had quite the sexual appetite. But perhaps they considered each other more as family than anything else.

Grabbing a glass of wine from the bartender, Rora joined them at the table.

"It's about time you got here!" Marzanna said with a mischievous grin.

"I got held up," Rora replied. "Good to see you, Gaius. Rosalee."

Tongue otherwise occupied, Rosalee didn't bother to turn around from her engagements with Akio, but Gaius smiled.

"How's the performance coming—" Gaius began but was cut off by screams and a whoosh of air from the street outside.

A hush fell over the pub, the silence broken only by the thumping of pints on tabletops. Several wenches and wards placed down trays of drinks for patrons and moved to the windows, grabbing fireproof sheets and preparing to cover the windows. Everyone waited at the edge of their seats for the telltale signs of a dragon raid—claws scraping against shingled rooftops, the slamming of shutters, the smell of smoke as fire and chaos descended over the city. If a dragon was close, sometimes it meant fleeing through the streets as the building you were just in was set aflame.

There was a creaking of gears, and everyone seemed to sigh in relief at the telltale sound of a ship lowering its sails as it flew above the city. Slowly, the musicians resumed their tune and the chatter once again filled the King of the Damned. It was probably nothing more than a quick robbery or mugging. Without the presence of the feds, such things were commonplace. And the cyborgs weren't paid enough nor had the ability to set up a policing force of their own.

Only the Mistress had a private guard.

"So," Marzanna began as Akio and Rosalee picked up where they left off. "Where's the tinkerer? I figured you'd invite her along. Especially after I saw her disappear into your rooms last night…"

Rora put down her drink. "You little gossip. Were you spying on me?"

"Hard to miss the watchmen lingering in the hallway."

"True enough."

"So…" Marzanna unslung her arm from over Gaius's shoulders. "Is she a good lay? By the look of those marvelous hips, I feel like she would be."

Blood rushed to Rora's cheeks.

"Fuck, Marzanna." Gaius leaned forward, elbows resting on the table. "Look at her. You're embarrassing the girl."

Clearing her throat, Rora opened her mouth to speak, but Marzanna cut in.

"Don't be fooled by those innocent eyes and sweet disposition." Marzanna's pointed finger seemed to encompass everything—from Rora's tight pants to her tighter shirt that scooped low between her breasts. "I've seen this girl screw her partners ten ways to Sunday when we go to our group fucking parties."

Rolling her eyes, Rora said, "I think you mean 'six ways to Sunday.'"

Akio managed to free his tongue momentarily as he added, "No, I think she meant orgies."

Chuckles rippled down the table.

"All right, all right, all right." Marzanna waved them off. "My point is, Rora is no virgin maid. So, where's the tinkerer? Was she that bad?"

"We didn't sleep together." Rora took a sip of her sweet white wine. "She tinkered my implant and kissed my hand before leaving. It was all perfectly respectable."

"Perfectly *boring*," Akio muttered between kisses.

Gaius crossed his arms. "Does she enjoy the company of men as well? I'll happily sleep with her if she'd look at my implant after hours."

Anger churned in her gut, and it took every ounce of self-control she had to remain seated and not dump her glass of wine in his lap. She couldn't let him know how threatened his intentions toward Gwen made her feel. He—and everyone else in this circus—needed to think Gwen and Rora were together, inseparable, *off-limits*.

If Rora had any hope of seducing Gwen and making her create a new hand against the circus rules, she had to keep the tinkerer wrapped around her finger—and her own pussy. Without a new hand, there was no knowing if Rora would survive the competition and perform for the emperor. And she would *not* let some firebreather get in the way of that.

"I'm not sure if she enjoys the company of both men and women. My instinct says yes." Rora had to force herself to unclench her jaw, quirking her lips into a semblance of a smile as she spoke the next words. "But don't get your hopes up. We're kind of a thing."

"Unless she takes multiple partners," Gaius replied, eyes full of challenge. "Half the people in the Union do these days."

"Hold up." Marzanna turned on Gaius. "What am I? Chopped liver?"

Leaning forward, Gaius wrapped an arm around Marzanna. "Who said I didn't take multiple partners too, babe? You know you're my number one."

Rora exhaled, thankful Marzanna was the jealous type.

Swallowing the last of her wine, she went to the bar to get a second glass.

Perhaps Marzanna was right, and it was time for Rora to put out. If her body's reaction to Gwen was any indication, it would be no difficulty to muster the desire to sleep with the tinkerer. Hell, she'd had half a mind to ask Gwen to stay last night after she'd tinkered her hand.

Why did I hesitate?

Instead of waking up to Gwen's warm body this morning, she'd instead had to work off some of the tension on her own.

Part of her thought that holding out might give Gwen more motivation to try to win her favor—more reason to create a new hand for Rora. But if other performers were more than willing to sleep with Gwen for nothing more than the hope of some extra tinkering, maybe Rora really did need to rethink her strategy.

As the bartender brought Rora's new glass of wine over, the door to the pub swung open and slammed against the wall. All too familiar loud voices filtered in.

Great.

Grabbing her wine, she moved to return to her table before—

"Evening, dyke." Abrecan sauntered over to the bar, leaning against the countertop. As he did, her gaze fell on curly black chest hair at eye level.

"Go away, Abrecan." She turned toward her table. "I'm not in the mood."

"What is it, little bird? Feeling sad I beat you in the first competition?"

Turning on a heel, she narrowed her gaze on Abrecan. "We *tied*. If you couldn't read our scores, feel free to ask the Mistress. Because they were the *same*."

Tapping a jeweled finger on his chin, he said, "If I recall correctly, I was on the platform before you. Either way, don't expect me to play nice going forward."

"Are you going to kill me, like you did to Asa and the others?" Rora snapped. "I'm sure the watchmen would love to hear that story."

Barstools scraped against the ground moments before Marzanna and Akio appeared beside her, sensing the growing tension. But Gaius and Rosalee hung in the background. Getting on Abrecan's bad side was dangerous, especially since he had a large following of performers who worshipped at his feet.

More than once, Rora had thought about telling the Mistress or watchmen what Abrecan had done during the first competition. But after Celeste had terminated contracts and reclaimed the implants, Rora doubted the woman cared about a cyborg bending the rules of a violent competition for his own gain. Not when she could reclaim the implant without any protest from the performer. No, the Mistress wouldn't do anything, which infuriated Rora even more. How was she supposed to win a competition with a fickle judge, murderous competitors, and unscrupulous rules?

Rage fueled Rora as she thought of everything going wrong—her fickle cyborg hand, her lost dream to perform for the emperor, what she'd had to give up to join the circus, the fact that the Union hated cyborgs, and the sexual frustration over not having screwed a tinkerer she so badly needed help from. Not to mention, the life-or-death competition looming over the performers.

To remain employed at Cirque du Borge, she'd have to fight every step of the way. Or lose her hand and any hope she had of performing for the emperor and convincing his Union Council that cyborgs weren't a threat.

Losing all sense of self-preservation, she pointed toward Thaniel. "While we're at it, perhaps we should talk about the first competition and how I saved your thug's life while you were off *killing people*."

She didn't mean to yell—really, she didn't—but she couldn't help it. Abrecan had this way of getting under her skin. He'd pushed her aside like she was nothing more than a child in the first competition. A challenger unworthy of his notice.

The music petered off as dozens of performers from nearby tables or leaning against the bar turned to look at them, their ears perking at Rora's accusation.

Behind Abrecan, Thaniel opened and closed his mouth. But the archer's other thugs—performers of equal stature— said nothing, seemingly unfazed by Rora's declaration.

"Didn't tell you, did he? I figured not." Rora's anger was a faucet she couldn't shut off as words poured from her. "I had to save Thaniel's sorry ass, *literally*. Because he managed to get stuck in the tubes. And what thanks do I get?" She leveled her gaze on Thaniel. "Threats for future competitions. So nice of you both to extend your hospitality for my trouble. I'm glad to hear you value Thaniel's life so highly."

As she finished the last sentence, her eyes slid to Abrecan.

The room fell utterly silent, everyone waiting on the archer's response.

A smile spread across his lips like a disease spreading over a city.

"Where are my manners?" He kneeled, placing hands on his knees as though he spoke to a very small, very foolish child. "To thank you for saving Thaniel's life, I won't break your neck tonight, little bird, for showing me disrespect. But make no mistake." Leaning forward, he whispered the next words into her ear. "By taking Gwendolyn from me, you've earned yourself more than an enemy."

Swallowing thickly, Rora couldn't manage to find any words to say in return.

Reaching out, Abrecan mussed Rora's hair. "You have a good night, now."

The wineglass in her cyborg hand cracked before shattering on the floor as her fingers curled into a fist.

When Abrecan, Thaniel, and their other cronies settled at a table in the back of the King of the Damned and conversation in the pub had resumed, Marzanna exhaled heavily. "It's so nice to make friends."

As though her hair were at fault for the direction the evening had taken, Rora pulled the tie out before shoving her curls back into a bun.

"Why does the Mistress let him do whatever he wants?" Rora snapped. "It's not fair."

Marzanna leveled sad, knowing eyes on Rora. "This world isn't fair—least of all for cyborgs. And you, my darling, just made an unfortunate enemy."

No kidding.

But she'd also made an important discovery.

Despite Gaius's words earlier, Abrecan—and likely the rest of the circus—thought Gwen and Rora were together.

Which meant there was still a chance to go through with her plan.

CHAPTER 14

Striding down long hallways toward the mess hall, Gwen passed glassless windows and stone archways leading to the gardens. Several resilient bushes sprouted from the earth, but very few flowers bloomed.

Damn bushes are just like this circus, she thought. *Stubbornly clinging to life.*

As she walked, her usual watchmen in tow, a flash of movement in the gardens caught her eye, and she paused. Turning, she spotted Bastian sitting on a stone bench in the gardens, leaning forward with his elbows on his knees, intently studying something in his hands.

Was Bastian Kabir reading?

Gwen hesitated.

Besides this morning, they'd hardly spoken after the first competition when they'd teamed up to harvest cyborgs. What was there to say?

Hey, how are you? Still traumatized as fuck from slicing apart perfectly healthy cyborgs? Me, too.

More than that, she was eager for time to eat and finish up the secret project she'd been working on.

Before she could move, Bastian looked up.

Not sure what else to do, she waggled her fingers in a halfhearted wave.

He rose to his feet, pocketing the book. "Ms. Grimm."

Taking a step back toward the hallway, she said, "Is there something you need? I really should get going."

He gestured to the stone bench. "Sit with me."

With a resigned sigh, she strode into the garden, noting the coarse shrubbery's hues of brown and green as they stubbornly clung to life.

The watchmen didn't follow her into the garden but remained in the hallway—out of hearing distance, for once.

When she moved to sit beside Bastian, a faint flash of color caught her eye. The bush opposite the stone bench hadn't been visible from the open hallway, tucked away as it was behind a wall with gargoyles.

She gaped. "Is that a—?"

He nodded to a single red rose, smiling at it as though it were a newborn babe. "I tend this bush every day I'm here, and I hire servants to oversee it while I travel. In all the years I've been a part of this circus, only a single rose blooms each year."

She hadn't seen a rose in person since she lived on Orthodocks. Many planets no longer had flowers after the industrialization period. Hundreds of factories had been built in years, and the resulting pollution had killed many of the pollinating insects. The owners of the factories and the governments that supported them argued space travel had never been so accessible or convenient as it was now.

Without space travel, ship tinkerers like Gwen would be out of a job—as would most people working in interplanetary trade.

"It's beautiful," she murmured.

Bastian smiled, and for a moment, she could have sworn he was a different man. Perhaps it was the way his eyes rounded or that he *actually* showed affection—even if it was for a flower.

Mesmerized by the deep scarlet petals, she reached out to the rose. Before her fingers touched the petals, a hand clamped over her wrist.

"I would appreciate it if you didn't disturb the flower."

Just like that, the temporary connection between them evaporated, replaced by rigid formality. "Is there something I can do for you, Mr. Kabir?"

Again, he gestured to the stone bench, and she flopped onto it.

"It's not what you can do for me, but what I can do for you."

You sound like Abrecan.

"Can you stop this ridiculous competition and allow the cyborgs to go free with their implants intact?"

It was the first time she'd dared voice the most obvious thing this circus needed—to be disbanded.

"No."

"Then there's nothing I want from you."

As she stood, he caught her elbow.

"I know what happened during the first competition was... trying. It was for me as well."

"It's traumatic as fuck is what it is." Slowly, she lowered herself back onto the bench. "How have you dealt with it?"

"With sleepless nights, mostly," he said, surprising her. "But I've come to terms with a single fact. For the circus to survive in the Crescent Star System, hurting the few to save the many is a necessary evil."

Anger bubbled in her veins.

Just when I thought he wasn't an imbecile.

"Your math sucks," she snapped. "Because if forty out of fifty acts are going to be eliminated over the course of this competition, that means eighty percent of the performers will have terminated contracts. That's not hurting the few. That's butchering the many."

Heat flared behind his eyes. "What would you have me do?"

"Stop the competition."

"You know I can't."

"Then get me access to books."

"What?" His gaze strayed to the hallway where Gwen had just come from—where the watchmen waited.

"The books in my office are useless and outdated." She watched as more watchmen marched down the hallway on what must be a patrol route. "I need textbooks from before the prohibition, implantation instructions, cyborg implant manuals—anything that will help me figure out how to do more than a sloppy patch job." She laughed humorlessly. Such things had been burned or confiscated by the feds long ago. "I might as well be asking for the stars."

A vein in his jaw bulged as his teeth clenched. "Follow me."

Unable to stop herself, her eyebrows rose. But she followed the ringleader in silence as he… led her to his chambers? He kept tinkering books in his *chambers?*

Tell me that's not how he gets women into bed.

Like hers, his room wasn't in the wing where the performers' dormitories were, but in a different, more secluded part of the palace.

The watchmen marched behind them. As they reached Bastian's door, he twisted a key in his fingers, seeming to debate something.

Then he turned to study her, his eyes tracing the scope of her face as though inspecting his precious rose. His hands came up, cupping her face gently.

What the hell was going on? Was he sick or something? Drunk?

Without preamble—or any warm-up—he pressed his lips to hers.

She raised her hand to slap him. But oddly, her thoughts melded together as his lips moved gently across hers. Why was her heartbeat quickening?

Bastian's thin body pressed against her chest and stomach. He smelled of sage, shoe polish, and peppermint. His olive skin was soft, and the beginning of a beard scraped her lips as he pulled away.

She couldn't help herself.

She gaped, chest heaving as though she'd been running from the feds.

"You twatlips. What the hell was—"

Before she could finish the sentiment, his lips were against hers a second time. He used his body to press her against the door as he nimbly unlocked it with his other hand. As he did, his lips roamed over hers hungrily—with as much fervor as she'd seen him dedicate to the circus itself.

As the door clicked open behind her, she had a single thought.

This was quite enough.

In a single motion, her hand cupped his balls in a vise grip. He groaned in pain as he hobbled into the room with her.

The watchmen stood silently in the hallway, unmoving from their posts.

Fucking perverts.

It was only when he shoved the door shut that she looked around.

Unlike Rora's room, Bastian's room was immaculate. There wasn't a single article of clothing or speck of dirt on the ground. His closet doors and dresser drawers were neatly closed and his bed made.

"What the fuck was that?" Despite herself, her voice was breathless.

"Would you—" he grunted. "Would you unhand me, please?"

Slowly, she let go, not taking her eyes off him as he removed his jacket, rolled up his sleeves, and gestured to the bed.

"Whoa." She held her hands up, backing toward the door. "This isn't the kind of help I was asking for."

Rolling his eyes, he gestured again. This time, she realized he hadn't been pointing at the bed, but toward the window.

She frowned, still not understanding.

Opening his closet, Bastian removed a rope, tying it to a stone pillar in his room near the window.

"While I enjoy using restraints on occasion with my partners," she began, "I think you have the wrong idea…"

Once he completed tying the rope to the pillar, he went to the window and dropped it.

Was he about to climb out?

"Care to explain what the hell is going on?" she demanded. "Is assaulting women how you get off?"

He held a finger to his lips, gesturing toward the door.

Where the watchmen were listening. Of fucking course.

"We needed a way to lose the watchmen and thus the Mistress's eyes and ears," he said in a voice so quiet she almost missed it. "If I'm going to help you with what you asked, they needed a reason to believe we wanted some time… alone." He gestured to the rope he'd tossed out the window. "But what you seek isn't in here, Ms. Grimm."

"It's just Gwen. And ask a girl next time, aye? Otherwise, I might be tempted to hack your pretty beads off."

"Of course. You have my apologies. I would have never kissed you without permission under any other circumstances."

Outside the door, boots shuffled—as though someone leaned forward to listen. Both of them looked at the door and then at each other.

He closed the distance between them, eyes laden with an intensity she'd yet to see from him. "So, Ms. Grimm—"

"Yeah, yeah. Little late to be asking now. If you must do it, just fucking kiss me."

As Gwen's gaze flicked back to the ringleader, she noted a distinct reddening to his lips and his chest rose and fell more quickly.

This time, when he kissed her, she was ready for it.

Rather than trying to go about foreplay quietly, she allowed her hands to roam the landscape of his body. His chest was hard beneath his clothes, his body lean and broad. It was the body of a man who wasn't afraid of hard work. She gasped as the flesh between her legs awakened.

This is all an act. This is to help the cyborgs. Rora will understand.

After today, she'd never have to kiss Bastian again.

But she couldn't keep her thoughts on the acrobat for long as Bastian's hands moved to her back, pulling her closely to him. Something hard pressed between her legs, and her thoughts swirled strangely, as though she'd been sucked into a black hole in space. It really had been too long since she'd bedded a man, or anyone for that matter.

"That's enough." His breaths were ragged. "Let's go before they suspect we aren't in here... getting to know one another."

"You mean fucking."

Taking a breath, he waited for the tent in his pants to deflate.

As he did, she couldn't dispel a strange twinge in her chest. Was that disappointment? She certainly wasn't bummed about not getting to bed Bastian Kabir. That was fucking ridiculous. This was a momentary act of necessity, and nothing more.

Slowly, he climbed out the window and moved hand-over-hand down the rope. It was then she realized his rooms overlooked the garden he was so fond of.

She followed him, far less graceful. Her boots scraped noisily as she struggled to climb down the rope. Bouncing off the wall several times, she eventually made it to the ground—crashing into some shrubbery.

"You're as graceful as you are lovely," he said.

Was that a smile on his lips?

Standing and brushing her pants off, she made a very unladylike harrumph.

He gestured to a hidden pathway through the gardens. "This way."

She trailed him in silence as he led her down secluded pathways outside and then back into the palace and down hallways with archways open to the elements. They had to stop and change route several times to avoid patrolling watchmen. The entire time, she couldn't help but wonder where they were going. What secret did he keep that even the Mistress and her watchdogs couldn't know? Eventually, they made it to the west-most section of the palace, where she assumed the show management and Mistress had their private quarters.

Stopping before an unmarked door in an unremarkable hallway, he removed a brass key from his pocket. Unlocking it, he ushered her inside. He grabbed a portable electric lantern and lit it before closing and locking the door behind him. They descended a winding set of stairs into darkness, and she was forced to take his arm or else lose her footing and send them both crashing into whatever waited at the bottom.

His touch sent the memory of their time in his chambers swirling through her thoughts, which she tried to shake off.

What's the matter with you? You're acting like a fucking schoolgirl. It was just a kiss, and an act, at that.

Besides, Bastian Kabir was a miserable fuck of a man. Even if he had lips of satin.

At the base of the staircase, the man attached to the satin lips hung the lantern on the wall and flicked on a light switch. A series of electric light bulbs flickered on, illuminating a long hallway with several massive oak doors.

"What is this place?" Gwen asked as she followed Bastian down the long hallway.

"A secret."

"Thank you, Sir Obvious."

They stopped at the massive door at the end of the hallway. After unlocking it, Bastian hesitated.

She crossed her arms. "You better not ask me to close my eyes. I've had quite enough surprises for one day, thank you. This whole endeavor has been cryptic enough."

Sparing a glare over his shoulder, he pushed the doors open.

Like the hallway, the room beyond was darker than night. The light from the bulbs in the hallway only faintly illuminated an antique rug with swirling red and gold patterns.

He disappeared behind the door. After a few muttered words, she heard the distinct sound of a light switch click. Rather than a few rickety old bulbs illuminating what she'd envisioned to be a dusty old cellar filled with outdated parchment, the light revealed something else entirely.

Dozens—no, *hundreds*—of light bulbs flicked on. Some were attached to wall fixtures, and more filled the massive chandelier at the center of the room. Countless smaller bulbs lined the edges of the walls, twinkling like starlight. All of which illuminated one thing.

They were in a massive library.

"No fucking way." Gaping, she studied the three-story walls filled with thousands of leather-bound books. The room stretched as far as the eye could see in either direction— perhaps as large as three ballrooms put together. "I've never seen so many books in one place."

"You like it?"

"As much as a bookworm in a library."

Bastian rolled his eyes. "Don't eat the parchment, please."

A thought occurred to her, and she turned. "You knew

about this place, and you didn't tell me? I could've used this knowledge *weeks* ago."

He patted the pocket where he'd stashed the key earlier. "I was recently promoted to honorary member of the show management team after my assistance in the first competition. It's a promotion I've been working toward for some time. I've only just been granted keys." He looked around, unable to disguise the wonder in his eyes. "I'd heard the Mistress kept a personal library. I just didn't know where or quite how large."

He shook his head as his eyes grew distant.

She eyed him. "Why do you want to be one of them?" When his gaze darkened, she pressed on. "The show management is a bunch of murderous pricks. And clearly, by showing me this place, you don't share their same homicidal inclinations."

"It's not that simple."

"It never is." She sighed. "Any idea how books are organized?"

"No," he said. "I imagine the Mistress has a filing system, but I haven't been made privy to it."

"Right." She pointed at one bookshelf. "You start there. Anything you can find on cyborg part implantations or even the specific manuals, I want it. Textbooks on cybernetic surgery would be good, too. I'm going to start over there." She pointed at the opposite wall, already walking toward it, eager to lose herself in work.

Anything to keep her mind off whatever the hell had happened in Bastian's room.

"You're welcome," he called after her.

There were dozens of ornate couches, armchairs, and small tables with matching chairs at the center of the room. She supposed it was intended to be a reading area since the room lacked window seating. They were too far underground for that.

She exhaled slowly. The bookshelf before her spanned the

length of several rooms and was taller than two inns stacked on top of each other.

Start at the bottom and work your way up.

Without further preamble, Gwen threw herself into her work. If there was a way to help save these cyborgs, she was going to find it.

CHAPTER 15

They were in the library for hours.

By the time Gwen thought to check her pocket watch, courtesy of her stomach alerting her to the passing of time, supper had long since passed.

I've spent an entire day in this library and still haven't found the books I need.

As she was unwilling to leave her work, Bastian left and returned with a tray of food for them both. They ate in silence before returning to the bookshelves. Rather, she ate in silence, and he pushed food around the tray.

"When's the last time you ate?" Gwen eyed Bastian's hollow cheeks and eyes. He'd always been a thin man, but his tall frame had become even wirier since she'd first met him. His suit hung more loosely now, and his knuckles stood out starkly on thin hands.

Regardless of his size, it was obvious he was a handsome man, and one to be reckoned with.

"I am eating."

Gwen groaned internally. Where was the maternal type when you needed one?

"Do you want to talk about it?" she began cautiously. "I've seen restrictors back when I worked on the ships. Sometimes, it seemed talking helped them with addressing their issues around food…"

Stars, I'm not the right person for this job.

How did you talk to someone who didn't want to acknowledge anything was wrong? More importantly, how did you show someone who refused to eat that they were harming themselves? Food was necessary to survival. But if he was restricting, then there had to be some reason or deep wound from his past that had led to this. What was it he saw in himself—or didn't see? What harmful thought process had been instilled in him, perhaps as a child? Could she possibly help him help himself?

"What are you, my physician?" Bastian said coolly. "I don't need you to psychoanalyze me."

"Fine."

Clearly, he wasn't ready to talk. And some small part of Gwen was relieved. What in the galaxy could she say, anyway?

To her surprise, her relief mingled with a growing sense of disappointment. Had she truly thought he'd confide in her? More than that, why did she want him to? Despite her initial dislike of the man—who always seemed to act more like a beast despite his formal speech—they'd become a sort of battlefield comrades. The kind that bonded over a hardship that could never be spoken aloud; a hardship that marked you for life.

Talk to him. The thought slid neatly into her awareness, and she slammed a metaphorical boot onto it. *A friendship can't be made without one person taking the first step.*

Could she possibly want a friendship with the infamous Cirque du Borge ringleader? The notion seemed ridiculous. And share her secrets? They could barely share a meal.

Returning to her work, she scanned shelf after shelf of

books. Anything that seemed promising, she brought down the ladder, which was attached to a track that rolled across the floor. She was careful to mark where she pulled the books from. Once she had a hefty stack, she hauled the books to a nearby table.

After flipping through countless titles that were dead ends, she looked to see if Bastian had made any progress. But rather than seeing him beside a stack of books and scanning a nearby bookshelf, he lounged on a chaise lounge chair with a small book in his hand. The very same book he'd been reading in the garden.

As she walked closer, peering over his shoulder, she read the title: *Hard of Desire.*

A laugh escaped her lips.

Turning, he tried to pocket the book in his jacket, but he missed several times.

"Are you reading a romance novel?"

"What if I was?"

"Hey." Gwen raised her hands. "I'm not judging. I like a decent amount of smut in my books. Keeps things interesting." Bastian raised an eyebrow, clearly not believing her sincerity. "It's just not something I would have expected from you."

Standing, he smoothed his pants and straightened his coat. "Assumptions are as pointless and harmful as stereotypes, Ms. Grimm. Surely you should know as much, given your choice of vocation and bedfellows."

"Why do you care who warms my bed?" She crossed her arms, smirking as she thought of what had happened in his bedroom a few hours before. "Could that be jealousy I'm detecting?"

"I'm jealous of no one," he replied smoothly. "Happiness should be found within ourselves. Nothing good can come from comparison."

She rolled her eyes. "So that's why you're starving yourself? Because you're so *happy* on the inside?"

He froze, his gaze growing utterly cold. "You go too far. What I do is none of your business." Slowly, he lowered himself back onto the lounge chair, returning his attention to his book. "Just like your sleeping with Rora is none of mine."

Heat blossomed in her cheeks. "If you're so keen on respecting another person's privacy, it would be difficult to notice such things."

"Do you honestly think you two have been subtle?" He barked a laugh as his eyes snapped up to her. "The whole circus practically knows. All the glances during rehearsals and your dancing at the ball—it's obvious for anyone with eyes the two of you are fond of each other."

Her thoughts careened to a stop.

They hadn't been that obvious... had they? Well, one thing was certain. She wasn't about to tell him they hadn't slept together yet. But *damn it*, he was right about one thing— she was falling hard for the acrobat.

"Piss off," was all she could manage to reply.

"Eloquent as ever, Ms. Grimm."

"That's Ms. *Fucking* Grimm to you." She moved toward the shelves but turned on a heel. "And just what the fuck do you think you're doing? Look for some books for stars' sake. You haven't pulled a single one off a bookshelf."

Crossing his legs, he didn't look up from where he sat on the lounge chair. "My job was to get you here, Ms. Grimm. It's your job to do the research."

"You suffering, lazy asshole," she hissed. "How do you expect me to... you know what? Never mind." Once again, she started to leave, only to turn back and glare at his novel. "I hope the sex scenes *suck*."

Stomping over to the pile of books, she picked up several and nearly threw herself onto the antique carpet in her fury.

Why did he get under her skin like that? Stars, he was so *infuriating.*

For a while, she thought he might have left to cool off. But the smell of shoe polish and sage filled her nostrils. Gaze snapping up, she was surprised to see him lowering himself to sit beside her.

"You are right," he said in his usual formal tone. "What you and Ms. Lockwood do is none of my business." He cleared his throat. "Regardless of my involvement with the show management team, I still think you deserve happiness. All of the performers do."

She exhaled noisily, recognizing the white flag for what it was.

How had she gotten to the place where cyborgs had become a sort of family?

Her thoughts strayed to her childhood on Orthodocks and the family she'd once had. Fear seized her chest as she realized there were more and more gaps in her memory. She still couldn't remember her parents' faces, and even their silhouettes had faded from her mind's eye. And now, she could no longer recall their names.

Tears pricked her human eye, which she roughly scraped away with the back of her hand. Her cyborg eye whirred in confusion, uncertain what to do with such human emotions.

"Have you ever thought about what it might be like if we didn't grow up in the Union?" she said at last. "Sometimes I wonder if life would be better outside of the Crescent Star System, especially after the Cyborg Prohibition Law."

When he didn't reply, she looked over at him. His gaze was distant as he stared past the bookshelves in front of them.

"It's not." His voice was soft, as though a louder volume might dissipate the strange energy forming between them.

Her eyebrows rose.

"I remember pieces of my life before—more than most, I suppose. Enough to remind me why I'm here."

As always, mention of the Forgetting sent ice through her veins.

"And why are you here?"

Bastian turned to look at her.

"Are you here to make a name for yourself or to protect the performers?" she asked. "I don't think you can have both."

Indecision swirled in his eyes. "I don't know. But I can't remain idle and watch all of my recruits be butchered to death. It isn't right. They deserve better than this."

"So do you."

"All I know is that to save the many, I must hurt a few." He sighed wearily. "If I'm to protect any of the performers, some of the performers must be sacrificed for the greater good."

She harrumphed. "That sounds like a cop-out to me. A way of avoiding responsibility in all of this."

He didn't respond.

They sat on the floor in silence for some time before she finally stood and extended a hand to him. "Let's get back to our search."

He studied her hand for a moment before taking it and standing.

Returning to the table, she gestured to one stack of books. "Read through those. *Please.* If we have any hope of finding anything useful, I'll need the help. Tell me if you find information on installation or upkeep. I also want to know more about how these chips in our brains work. I'll start over here." She waved at a different pile.

A shiver crept up her spine at the thought of her checkup with Celeste.

Hours later, Gwen's head swam almost as much as the words on the pages as she scanned book after book. It had to be late into the night by now.

"I found something."

Bastian's words yanked her from her thoughts.

"This one is a textbook about cyborg foot re-installations.

There's text in here about how to proceed if the first unit was installed improperly."

Nearly leaping from her chair, she stood and dashed to his side, snatching the book from his hand. "Yes! Just what I needed for Marzanna. I could kiss you, you bastard." She hesitated, realizing what she'd said. "Well, we already did that, I suppose."

She plopped onto the floor, studying the index before flipping to the pages she sought. "Marzanna's foot wasn't installed properly. It lags when she moves too fast, and I've seen the unit drag when she's rehearsing. I tried rewiring the unit, but without a manual or some type of instruction guide, it's all guesswork."

As she scanned the text, her heart froze. She turned to Bastian. "When's the next competition?"

His brows drew together. "I shouldn't be telling—"

"I don't have time to pussyfoot around this," she interrupted. "Someone's life is at stake. When does the second competition start?"

He sighed heavily. "Tomorrow."

For a moment, she forgot how to breathe as dread tightened her chest.

"What is it?" he asked.

She licked suddenly dry lips. "I might have killed her."

"Who?" he asked. "Marzanna?"

She managed a nod. "I have to get to her—before the competition. If I don't fix the wiring before the machine gets too hot, it might short-circuit. If it does, she could…"

Die.

Bastian removed a pocket watch from his coat, which hung on a long chain. His features went suddenly pale.

"What is it?"

"It's nearly dawn." He looked up to her then, his eyes wide. "They've likely already been brought to the theater for the second competition."

Leaping to her feet, she bolted down the hallway, her heart slamming in her ears.

She had to get to them before the competition started.

Behind her, Bastian's footsteps pounded in time with hers. But she feared it was already far too late.

CHAPTER 16

There was a loud bang, and Rora opened her eyes.

"Get up." A masked watchman hefted an electric lantern at the threshold of her room. "You've been summoned."

In his other hand, he held a baton. The threat was as plain as a Black Hole. Calls from additional watchmen echoed down the hallway as other performers were roused from their rooms.

Standing, Rora rubbed her eyes. As she did, she noticed for the first time the second masked watchman in her doorway held a key. Had they *unlocked* her bedroom door? No one was supposed to have keys to the dormitories other than the performers themselves.

What else has the Mistress lied to us about?

Normally, she didn't think much of the watchmen's attire. But as she studied the usual black pants and button-up shirt with two pistols strapped to his back and a sword at one hip, she couldn't help but notice how heavily armed they were for a circus guard. Not to mention, they never stepped out of line and never spoke to the performers outside of what was strictly necessary to perform their job. Ever.

How much did the Mistress pay the hired soldiers for their obedience? It had to be a hefty paycheck to wordlessly usher cyborgs to their deaths.

Rora slipped into her shoes.

Since the first competition, she'd slept in her performance gear every single night. She refused to be caught off guard a second time. Therefore, she didn't hurry to grab clothes and get dressed as the watchmen ushered her out into the hallway.

Dozens of other performers filtered out of their rooms in the dormitory wing and joined Rora in the hallway. Everyone had the same question on their lips.

Was the second competition about to begin?

"Can it be time already?" Akio whispered as he and Marzanna joined Rora in the hallway. "I swear, it's only been... what? Two weeks since the last contest?"

Dread weighted Rora's tongue, and she couldn't reply.

"It's my turn," Marzanna said to Akio as they neared the theater. "You competed in the first competition. I should go this time."

Akio shook his head. "Not with your foot. That's the worst idea I've heard all day."

Rora's brows furrowed. "The day just started."

Marzanna stifled a chuckle as the performers around them fell into a strange, hushed silence.

"Regardless," Akio whispered. "I can compete again. You're my only family. Let me do this."

But even as he spoke, Rora could see sweat beading on his temples.

They'd never spoken about what they'd had to do during the first competition, but she knew the obstacle course had deeply distressed her friend.

She swallowed thickly.

The last competition had brought about the death of three cyborgs. What could possibly be in store for them today? Who would meet their end at the hands of the competition—and the tinkerer who took their parts?

The hands I want all over me, she thought, and then shook herself. *Focus.*

"No," Marzanna said firmly. "You went last time. It's my turn to face the crazy."

Reluctantly, Akio nodded.

When they entered the theater, Celeste Beckett, the Mistress of Cirque du Borge and Keeper of Beasts, stood at center stage and watched the performers as they were ushered into the room. Although it took a while for the performers to filter into the theater, there were noticeably fewer people than there had been a few weeks ago.

Watchmen stationed themselves around the theater at the exits.

"Welcome to the second competition." Celeste crossed her arms, the tight leather jacket creasing as she tapped her red-manicured nails against her lower lip. She was dressed in black leather from neck to toes, her heeled leather boots impractical for anyone—especially the Keeper of Beasts. Rumor had it she used her heels to keep misbehaving animals in check.

Why was she introducing this particular competition?

Matthieu Eaves, the set designer, had introduced the first competition, which had been an obstacle course of his making. What could the second competition involve? Something with animals?

The doors to the theater slammed shut, echoing in the room as whispers tapered off. All eyes were on center stage.

"The first competition tested your agility. Now, your determination will be put to the test." Celeste's eyes swept over the room. "For this competition, performers have a single objective: to locate and bring back the red dragon."

The silence that fell was deafening. It was so complete that Rora heard the distinct patter of water hitting the floor.

As though someone had just wet themselves.

Fear knotted her stomach. This was utter madness and worse than the first competition. Dragons regularly attacked the city of Apparatus. Half of the time, citizens were putting out fires and repairing buildings the dragons destroyed during raids. How in the galaxy were a bunch of performers supposed to *capture* a wild dragon?

"Like cyborgs, the dragons have been misunderstood," Celeste continued.

I'll say.

"They have been exiled to the planet of Grandstand, same as us. But now we are going to bring them into the fold.

"The dragon lives in a cave on the tallest mountain beyond the forest. Your job is to subdue the creature and bring it back. The performer who brings it back alive wins.

"There are no official teams. But given the nature of this competition and the challenges you will face, any performers who work together to bring the dragon back will not be selected for the lottery and be allowed a shared victory.

"In addition, you are to select a single representative from your acts to participate in today's competition. It may be the same performer as last time or someone else. But one cyborg must go on behalf of the act, and everyone will share their fate.

"As was the case for the first competition, you will be judged by the show management team. The losing performers will have their names entered into the lottery, and thirteen acts will be selected for contract termination.

"Once the thirty-six performers have been selected to participate in the competition, you will exit the building and receive your supplies. The dragon's cave is less than a day's march from here. Watchmen will then escort you to the forest at the edge of the city, after which time you have until sunset tomorrow to bring it here."

The Mistress paused, studying the audience with narrowed eyes. "Should any of you be tempted not to return, remember that the remaining performers from your respective acts will automatically have terminated contracts and be selected for harvesting. And if you are found in my city… you will wish for a swift end."

Celeste waved a hand to the opening doors at the back of the theater. "Break a leg."

For a moment, Rora struggled to breathe as her head swam. She couldn't think, let alone move. It felt as though her feet had been replaced with cinder blocks.

Sensing this, Marzanna grabbed Rora's elbow, pulling her toward the open doors. "Come on. Now is not the time to lose your shit. We have a competition to win."

Rora spared a glance back toward Akio, who was being ushered with the other performers who weren't competing back toward the hallways.

"*Good luck*," he mouthed.

Rora could only manage a nod. Her heart thudded a rapid melody to what must surely be her death march. In the first competition, she'd couldn't even pass Abrecan to climb up the rope. How was she supposed to stand up to a dragon that had to be two or three times Abrecan's size?

The dragons of legend had supposedly been the size of war ships. The ones that remained today were little more than the size of two lions in length.

Still, it was big enough to kill her.

Once the thirty-six performers exited the theater, the doors were rolled back down and locked in place.

Watchmen passed out boots, jackets, and backpacks. When Rora received her backpack, she glanced inside, noting water, food supplies, and… Was that climbing gear? There was rope, grappling hooks, and other supplies she couldn't identify.

By the looks of what was in the bag, the circus wasn't concerned about the performers spending a night in the wilderness. Had the dragon killed off most of the predators?

Heels tapped against cobblestones, and Celeste emerged from a side door of the theater, coming to stand before them.

"One more thing," Celeste began. "Due to the dangerous nature of this particular competition, the show management team has revised how contracts will be terminated for the remainder of the competitions. Should any of you die in the attempt of capturing the dragon, your performance act will automatically be selected for termination—so long as the bodies are brought back or located by our cleanup crew. If thirteen people lose their lives to this competition, there will be no lottery in this round. Understood?"

Across the group of thirty-six performers, dozens of eyes widened.

But Abrecan... he smiled, his gaze shifting to Rora and Marzanna.

Celeste had just given Abrecan and his followers a reason to pick them off one by one.

The performers shouldered packs and followed the line of watchmen into the palace's courtyard. At the gate, there was a table of weapons, consisting of bows, swords, and spears.

Pushing forward, Abrecan grabbed a bow as tall as he was and a matching set of arrows. The other performers rushed the table afterward. By the time Rora and Marzanna made it to the front, there were two spears left. Two spears to protect them from the dragon and whatever else might be lurking in the forest—human or beast.

Fantastic.

As they walked toward the outskirts of the city, surrounded by watchmen, the sun crept above the horizon.

I can't give up now. There are only two competitions left.

She was so close to meeting the emperor and fulfilling her lifelong dream of securing patronage. Two more competitions, and she'd be home free. Soon, she would prove to everyone she was the best performer at Cirque du Borge. And with the way things were going with Gwen, she might have a new hand in no time, too.

But she couldn't help the feeling that the tinkerer had Rora wrapped around her finger, rather than the other way around. After Gwen had showed up at Rora's room and explained what had happened at the ball, Rora hadn't been able to stop thinking about her.

Forcing the beautiful tinkerer from her thoughts, Rora tried to focus on what lay ahead.

Thinking fast, she came up with a desperate plan.

Slowly, she made her way over to a small group of acrobats who weren't allied with Abrecan or his followers.

"Join us," she whispered. "Our odds are better together than apart."

"Our odds suck," Sara, one of the acrobats, said.

"Better than each of us individually against a dragon." Rora watched Abrecan strut confidently at the head of the group beside the watchmen. "At the very least, we can watch each other's backs until we make it to the cliffs."

There weren't official teams, but it couldn't hurt to form alliances with other performers. Even if they did somehow manage to subdue the dragon, Rora and Marzanna would be hard-pressed to bring it back to Apparatus—awake or unconscious. Not to mention, the dragon wasn't the only beast in these parts.

Sara remained silent for an impossibly long time.

"Fine," she said at last. "We'll join you as we travel through the forest. But when it comes to the dragon, I'll fight you for it. I'm not coming back without that scaly beast."

Rora nodded. "We'll see."

When they neared the city's limit, she slowed, her friends and new allies doing likewise. Abrecan and his followers went ahead of them into the line of trees. She'd need to keep them where she could see them. She didn't fancy an arrow between her shoulders.

Before he disappeared, Abrecan turned around and smiled broadly at her. Then he strode into the forest, the others in his group yipping and cheering like wild dogs.

Taking a deep breath, she said, "Everyone, keep your eyes peeled and stay alert. We have more than just animals to worry about in this forest."

Sara sniffed. "They *are* animals."

Rora shifted her pack. "No arguments there. But to beat them, we might have to be animals, too."

She wondered just what she'd do in the name of self-preservation—and to achieve her dream of patronage.

Taking a deep breath, she strode ahead of the group and into the forest.

It was time to find a dragon.

CHAPTER 17

As Gwen ran up the staircase and into the hallway, a hand caught her arm.

"What are you doing?" Bastian hissed, pulling her behind a curtain as watchmen marched down a nearby hallway. "Are you trying to get us both caught?"

"It doesn't matter," she said. "Marzanna's life is in danger."

He didn't release her arm even after the watchmen's footsteps faded into the distance. "It's too late. The performers are gone."

She growled even as her heart plummeted into her boots. "Gone *where?*"

Slowly, he peered from behind the curtain before striding down empty halls with her in tow.

"Their mission is to find and bring back the red dragon— the beast that keeps attacking the city—by sunset tomorrow." He pulled her into the gardens. "It's rumored to live in the cliffs beyond the forest outside of Apparatus."

She stopped beneath the rope leading to Bastian's room. "You're fucking with me, right?"

His lips drew into a thin line. "Do you honestly expect me to respond to that?"

"They have to find a *dragon*? What fuckarsery is this? Are you people all out of your minds?"

Glancing to the empty hallways and then back to her, he gestured to the rope. "Will you just climb up before someone sees us?"

She scowled. "How can you be talking about sneaking around at a time like this? I'm just going to walk up to my room, get my tool kit, and—"

As she started walking back toward the hallway, Bastian caught her wrist again.

"I must insist." He practically *dragged* her back to where the rope dangled in the garden. "It's too late. You can't help Marzanna. But you can still help the others with the knowledge we learned last night."

She pulled against him, but he didn't stop.

"If I'm ever to help you again, our movements must remain a secret."

"I don't have time for this." She twisted, her body spinning.

Elbowing Bastian in the chin, she tore her arm free of his grip.

Stumbling backward, his eyes widened. "Did you just *hit* me?"

"Have you not been listening to me this entire time? I have to get to Marzanna *now*. I don't have time to attempt to scale a castle."

"You can't help Marzanna. Not without interfering with the second competition, which I cannot allow."

She rolled her eyes, her look saying one thing, *"Fuck what you allow."*

Again, she moved toward the hallway, but something smacked hard against her ankles. Her feet went out from under her, and she crashed into nearby shrubbery. Flipping onto her back, she narrowed her eyes on the bastard who'd just fucking *tripped* her.

She leaped to her feet, only for Bastian to kick at her ankles again. Only this time, she dived out of the way. His leg swiped at air as she landed another blow to his jaw.

Running a thumb along his cheek, he said, "I didn't see combat training in your files."

"First of all, that's the creepiest thing you've ever said to me," she said. "Second, any bastard carrying cargo between planets learns how to fight or they get killed by pirates. You should know as much, traveling with the circus."

Slowly, he moved, circling her. "I won't let you interfere with this competition."

She barked a laugh. "As if you can stop me."

If she had any hopes of being a true cyborg tinkerer, she had to fix this mistake. More than that, she had to save Rora's friend.

Bastian positioned himself between her and the hallway, blocking her exit. But that wouldn't matter for long.

She lunged at him, landing several blows to his gut and sides. But as she struck, her fists collided with something far harder than human flesh. Stumbling backward, she shook out the zinging pain in her hands.

Looking closely for the first time, she used her cyborg eye to scan Bastian's frame. How had she never noticed it before? He was practically glowing with metal.

"Are you made of fucking *steel*? Just what kind of implant did you get?"

Bastian didn't reply. Instead, he charged.

She struck out at him, and he didn't bother deflecting her blows. Again, her hands collided with his hidden implant. Her arms screamed with pain, but she ignored it. Spinning away, she reached for the knife in her boot. She didn't want to hurt him, but there wasn't time for this nonsense.

Something slammed against her back, and she staggered forward.

Bastian's hand encircled her wrist—yet fucking again—and he spun her to him. There was a clicking sound as he cocked Gwen's own pistol.

How had he gotten that?

He nodded toward the rope at the opposite end of the garden. "If you please, Ms. Grimm. Climb the rope *now*."

Smiling, she tightened her grip on the knife she had pressed against Bastian's fucking testicles.

"I don't think so."

Glancing down, he sighed in exasperation, belatedly realizing his predicament.

"You knew this competition was going to happen when you recruited me, and you told me *nothing*." She pressed the knife harder against his crotch. Hard enough to make him gasp. "Why? Just so you could get me to sign that farce of a contract? Think I would have preferred dying to butchering other cyborgs? Well, I do, in case you're wondering."

When he didn't respond, she snapped, "Say something!"

"I didn't know."

Surprised, she lessened the pressure of the knife. "What do you mean you didn't know?"

"I'm not part of the show management team," he said through gritted teeth. "They didn't tell me what they were planning. A watchman slipped a letter beneath my bedroom door the morning of the ball with a notice that the first competition would be that evening and that all of the performers must be present. Knowing Celeste, I suspected the competitions wouldn't be pleasant, but I had no idea what she'd planned or that she intended to employ the contract's fine print and begin extractions. She'd never done it in the past. It wasn't until after the first competition—after you and I harvested the implants—that I went to a show management meeting, uninvited, and demanded to be informed about the competition."

Bastian lowered the pistol. Slowly, Gwen lowered her knife as well.

Glancing away, he ran a hand through his thick black hair. "I didn't know, Gwendolyn. I had no fucking clue."

She wasn't sure what was more surprising—the fact that he had used her first name or that he cursed.

"And my recruitment?"

His gaze was distant as he stared off into the gardens. "Pure chance. I'd heard from one of the manufacturers that a talented ship tinkerer was in town. It wasn't until I located you in Anchorage's prison that I learned of your illness and thought you might be a good fit for the circus."

She sniffed. "You mean desperate enough to join."

Eyes connecting with hers, he said, "We need a better tinkerer than Celeste. One who shows a modicum of remorse, at the very least. She's the only one we had after our last tinkerer disappeared more than a year ago."

As though something snapped inside him, anger filled his gaze—a deep, bottomless fury.

"You want the truth? Then here it is. The circus didn't have any funds. Hasn't for months. It's why you haven't been paid yet. I used every last mark I personally saved up over the past ten years to pay your bail and additional parts for your implant, but it wasn't enough. So, I used the last of the circus's recruitment funds as well. The Mistress didn't approve, but... she came around when I insisted you would help to remove some of the responsibilities from her plate."

For the first time, Gwen looked at Bastian, truly *looked* at him. At the way his eyes were drawn, the deep, purple smudges beneath his eyes, and the terror lurking in the back of his gaze.

"What did she do to you?"

Shaking his head, he sighed. "I think the better question is, what *hasn't* she done to me?"

She thought of his restricting habits, how she'd never seen him eat. How he was always dressed immaculately, as though he was trying to hide a part of himself that he was ashamed of.

Suddenly, it clicked, and the words were out of her mouth before she could stop them. "Did she... force herself on you?"

His gaze fell from hers. "No. But she's done just about everything else." He swallowed thickly, a spark of anger alighting his features. "And the watchmen are loyal to only her."

A fury bright as starlight burst in her chest. Heat blossomed in her cheeks, and her arms shook. How could Celeste do this to him? How could *anyone* do that to another person—use someone as though they were worthless tools?

Some strange instinct took over, and she sheathed her knife and wrapped her arms around him. At first, he was stiff with his arms at his sides. Moments later, his arms enveloped her, wrapping tightly around her back to pull her close to him.

"I'm so sorry." She murmured the words into his jacket, realizing for the first time that he was slightly taller. "I'm so damn sorry."

A thought occurred to her, and she ripped herself out of his arms.

"What is it?" he asked, looking around.

"I-I..." She was at a loss for words. "I shouldn't have touched you like that... without your consent. Even if she didn't... well... after whatever she did to you. I'm sorry."

She took several steps back from him, shaking her head. How could she be so *stupid?*

Understanding flickered across his features. "I didn't mind. It was... nice, actually. Thank you, Ms. Grimm. For your kindness."

Clearing his throat, he pointedly eyed the rope that swayed faintly in the wind.

"I'm going to help them," she said. "I *must* find Marzanna and fix my mistake. More than that, I can't leave them to fight a dragon alone. Can you?"

His eyes flicked to her human one, eyebrows furrowed.

"I don't know the geography of this planet, and I don't have time to find a map." Desperation tinged her voice, but she pressed on. "Not to mention, you've worked with Celeste. You know animals and how to handle them. I need your help. Please."

She tried not to think of Celeste's threat after the first competition—and the very real possibility that the Mistress might try to take her eye if it was ever discovered she helped the performers during the competition.

I have to protect the cyborgs. And I won't let some bully like Celeste fuck with my new family.

A deep heaviness settled on her chest.

Sighing, he nodded. "Fine. But we do this my way. Climb the rope and don't leave the room until I get back." Turning back toward the hallway, he said over a shoulder, "I have to get something if we have any hope of bringing that dragon back."

Hours later, Bastian returned through the window with swords and shields and some strange item that bulged in his pocket. They packed bags before Gwen retrieved her skimming board and tool kit from her room.

When night fell, she finally convinced Bastian that the skimmer was the fastest way to get out of the city and catch up with the performers.

Kicking on the engine, she stepped onto the board, and he got on behind her. Wrapping his arms around her waist, which was heavy with the sword, she pushed off the window and flew into the night.

They soared to the edge of the forest near the cliffs before descending and setting up camp.

They ate dried food in silence and filled their water canteens in a nearby stream. She prayed the stream was clean enough that they wouldn't be violently ill from drinking toxins.

As they lay down, pulling jackets over them as blankets, she voiced a question that had been lingering at the back of her mind. "Why did you join Cirque du Borge?"

Bastian lay on his back, staring up at the leafy canopies above them.

She didn't think he'd actually answer her—not after the sleepless night and heartwarming day they'd had—but he eventually spoke.

"I was sentenced to death by hanging when the former ringleader found me," he said. "It was more than ten years ago now, and I can only remember pieces."

He could remember things from ten years ago? But how? Her memories were already fading and fast.

Surprise streaked across her face. "That's terrible."

"It was well deserved from what I can remember. As the eldest child, I'd been set on a course to inherit my father's estate. Where I'm from—outside the Union—first children must prove their worthiness to their parents before they can take over the family business. I'd worked hard and made parts of the estate more efficient.

"But when I refused to take part in a certain aspect of my family's estate, my father withdrew my inheritance. Not long after, I became ill and needed money for a medical procedure. When I asked my father for assistance, he wouldn't allow me a portion of the inheritance, even as a loan for the procedure.

"I didn't have any options. If I didn't have the procedure, I'd likely die. I was forced to participate in my family's illegal operations and prove myself to them. Only then would I receive the money I needed.

"I hated every moment of it. Eventually, I turned myself

in to the authorities. In the process, I lost everything—my family, my fiancée, and my inheritance. I had been about to lose my life as well when Carlisle found me and offered me a second chance at life."

Gwen was surprised by how similar their circumstances had been that led them to the circus. Both she and Bastian had been about to die when a ringleader had found them and offered a way to evade death.

"It sounds like you and this Carlisle got along." She rolled onto her stomach, resting her chin in a hand. "Was he the ringleader before?"

He nodded. "I loved that man like a father. Perhaps more than my father."

"Did you get the procedure you'd needed when you joined the circus?"

"Yes. I have a bad heart, you see. When I got here, they gave me a pacemaker to keep my heart going." He scratched his head. "When I joined the circus, the role of ringleader was already taken. I'd been apprenticed to Celeste. At the time, there'd been a lot of experimentation on animals to try to make them cyborgs, too. Bigger crowd appeal, the Mistress had said. It had been before the emperor's rise to power.

"But the implants didn't take. We later learned it was because of the anesthesia. After that, we did surgeries under the lightest anesthesia possible. When the animals awoke and saw me mid-surgery, most attacked. After several near-death experiences, I was given a second cyborg implant—plates beneath my chest and back—to protect my vital organs from the beasts we were attempting to turn into cyborgs."

Gwen's eyes widened.

That's why you nearly broke my fucking hands today.

"This competition isn't the first of our unspeakable crimes," he said. "It's simply the first against our own people."

"So... you can't be killed, then? With your second implants?"

"Not with swords or knives to the back or gut, no," he admitted. "A bullet to the head or a knife to the throat would suffice, I suspect."

Interestingly, he didn't look at her, keeping his eyes on the trees above.

Some time passed, and he didn't say anything for so long that she thought he might have fallen asleep.

"I have no home or family to return to at the end of my contract," he said at last. "The show management position—it's all I have left."

She sat up. "I'm sorry for what happened to you. But you're wrong."

His gaze snapped to hers.

"I wouldn't call us friends, exactly," she began. "But for what it's worth, you're not alone. You have me. You also have the circus and all the performers you've recruited. They need you."

I need you.

Where the hell had that come from? Since when was she cozying up to Bastian?

Chill the fuck out.

Clearing his throat, he said, "We'd best get some sleep. I expect we'll make it to the dragon's cave tomorrow."

Slowly, he sank to the ground and pulled his coat over him.

As she drifted off to sleep, she thought of Rora, praying that she was all right and her hand was working. When sleep finally came, she dreamed of both Bastian and Rora—and the feel of their naked bodies pressed against hers.

Gwen awoke the next morning when a sound ripped through the trees, sending birds squawking and soaring into the air. It was a sound she'd never heard before on any of the Union's planets she'd traveled to as a tinkerer.

Somewhere above them, a dragon roared.

CHAPTER 18

Taking a breath, Rora swung her arm up, letting go of her previous handhold on the cliff to grab the nearest ledge. She hung in the air from one arm for several long moments before her feet found purchase and she scrambled up.

Eventually, she made it to the top of the next ledge, tied off the rope to a nearby rock, tested it, and tossed it down to Marzanna and their wayward allies. When the rope drew taut, she knew someone must be climbing up.

Besides the whistling of the wind, it was eerily quiet.

Where is Abrecan?

Rora had expected him to make a move against them hours ago before they started climbing the cliff where the Mistress had said the dragon lived. Thus far, Abrecan, his followers, and the dragon were nowhere to be seen.

As the most skilled climber, Rora led the way as they climbed hundreds of feet. For every cave they passed, she scanned each before tying ropes off so their teams could ascend without the need to climb unassisted up the cliff. However, it had been hours since they'd started their ascent.

After searching countless caves, they were all growing restless and tired.

There was another cave a short distance down a narrow ledge.

Just one more, and then we can rest.

Marzanna appeared first over the ledge, followed by their reluctant allies. Rora helped them up as quickly as she could. Once they were all there, she wiggled her way to the head of the group again, peering down the narrow path.

When Marzanna came up beside her, Rora stopped short. "Are you hurt?"

During their march up the mountain, they'd been forced to go slower as Marzanna struggled to maintain their pace. She'd insisted she was fine before, but she hadn't been limping. Now, her cyborg foot dragged visibly, far worse than before.

"It's my damn foot," Marzanna replied. "Nothing to worry about now. We have a dragon to find."

Rora wanted to object, but there simply wasn't the time or resources to help Marzanna. "Stay at the back of the group. If we need to get away in a hurry, I want you safe."

Marzanna's mouth drew into a thin line. Clearly, she didn't like Rora's orders as much as Rora disliked giving them.

Slowly, Rora moved toward the cave.

Unlike most of the other caves they'd searched, this one was nestled into an alcove that protected the mouth of the cave from the gusting wind. The strands of hair that had fallen loose from her bun settled around her face, tickling her cheeks. She nearly sighed in relief at the lack of wind.

As they crept toward the cave, they were forced to shimmy sideways as the path grew dangerously thin. Was the air getting warmer?

Once a few feet from the cave, she leaped, her pack jingling as her feet hit the ground outside the cave. A rock bounced, skittering off the side of the cliff. Below, the trees were the size of her little nail. Forcing her eyes ahead, she scanned her surroundings. This cave was far bigger than the others they'd seen so far, which had simply been indents in the cliff.

Deep in the darkness, she thought she could hear something. Could it be a rustling? The hair around her face lifted from her cheeks as though from a wind deep within the cave. Could there be an opening on the other side? It would certainly make navigating this cliff a whole lot easier if they didn't have to climb the entire thing and could walk through it instead.

As she stepped into the cave, the air grew definitively warmer, sending gooseflesh across her skin at the sudden heat.

But rather than being relaxed by the warmth, fear rocketed through her.

They'd found the dragon.

Behind her, boots crunched on the rocky ground. Rocks pattered into the cave, echoing as they went deeper into the dark abyss. Rora spun around, waving her arms frantically as Marzanna jumped into the mouth of the cave, followed by their allies.

Seeing her, they froze in place.

Pointing toward the depths of the cave, she mouthed, "*Dragon!*" as she crept toward the wall. The others did likewise.

Blinking, she tried to force her eyes to adjust to the dim light of the cave, but she could see little beyond the sharp ridges along the wall. Removing her pack, she pulled out a portable lantern.

It took several tries with her shaking hands, but she managed to light it. She paused only long enough to grab the spear she'd tied to her pack. Extending the lantern up, she gaped as the cave glittered. The firelight reflected off thousands of clear crystals lining the walls of a cave the size of the theater. Down the tunnel at the center of the cave was a scarlet dragon.

For a second, Rora was tempted to shit herself.

It would have been a very glamorous first reaction to the most dangerous thing she'd ever done. Her second reaction was to run, to shove past everyone and climb back down the rope to the safety of the hills and trees far below. But if she did that, she'd be condemning herself—and the lives of her friends—to beggary or worse.

Clenching her butt, she swallowed and crept forward, leaving her pack in the tunnel behind her. Hands sweating, she clutched on to the spear and lantern as she moved forward.

The dragon's scarlet scales rose and fell in the rhythmic pattern of sleep as it breathed deeply. Its eyes were closed and its head nestled atop crossed claws. The position looked positively feline.

What *now*?

Turning, she realized Marzanna had followed quietly behind her. "What's the plan?"

Hell if I know.

"We wake it," Rora replied, "and try to befriend it. But we should be ready if things don't go our way."

Marzanna shook her head. "What creature in this galaxy wants to be woken up from a nap? You'll just piss it off."

"Do you have a better plan?" When Marzanna didn't reply, Rora continued. "We have to gain its trust and get it back to the palace before Abrecan does. Otherwise, we'll all be entered into the lottery."

Marzanna pointed at the dragon with her own spear. "How are we going to get down a cliff with an unwilling dragon?"

"Excellent question."

Everyone else hovered at the mouth of the cave, looking as scared as Rora felt.

Before she could figure out what she was going to do, a

low rumbling came from the back of the cave, sending loose stones bouncing and some of the crystals along the walls rattling free.

Swallowing, she turned toward the sound.

The dragon raised its head from its legs, exposing its fangs in a snarl. The white of its teeth contrasted the bloodred of its scaled flesh, which shimmered in the firelight as it stood. It loosed a roar and pawed its talons on the cave floor.

Rora's pulse thumped like a hammer striking an anvil. For a moment, she feared her legs wouldn't move or that she'd actually shat herself. Licking dry lips, she placed her spear on the ground. She didn't want the dragon to feel threatened. Then she forced herself to take a step forward and then another. The dragon was dozens of paces away from her. Shattered crystal crunched beneath her boots.

"We're not here to hurt you." Her voice trembled, and she nearly dropped the lantern several times. "We have friends who'd like to meet you."

Again, the dragon pawed at the cave floor, leaving sharp grooves in the rock face.

This was the creature that had ravaged their city countless times, and she wanted to have a *chat* with it?

"I've never met a dragon before." She could barely hear her voice over the whooshing in her ears. "I've only read about your kind in storybooks. You're far more impressive in person."

Stop rambling. It can't understand you anyway. Get your act together, or your friends will die.

To her surprise, her words seemed to calm the beast. Smoke plumed from its nostrils, but it no longer growled or showed its fangs.

The center of the cave was hollowed for a sort of nest. As she strode down the tunnel, deeper into the cliff, the cave opened up to a space far larger than the theater. In addition to the crystals lining the walls of the cave, bones littered the floor, pushed to the outskirts of the room.

The dragon was mere paces from her now, eyes narrowing. Compared to the others, she was the shortest and, hopefully, the least threatening to an agitated dragon.

Some of the fictional stories she'd read about dragons had said the creatures could speak, but as she neared the red dragon, she knew it to be a fantasy. There was primal instinct in those eyes, some intelligence, but mostly vague, irritated curiosity.

"My name is Rora, and these are my friends." She gestured over her shoulder. "We're in a bit of a pickle. I'm hoping you might be able to help us."

She raised her cyborg hand toward the dragon's shoulder, the closest thing to her.

Please don't eat me. Please don't eat me.

Not for the first time, she wondered at the complete idiocy of this entire task. How was anyone supposed to retrieve a dragon from a cliff without a fleet of air vessels?

They were doomed. She was going to die. They were all going to die. There was no way anyone could pull this off.

Unable to stop herself, she closed her eyes, preparing for the feel of sharp teeth sinking into her cyborg hand. Instead, she started as her fingers clinked against its scales. The sensation of touch was quite different from her human hand. She could sense the sharp scales on its shoulder but not the warmth of it or the fine ridges. Slowly, she ran her hand back and forth over the scales, as though petting an animal.

"The people who want to meet you sent us to find you."

Hot air tickled her neck as the dragon watched her.

They're more beast than you are.

Slowly, she looked up at the dragon. It wasn't looking at her, but toward the mouth of the cave. Following its line of gaze, she saw what she'd feared since they'd entered the forest.

A group of performers stood in the mouth of the cave, and Abrecan directed a nocked bow at the dragon.

The bow was massive, of a height with him, and the arrow was the size of a spear.

"I must thank you for leading us to the beast."

Without his training as a hunter and his experience at Cirque du Borge, he likely wouldn't have been able to draw the bow. It was as if the weapon had been made for him to use in this competition. The only bow powerful enough to pierce a dragon's scaled hide, and the only performer with enough strength or skill to use it.

Slowly, realization dawned.

Abrecan didn't try to kill Rora or her friends before because he wanted to use them as bait for the dragon. He'd thought the beast would be picking them from its teeth by now, and he could swoop in and capture the dragon while it was otherwise preoccupied.

As he stepped toward them, not letting go of the bow's string, his followers grabbed two of the acrobats from their allied team and tossed them over the edge of the cliff.

There wasn't even time for Rora to call out.

Abrecan directed an arrow at the dragon's chest.

"No!" Rora placed herself between the dragon and Abrecan. For reasons she couldn't explain, the idea of killing this majestic creature was unthinkable. It might have ravished their city in the past, but it hadn't harmed her. "We have to bring it back alive."

She didn't move from where she stood in front of the dragon. "Dragons are nearly extinct. We can't just—"

"How did you expect us to bring back the dragon? By riding on its back into the sunset?" Abrecan spat. "The creature must be incapacitated if we're going to bring it back to Apparatus. And I have no intention of losing this competition." To her surprise, he winked at her. "I'll be sure to comfort our little tinkerer when she learns of your death. She'll be in need of a man's touch, I think."

Before she could reply, he released the arrow.

A massive force collided with Rora's back, sending her flying to the side. She bounced once, sliding across the cave floor.

A rumble bubbled up from within the dragon's belly before its roar erupted throughout the cave, sending crystals shattering onto the floor. Throwing her arms up, she covered her head as hundreds of crystals pattered against her skin.

Looking up, she saw the massive arrow wedged between the dragon's scales on its flank—deep enough to be painful but not deep enough to kill.

Had the dragon protected her?

As the beast breathed, the space between its scales grew bright orange. Abrecan nocked another arrow, which he sent flying just before the dragon released a wave of fire. The arrow bounced off the cave walls, sending more crystals raining down upon them.

Everyone at the mouth of the cave ducked outside, taking cover.

As the dragon's fire billowed outward, Marzanna leaped toward them. She narrowly made it into the dragon's nest, out of reach of the flames engulfing the mouth of the cave.

Others were too slow. The smell of roasting flesh filled the air as the dragon barreled forward.

Rora rose to her feet on shaking legs. As she stumbled forward, the soles of her boots were warm against her feet. All around her, the crystals that hadn't come crashing down melted into the walls.

Abrecan shot more arrows at the dragon, and Rora ducked as several bounced off the walls near her.

Marzanna got to her feet as well, and Rora breathed a sigh of relief to see her friend wasn't harmed.

At the cave's entrance, the dragon snapped at Abrecan,

who rolled out of the way. Several of his followers, including Thaniel, descended from ledges on either side of the cave's entrance to help him fight the beast. But with the swipe of the dragon's tail, more performers were sent to their deaths over side of the cliff. From where she stood inside the cave, Rora thought she saw several cyborgs descending the cliff.

They're running away.

Slowly, the dragon forced Abrecan and his friends toward the edge of the cave's entrance. More and more performers tumbled off the cliff or retreated. If they didn't do something, and quick, they would all be dead.

Suddenly, two forms appeared, hovering before the mouth of the cave.

"Gwen!" Rora cried.

Like a tall, foul-mouthed savior goddess, Gwen appeared, riding a skimmer with…

Was that Bastian Kabir?

The ringleader leaped into the mouth of the cave beside Abrecan and Thaniel. He brandished a sword and shield, swiping at the dragon's flank. Gwen flew into the mouth of the cave, narrowly skimming out of the dragon's reach.

I have to help.

Looking around for a weapon, Rora realized her spear was nothing but a line of ash and a small metal tip.

"Stay here," Rora said to Marzanna before grabbing the tip of the spear and running toward Gwen and the enraged dragon.

The dragon snapped at Gwen, its teeth nearly sinking into her skimming board as she slashed with her sword. Then its tail collided with Bastian, sending him flying into the cave's wall.

"Hey!" Rora waved her arms. "Dragon! Over here!"

The creature didn't turn toward her, perhaps having forgotten her entirely. But as teeth flashed, reflecting blinding sunlight, Rora's heart slammed in her chest. Catching Gwen's sword between its teeth, the dragon snapped it in half.

Eyes widening, Rora's gaze skirted between Gwen's shattered sword and the arrow sticking out of the dragon's flank. For an impossibly long moment, she watched as long shards of metal pattered onto the ground alongside crystal.

If I don't do something, Gwen and the others might die.

She didn't want to hurt the dragon. But more than that, she couldn't let anything happen to Gwen. Plan or no plan, an instinct swelled within Rora that had her charging forward.

Before the dragon could lunge for Gwen, Rora swung her cyborg fist down—and onto Abrecan's arrow, driving it deeper into the dragon's flank.

Blood oozed as the beast roared.

Turning, it lunged for her. She stumbled backward but not nearly fast enough. She held a hand up to shield her face. Powerful jaws sank into her cyborg hand, crunching it into useless scrap metal and sending sparks flying.

For a moment, time seemed to slow. As sparks hovered in midair, all she could think of was her shattered dreams of performing for the emperor. She thought of everything she'd gone through—everything she'd done—to get a new hand. All to keep performing and to be the best. Last of all, she thought of how she'd knowingly coerced Gwen in the hope of getting a new implant. And how, even now, she was no longer certain of anything, least of all her feelings toward the tinkerer.

Had it all been for nothing?

Then time resumed, and deep, all-consuming pain crashed into her like the ocean tide. The dragon's eyes widened as electric shocks bolted through its jaw. It released her, shaking its head furiously.

Screaming, Rora fell backward as more electric bolts shot up her arm. Agony exploded through her senses as the battery in her implant went haywire. It was as though every nerve was on fire. Her world narrowed to the electricity pulsing from her hand.

Writhing on the ground, she screamed until her voice became hoarse. But wave after wave of agony hit her senses. Her body spasmed and convulsed on the cave floor.

Somewhere above her, the dragon roared. She prayed it would end her swiftly. Anything to stop this endless torture.

A form appeared before her, her foot dragging. She stood between Rora and the dragon.

"No, Marzanna—" Rora tried to say, but the words were choked as another scream tore through her.

Marzanna did her best to move quickly, but the dragon was faster. It swiped its tail and hit home. As the trapeze artist flipped through the air, sparks erupted in her foot, and she tumbled to the floor.

"No!" Rora screamed, but she could do nothing as her body convulsed. Bolt after bolt of electricity ricocheted through her.

Blinking through the tears blurring her vision, Rora peered at Gwen. She, Bastian, Thaniel, and Abrecan fought to get the dragon's attention and lead it away from them. Feet pounded as the dragon stormed toward the mouth of the cave, enraged.

Gwen went for its injured flank, following Rora's lead by slamming a shield onto the arrow already embedded in its flesh. The dragon spewed smoke and fire. Bastian ducked beneath the dragon's wings before leaping onto its back. Twisting its head, the dragon tried to shake him off. When he held fast, it shuffled toward the mouth of the cave.

Abrecan and Thaniel dived to the side as the dragon ran toward the cliff and leaped into the air—with Bastian on its back.

Sudden silence enveloped the cave.

The electric bolts had stopped, replaced by a throbbing

agony in Rora's hand. She blinked. Remaining awake suddenly felt like a tremendous effort.

Gwen's beautiful face appeared above hers, smeared with ash, her hair in disarray. The tinkerer moved swiftly, checking Rora's vitals and studying her destroyed hand. Rather than her usual tinkering, Gwen stood and hurried over to another body lying beside hers.

It was then Rora realized Marzanna lay beside her. And she wasn't moving.

CHAPTER 19

Marching toward the mouth of the cave, Gwen grabbed her skimmer.

Abrecan and Thaniel stared slack-jawed at where Bastian rode atop the dragon's back over the forest below.

"If those two women aren't alive when I return..." Gwen pointed at where Rora and Marzanna lay on the cave floor behind her. "So help me, I will kill you myself and make it look like an accident. Have I made myself clear?"

Abrecan's eyes swept the length of her. "Implicitly."

"Excellent. I'll be back. I seem to have misplaced my ringleader." Despite her casual tone, fear tightened her chest. But the fear wasn't for herself. Interestingly, it was for the idiot riding on the dragon.

Kicking on her skimmer, she flew after Bastian and the damned dragon.

Crouching low, she headed straight toward them, throttling the engine's gears.

To her surprise, catching up wasn't difficult. The dragon didn't fly straight but twisted. The creature turned, teeth snapping, trying to buck Bastian off its back. But Bastian was somehow managing to hold on just out of reach of the dragon's jaws.

Rather than holding fast to the dragon's scaly hide as it continued to buck, Bastian rummaged through his pocket.

"What are you doing?" Gwen shouted as she flew alongside them, just out of reach of the dragon's slashing tail.

He pointed at his pocket, nearly losing his grip on the dragon. "I have syringes, but I can't assemble them."

That's what you went to get yesterday.

"Toss them to me!" she screamed. "Now, Bastian!"

She idled her skimmer as the scarlet dragon wheeled around to face her. Fumbling, Bastian pulled the box of anesthetics from his pocket as the dragon flew toward her, closing the distance.

Throw it. Throw it now!

As he threw the box to the side, she dived out of reach of the dragon's claws just in time. Flying forward, she caught the box before idling again, removing a vial, and filling the syringe.

In her periphery, she sensed the dragon's flapping wings and heard its breathy intake as it neared once more.

"Gwen!" Bastian shouted, his voice close.

She pocketed the box before tossing the empty vial. "Got it!"

Then she flew straight toward the approaching dragon. "Catch!"

She lobbed the syringe of anesthetics at Bastian, needle and all.

Reaching out, he grabbed the syringe without stabbing himself. Too soon, the dragon was on her, and she veered skyward. Its claws scraped against the bottom of her board, but she remained airborne.

Looking down, she watched as Bastian jammed the syringe between the dragon's scales on its neck.

The beast roared, which was followed by a pitiful, whining

sound. It shook its head like a dog out of water. Its wings toddled first before its head dropped, and they descended headfirst toward the forest below.

"Oh, fuck."

She revved the engine again as both dragon and rider fell from the sky.

As she neared them, she reached out, trying to catch Bastian's reaching hand. But she was too slow. Bastian and the scarlet dragon collided with the canopy of trees. Branches snapped noisily as they fell toward the ground.

She flew after them.

It took a moment to find an opening in the trees and another to locate Bastian. He lay on his back on the ground, eyes closed.

Soaring low, she kicked off her skimmer's engine, jumped to the ground, and ran over.

Nearby, the scarlet dragon lay unconscious, its tongue lolling from its mouth as its chest rose and fell in a deep sleep.

"Bastian!" She ran a hand over his face and then over his chest. "Are you okay?"

Stars, was he breathing?

There was a notable intake of air before the ringleader grunted.

"I'm fine," he wheezed, eyebrows furrowed. "My implant took the worst of the fall."

"Good." Without further preamble, she slapped him across the face.

"Hey!" he barked. "What was that for?"

"Don't you dare jump on a dragon's back again. You scared the shit out of me."

Slowly, he pulled himself to a seated position. "Is that concern I detect, Ms. Grimm?"

"Shut up, wenchwad." She stood, hopped back on her skimmer, and kicked the engine on. "I'm going to get the others and check on Marzanna and Rora. Watch the dragon while I'm gone."

Without waiting for a response, she took to the sky.

Why am I getting so worked up over Bastian Kabir?

When she made it back to the cave, Abrecan and Thaniel sat—rather unhappily—beside Rora and Marzanna. Marzanna remained motionless on the ground. But Rora was upright, leaning against the wall. Her chest rose and fell rapidly, and there were burns up her arm, but she was blessedly alive.

Gwen rode her skimmer through the cave and directly to Rora.

Kicking the engine off, she leaped down and kneeled before the acrobat. "Are you okay?"

"I'm fine now that you're here." Rora managed a small smile, but Gwen could tell the other woman was in a world of pain.

"What were you thinking, trying to distract the dragon like that?"

Rora's shoulders rose and fell, teeth sinking into her lower lip. "I wanted to help."

For an impossibly long moment, they stared into each other's eyes, not saying a word.

Something unspoken hovered in Rora's eyes as they filled with tears. "I was scared of losing you, too."

Instantly, the moment in Rora's room came to mind where Gwen had revealed why she'd wanted Rora to join another act after the horrors of the first competition. At that moment, she'd been vulnerable and told the acrobat the truth. She was scared of losing her.

And Rora felt the same about her.

Butterflies flitted through Gwen's stomach, pushing past the fear and worry that had turned her thoughts black.

Nodding, Gwen cupped Rora's face. "I was scared, too."

Stars, she wanted to do this right, to move slowly with

Rora. But as she looked at the acrobat, her eyes filled with longing and agony, Gwen found herself leaning down.

Ever so slowly, she moved until their lips were nearly touching. Her eyes, one cyborg, one flesh, flickered back and forth between Rora's—waiting, hoping.

Then Rora leaned forward.

The touch of her lips was ecstasy. It was as though a thousand dragon fires burned through Gwen at once, purging her of everything except for the desire for Rora. For more.

It was a hungry, desperate kiss of lips and tongue and teeth. Rora's human hand tangled in Gwen's hair, and Gwen cupped Rora's cheeks as she pulled her close. All Gwen could think of was the feel of Rora's dark skin against hers, and how she longed for the time to learn every curve, every freckle, every scar. And Rora would have a few of those after today.

All too soon, the kiss ended.

Gwen pulled back. "I'll get you fixed up as soon as I can. But right now, I need to check on Marzanna."

Rora nodded.

As Gwen feared, Marzanna's foot had been unable to handle the electrical current from the incorrect wires she had installed. There hadn't been an electrical fire, but there'd been enough sparking to leave Marzanna's entire body covered in burns.

What have I done?

Brushing the tears and guilt away—knowing both would consume her the moment she was alone—Gwen worked quickly. She replaced the wires with the proper ones she'd read about in the book from the Mistress's library.

Checking Marzanna's vitals for the thousandth time, Gwen was relieved to feel a steady heartbeat, though it was far fainter than she'd like.

Briefly, Gwen examined Rora's hand. Now that the sparking had passed and the implant's battery was dead, she wasn't in danger of it happening again. But her body needed time to recover.

Glancing toward the sky, Gwen knew they couldn't stay here for long. If the performers were going to get back to the palace with the dragon before sunset, they'd have to start the journey back down the cliff and through the forest immediately.

Gwen flew Marzanna down first, leaving her with Bastian, before returning to the cliff for Rora.

"Aren't we going to get a ride?" Abrecan called from where he climbed down the cliff.

"Are we friends?" Gwen shot back.

Once in the cave, she helped Rora stand on the skimmer behind her.

As Rora wrapped her arms around Gwen's waist, a sense of safety and belonging swelled in her chest. Images of the moment they'd shared before flitted across her mind. She forced herself to focus on the present as she flew as smoothly as she could, careful not to jostle Rora too much.

After dropping Rora with Marzanna and Bastian, Gwen circled back to the cliff, checking for survivors.

There weren't any.

Only a pile of broken bones and flesh lay at the base of the cliff. Scavengers were already picking at their bodies and circling in the skies overhead.

When she returned, more performers had joined Bastian and the others. Abrecan and Thaniel stood at the head of the group, eyeing the dragon with nothing short of hunger.

The truth of the matter was—Rora and Marzanna were in no shape to bring the dragon back themselves. And Gwen and Bastian couldn't be seen helping them, for their own safety and for the safety of the performers. There was no saying what the Mistress would do to those who had... assistance in winning the competition.

So, it was time they had a little chat with the other performers.

Gwen placed herself between the group and the dragon, which was neatly tied up. It appeared as though Bastian had found vines to tie the beast's front and back legs together and its mouth shut. There was also a makeshift net on the ground. To drag it, she realized.

Removing the box with the remaining vial of anesthetic from her pocket, Gwen filled another syringe and held it up for everyone to see.

"Listen up," she shouted. "It's time we lay some groundwork for how things are going to go for the rest of the competition." She eyed Abrecan before gesturing to Bastian. "Thanks to our assistance and these handy little anesthetics, you now have a dragon willing to return to Apparatus. You're. Fucking. Welcome. However, if the dragon is to remain docile, and if you don't want the Mistress to learn you had no part in successfully luring the dragon from its lair, the Mistress will never know Bastian or I were here. *And* the victory will be shared."

Fists clenched, Bastian added, "If the Mistress learns we helped you, no one will win this competition, and all of your names will be entered into the lottery."

And Bastian and I will have terminated contracts.

She stuffed down the fear rising up her throat, careful to keep her expression neutral.

Abrecan shook his head. "If I'm to drag its carcass back to Apparatus, then I'm going to claim the victory."

"Then I guess you won't be needing this." Squeezing the plunger, she sent some of the precious anesthetic pattering onto the dry ground.

Hand outstretched, Abrecan stepped forward. "No!"

"Do I have your attention?" When she stopped, the syringe still held most of its contents.

The veins in Abrecan's jaw bulged as he nodded. "I see you've chosen your friends, Ms. Grimm."

Briefly, Gwen's gaze flicked to Rora, whose head hung limp between her knees where she rested on the ground.

She turned to the group. "How many died on the mountaintop?"

The performers spoke amongst themselves in soft whispers.

At last, Thaniel said, "Eleven."

She nodded. "That means only two more acts have to be eliminated from among you. And a number of performers aren't here at this moment. If you want my help and my silence, you will work together, and you will win together—and you won't say a damned thing about Bastian or me. Understood?"

Abrecan crossed his arms but said nothing.

Bastian came to stand beside Gwen. "Do as she says, or there will be consequences."

A humorless smile traced Abrecan's lips. "You're lucky I know yours aren't idle threats. Otherwise, I might think you were kidding."

"I don't joke."

"Clearly." Abrecan turned to Gwen. "You have a deal, Ms. Grimm."

After Gwen returned the vial to Bastian and he administered the second dose, Bastian, Abrecan, Thaniel, and several of the uninjured performers hauled the dragon onto the net. Meanwhile, Gwen went to help the injured, placing Marzanna on her skimmer.

It took several hours to drag the dragon back to the city of Apparatus. During that time, Marzanna didn't open her eyes once, though she clung to life.

When they neared the line of trees before the city, Gwen spoke with several performers before passing the unconscious Marzanna to them.

"I want to see Marzanna and any more of the critically injured after... after the contract termination process is complete." Gwen's gaze settled on Abrecan. "Congrats on your combined victory."

She could barely think past the racing of her heart.

Now that they were back at the palace, she could only think of one thing. How was she going to harvest thirteen more acts tonight?

She was still exhausted from her sleepless night in the library with Bastian—not to mention the day spent in the company of a dragon. All she wanted to do was fall into her bed and never wake up. But if she was to protect herself and the cyborgs from the Mistress, she had to reclaim their implants.

With a final nod to Rora, Gwen turned toward Bastian.

It was time they snuck back into the true dragon's lair.

Without another word, they headed for the city.

For the second time, they climbed up the rope in the garden to Bastian's rooms. They bathed and stashed their things before leaving his room to an escort of watchmen.

By the time they entered the theater, the final acts had been selected from the raffle, and the winners congratulated on their victory.

In the corner of the theater, the scarlet dragon crouched in a massive, fireproof cage. Fully awake now, it studied them with catlike eyes, its pupils narrow and alert. It tried to stand but slammed back down in the small cage. The dragon's wings were curled around itself, and it let out a rumbling growl from deep within its stomach, its mouth collared shut.

"Isn't she a beauty?" Celeste appeared before them.

Gwen didn't bother to speak. Not that she could, anyway, with the fear squeezing her chest.

I can do this. I must do this.

But the idea of retrieving implants from the losing cyborgs again made Gwen want to retch.

"You know." Celeste paused, turning to Bastian as several of her apprentices carried the caged dragon on supporting beams toward the animal housing center—a separate warehouse within the castle. "If you ever want to return to the fold, we could use an experienced hand with the dragon. It will take some time to make sure it's... docile."

"Good luck potty-training the dragon," Gwen said, somehow finding her voice. "Bastian is done being whipped like one of your beasts."

After the day's events, she'd lost whatever tact she might have had.

Beside her, Bastian stiffened.

Celeste turned to Gwen, perfect eyebrows arching. "Ms. Grimm, I'd been looking for you today. Where have you been?"

Gwen did her best to keep her expression carefully neutral. "I... spent the day with Bastian."

We were just fucking. Nothing to see here.

She recalled their farce—the story they'd wanted the watchmen to believe.

Celeste nodded. "My watchmen told me you'd spent several days in Mr. Kabir's chambers, not coming out for food once. But when I summoned you a few hours ago, I was told no one responded when they knocked on your door."

"We must have been asleep," Gwen said.

"Were you?" Celeste's nails clicked together where her hands were folded demurely in front of her. "Because when my watchmen unlocked the door, they said no one was in the room. Care to adjust your story now?"

Several watchmen who'd been lingering not far off came closer to them, somehow sensing the turn of the conversation.

"We wanted privacy." Sweat beaded on Gwen's brow. "The watchmen have been constantly on our heels, so we made a little escape."

"The watchmen are here for your safety," Celeste said.

Liar.

"So, where were you?"

Swallowing, Gwen couldn't find the words, the right lie.

Celeste stepped toward Gwen, eyes skirting down to her legs. "I told you what would happen if you stepped out of line again."

Several watchmen swooped in all at once.

When they hit Gwen with the club this time, it wasn't a warning strike. They swung at her legs to break.

But Gwen was ready.

When the first wooden baton struck, she punched the watchman in the throat. He stumbled back before he could strike again. Pain shot up her leg, but she ignored it. More watchmen moved in. Did she dare use her pistol or the knives sheathed in her boots? Somehow, she knew bringing out her own weapons would earn her a far worse punishment.

She managed to avoid several more blows, swinging out of the way, but she moved right into the arms of another watchman.

He latched on to her, hands encircling her biceps.

When the batons struck this time, pain ignited in her legs. Again and again, they struck, hitting her thighs and calves. They hadn't broken bones yet, but *fuck.* They would soon.

Her traitorous eyes skirted up to Bastian, pleading with him.

Help me.

But why would he? Despite his intervention with the dragon, he wanted to be a part of the show management team more than anything. Why risk his position and contract for her? Especially if she was clearly a lost cause. Not to mention, he'd been willing to let Marzanna die all so they could avoid intervening in the competition. He wouldn't intervene now.

Air and hope whooshed out of her as another baton struck. Head hanging, her body absorbed blow after blow. She tried to hold on to the image of Rora in her mind's eye, but she couldn't think past the agony in her limbs.

"The library," Bastian cried. "We were in the library."

For some reason, the watchmen stopped, as though by some unspoken command. They didn't release Gwen, but they looked at the Mistress, awaiting her order.

Gwen gasped, uncertain if it was from shock or pain.

Did he just choose me over the circus?

Above, Celeste studied Bastian, her eyes narrowed. "Why?"

"To find a safer way to extract cyborg implants and fix the ones that aren't working," Gwen grunted. "And to have some stars-forsaken privacy to fuck in peace and quiet around here."

Celeste nodded to the watchmen around Gwen.

Before she realized what was happening, the watchmen landed a few more blows in quick succession with their wooden batons to the gut. Several landed punches to her face. One slammed into her human eye, and she knew at once she'd have a black eye. Though they carefully avoided her cyborg eye.

Two strikes.

A third meant the Mistress would take Gwen's eye, and she didn't doubt the woman's word for a second.

Then they dropped Gwen like she was a sack of useless performance props.

She crashed to the ground, her entire body throbbing. Biting back a groan, she couldn't stop a hiss from escaping her lips as she tried to stand and couldn't.

"Next time you go to the library, I want to be informed," Celeste said.

"Yes, Mistress." Bastian waited until the Mistress and watchmen strode to another part of the theater before coming to Gwen's aid. He looped an arm through hers, hauling her to her feet.

"I didn't think you were going to step in there." She hissed at the pain and was forced to lean heavily on Bastian.

"This is why we should never have intervened," Bastian said. "I warned you what happens when you cross her."

"She's a raging bitch having a temper tantrum."

That much was true. But Gwen had been injured before during pirate raids when she worked as a ship tinkerer. This beating—uncomfortable as it was—was nothing compared to when she'd been run through with a blade and nearly died from the resulting fever.

"It's a few superficial wounds. It could've been worse," she admitted. "Celeste was just flexing to get the information she wanted. Lucky for us, we broke a few rules, so she only needed to know about one."

He sighed. "We'll have a healer see you as soon as we finish harvesting tonight. I'm afraid there isn't time now."

Slowly, they hobbled over to Gwen's office.

In the theater behind them, the watchmen gathered the acts selected from the lottery for harvesting, forcing them into a line outside of her office.

Bastian located a tall stool somewhere, which he placed in front of the table. Nearly falling into it, Gwen clutched the table in front of her. Her knuckles were white where she gripped the edges.

The pain in her legs and face was nothing compared to the terror churning in her gut for what was ahead.

"I can't do this again."

I've all but killed Marzanna. How can I possibly hope to help these cyborgs?

She was no more a cyborg tinkerer than she was an ally to these people. Who was she kidding? She wasn't actually helping them. She was the fucker wielding the blade in the slaughterhouse.

A hand gently squeezed her shoulder. "We must. Let's try to save as many as we can tonight."

She didn't miss his use of "*we.*"

Shaking her head, she bit back the resulting wave of pain. "Thirteen acts to terminate tonight. And thirteen more acts after the final competition. That's at least twenty-six people who will leave here in the coming weeks crippled or dead at my hands."

"One more competition," he persisted. "Then the ten final acts will perform for the emperor, and this will all be over."

"Do you know what the final competition is?"

"No." His eyes strayed to the unmoving watchmen standing outside her office door, at each exit, and the ones surrounding the tearful performers awaiting their fate. "After being unavailable for the Mistress today, I doubt I'll be given any details. It will be a surprise for us both."

She made a disgusted noise in the back of her throat. "I hate surprises."

They gestured for the first performer from one of the losing acts to enter. Two watchmen dragged a man into her office and strapped him to the table.

Gwen swallowed back tears. Whether it was from the pain in her legs, from having nearly killed Marzanna, or from the thought of what she was about to do, she wasn't sure.

The screams of the cyborgs echoed in the theater throughout the night. She lost all sense of time, place, of herself.

Blood soaked her tunic and pants, running into her boots until she left scarlet footprints. Somehow, they kept going until they reclaimed all but one implant.

As she sliced through skin and tendons, reaching for the final performer's implant, the man looked up at her, his face splattered with his own blood.

In a gurgling hiss, he uttered two words that cut down to Gwen's very core.

"Grimm Reaper."

CHAPTER 20

As Gwen poured a bucket of water over her head, body wracked with sobs, a fist pounded on her bedroom door.

What now?

Her bath was dark pink from the blood the Grimm Reaper drew.

Again, a knock sounded at the door. Swallowing back tears, she finished washing, wrapped her hair in a towel, and hopped out of the tub.

She still shaved half of her head. The scars from the incisions had started to fade somewhat. She wondered just how many scars she'd left tonight.

Don't think about that right now.

There wasn't time to deal with that. If she allowed herself to linger for too long on the hours she'd spent disfiguring perfectly healthy cyborgs, she'd never leave her room again. She'd address the horrors she'd committed once the competition was over and the cyborgs—those who remained —were safe.

Slipping into a bathrobe, she swiped her pistol from the bathroom counter. She was under no illusion that the remaining performers held any fondness toward her. They were scared, and scared people tended to lash out. As she walked across the room, she paused.

The project she'd been tinkering with for weeks sat on her bed. She'd pulled it out before stepping into the bath. Gears and wires stuck out in all directions, which held a strange metallic glow in the artificial light of her gas lamp. Now, anger swelled within her at the sight of it, and she shoved it into her wardrobe before heading toward the door.

The person outside her door knocked again as she opened it.

Behind her back, Gwen cocked her pistol. When she saw who it was, she lowered her weapon.

The shorter woman's dark skin paled. "Oh my gosh, Gwen. Are you all right?"

Having glanced in the mirror before her bath, Gwen knew her human eye was purple and swollen. She was covered in matching bruises, which her bathrobe did little to hide.

"No." Gwen looked over Rora's shoulder to the watchmen in the hallway. "I'm terrible company, but you're welcome to come in."

Slipping in, Rora shut and bolted the door behind her.

"Don't bother." Turning, Gwen strode into her washroom and placed the gun on the sink. Dropping her bathrobe, she pulled on a clean pair of sleeping trousers and a shirt. "The Mistress doesn't respect anyone's privacy around here anyway."

The acrobat nodded. "Celeste had the watchmen unlock everyone's rooms the morning of the second competition. Trust me, I know."

Gwen toweled her hair before sitting on the bed. Rora sat down beside her. As she did, Gwen noticed how she carried her cyborg hand, cradling it in her human one.

With half a glance, it was obvious the implant was completely destroyed.

There were deep indents from the dragon's teeth. Gouges in the metal exposed the wiring beneath.

Rather than asking for help—help she so clearly needed—Rora stroked Gwen's cheek with her human hand.

"I ran into Bastian when he was returning to his rooms. He told me what the Mistress did to you." Dropping her hand, Rora shook her head as her eyes fell to her lap. When she looked back up, tears filled her eyes. "You shouldn't have come."

Gwen flinched as though slapped. "And let you and the other performers be the only ones to risk your lives? Not happening. Besides, I had to help…"

Marzanna.

She'd hoped to get to Marzanna in time and fix her foot. And she'd been too late.

"But I didn't help." Bitterness rooted in Gwen's chest. "Nothing I did made a difference, and I had to harvest innocent people anyway."

Turning away, she studied the stone walls of her room. Stars, she couldn't cry. Not right now. Not with Rora right there.

"It can't be easy… being forced to hurt someone." Rora's voice was soft and not unkind.

The damn woman was trying to sympathize with her when she had a broken implant and was probably in as much pain as Gwen was, perhaps more.

Swallowing, she tried to push back the lump in her throat. "It's not the first time I've killed someone."

Her voice was harsh, wavering.

But she *had* killed several people tonight. Unlike the first competition, there were many performers who'd relied on their implants to live. And she'd taken those implants from them. Unfortunately, several of the eleven performers who'd died in the forest had been a part of larger acts. Acts she'd been forced to harvest.

A soft, human hand found hers. Still, she kept her eyes trained on the wall. Eventually, the tears came, trailing soundlessly down one cheek.

Rora's thumb swiveled back and forth atop Gwen's hand, her calloused skin rough.

"I killed in deep space," Gwen said. "There were pirates, thieves, and other delinquents who always cropped up. When we were boarded, I killed plenty of people. It had been in defense of my trade and my life. But this... this was murder."

Gwen wiped her cheek with the back of a hand. "Celeste threatened to take my eye back, among other things, if I don't do as I'm told."

The bruises peppering her skin said as much.

"Even still, I can't do *nothing*." Letting go of Rora, Gwen leaned forward and cradled her head in her hands. "Bastian insists that the Mistress will terminate my contract, and I won't be able to help anyone—to remove their implants safely or fix the implants of the performers who are still at this stars-forsaken circus. But all I can see—all I can think about—are the people I'm forced to harvest."

Anger ripped through her as tears streamed down her face in earnest.

"And I haven't helped a single person. I can't even do my fucking job right. Marzanna is all but dead because of me."

How had everything gone so *wrong*?

She'd taken the job with the circus not only to save her life but because she liked a challenge. She'd wanted to figure out just what it meant to be a cyborg tinkerer—and a good one at that. After the first competition, she'd stayed to help the cyborgs. People unwanted in the Crescent Star System. People like her. She wanted to protect them from the monster they called Mistress.

A monster who was willing to murder within the walls of her own home.

But Gwen had done nothing but hurt the people she'd

stayed to protect. She was nothing like her parents, whatever their names were.

Helpless rage splintered through her as more of her memories were lost, slipping from her grasp like oil between her fingers.

How could you lose your memories from a simple cyborg implant? None of this made any sense.

The smell of rose and peach blossoms filled Gwen's nose. Rora didn't reach out to touch Gwen. Instead, she sat quietly.

Waiting for me to calm the fuck down.

Eventually, she sighed. "I'm sorry you had to see this. I just... I can't stand feeling... useless."

Rora's brown eyes were bright. "If not for you and Bastian, we'd all be dead right now. You *did* help us today. You risked your lives to save ours."

Gwen winced, unable to hear those words right now. Not when something even larger loomed over her thoughts. "How's Marzanna?"

"She still hasn't woken up," Rora said. "But the healer is doing everything he can."

After she'd finished reclaiming implants of the thirteen losing acts, Gwen had spent *hours* with Marzanna. She'd done everything she could think of, but nothing helped. Nothing at all.

"I did this." Those damn tears came again. "It's my fault her foot malfunctioned and she isn't waking up."

"It was an accident," Rora said, and it sounded like she believed it. "You've been fixing implants for weeks, and so many people are better for it. I've..." Her gaze slid down to her useless hand. "I've been able to get by longer than I thought possible with my old hand."

Rora looked up, and their gazes locked. "The first time I saw you, something inside me changed. I've made plenty of friends in my time at the circus, but I've always felt alone. I never realized it until the first time we spoke. You sparked something inside me. I felt something I hadn't felt in years, perhaps longer…"

The Forgetting, Gwen realized. Rora couldn't recall if she'd always felt this way.

Throat tightening, Gwen tried not to think about her own past that she struggled to remember.

"You made me feel cherished," Rora said. "Like I had value beyond my performances. Like you wanted me for me."

"I do," Gwen said simply.

And damn her, she meant it.

Looking down, Gwen studied Rora's useless implant. Could she make it through the final competition without it if Gwen uninstalled the unit entirely? Or if Gwen dared to tempt fate and intervene, would Rora fall into a deep sleep just like Marzanna, never to awaken again?

Fear swam through Gwen, making her dizzy. She'd nearly killed Marzanna. There was no way she could…

But before she could finish that thought, Rora's eyes skirted around the room and locked on an object within the open wardrobe. Gwen hadn't bothered to close the doors when she'd stashed her secret project earlier. And she wasn't sure if she regretted that decision.

In the center of the wardrobe, easily viewable from Gwen's bed, was the cyborg hand she had been tinkering with for weeks, creating nearly from scratch.

Standing, Rora went over to the hand, her eyes round. She picked it up and turned back to Gwen. "Is this… Is this what I think it is?"

Biting her lip, Gwen felt as though she might drown in fear —fear of what she might do to the woman she was falling for.

But she couldn't find it in herself to lie to Rora. Not with those beautiful brown eyes full of hope. Not when a new hand could make the difference between Rora winning the third competition and being banished from the circus forever.

"I've been working on it since the first time I tinkered your hand," Gwen admitted.

After joining the circus, she quickly learned from the ever-present watchmen the rule surrounding new implants—largely that performers never got new implants, refurbished or otherwise. They were expected to live out the thirteen years of their contract with a single implant.

Thanks to the Cyborg Prohibition Law forbidding the manufacture of implants, they were incredibly rare and disgustingly expensive. With pricey new implants out of the picture, that left only the Mistress and perhaps a tinkerer with the appropriate skill set to create refurbished implants—under the assumption that there were enough parts lying around.

Fortunately for Gwen and Rora, there were.

Unfortunately, Gwen's cyborg tinkering skill set was juvenile at best.

Regardless, by creating a new implant for Rora, she would be breaking the circus's rules of no new implants. But she deeply cared for the acrobat, and she'd do anything to help her. They could only hope no one noticed Rora's old implant had been used as a dragon's chew toy.

Rora's mouth dropped. "That long?" She shook her head, turning her gaze from the polished implant to Gwen's eyes. "I can't believe you did this for me."

"I want the best for you." Gwen looked away. "I wanted to help."

Slowly, Rora sat beside Gwen, placing the new hand on the bed. It was made from scavenged parts and in far better condition than the acrobat's current hand.

Reluctantly, Gwen met Rora's eyes.

"Today has sucked," Rora said, rather bluntly. "You've had to do horrible things, and I'm sure you're exhausted. But what happened with the implant extractions wasn't your fault. The Mistress forced your hand. You were *not* responsible for those deaths. The blood of those cyborgs is not on your hands.

Do you hear me?" As Gwen started to look away, Rora grabbed her chin. "You also faced a dragon, and you beat it. You saved my life in the process. Sure, bad things happened. But I believe Marzanna is going to get better. I believe in *you*."

Overwhelming gratitude swelled in Gwen's chest. Words utterly escaped her as tears rolled down her cheek. But she managed to grab Rora's hand, nodding.

As the tears subsided, she took a deep breath. And then three more.

"I'll install it if you want me to." Fear tightened Gwen's chest, but she pressed on. "I'm terrified of hurting you like I hurt Marzanna."

"I trust you." Rora gestured to her limp hand. "Besides, you can only go up from here, right?"

Sighing, Gwen moved back toward the wardrobe and rummaged among the things for her tool kit. "We'd better get started if we want to get this thing installed."

"Right now?" Rora's eyes grew wide.

Placing her tool kit on the floor and sitting down beside it, Gwen nodded. "I want plenty of time before the final competition to make sure it's installed properly. I don't want to risk another massive malfunction out in the wilderness or wherever. Because who knows what asinine idea will be concocted for the final competition."

"You don't know what the competition is?" Rora asked as Gwen gestured for her to lie on the ground.

Gwen disinfected her equipment. To her surprise, she found herself wishing Bastian was there. If only for his calm temperament and steady hands to assist her. It certainly wasn't for comfort as she wondered if she was about to kill the woman she cared deeply for.

"No." She passed a flask to Rora, who took a deep swig. She then placed a leather strap between her teeth. "Rumor has it we should find out tomorrow."

Pausing, they looked at each other—Gwen with uncertainty and Rora with utter trust.

Rora nodded, the gesture seeming to say, "*Just do it.*"

With that, Gwen started uninstalling and reinstalling a new cyborg implant, praying the whole time she wasn't about to send Rora to the Reaper's door right beside Marzanna.

As they worked through the night in near silence, Rora's grunts of discomfort muffled by the leather strap, Gwen wondered just what was in store for them tomorrow.

There was only one competition left before they saw the emperor.

CHAPTER 21

P ain tore Rora from sleep.

As she jolted upright, soft sheets fell from her chest, revealing a gleaming cyborg implant on her right arm.

Is this actually real?

For so long, she'd dreamed of getting a new implant—one that actually worked—and now that she had one, she was speechless, numb.

She should be happy. But instead, her mind was strangely blank.

Glancing around at a bedroom far larger and tidier than hers, Rora's gaze settled on a tinkering table with tools. Belatedly, she realized she was in Gwen's room. More specifically, she was in the tinkerer's *bed*. Her cheeks heated as she spotted Gwen curled up on the floor with several throw pillows and a quilt blanket. Even in sleep, exhaustion marred her features, but it didn't diminish the stubborn vibrancy that was Gwen.

Against all odds, Rora had successfully seduced Gwen, manipulating her to break circus rules and create a refurbished hand.

I should leave.

The thought zipped through her mind, unbidden.

Instead, her cyborg fingers curled around the sheets and pulled them to her face. Beyond the faint smell of oils and metals, typical of tinkerers, was Gwen's aroma of vanilla and lilac. Scrunching the sheets, she pressed them to her nose as her gaze moved across the room to the woman sleeping on the floor.

The woman who'd risked everything for her time and again.

First with the dragon and now with installing a new implant.

But if Rora was to perform for the emperor, she had to make it through the final competition—whatever it was. She couldn't let herself get distracted by a pretty face, especially now that she had her new hand.

Slowly, she lowered the sheets from her face and swung her legs over the bed.

Pain zigzagged up her arm from the movement. Installing machinery into bone and sinew was never easy, particularly without anesthesia, but she had made it through. The pain would pass. It would be worth it.

Slowly, Rora slipped into her shoes and crossed the room.

When she came to where Gwen slept near the door, she hesitated.

I didn't even have to sleep with her to get a new hand. She did this for me willingly and without strings.

Interestingly, disappointment swirled through Rora, and it felt like her feet were rooted to the ground.

Biting her lip, she glanced back and forth between Gwen and the door, and made her decision.

She headed for Gwen's work station in the corner of her room and wrote a quick note using a spare quill and parchment. Placing the note beside where the tinkerer slept,

Rora grabbed one of Gwen's large sleeping shirts and pulled it over her head, covering her cyborg arm.

She'd need to figure out how to keep her new arm a secret from the show management team. First, she'd talk to the performers who'd seen the dragon bite her implant and somehow convince them not to say anything.

For now, she'd need to keep it covered.

As Rora stepped over Gwen and reached for the door handle, she paused, looking back.

The tinkerer rolled over in sleep, a breathy sigh escaping her.

I'm sorry.

Then she opened the door and strode out.

Glancing up, she nodded at the waiting watchmen before heading for her dormitories, trying to ignore the guilt churning in her stomach.

It would be worth it. Soon.

CHAPTER 22

Gwen peered down at her steeped morning brew, which smelled suspiciously like last week's stew.

As had become her habit, she sat at the table for circus staff in the mess hall with Bastian and several other cyborgs. The healer, Barbosa Brower, ate his food with an open mouth while Bastian didn't eat at all. Despite the riveting company, her gaze strayed toward Rora's table, where the acrobat sat alongside her friends, laughing and chatting.

Darkness settled over Gwen's thoughts as her stomach twisted in knots.

Sensing her gaze, Rora looked up, and their eyes locked. She flashed a set of perfect square teeth. A look Gwen couldn't read caught in Rora's eyes before she turned her attention back to her friends.

Not until the early hours of the morning had Gwen finished installing Rora's new hand. Somewhere near the end, Rora had passed out on the floor. Not having the heart to wake her, Gwen carried her to her bed before falling asleep on the floor.

When Gwen awoke later that morning, already late for breakfast, Rora had been gone. Rather than waking up to the face of the woman she was falling for, Gwen found a note beside her on the floor, which said, *"Thank you! See you later today?"*

It shouldn't have stung as much as it did. Dark suspicion clouded her thoughts, and she tried to push it back. But it came to the forefront of her mind again and again.

Did Rora use me?

Why else would she conveniently disappear the morning after Gwen installed her new hand? It felt a hell of a lot like waking up to cold sheets beside her the morning after a good fuck.

Calm the fuck down. She probably had to do something this morning.

Not to mention, Rora *had* asked to see her later today.

The sound of a fork scraping against a plate grated Gwen's senses, bringing her back to the present. Her eye twitched in response, sending a wave of pain through her. The swelling had yet to go down from Celeste's recent beating.

"Rough night?" Bastian raised an eyebrow, setting his fork down and leaning forward on his elbows.

"Couldn't sleep," Gwen lied.

The few hours of sleep she'd gotten last night weren't enough to make up for a sleepless night and the horrors within those days.

"Couldn't or wouldn't?"

Swallowing a gulp of the loathsome brew, Gwen forced a smile. "Why so curious? Does the great Bastian Kabir want to give me a reason to stay up late?"

"While I appreciate the offer, I prefer my women to sleep only with me."

"How terribly boring."

"Some people would call it intimate."

Mirroring Bastian's position, Gwen leaned forward so that her breasts pressed against the tabletop. "Those people are prudes." She eyed Bastian's spotless collared shirt, vest, and jacket, wondering just what it would be like to unravel the stoic ringleader.

Without another word, she turned her attention to the healer, who studied his bowl as though performing surgery. "How's Marzanna?"

Looking up, Barbosa goggled, cheeks flushed. It was then she realized one of his hands was still beneath the table.

She rolled her eyes. "I hope you wash those hands before you return to work."

Stuttering, he blathered as he attempted to form sentences. Though she suspected the blood hadn't yet returned to his brain. "Ms. Southerland was asleep when I checked on her this morning," he managed after several failed attempts to reply.

Before she could inquire further, the room quieted. The sound of chatter morphed into a thunderous silence. The Mistress and her show management team stood at the front of the dining hall. The masked watchmen followed them, standing guard around the perimeter of the large room.

Half the tables were empty of the performers that filled them only a few short weeks ago. The mess hall had once been barely able to accommodate all of the performers. Now, countless cyborgs were gone, leaving shadows and memories of violence.

Images of carnage and severed limbs sprouted in Gwen's mind. She could see with vivid clarity when she'd sawed a shoulder the night before, scarlet spurting onto the floor. One man had ripped through his restraints in his desperation to keep the cyborg elbow that connected his human hand with the flesh of his upper arm. The watchmen had bloodied him before restraining him. Another performer, a woman, had reached for her, desperately begging for mercy before she'd pissed herself.

Something touched Gwen's shoulder, and she flinched away. When the touch came again, she opened her eyes, not recalling having closed them in the first place. She sat at her table, shaking, having completely missed what the Mistress had said… Something about the next competition?

Beside her, Bastian looked at her with worry in his eyes, his hand on her shoulder.

Sweat beaded on her brow. Her hands trembled, and she held them together in her lap, unable to make them stop.

I killed them. It's my fault they're dead or worse. I should have done something. I should have stood up to the Mistress. I should have kept her from turning me into a monster. I should have—

Bastian slid into the seat beside her. His hand found hers, holding tight.

Squeezing her eyes shut, she prayed for the moment of panic to pass.

As Bastian leaned toward her, her hair caught on the start of his beard. "Take deep breaths. In for four seconds, out for two."

She did as instructed, breathing deeply before exhaling, counting the entire time in her mind.

A warm burst of peppermint air tickled her cheeks in time with her own breathing. When she opened her eyes several moments later, Bastian still had a hold of her hand.

"Better?" he whispered.

No, Gwen wanted to say.

Fear, panic, and regret tightened her chest, squeezing until she felt she couldn't breathe.

"Keep breathing," he urged.

She felt like she had been wrung out and left to dry. Her body screamed to move, to take action, as a deep restlessness settled on her chest—tightening, squeezing. Meanwhile, her emotions felt raw and distant, as though they were someone else's. Yet any time she thought of the competition, a crippling anxiety descended over her, and the feelings once again bombarded her like a meteor shower in space.

Nodding, she took a breath before exhaling slowly. As she did, the Mistress's words slowly registered.

"It's my pleasure to inform you that you'll be performing on Jinx for the final competition."

Had she heard that right? The moon known as the home of pirates, runaways, and the lawless type? *That* was where the circus would be performing?

What was the Mistress thinking? Their ships would be robbed within moments of docking, if not shot down before and sold for scrap. And why would this be a proper test of skill for the emperor?

"As performers, you must be able to win the hearts of the people," the Mistress continued. "Unlike our previous competitions, there will be no lottery. The people will decide your fate. After our final twenty-three acts have performed, the people will vote for which ten they like the best. Those acts will go on to attend His Imperial Highness, and the rest will remain behind on Jinx as humans."

Gwen's heart raced at the implication behind those words. *Remain behind as humans.*

She still had a job to do. One job left in this barbaric competition. Could she remove cyborg implants from thirteen more acts? She wasn't sure she had it in her. But dare she defy the Mistress? She already had two strikes against her.

More than the threat to Gwen's cyborg eye or physical well-being was the threat to Rora. Bastian had known about their nights together. Could the show management team know as well? Would they punish Rora or her friends for Gwen's noncompliance? Would the Mistress dirty her hands and butcher the losing performers for their parts?

On a Union planet—besides Grandstand—the feds would arrest them as murderers. Even Grandstand, the dumping ground for cyborgs and other undesirables, had limited fed supervision—hence this ludicrous competition going uncontested. But on a moon of pirates and lawbreakers? The

Mistress could simply say the cyborg implant retraction had gone sour for the final acts and dump the bodies in an alley. No feds would object. They'd be several planets away within Union territory.

"The next few days are yours to do with as you see fit," the Mistress continued. "Our ship departs in five days at dawn, and the journey will take more than a week by solar waves. Prepare yourselves for the competition. I expect it to be our most exciting one yet."

The watchmen moved to either side of the exit as the Mistress and the show management team strode from the silent room. Long after their guard departed, additional watchmen stood at every exit.

They are keeping us from running away.

Standing, Gwen carried her tray over to the rotating platform for cleaning, behind which was the dishwashing room. Other performers and circus staff did the same. It would seem most everyone had lost their appetite after the inspiring speech.

Bastian appeared beside her, putting his tray full of food on an empty rotating platform before it disappeared into the room beyond the wall.

Taking a deep breath, she said, "Walk with me? There's something I'd like to talk to you about."

Despite Bastian's aid during her moment of panic, he was all stoic ringleader once more. Pressing his lips into a thin line, he nodded, eyes full of skeptical disinterest.

He doesn't want to get in trouble again, she realized. More than likely, he was no longer interested in their strange partnership to save the performers. Some part of her suspected an awful truth. Once again, he prioritized the Mistress and show management team position above all else.

If so, she'd lost one of her greatest allies.

As they walked out of the dining room, down the halls, and into the theater, they passed countless watchmen, none of whom acknowledged the presence of any cyborg. It was as though they'd become mindless statues, somehow worse than before.

When they entered the theater, several of the performers followed them inside, moving to their respective locations— the trampolines, rings, boxes, ramps with bicycles.

Gwen strode into her office with Bastian at her heels. Someone had cleaned up the blood and gore from the night before because it was immaculate.

Bastian nodded to the two watchmen standing guard at the door. After he entered, Gwen rolled the door shut behind him. There was no point in asking for privacy with the Mistress's orders to trail her.

"I... I can't do it again," she blurted. "I can't hurt any more people."

For a moment, he studied her. "What if it's Rora? What if she loses, and either you could remove her hand properly, or she could die from blood loss?"

"Don't you dare—"

"As the tinkerer, you have a job to perform at this circus."

The words were so cold, she flinched. It was as though, in a single day, any warmth that had developed between them— frail as it was—had disappeared entirely.

For a moment, she wondered if she could run away with Rora and her friends. But they wouldn't get far. With the number of guards she'd seen on her walk through the halls to the theater, there was no way they could make it past without being seen, especially while carrying Marzanna. They would all be killed and harvested before reaching the docks.

The Mistress had prepared for this and was already one step ahead.

But Gwen wasn't about to give up. After what happened with Marzanna, she was more determined than ever to do *something*.

"I have an idea," Gwen said. "For the third competition. And I'll need your help."

"We fought a dragon," he hissed, his stoic expression fading momentarily. "Isn't that enough for you?"

"No," she bit back. "Not with everyone's lives in this circus at stake. The performers *you* recruited."

"I'm well aware that I recruited them, Ms. Grimm."

"Good. Then how do we save them?"

"There is no 'we,'" he said, speaking the words she feared. "Did you learn nothing of the Mistress's ire yesterday? If you cross her again, things will end poorly for you. And I won't be there to save you this time."

"Where's the bastard who rode a dragon into the fucking sunset? That guy had *balls*. He was willing to take a risk to do the right thing. And you still can. Come to my room tonight. Just hear what I have to say. I have a plan that could save our friends."

A plan that I came up with just this second.

There would be time to perfect it.

Bastian opened his mouth to speak when a knock sounded at the door.

Sighing, she said, "Enter."

The door slid aside, revealing a performer with a busted implant.

Bastian turned on his heel. "I'll see myself out."

"Think on it," she called as he left the room.

Something inside her twisted, but she pushed thoughts of Bastian aside.

After tinkering with implants for several hours, Gwen eventually excused herself and went out into the theater. If her plan was going to work, backup would be handy.

As she neared Rora's slackline, she was thankful to find Akio and Rora together, the two speaking animatedly.

Slowing, Gwen cleared her throat.

Rora and Akio turned to her. Something strange crossed Rora's features, but it disappeared in an instant.

"How are you feeling?" Gwen asked, glancing at Rora's hand.

"Doing great," Rora said with a stiff smile. "Thank you."

Ignoring the sinking of her heart, Gwen turned to Akio. "I was actually hoping I'd catch you. I... Well, I wanted to apologize for my part in what happened with Marzanna."

Akio ran a hand over the back of his neck before saying, "Thanks for saying that. For the record, I don't blame you for what happened. It was an accident."

"She'll come around," Rora said. "I know she will."

Gwen's throat tightened as she swallowed back the waterworks threatening to make an appearance. "What happened to Marzanna *is* my fault. I replaced the wiring incorrectly. That's why her foot malfunctioned and she hasn't woken up."

"No," Rora said, her voice rising. "If anyone is to blame, it's the Mistress. She's the reason for these competitions happening."

Releasing a series of hacking coughs, Gwen jerked her human eye toward where the watchmen stood guard around the theater—hoping Rora and Akio understood.

Gwen waved a hand to the performers glancing sideways at her.

"Allergies," she lied. Lowering her voice, she turned back to Rora and Akio. "I don't know about you guys, but I'm done being a pawn in this competition."

Rora cocked her head to the side. "What do you have in mind?"

"Meet me tonight in my room, and I'll tell you all about it."

For a moment, Gwen thought Rora would say no, that an excuse for why she couldn't come tonight would fall from her lips. Instead, she nodded. The gesture was hesitant, her brows drawing ever so slightly. But she said yes, as did Akio.

No one knew what awaited them in the emperor's court. But what other option did they have other than to press forward? Either they would die in this competition, or they could hope there wasn't anything worse than remaining as part of Cirque du Borge.

Just like that, it was settled.

CHAPTER 23

As the performers filtered back from the mess hall that evening toward their bedrooms, Rora and Akio turned down another hall, heading straight for Gwen's rooms on the dormitory hall for the circus staff.

Watchmen lined the hallway and were stationed at every exit. Were there always this many?

What am I doing? I should be focusing on my performance now more than ever, not running to Gwen the moment she calls.

Somehow, Rora found herself saying yes to Gwen, despite her intention to keep some distance between them. She had patronage to secure, after all. If she could convince the emperor and the Union Council cyborgs weren't a threat, he could easily purchase her contract from Cirque du Borge. All of her dreams could still come true.

So why was she risking the fate of that very attainable dream?

Because I'm a stupid, foolish woman with no self-control.

Guilt gnawed at her stomach, and it was a struggle to keep Gwen from her thoughts.

As Rora and Akio neared Gwen's room, one of the hired mercenaries emerged from the shadows and stopped them.

"What is your business here? All performers are to return to their dormitories after the evening meal."

"We—" Rora began but was interrupted.

"I asked them to come see me." Down the hall, Gwen poked her head through her bedroom door. "Their implants need tinkering, and I didn't have time to see them during my regular office hours." She gestured to Rora and Akio. "Come on in."

Slowly, almost hesitantly, the watchmen took a step back and allowed them to pass.

Rora and Akio hurried into Gwen's room and closed the door.

"Thanks for coming." Gwen plopped herself on her bed. "Just a heads-up, Bastian might be joining us."

"I don't think I properly thanked you for your help last night." Rora ran a hand over her very new, very functioning cyborg hand. "It hurt a lot, but it's infinitely better than the old one."

Biggest understatement of the year.

Despite the vulnerable moment they'd shared last night, and the utter devastation she'd seen in Gwen's eyes, today, the tinkerer was all cool and collected. She wore a clean, loose blouse—nowhere near as see-through as the one she'd worn the night before—and clean trousers. They hugged Gwen's hips, highlighting a lean, tall figure. Rather than Rora's hourglass shape, Gwen had a small chest and large, full hips.

Hips she so very badly wanted to grind against.

Rora swallowed thickly as arousal stirred the flesh between her legs.

Get a grip. You have your hand. Time to listen to whatever Gwen has to say and then get out of here.

With a small smile, Gwen nodded. "I'm glad to hear that. Tell me if it starts making strange sounds or not responding, okay?"

"Of course."

"Before anyone else gets here," Akio said, interrupting what had quickly become an awkward conversation. "We should probably talk about something."

It was a struggle to tear her eyes from Gwen, but Rora turned, brows furrowed.

Akio cleared his throat, clearly uncomfortable. "Are we sure it's a good idea to include Mr. Kabir in on this?"

Gwen opened her mouth, but Akio spoke first.

"I like you, Gwen," Akio continued. "But I've known Bastian for years. He was the Mistress's man before he was the ringleader. He's hungry for power. It's what drives him. Helping us, sacrificing all the power he's worked for over the years... It's not something the Bastian Kabir I know would do."

Rora understood where Akio was coming from.

Bastian had always been a man hungry for power. So, what had changed in him now, if anything? Why had he intervened in the second competition? Could he be working undercover for the Mistress?

There was a sound, and they all turned.

Bastian stood mutely in the doorway.

If Rora hadn't been watching Bastian, she might have missed the pained look—like a wounded animal—that crossed his features. As quickly as it appeared, it was gone, and he wore the same impassive mask she'd come to associate with the ringleader.

Gwen's cheeks flushed. "Bastian! You came."

Bastian? When had they started on a first-name basis?

"Tell us, Mr. Kabir, why the sudden change of heart?" Akio asked, not unkindly, as Bastian closed the door.

Gwen opened her mouth to speak, but Bastian placed his hand on her shoulder. The gesture was so familiar that Rora ground her teeth.

"You make a fair point, Mr. Yamamoto," Bastian said.

Gwen pinched the bridge of her nose. "Enough with the formalities, people."

"I have been loyal to the show management team for years," he continued before turning to Gwen. He looked at her with a softness Rora had never seen before. Could that be…? No.

Had the ringleader fallen for Gwen?

"Working with Gwen in extracting the cyborg implants after each competition has reminded me of one thing," Bastian said. "You are *my* people. For the past seven years, I handpicked each one of you. I found you and offered you another life—one I thought might be mutually beneficial. I stood by every one of you as you received your implant. I trained you in the ways of the circus—how to succeed and how to gain the favor of the audience. You are my greatest masterpiece."

Bastian's gaze met Rora's and Akio's before his eyes settled on Gwen. "And I will no longer stand idle while the Mistress destroys everything we have done to make this circus a home."

"Why us?" Rora asked, trying to restrain the edge forming in her voice. "Why not help anyone else?"

"We'll help the others," Bastian replied. "But not everyone can be knowledgeable of our intentions, or else the Mistress might get word of it, and we'll all have terminated contracts.

"Any performers who lose and are left behind on Jinx are receiving a death penalty. Few survive on the streets while healthy, let alone while recovering from a traumatic implant removal. No one will take pity on them there. We need to do everything we can to ensure the safety of as many as possible."

Clearing her throat, Gwen said, "Which is why I came up with a plan to sabotage Abrecan and his friends' performances."

Rora gaped.

Was Gwen serious? She wanted to take on *Abrecan*?

They were what… four against twenty? Not to mention,

neither Akio nor Rora were the I-can-defeat-muscle-heads-twice-my-size type. If it came to a confrontation with Abrecan, Thaniel, or the others, they'd be done.

More than that, Rora wanted the very thing that made her seek out Bastian Kabir two years ago. The thing that moved her to action after she'd broken her hand beyond repair. The thing that made her cut off her right hand with a kitchen knife in order to become a cyborg.

She wanted to be the best, but she wouldn't do it through cheating.

"No." When Rora spoke, she couldn't hide the disbelief—the disgust—from her voice. "I won't cheat. It's not right."

Surprised disappointment bled into Gwen's features. "You're still going to do your performance, same as always. That won't change. I'll only be fucking with Abrecan and his friends' props. The people who tried to get you killed in the second competition." She paused, clearly waiting for that to sink in for Rora. "I'll weaken the supporting beams of Abrecan's target, swap out Thaniel's weighted balls for lighter ones—small things. If Abrecan happens to miss his target and an arrow connects with a member of the audience... Well, he wouldn't exactly have the love of the people, would he? And that means you would be that much closer to achieving your dream of performing for the emperor."

"How is stooping down to their level any better?" Rora said, trying to make Gwen understand. "If we cheat, we'll be no better than them."

Rora wasn't the purest among them, but she was surprised by Gwen. The very person who'd said she wanted to protect the cyborgs was plotting to help exile some of the performers on Jinx? It felt somehow... disingenuous.

But didn't Rora want to keep her hand and perform for the emperor? This would essentially secure her place. It would also help ensure the safety of her friends. But cheating meant she wouldn't have earned her place to perform for the emperor. Despite everything, she still wanted to prove she could do it on her own.

Hurt streaked across Gwen's face. "I'm doing this for you —to protect you. I don't want to leave anyone behind on Jinx, let alone take their implants before doing so. But what choice do we have? I need you to live, Rora."

Gwen came to stand before her, eyes pleading. "If you have a better idea, please tell me. I'm doing everything I can think of to keep you safe." A calloused hand touched Rora's cheek. "I don't know what I would do if I lost you. I…"

Rora's heart pattered, knowing and fearing the words that came next.

"I love you," Gwen said.

All of the objections on the tip of Rora's tongue fell away. What could she possibly say to that? Well, she knew damn well what she *should* say, but the words felt heavy on her tongue.

It wasn't supposed to get this far.

The plan had been to seduce Gwen, coerce her into making a new cyborg hand, and then put all of her focus into winning the competition and then securing patronage from the emperor or his court.

But now…? Things were changing, and Rora couldn't deny the quickening of her heart the moment Gwen walked into the room nor the way she wanted to be the one to comfort her when the world crumbled around them. She'd seen a glimpse of Gwen's core last night, and Rora found herself wanting to support that woman and watch her flourish.

But could she give up her dream of being a court performer? She wasn't sure.

She couldn't return the sentiment to Gwen. Not at this moment. So, she did the only thing she could.

Rora took Gwen's hand, squeezing tightly. "What do you have in mind?"

Hurt mingled in Gwen's eyes for a moment before

disappearing, but she rallied and told Rora and Akio her plan for the next competition. But as Gwen spoke, her gaze flickered back and forth between Rora and Bastian.

Rora's cyborg hand curled into a fist.

Eventually, they finished making plans, and it was time for them to go to bed. With a quick farewell, Rora made her way back to the performers' dormitory wing.

"I know you and Marzanna are usually the ones to talk about these sorts of things," Akio began. "But do you want to talk about that three-word phrase a certain tinkerer said tonight?"

Despite herself, Rora smiled, shaking her head. "I like her. But everything is so confusing right now, especially with the competition. I don't want to cheat. I don't know if I could live with myself if I did."

Akio exhaled heavily. "Times are changing, and if this means we live to perform another day, I don't see why it's such a bad thing. Especially after what they did in the first competition. They killed people, Rora. Who's to say they wouldn't do the same to us? Or don't already have something foul cooked up?"

Not for the first time, Rora thought about Abrecan's very bold, very public threat he'd made weeks ago in the King of the Damned.

By trying to take Gwendolyn from me, you've earned yourself more than an enemy. It might not be in the next competition or the one after that, but one day soon, I'll have my revenge.

They paused before Rora's door.

"I know you're right. It's just... I want to win fair and square." Rora ran a hand over her face. "I have to do something. I just don't know what."

Akio patted her on the shoulder. "Sleep on it. Things will be clearer in the morning."

Rora nodded, entirely unconvinced. "Sure."

After bidding Akio good night, Rora went into her room,

locking the door behind her and sighing. Not that locks did much these days.

As ever, everything in her room was in complete disarray —clothes strewn on the floor, dresser drawers half-open and bulging with items, bed unmade. It was a strange reflection of her life.

"What am I supposed to do?" she muttered. "Tell Abrecan, 'Hey, mortal enemy. Hope all is well. I want to beat you fair and square, so I thought I'd let you know that someone plans to sabotage your act in the third competition.'"

She shook her head.

The thought of telling Abrecan anything—or even talking to him—was ludicrous. He was a prick and a bully. Still, he *was* a cyborg.

Leaning her head against the door, she closed her eyes, feeling defeated and resigned.

There are no good people at Cirque du Borge. Just survivors.

There was a strange sound, like the shifting of feet, and Rora opened her eyes. Were watchmen in the hallway? Turning, she pressed her ear to the door.

Nothing.

That was odd. She could have sworn she'd heard—

"Hello, dyke," a deep voice hissed behind her.

Before Rora could scream, a hand encircled her throat, slamming her head against the door. She went limp for a moment, nearly blacking out before someone turned her around to face the room.

The two figures were garbed in shadows. Even in the darkness, she knew who they were. Abrecan and Thaniel loomed as imposing and cold as a winter storm. At that moment, she felt small enough to drown in a raindrop.

Pain muddied her thoughts, and she blinked back the blood dripping into her eye.

"Care to repeat what you just said?" Abrecan squeezed her neck harder, his rings cutting into her neck.

Clawing at his hand, she tried to free herself, to breathe. After a moment, the archer loosened his grip, and she gasped.

"Speak," he demanded.

Mustering her strength, she spit in his face. "I won't tell you a damned thing."

Sniffing, Abrecan removed a knife from a sheath at his waist, pointing at Rora's new hand. "Oh, you will. It's that, or I destroy that pretty new hand of yours."

Fear frosted her senses so completely that she nearly passed out.

"No," she gasped. "Please."

She needed her hand if she had any hope of making it through the third competition and performing in the emperor's court after that. If she lost the competition, she would be left behind on Jinx. More than that, she'd be dead before the week was up.

Abrecan's hand tightened around her throat, and he slammed her head into the door a second time.

Gasping and coughing, she clawed at his grip. But he was as immovable as a mountain.

"The props," Rora gasped, and Abrecan's grip loosened just enough for her to take a shallow breath of air. "Someone plans to sabotage your props in the third competition."

"I think we know who that 'someone' is," Thaniel hissed behind Abrecan's shoulder.

"Indeed, we do," Abrecan said.

Suddenly, the grip on Rora's neck loosened, and she tumbled to the floor. Stars pattered across her vision.

Footsteps sounded across the room. Slowly, she looked up.

The archer emerged from the shadows with a massive electroshocker in his hands.

Eyes widening, she reached for the door handle behind her.

"I wouldn't do that."

She froze, her fingers touching the cold handle. Releasing

the door and turning back to him, she studied the illegal electroshocker in Abrecan's hands. Celeste's apprentices used the weapon on larger predators when the implants made them go mad and attack people. The very same weapons had killed just as many beasts as debilitated them.

Her heart hammered loudly, and she didn't dare move.

"I thought it would be difficult to punish Gwen, make her regret not joining my crew," Abrecan said. "But I didn't think the timing would be so perfect." He aimed the weapon at her chest. "I appreciate the insight, little bird. It will make beating your friends that much easier."

Before Rora could scream, he pulled the trigger.

She only managed to throw her hands up in front of her. One barb sank into her chest, and the other wrapped around one of her cyborg fingers. Pain ignited in her veins and her body seized as the electric currents shot down the wires connected to the barbs.

Her brand-new cyborg hand twitched, the fingers spasming, before her entire world went black.

CHAPTER 24

The next morning, Gwen arose feeling hopeful.

Finally, she was making a difference.

Rather than heading to the mess hall for breakfast, she walked to the performers' dormitory wing. Her eye and legs still ached, but she didn't let that slow her strides to Rora's room. Nervousness swirled in her stomach as she knocked on the door. When no one answered, she knocked again. Still nothing.

Akio appeared in the hallway, and Gwen turned to him. "Have you seen Rora this morning? I was hoping to talk with her."

She hadn't expected to tell Rora she loved her last night, nor had she expected Rora to say it in return. But she couldn't deny the sting of the unspoken words. More than that, she hadn't expected Rora to be so vehemently against their plan.

He gave Gwen a knowing look. "If by talking, you mean 'screw each other's brains out,' then no. I haven't seen her. I'm pretty sure she's still in her room."

Gwen smirked. "Thanks."

I really should talk to her. To clear the air, if nothing else.

Slowly, she turned, about to head downstairs. Hesitating, she turned back and knocked on the door again, louder this time. Maybe Rora was bathing and hadn't heard her.

"Rora?" Gwen reached for the door handle.

It was unlocked. How strange.

Slowly, she opened the door, keeping her eyes on the floor in case Rora wasn't dressed. "It's me. I was hoping I could walk you down to breakfast."

Rather than the sounds of Rora in the washroom, the room was utterly quiet.

Slowly, Gwen looked up and screamed.

Rora lay as though her body had been tossed carelessly onto the floor. Her hair was in disarray, and her arms and legs were splayed. Had she passed out?

But, no.

The closer she got to Rora, she could see dried blood on her forehead. Had Rora hit her head falling down? And were those bruises on her neck?

"What is it?" Akio stormed into the room. "Oh, fuck. What happened?"

"Go find Bastian and the healer *now*," she said before closing the door and running over to Rora.

She knew she'd already drawn too much attention to herself and Rora by screaming. And stars, she didn't want the watchmen or show management team intervening. It would only make things worse.

Holy fucking stars. Did my tinkering kill her?

Swallowing back bile and her panic, Gwen rolled Rora fully onto her back before checking her vitals. Then she sighed with relief.

She still had a pulse.

"Rora!" Gwen held her face between her hands, tapping her cheek gently. "Rora, wake up!"

Nothing.

Slowly, she examined Rora's implant. Everything seemed to be in order, but she wouldn't know until she had her tool kit. And she wouldn't leave Rora until help came.

Not knowing what else to do, Gwen picked Rora up and placed her gently on the bed.

A few minutes later, Akio appeared with Bastian and Barbosa in tow, closing the door behind them.

With a nod to Gwen, Barbosa took her place at Rora's side. He removed a number of things from his healer's bag before examining her.

Bolting from the room, she ran down the hallways with the watchmen on her heels. But she didn't care. She grabbed her full tool kit from her room before hurrying back to Rora's room.

When she returned, Barbosa was shaking his head as he examined Rora.

Gwen fell to her knees beside the bed.

If she didn't know any better, she would have thought Rora was resting peacefully with her dark hair splayed prettily out over the pillow and her lips the bright red of life and youth, not the graying color of imminent death.

"What did you find?" Tears slid down Gwen's cheeks as she held Rora's cyborg hand.

"Nothing is physically wrong with her besides a few cuts on her head," Barbosa said. "I can't explain it. I was hoping you might know. It's as if her entire implant system is shutting down, and her body with it."

Akio stood in the corner of the room, his cheeks covered in silent tears.

"She's not responding to treatment?" Bastian asked.

The healer shook his head. "There's nothing actually wrong with her. Her heart is healthy, and there's no fluid in her lungs… It's like what happened to Marzanna. Her body is rejecting the implant."

For a moment, the entire world slowed to a stop. It was as though the planets within the Crescent Star System had stopped orbiting.

Her hand slipped from Rora's as she stood. Body shaking violently as though from cold, her heart plummeted into her bowels. She took a step, surprised the ground tilted beneath her, before promptly passing out.

When she awoke, Bastian cradled her in his arms. Had he caught her?

Barbosa hovered, trying to examine her, but she pushed him off and stood.

"It's my fault." Words tumbled from her lips. "I did this. I installed her new hand even when I knew doing it could kill her. She insisted I do it anyway, but I should have refused. And now she'll die just like Marzanna."

"They're not dead." Bastian's voice sounded strangely distant.

"If Rora and Marzanna don't wake up in the next four days, they will be disqualified from the competition," the healer said. "They will be selected for contract termination."

"Not now," Bastian growled.

Slowly, the ringleader approached her, raising his hands as though to calm a spooked horse. "There's still time. We can still try to save them both."

"I couldn't save Marzanna," she sobbed. "I tried for days, but her implant is fine. There's nothing to fix…"

"Look at Rora's hand. See what you can do," he pressed. "Maybe we learned something new from… our research. Something that would help."

After several long moments, she nodded, wiped her tears with the back of her jacket sleeve, and rose to her feet. Barbosa passed her a cleaning solution and cloth, with which she cleaned her hands in silence. She opened her tool kit and got to work examining Rora's hand.

As she opened Rora's panel and examined the implant, she heard Bastian speak.

"Not a word of this is to be spoken to anyone." There was a hint of menace in Bastian's voice—a hint of the beast she had seen when she first joined the circus. It was a whispered threat, promising violence.

"Of c-course," Barbosa stammered. "I w-wouldn't say anything."

"I appreciate your discretion."

Gwen worked like she'd never worked before, using every ounce of knowledge she'd gleaned from her research in the library. She checked the wiring, the mainframe, the connection points, the battery. *Nothing. Nothing. Nothing.*

"It's the same fucking thing," she snapped. "Only, with Marzanna's foot, I knew I had installed the improper wires. Now... There's nothing wrong! Not even a wire is out of place."

Everyone stood in tense silence.

"What's that?" Bastian's voice held a strange note to it, and she looked up sharply.

He walked to the edge of Rora's bed and picked something off the ground. It was a small slip of parchment. As he studied it, his brows drew together. Looking up, he eyed Gwen before his eyes skirted back down.

"What is it?" she barked. "Spit it out, damn it."

With a sigh, he read it aloud.

This little bird told us a pretty tale before she passed out. Think carefully before you cross us. There will be consequences if you do.

Bastian shook his head, disbelief written all over his face. "Rora betrayed us?"

"She seemed upset last night when we walked back to our rooms," Akio said, his voice small. "She told me she couldn't live with herself if she cheated, that she had to do something. But I never thought she would tell *them*."

"Are we sure these people didn't hurt Rora?" Barbosa said. "Could they have been the reason for whatever is happening to her?"

"No," Gwen said, her voice hollow. "If she's rejecting her implant just like Marzanna, I know full fucking well who's to blame."

Shaking his head, Bastian's eyes widened with disappointment. "I knew she was ruthless. Because only ruthless people cut off their hand to become a cyborg, which is exactly what she did when the circus came to town and she asked to join us. But this? I would never have taken her for a rat."

For a long moment, Gwen didn't register his words.

She did *what*?

The Rora who never cursed, who always followed the rules, the Rora who didn't want to cheat in the third competition—*that* Rora cut off her own fucking hand?

Clearly, she didn't know Rora at all.

More than that, she'd been played. If what Bastian said was true, Rora was more than ruthless—she was calculating. And Gwen had been played like a fucking fool.

That explained everything. It was why Rora didn't say she loved Gwen back—because she never did. She loved performing above all else.

Mouth hanging open, Gwen clutched her stomach, feeling like she was going to retch. "I can't do this anymore." She rose to her feet. "I won't kill anyone else. And I won't fight for people who don't want my help to begin with."

She pushed past Bastian and out of the room. The others stood in silence as the door slammed shut. She had been trying to help them. But they had never wanted her help.

Everything she'd done, everything she'd been fighting for was a lie.

All she could do was hurt people—people who never wanted her to begin with. She'd outstayed her welcome.

On bruised legs, she hurried back to her room. She wouldn't stay in Apparatus a moment longer.

CHAPTER 25

Night had finally fallen.

Shouldering her pack, Gwen opened her bedroom window. With only a single month's pay in her pocket, she hoped it would be enough for passage off this planet.

It was time she left Apparatus—and the whole planet of Grandstand—behind her.

Before she kicked her skimmer's engine on, she hesitated. Looking back at her room, she recalled her vow to help the cyborgs during the competition. Like her, they were outcasts, unwanted members of the Union. And she'd vowed she wouldn't stand by and watch them be slaughtered.

But now, she knew she couldn't help them. As a ship tinkerer, she could only extract the implants and care for the machine—not its host.

Rora and Marzanna were dying because of her.

But the performers didn't even *want* her help. Rora hadn't wanted her help.

Not only had Rora used Gwen to make a new implant, but she had also revealed their plan to Abrecan. The betrayal turned Gwen's stomach, and she swallowed back tears.

Smoke billowed into the room as her skimmer roared to life. Without another look back, she kicked off her bedroom window and soared toward the setting sun.

Gwen hoped a captain could be swayed to take on an additional crewmember, or a passenger at the very least. She'd also need to leave the name of Gwendolyn Grimm behind. Although her memories slipped between her fingers more and more every day, she'd become a cyborg after the Cyborg Prohibition Law had been put into place. If the feds discovered as much, her life would be forfeit—whether she spent what remained of it behind bars or beneath an executioner's ax.

Soaring over the palace, she turned toward the docks. As always, her skimmer pulled her toward the edge of gravity, but she resisted it, flying lower over the small city. It had far less industry than Anchorage, though some dockworkers carried cargo in crates and bags to and from the ships.

As night began in earnest, she could only hope the darkness would be enough to obscure her from the pedestrians on the street. Far behind her, she could vaguely see the outline of the mountainous forest, which had once housed a red dragon. For the first time, she wondered what had become of the creature.

Had all of what she and Bastian done in the second competition been for nothing? She shook her head. There was nothing else she could do for the performers of Cirque du Borge. Not that they wanted her help, anyway.

Rora.

Her heart ached like a physical pain at the thought of the woman she thought she loved. But she pushed it down, forcing herself to focus on the present.

At the docks, laborers not carrying loads from the ships moved toward inns and taverns.

Gwen brought her skimmer to a lower speed, hoping the rowdy singing from a nearby tavern would drown out the hum of the engine. Dropping into an alley, she kicked the skimmer off and landed neatly on her feet. Rather than feeling relief at being out of the Mistress's castle and on her way to freedom, she felt something else entirely.

The hairs on the back of her neck stood up.

Someone was watching her.

Looking around, she didn't see anyone except the people passing by the end of the alley.

Heaving her skimmer under an arm, she marched out of the alley and into the open, as if such things were commonplace for her. Nothing out of the ordinary. No cyborg tinkerer violating the contract of the most powerful person in this city.

As she walked toward the docks, several tavern wenches and wards stopped pouring buckets of stars knew what into the street to stare at...

Gwen's eye whirred.

Ducking into the shadows, she pulled up the hood of her long-sleeved tunic and then the collar of her leather jacket.

Damn it.

She hadn't thought of wearing a hooded cloak. She hadn't needed to hide her cyborg eye before. Her hood wasn't deep enough to hide her face, but it would have to do. For a moment, she thought about ditching her skimmer, if only to have both hands open to reach for weapons. But if she needed to escape in a pinch, she'd have need of it.

After ducking from the shadows of one tavern to the next, she slowly made her way toward the docks. When the shadows ran out, she sighed and stepped into the darkened light of early evening.

Time to find a ship.

Four ships were docked. The sailors on the first two refused to speak to her as soon as they caught a glimpse of her cyborg eye, despite her insistence that she speak with the captain.

I'll just have to hitch a ride with one of the other two ships.

By the looks of the empty crates and pallets, the ship at the end of the docks appeared to transfer lumber and coal. The other ship appeared to carry—

No. It couldn't be.

Gwen strode closer to the third ship, which was docked nearer to land. Her traitorous heartbeat drowned out all sounds as she drew nearer. There were chains with empty manacles along the deck's railing, and below deck she thought she heard the crack of a whip.

A flesh trader? On Grandstand?

Slavery was illegal in the Union. Just like creating cyborgs was illegal... and performed on this planet anyway. She supposed there were bound to be other laws the Mistress broke.

It's time I'm off.

She didn't dare linger too long by the flesh trader vessel.

As she headed for the ship at the end of the dock, a whistle sounded behind her. Turning, she noticed several crewmembers emerge from the shadows of the lower decks of the flesh trader ship.

"Oy!" one called to her. "What're you doing?"

She bit the inside of her cheek, careful to keep her chin low to hide her cyborg eye. Did she dare turn away now? This ship was one of two ported at Apparatus that she could board tonight. It was her only way out of the city and off Grandstand. Worse yet, what if the captain on the fourth ship refused her like the first two? Then it would be the flesh trader or return to her rooms—and a dying Rora.

Heavy booted steps rocked the docks as several of the sailors approached her from the flesh trader vessel, striding across the gangway. She'd already taken several steps toward the fourth vessel farther down the docks, and now the flesh trader vessel was between her and land.

"You here to drop off more of Ms. Beckett's cargo?"

Gwen stiffened.

What did the Mistress have to do with a flesh trader?

"No."

"Fine enough. She's been giving us a bunch of cripples lately anyway." The man stopped at the edge of the gangplank, eyes skirting the length of her. "Looking to explore a new trade, then? We usually prefer our girls to be feminine and not quite so roughed up, but I'm sure you'll be to someone's liking. Everyone has a type."

She paused. Did that mean what she thought it did? Had the Mistress sold the performers to flesh traders? No. There was no way...

"I'm here to speak with your captain." She took a step forward, but whether it was toward the sailor or toward the taverns and civilization beyond him, she couldn't be sure. "I'd like to discuss rates for travel."

"We aren't taking passengers." The man smiled, revealing a single gold tooth in a mouth of crooked, yellow teeth. His hands rested a little too casually at the sword sheathed at one hip and the pistol on the other.

More sailors strode down the gangway and onto the docks, blocking her route of escape.

"I'd like to speak with your captain all the same." Her fingers twitched. Did she dare try to start her skimmer? The men were paces away now. She couldn't get on it with them so close.

There was a moment of tense stillness when neither she nor the sailors moved.

Then she sighed, expecting what came next.

So much for civility.

One man lunged for her arm. Moving on instinct, she unsheathed the knife at her hip and sliced upward, cutting deeply. Blood sprayed, hot and sticky. Another sailor made for the skimmer under her other arm. Spinning her weight into him, she used her board like a battering ram. He stumbled backward into nearby sailors. But, somehow, he kept his grip on her skimmer, pulling it down with him as he fell.

More men appeared on the main deck of the flesh trader ship, drawn to the commotion. They dashed down the gangway as Gwen leaped over the fallen sailors. Before she'd taken several steps, someone caught her wrist, twisting it and forcing her to drop her knife. As the man pulled her backward, she kicked up, flipping herself into the air and landing behind him.

Too late, she realized she'd flipped into the center of the ring of men hurrying off the flesh trader vessel and onto the docks. She slammed the first man in the back, sending him careening off the side of the docks.

Crouching low, she freed two more daggers from hidden sheaths up her sleeves. If the men surrounding her managed to disarm her again, she had only the knife in her boot and pistol at her hip. The gun was only good for a single shot. She'd have to make it count.

Without feds in this city, she wondered if a shot would draw attention—or help. Likely not.

She was on her own.

Crouching low, knives ready to strike, she said, "I'd like to speak with your captain about passage. But if he'd like me to kill more of his crew to necessitate my assistance in his departure, then by all means."

The men laughed.

"We aren't short on bodies," one said. "Plenty of hands to pick up extra work."

She hadn't thought about that. If they held slaves below deck, they likely did have plenty of extra hands.

"Are you so eager to die, then?" Slowly, she rotated in a circle, trying to see all of the men at once.

It was only a matter of time.

"We've dealt with plenty of runaways before," the man

with the gold tooth said. Only now, he had a bloody lip to go with it. "Bringing unwilling women isn't new for us."

"I'm sure that looks good on a resumé."

As the sailors closed in, their steps perfectly timed, she realized the man was right. She could get away if the men made a mistake or tried to work on their own. But working in unison? She didn't stand a chance against this many experienced flesh traders.

If they were going to take her, then she wasn't going down without a fight. She'd kill as many of them as she could.

Hands locked on to her, and she slashed, not knowing what her knives connected with.

Two bodies dropped before her knives were wrenched from her hands. Arms wrapped around her, pinning her hands to her sides. Someone yanked her hood backward, revealing her cyborg eye.

"A circus runaway?" The voice came from the gangway behind her. It was a woman's voice. "We have a special place for cyborgs in our trade. As the least liked people in the Union, they get the undesirable jobs."

The sailors parted to reveal a woman descending the gangway toward them.

"Captain," several of the men murmured.

Gwen spat. "A woman forcing other women to fulfill the desires of men? You should be ashamed."

A sailor's fist connected with Gwen's gut, and the air whooshed out of her.

"It's the way of the world, my dove," the captain said. Like Gwen, she wore trousers, a loose tunic, and a leather jacket— which likely hid a number of sheathed weapons. "But don't worry. Plenty of women enjoy the pleasures I provide them as well—if you're lucky enough to land a position at a pleasure house." She nodded toward her crew. "Lock her in with the others."

Before the men could haul Gwen onto the ship, a roar

sounded from down the docks. A gun was shot off into the air, and the docks rumbled.

The sailors stopped, turning toward the newcomer.

Between the men, Gwen spotted someone she never thought she'd see again.

"Good evening, gents, Captain." Bastian's heeled shoes clicked on the wooden boards as he reloaded his gun.

You idiot. What are you doing?

"It appears one of my performers has strayed from the herd." He cocked the gun. "If you would be so kind, I'd like to have her returned to me. At once."

A performer? Did Bastian think she'd be seen as less valuable if they thought she was a performer, rather than a tinkerer? Either way, the flesh traders had only to look at her tinkerer's belt and clothes to discover her true trade.

"A performer, you say?" The captain crossed her arms. "She killed several of my men. What kind of performances do you put on in that circus of yours?"

"The kind that captures hearts." Bastian positioned himself out of reach of the sailors' swords, though he was easily within the firing range of a gun. Or the ship's cannons.

"With a sword or theater, I wonder?"

"She's a… singer," Bastian said. "She's got the pipes of a nightingale."

Gwen rolled her eyes. He *had* to say singing.

"Is she now?" the captain intoned, eyes locking with the tools hanging off Gwen's belt. "I'd like a demonstration. Let's hear our little dove sing a pretty tune."

If she could move, she would have slapped Bastian upside the head.

"If you prefer song over marks, far be it from me to point out your idiocy," Gwen said. "I'll gladly compensate you as soon as the ship has left the dock."

She appreciated what Bastian was doing, really. But she had to get off this planet. And if that meant she went with the flesh trader... Well, it certainly wouldn't have been her first choice.

The captain gestured to Gwen, though her eyes hadn't left Bastian's. "You see? This little dove is inquiring about passage. It would seem she's not eager to remain at the circus. I'd say that makes her fair game. She was the one who approached me, after all."

"If you'd like to be welcomed to our city in the future, you'd do well to remember that we don't take kindly to traders who defile our performers," Bastian bit out. "I'll not ask again. Hand her over."

The captain eyed him for a long moment. "You look familiar. Have we done business before?" She took several steps forward, eyes sweeping the length of him. "Aye. I recognize you."

Bastian appeared unimpressed by this knowledge. "I'm the ringleader of Cirque du Borge. Many know my face."

The captain tapped a thumb to her chin, as though debating between stew and soup for dinner. "Have it your way. We'll be taking the nightingale aboard. I don't appreciate being given cripples after being asked to come all this way for *good property*. Bring her in, boys."

In a single movement, Bastian removed a second pistol from his jacket. With a gun in each hand, he shot down the two nearest sailors.

Gwen would have gaped at that pinpoint accuracy if she wasn't being manhandled by the other sailors, who did their dandiest to drag her up the gangway. Swinging, she tried to elbow the man holding her left arm. He blocked her easily. Instead, she slammed her booted heel into his foot. Yelping, he let go, and she slammed her elbow into his teeth. He cried out, stumbling backward and splashing into the water.

Before she could move, another sailor grabbed her around the waist, hoisting her over his shoulder like a sack of grain.

Suddenly, there was a flash of movement. Knives slammed into chests, including the sailor carrying her.

She toppled back onto the docks with the dead sailor, rolling forward and out of reach of the hands grasping for her.

One of her knives lay a few feet away. She grabbed it and turned, slashing upward and killing two men in moments. Their blood oozed from the deep cuts to their throats. For the first time in weeks, the sight of blood didn't make her want to vomit or freeze with fear. Instead, a thrill charged through her at the fight, at the ability to finally do *something*. She felt no regret at killing these men. They were vile creatures who made their money off others' suffering. They deserved far worse than a swift death.

Three sailors surrounded Bastian. The dingbat had a rapier with him, of all weapons. *This isn't a fucking sporting match.* The blade bent back as he blocked several blows from the sailors' far thicker blades and arms. Compared to the meaty sailors, Bastian seemed small enough to fit in a matchbox, regardless of his height and broad stature.

One of the sailors managed to get around him and sliced his side. Grunting, Bastian caught himself, bringing up his scrawny sword in time to block what would have been a fatal blow.

Running forward, Gwen slid on her knees and sliced into the heels of the nearest sailor. The man screeched as she kicked him off the dock.

Bastian ran the final two sailors through with a knife he got from stars knew where.

When she looked at Bastian, breathing a sigh of relief, her heart froze. His eyes widened, and he ran toward her, shoving her back. Stumbling, she fell over several bodies on the dock as a shot rang out.

Bastian clutched the side of his neck as blood spurted everywhere. Through the once immaculate black fabric of his jacket, blood wept from a gunshot wound at the base of his neck. She prayed it was his shoulder and nothing more important.

Instinct seized her, and she rolled, another shot flying wide and thumping into one of the corpses on the dock beside her.

Grabbing her loaded pistol from its holster at her hip, she dodged yet another bullet before rolling into a crouched position and firing.

The captain stood on the gangway and flinched as Gwen's bullet found its target. Blood seeped from a wound to her gut. She toppled sideways, splashing into the bay.

Voices called out somewhere below deck on the flesh trader vessel.

"Gwen." The voice was weak and came from behind her.

Bastian.

Spinning, she dashed for him. Leaping over bodies, she caught him before he fell off the docks.

"Before you ask," he hissed through clenched teeth. "I'm fine."

"And I'm a fucking nightingale."

She felt the wound at his neck, and her fingers drew blood.

"I have good news and bad news," she said as she examined him, still holding him upright. "The bad news is you've been shot."

"Thank you, Madam Obvious."

A faint smile quirked Gwen's lips. "Don't recycle my jokes. Get your own."

This produced a fainter smile in return. His eyes fluttered, near to closing.

Panic seized her, and she shook him, pulling his good arm over her shoulder. "The good news is the shot missed your head and didn't hit your heart, though I don't know where the bullet went. For now, we need to put pressure on the wound to staunch the bleeding—"

"Save them." His voice was soft.

She hesitated, hearing the cries of the slaves below deck. If they didn't move, and soon, more flesh traders could come and surround them.

"The slaves. On the ship." His voice grew weaker with each word. "I'd bet anything they're our former performers."

Her heart stilled.

She hadn't wanted to believe it. But if the Mistress could order Gwen to hack people apart for outdated cyborg implants, that meant Celeste would also be capable of selling the former performers to flesh traders. Was she so desperate for money? What did she hope to gain?

Still, Bastian—the man she'd grown to care about—was dying. He needed help, and soon.

"In case you haven't noticed, you need immediate medical attention."

Gwen glanced over her shoulder at the empty deck of the flesh trader vessel. She could go below deck and free the former cyborgs. Hell, she could even try to fly the ship herself. She knew enough about how ships worked to get it into open space. But she knew little about navigating or bringing a ship into port.

But there were probably also more flesh traders below deck, not just the people who needed more help. They might object to her stealing their vessel and freeing the prospective slaves. But... if she freed the former cyborgs, that meant she not only had helped these people, but she might have a very willing crew. If the flesh traders didn't capture or kill her first.

She glanced back toward Bastian, who blinked slowly.

Then, she shook her head.

Stars, she wanted to help these people. But it was a longshot. Daring a rescue below decks would assure Bastian bled out on these docks. She couldn't guarantee she'd save the former cyborgs. But if she tried to help them, it'd mean she'd lose Bastian.

She realized then she did have something to fight for, after all.

"There'll be no naps just yet."

Looking around, she spotted her skimmer under several corpses. Laying Bastian down, she extricated it, ignoring the smears of blood across her perfectly rusted skimmer. Placing the board beside Bastian, she looped her arms under his and heaved his body onto the board. He was much lighter than she'd expected.

"As soon as I have you settled," she said through gritted teeth. "I'll come back for them."

It wasn't a perfect solution, but it was the only one she could live with.

As quickly as she could, she kicked the sailors' bodies off the docks. They splashed into the bay. She prayed the bodies wouldn't be discovered at least until morning—or, better yet, were carried out to sea. It might be enough cover to not arouse suspicion for long enough that she could see to Bastian and get back to the slaves.

I'm sorry, she thought to the former cyborgs below deck.

Somehow, she knew she'd be too late.

Then, she turned on her skimmer's engine, grabbed hold of the edges, and guided Bastian toward the inns, praying there would be a healer nearby.

"Stay with me," she said. "I'm going to get you help."

As she hurried toward civilization, Bastian's fingers wrapped around hers before going limp.

CHAPTER 26

Gwen paced in the tiny inn room as the healer tended to Bastian's wounds by the light of a single, flickering light bulb.

The woman, who apparently had experience as a midwife and Union army nurse, was the best healer they could find on short notice. But it seemed her experience had given her an eye for combat wounds.

A metal bullet clinked into the tray on Bastian's bedside table. As the woman cleaned where his shoulder met his neck, she made tsking sounds in the back of her throat before stitching the wound.

Once finished, she stood. "That's all I can do for him."

Rising to her feet, Gwen removed several marks from her pack. Only hours ago, she'd hoped to use the money toward her passage off Grandstand. Instead, she passed the inflated fee to the healer who'd helped save Bastian Kabir.

"For your work and your silence."

The healer sniffed. "This isn't the first alleyway mugging that has gone awry. I've been summoned for others. I know how to hold my tongue. Your Mistress won't hear of the incident from me."

Gwen winced.

Your Mistress.

It was an unfortunate reminder of her current circumstances. She was still part of Cirque du Borge.

And Bastian was alive. So, there was that.

She'd told the healer Bastian had been mugged in an alley and shot. Thankfully, the woman had been smart enough not to press for more details.

When the woman left in a flurry of skirts, Gwen slumped into the chair beside the bed. Leaning forward, she assessed the healer's work. The stitches were neat and tidy. Still, Bastian would have to be careful about how much he moved his neck and shoulder in the coming days, or the wound might open again.

After watching the rise and fall of Bastian's chest in a deep sleep for nearly an hour, trying to reassure herself he was fine, she left the inn with her pistol and bloodied knives.

When she returned to Bastian's room hours later with food, he was awake.

"Morning," she said, placing the tray on the side table. "How are you feeling?"

"Like I got shot."

Slowly, she helped him sit up in bed. She then placed the tray of potatoes, eggs, and fresh-brewed lunar tea in front of him.

"I'm not hungry."

"I thought you might say that." She grabbed a second tray with a biscuit, milk, and tea and placed it onto his lap. "You really should eat something. You need your strength to recover."

Eyes narrowing, he studied her before picking up the biscuit and nibbling on pieces. She ate the eggs and potatoes beside him in silence.

"Did you go back for the others?" he asked. "Did you save them?"

She had to clear her throat before she could speak. "Once you were settled, I went back to the docks, but the ship had left port sometime in the night."

Guilt weighed heavily on her chest. But she tried to reassure herself with a single thought.

Bastian was alive.

Despite everything that had happened between them—the butchered cyborgs, traveling into the wilderness, fighting a dragon, and now facing a pack of wolfish flesh traders—she'd come to rely on Bastian's reassuring presence and iron will. Despite the gray waters they treaded through, he somehow clung to a moral compass, knowing exactly what he needed to do and when. And what he was fighting for.

Yet for her, it took Bastian getting shot and nearly dying for her to realize she had someone else to fight for. There was still time to try to save Rora and Marzanna. Regardless of what Rora had done to betray them, she still deserved a chance to live. It was Gwen's fault Marzanna and Rora weren't waking up, and she would find a way to fix it. It didn't matter how hurt she was by Rora's actions. Even if neither of them pulled through, Gwen couldn't run away. She had to protect Bastian, Akio, and all of the other cyborgs who were fighting to stay alive in this competition.

Bastian studied her with dark, narrowed eyes. "Why did you leave?"

Exhaling heavily, she opened her pack beside the bed and removed her tool kit. "If we're going to talk feelings, I might as well do something productive in the meantime."

"Is talking about your feelings unproductive?"

"Maybe. Sometimes. I don't know… It's sure as hell uncomfortable." She gestured to the remains of his normally pristine dress shirt. "I'll need to remove your shirt to check your plating. It'll be hard to see what kind of damage was done last night without cutting you open. But I'd like to do a preliminary check anyway."

Nodding, he handed her his tray of food, which she placed on his side table. After unbuttoning the front of his shirt, he attempted to remove the sleeves. Pain flickered in his eyes as his jaw set in that usual stubborn way of his.

"Will you stop trying to do everything yourself?"

"I can't," he snapped. "If I don't do something, no one else does." He pointed a finger at her, his unbuttoned shirt hanging loosely on him. "You abandoned us. You left without any explanation."

"Did I need to explain myself? I'm the reason Marzanna and Rora are dying." She was surprised to find herself nearly shouting.

Clenching her jaw, she tried to calm herself.

Why was she so glad about Bastian being alive again?

"I couldn't be the reason any more people die," she continued. "I thought I could help them. I thought, as a cyborg tinkerer, I could make a difference. But the only difference I've made was securing early graves for two performers."

Bastian's chest heaved as he breathed. For the first time, she noticed the dark, coarse hair at the center of his chest, and she swallowed instinctively.

She scratched her head. "I'm not a mass murderer, and I'm certainly not a cyborg tinkerer. Butchering cyborgs wasn't in the job description when you shoved that stupid contract in my face." She sighed. "If you had known about the competition and what I would be expected to do, would you still have recruited me?"

He started as if surprised by her question. "Yes."

"Why?"

"Because I need you!" This time, it was he who shouted.

On instinct, she stepped away from the bed. "What are you talking about?"

He had the good grace to look away, blushing. "It's the Forgetting."

She frowned, not understanding.

"What do you remember of your past?" he asked.

Slowly, she thought of her family and how they'd done something to protect her and her siblings. But the story behind it was completely gone.

"My earliest memories are my first tinkering jobs when I worked as an apprentice," she said. "Why?"

His eyes widened. "Your memories are fading faster than what's typical, but it's not unheard of. I've been a part of this circus for ten years. At this point, I shouldn't remember anything about my past. But I do. I remember working for my family and what happened toward the end when Carlisle found me. And more than anything in the world, I want to forget it."

"What?" She shook her head, at a loss for words. "You want to forget your past? Why?"

"I wasn't a good man, Ms. Grimm," he said simply. "I don't wish to remember the man I was."

She frowned. "How do you expect me to help you?"

His shoulders rose and dropped in a shrug. "Our old tinkerer couldn't figure out what was wrong with me. Toward the end, I thought he might have found something, but then he disappeared without a word. I hoped a new tinkerer with a fresh perspective would be able to help with my situation."

Crossing her arms, she said, "I don't see how a lack of memory loss is a bad thing. Hell, I want to *stop* the Forgetting, not try to help you lose your memories." Anger surged through her veins, and she clenched her fists to keep them from shaking. "Was all that you said the other night about saving the performers some bogus lie to keep me here? All so I can be your cyborg tinkerer?"

"Of course not!" He swung his feet off the side of the bed.

"What are you doing, you oaf? Are you trying to kill yourself after I worked so hard to save your life? Sit down."

Slowly, he rose to his feet. Despite the anger coursing through her, the sight of him, injured and limping toward her, cooled some of her anger.

With his shirt unbuttoned, she could see the outline of his implant when he exhaled—where she normally would have seen abdomen and ribs. Dark bruises and welts peppered his skin. The flesh traders had hit him.

He'd risked his life for hers.

With a sigh, she came forward and looped his arm around her shoulders. She tried to guide him back to the bed, but he resisted.

"Is it so wrong to want to help myself and the others at the same time?" His eyes locked on hers. They were so close she could feel the heat radiating off his body.

"In the process, I also saved you." His voice a low rumble. "Without the surgery, you would have died."

Damn it, she couldn't think with his body pressed so close to hers. The heat of him muddied her thoughts.

"You're killing yourself, you know." She forced the words out. She didn't want to say them. Hell, he probably wouldn't be able to hear them, but they needed to be said. "I've known you for several months now, and I've rarely seen you eat a full meal. When I picked you up last night, you weighed little more than a child half your age—assuming you're thirty after ten years at this circus. There's no point in helping you if you can't learn to love yourself first."

Paling, Bastian looked away. Was that shame she saw in his eyes?

"What is it you see when you look in the mirror?" she pressed.

"A man far larger than Thaniel." His voice was small. Not the loud, commanding voice of the ringleader, but the one of a forgotten son.

In her mind's eye, she could see the overweight juggler.

"I see the man I once was—the man I'm scared to be again."

"That was why you had heart problems," she realized, recalling the first cyborg implant Bastian had been given—a device for his heart.

He nodded. "I was a large man once. But it wasn't simply my size that led me to need my first implant. My family had a history of heart problems. Many died before their time, clutching their chests. But the weight, how I was... Well, it didn't help."

"So long as you're healthy, who the fuck cares what size you are?" Again, she tried to bring him toward the bed, but he stood rigidly in place. "I don't care if you are tall or short, bony or curvy, or what color your skin is. If you were an asshole, I would have left you to die on those docks. But you're not. You risked your life to save mine. You came after me and fought flesh traders. The Mistress could have both our implants for this."

As she spoke, she noted the closeness of his lips to hers. She could feel his stale breath heating her cheeks, and she didn't care. Her heart raced as she felt the weight behind the arm slung across her shoulders. Now, his arm around her felt far too similar to an embrace.

"You're a good person," she continued, her voice soft. "You are strong and handsome and capable."

He started. "You think I'm handsome?"

"I just said so, didn't I?" Her cheeks heated. "I wish you could see what I do—the man behind the ringleader. Why do you want everyone to think you're such a beast?"

Finally, he let her guide him back toward the bed. She lowered him onto the mattress. Rather than lying back down, he sat at the edge of the bed. Slowly, she sat beside him.

Then, he did something she didn't expect.

Reaching out, he traced his fingers over her shoulder to

the soft skin of her neck. His hand lingered before he ran his fingers through her hair. She froze, her breath hitching.

"I don't have to push people away if they're too afraid to get close."

His hand moved back down her neck before his fingers traced her shaved scalp. Her breaths were ragged, and she surprised herself by leaning into his touch.

Slowly, he ran a finger down the side of her cheek before removing his hand.

To her surprise, she found herself longing for his touch again.

"You've made me want things that I... I told myself couldn't happen," he continued. "And you were right. I was selfish in my recruitment of you. I needed you not just for the circus, but for myself. I thought you'd prefer a life as a cyborg to no life at all. Was I wrong?"

Her eyes lingered on Bastian's hands, which rested in his lap. With more effort than she cared to think about, she tore her gaze away.

"No," she said at last. "Even if I had known the reason for your recruiting me, I probably would have still taken the second chance."

She thought about what it must be like for Bastian. How he spent years watching every other cyborg lose their memories when he longed to forget and didn't. But what about his past was so bad that he was desperate to wipe it from his mind?

Perhaps it was from watching Rora fade slowly from this life, but Gwen found she didn't have the heart to be mad at him.

"I'm sorry," he said. "For bringing you into this mess and for not being completely honest with you sooner."

"I'm sorry for almost getting you killed." She opened and closed her hands. "Thank you for coming after me, for showing me I have something left to fight for." She cleared her throat, careful to keep her eyes off his bare chest. "Now, let's see what type of damage that bullet did to your implant."

Together, they removed his shirt. As she pulled each sleeve off, his fingers grazed hers, and she had to consciously remind herself it was no big deal. It didn't mean anything.

With his shirt off, she noticed a shallow cut in his side, and she remembered how a flesh trader had sliced him with his sword. "It appears our healer missed a spot." She got to work cleaning the wound before examining his implant. Moving her fingers across his chest and back, the plating beneath felt intact. There were a few sections with indents—possibly from their exchange with the dragon or from the night before—but the implant seemed well-constructed. When she examined where it attached to his backbone, she was amazed by the complexity of how the machine wove into each vertebra.

"I want to see your chip."

From where Bastian lay down on the bed, he tried to peer up at her. "Why?"

"Humor me." She shoved him unceremoniously back onto his stomach.

As he muttered something ungentlemanly into the pillow, she felt for the faint outline of where the chip would be inserted into his brain. She knew from some of the books that the slot used to be a bright metal material, but after pirates had stolen a number of chips from cyborgs, it had been changed to match the skin tone of the cyborg to make it more difficult to locate.

Finding it, she popped the panel open and removed the chip.

Most chips were small rectangular devices made of metal and sometimes polymer as well. Bastian's chip consisted of the metal she'd anticipated, but it also had a far darker material marbled into it. As she studied it, she could have sworn the chip pulsed. What was that darker material, anyway? It didn't look like any polymer she'd seen.

When she replaced the chip and closed the panel, Bastian pushed himself up and turned to face her.

Panic filled his eyes, and his cheeks were flushed. "Warn me next time. It felt like you were going inside and tampering with my brain. I couldn't think... I couldn't do anything until you put the chip back."

She froze. "Say that again."

"It's like my thoughts froze the moment you removed the chip." His eyes grew distant. "I couldn't recall anything—not your name or mine or anything about my past. All I could think about was this strange... *need* to return to the circus."

Just like what I felt after Celeste removed my chip.

Then everything clicked into place.

"It's the chips!" she exclaimed. "The Forgetting and Rora's and Marzanna's body rejecting their implants—I think it's all because of the chips. There must be some issue with the coding. I'll need to find a portable mainframe or data processor to confirm this. This isn't Union-grade technology, after all. But fuck me, I think it's the chips."

A properly functioning cyborg chip shouldn't impact the function of the host's mind or body—only the functions of the implant it had been created to control without the need for internal wiring across the cyborg's entire body.

Something—or someone—had tampered with the chips.

Her mind raced. "Is there anyone we can borrow or purchase a portable mainframe from?"

Slowly, Bastian nodded. "I know someone from this side of town who might have what we need. But it's going to be expensive."

"Of course, it is. Once we have it and get back to the castle, we'll have a look at your chip."

And Marzanna's and Rora's, she added silently.

"As soon as you're feeling well enough to walk, we'll head back."

There were only three days until the final competition, which meant they were running out of time.

This discovery could mean everything, and not just that she wasn't the world's worst cyborg tinkerer. But if Bastian couldn't form coherent thoughts without the chip—a technology that was supposedly only there to allow him to remotely control his cyborg implant—then maybe, just maybe, this could be the key to discovering the true origin of the Forgetting.

And how she could save Rora and Marzanna.

One strange incident with the chip was a coincidence. Twice was a pattern.

Now that she thought about it, she'd started losing her memories in earnest after her first implant check-in with Celeste.

Perhaps the Forgetting wasn't an accidental side effect of becoming a cyborg, after all.

CHAPTER 27

I f there was anyone who could make dying look good, it
was Rora.

Like the last time Gwen had seen her, Rora lay on
her bed with her arms folded delicately across her stomach.
Only this time, her fingers rested atop a single red rose. All
around the pillow, her curly brown hair was loose. The sight
startled Gwen more than anything, as Rora rarely wore her
hair down. Her lips were the color of a blooming, pink rose,
and her skin glowed as though she'd just spent a day in the
sunshine.

Even at death's door, Rora managed to take Gwen's breath
away.

Guilt burrowed inside her, pulling her attention away from
the sleeping beauty. No matter what Rora had done to betray
them, it was Gwen's fault she was here.

Hours earlier, Gwen and Bastian had purchased a portable
mainframe with their combined remaining funds. They then
snuck into the palace, which took the better part of the day to
get to the performers' dormitories unnoticed. Akio had
remained in Rora's room, standing guard over her while
they'd been gone.

Once in Rora's room, Gwen removed the portable mainframe from the bag they'd stashed it in and set it on Rora's bedside table. She then instructed Akio to roll Rora onto her side. Afterward, she opened the port and removed Rora's chip. Like Bastian, Rora's chip had the same mysterious marbling.

With trembling hands, Gwen inserted Rora's chip into the small machine, which had a keyboard and screen with bright green text.

This has to work. I can't fail them again.

Trying to ignore the tap dancer in her chest, she could barely think past the racing of her heart. Green text scrolled across the screen in an endless wave of coding. Gwen was no engineer or mainframe expert, but all tinkerers had to understand basic coding in case machines malfunctioned. She could tweak the coding, but she couldn't write it.

Nearby, Bastian was on his feet. His cheeks were hollow, his face pale.

"Sit down before you pass out," she muttered, not removing her eyes from the scrolling text.

Why is there so much fucking coding?

Although she'd anticipated the cyborg implant system to be complex, she'd never realized just how complex. There were data systems for mechanoreceptors, thermoreceptors, pain receptors, proprioceptors, and so much more that she couldn't entirely grasp. It was an entire data pool to ensure the cyborg implant functioned like a biological limb.

After several hours of tapping keys, she'd made it past the basic functions of Rora's cyborg hand when she spotted something out of the ordinary. "That's not possible."

Bastian stood from where he'd slumped on the floor beside her. "What is it? What did you find?"

Barely blinking, not wanting to miss anything, she studied the rolling text on the small screen.

"Rora's system was rebooted," she said. "It appears to be

an automatic programming for when trauma happens to the implant. Something must have happened before she passed out. The parts of the chip that rebooted included the control of the host's cognitive function. It's why she fell into a deep sleep—and likely why Marzanna has, too. This 'sleep' allows both the technology and its host to recover. I think I can kick-start the implant system with a simple coding."

She prayed she was right and that both Rora and Marzanna could still be saved.

At that moment, it didn't matter that Rora had used her. The acrobat still deserved a chance to live. Everyone did. For now, Gwen shoved her personal feelings toward Rora to the back of her mind. There would be time to address it *after* she was awake.

Bastian squeezed Gwen's shoulder encouragingly. But she couldn't look back. Typing as fast as she could, she restarted Rora's system. All the while, her heart thundered inside her chest.

Several minutes later, she unplugged the chip and reinserted it into Rora's head before rolling her onto her back. "That should do it."

Everyone waited in silence.

Sweat streaming down her face, Gwen lowered herself onto the edge of the bed beside Rora.

Please wake up.

With nothing left to do but wait, her suppressed feelings surged to the surface. Anger raged inside her like a bubbling furnace, mingling with hurt and betrayal. But when she'd told Rora she loved her the other day, she'd meant it. Even if she could never trust Rora again, she needed her to be all right. She needed to know Rora wasn't going to die because of her.

Time passed, and Gwen prayed on every star she'd ever heard of, asking every god of every religion to help her—if only this once. She knew her soul was likely damned from the blood staining her hands. But Rora didn't deserve to die because of Gwen's ineptitude.

Moved by impulse, she leaned down and placed a kiss on Rora's forehead. Whether or not Rora woke up, things could never go back to the way they were. This kiss was a goodbye to her dreams for the two of them, fleeting as a shooting star.

When she pulled back, Rora opened her eyes, blinking.

"She's all right!" Akio cried.

Tears streamed down Gwen's cheeks as relief flooded her chest. But she reined her emotions and stood to her feet, creating distance between herself and the acrobat.

She had done her part to make sure Rora was okay. But this woman had betrayed them to Abrecan and used Gwen to get a new hand. She wasn't about to forget that nor let her guard down so easily.

Lines formed between Rora's brows. "Where am I? How long have I been out?"

"One day," Gwen said, crossing her arms as if that gesture could put a distance between her heart and the beautiful, treacherous acrobat sitting up in bed. "I shouldn't have tried to install your new hand. It's my fault you were hurt, and I'm sorry for my part in this."

Rora paled. "Don't—I should be the one apologizing."

Yes, you should.

Instead, Gwen said, "There'll be time for that soon enough."

Rora flinched, but Gwen ignored her. "Let's see to Marzanna's chip."

Hours later, Marzanna was awake. At the moment, Akio held her in a hug, crying and swaying, while Marzanna tried to pry herself free. The two trapeze artists were a strange and beautiful sort of family—as harsh as siblings and as fiercely protective as parents.

From where Gwen sat on the edge of the bed, she watched them, smiling.

Bastian ran a hand over the back of his neck. "Would you look at my chip as well? See if you can... remove my old memories?"

"Are you sure you don't want to remember your past?"

He nodded. "I wasn't a good man. I... Well, you showed me that I can be a better one now. And I don't want to lose sight of that."

That was a blatant cop-out if she'd ever heard one.

What part of his past was he running from?

But who was she to deny Bastian this request? This was his life after all, and she certainly wouldn't take his choice away. Even if it was clearly a bad choice.

Sighing, she gestured to the bed. "No promises, but I'll see what I can do."

Like the others, he lay down on the bed on his side.

Before she removed the chip, he turned to look at her. Then he reached for her hands, clasping them tightly. For a moment, she was so surprised she forgot to move.

His eyes locked with hers, and she saw deep-rooted fear.

He's afraid of losing control.

She squeezed his hand tightly. "I'll be as quick as I can."

Then she let go and opened the port at the back of his neck, removing the chip.

As she worked, studying the rolling green text, Akio appeared beside her.

"I've always been skeptical of the ringleader," Akio said as he studied Bastian. "After today, he's proven his good intentions in my book." He looked directly at Gwen. "You did this."

She frowned, not understanding.

"He's a different man because of you," Akio said. "A better man."

"I didn't change him," she said. "People only change if they want to."

Akio shrugged noncommittally. "People don't really change. But you gave him a reason to want to change himself. If you asked me a month ago, I would've told you not to waste your time and that he couldn't be changed or reasoned with. But I'm glad, deep down, he wanted to be a better man."

A smile touched her lips. "Bastian is a good man. Here's to hoping I can help him."

His coding was fucking complex. Unlike everyone else's chips, chunks of text overlapped one another, layering in disorganized patterns. Typing, she scanned the coding.

"Fuck," she muttered sometime later after staring at the rolling text on the portable mainframe's screen.

"What is it?" Rora asked.

Gwen scratched the shaved half of her head. "The coding is so damn complex. It's like the person who created and installed the chip had conflicting intentions with the person who updated it. There are two distinct codings."

When Rora came to stand behind Gwen, she had to ignore the itch between her shoulder blades at the closeness to the acrobat.

"What do you mean *conflicting intentions?*"

"It's as though the person who installed the chip encoded the same functions to Bastian's chip as everyone else," Gwen said. "Then, a second person came in and did a second layer of coding."

His second implant, she realized. The two codings must have been for each of his implants.

Unlike the rest of the circus, Bastian had two cyborg implants. The first was for his heart, while the second implant was a plating protecting his vital organs when he worked with the cyborg animals as an apprentice for the Mistress. Could the person who installed the plating have accidentally written conflicting coding? Or was it intentionally malicious?

"Can you fix it?" Rora asked.

As Gwen exhaled, her heart sank. "No. The two codings are woven over each other. If I try to erase some of the second coding, there's a good chance I could wipe out his memories or personality. He might not be the same person afterward. This is beyond my skill level."

Slowly, she unplugged Bastian's chip from the machine and returned it to his head.

The ringleader sat up in bed, hope filling his eyes. "Did it work?"

She shook her head. "I'm sorry. I couldn't help you. But I think a qualified engineer, coding specialist, or an actual cyborg tinkerer would be able to do more than I can."

"I see." He cleared his throat. "Thank you for trying, Ms. Grimm. It was a kindness I won't forget."

As though this week wasn't full of enough surprises, Bastian swung his legs to the side of the bed where Gwen sat and hugged her. When he pulled away, he cleared his throat and then shook her hand.

"Well, that was awkward for everyone," Marzanna said, a hint of a smile in her voice. "So... what now?"

"I should apologize." Rora's eyes fell to the ground. "Before I passed out, I... I told Abrecan and Thaniel about the plan to sabotage their props. He used an electroshocker on me and must have dumped my body in the room after. He said something about punishing Gwen for not joining his crew."

Gasps echoed around the room, though every face still held a mark of disbelief.

Realization hit Gwen.

When she first joined the circus, Abrecan had offered her an alliance, and she'd turned him down. In the second competition, she'd forced Abrecan, Thaniel, and the others into a joint victory to save Rora, Marzanna, and Akio from extractions. This must have been how he'd intended to get back at her—by attacking someone she cared about. Or thought she cared about.

He must have intercepted Rora on her way back to her room last night.

But Gwen had seen Abrecan's note. She knew what Rora had done.

A cold anger seized her chest. The feelings of anger, betrayal, and utter fucking devastation finally caught up with her. "Why? What reason could you possibly have to reveal our plan to Abrecan? I was trying to save your lives!" She swallowed the lump wedged in her throat. "I thought we... that you and I were..."

Endgame.

How could she have been so wrong?

"He threatened to break my hand if I didn't." Rora's cheeks pinked, but she held Gwen's gaze. "I knew I'd need the help of the tinkerer with my new hand if I was going to get into the top ten acts. After everything I worked toward, after everything you'd done to make me this hand, I couldn't let Abrecan destroy it. Even if that meant revealing your plan." Then she broke Gwen's gaze, eyes growing distant as she studied the floor. "I'm sorry, Gwen. I didn't mean for it—for you and I—to get this far."

Gwen's mouth hung open. She tried several times to speak but couldn't.

It was true. Rora had betrayed her, used her.

She had known it from the moment Bastian had revealed the circumstances surrounding the circus's recruitment of Rora. Only someone who was utterly ruthless and calculating —and moderately insane—would cut off their own hand. And anyone willing to cut off a limb for personal gain would be more than willing to use others to their own ends.

But hearing Rora admit that she'd used Gwen, that she hadn't meant for what they shared to get this far, it was like everything finally hit her.

Whatever they had shared was over. It had been nothing more than a convenient lie, and she'd fallen for it like a fucking fool. She'd fallen for *her*. Even now, a distant part of her screamed that this was all a dream, that the Rora she knew would never do this to her. But this was life. There were no saints at Cirque du Borge.

Gwen's heart sank into her boots as the betrayal settled on her shoulders like a physical weight. But she clung to her anger like an anchor, allowing it to fuel her. Without it, she was afraid she would succumb to the dark devastation clouding her thoughts.

"Beyond fucking with me, do you realize you've possibly killed some of your friends?" Gwen demanded. "This plan wasn't just for you. It was for Akio, Marzanna, and all of the other innocent cyborgs. It was to keep you all safe. Do you want me to be forced to remove your hand? Don't you know what the Mistress has done to the former performers?"

Confusion marred Rora's features.

With everything going on, Gwen hadn't had a chance to share her and Bastian's discovery with them.

"The losing performers are being sold as slaves to flesh traders. That's where Bastian and I were last night. She sold the performers and their contracts to fucking *flesh traders*. Do you want to be a slave?"

Rora shook her head. "The Mistress wouldn't... She said... I never meant to..."

Anger filled Gwen's chest, making it hard to breathe. "Was any of it real? Or are you still playing me, playing all of us, just so you can get what you want? Are you really that selfish?"

"You're one to talk!" Rora yelled back. Marzanna placed a hand on her shoulder, but she shook it off. Pointing an angry finger at Bastian, Rora fixed her eyes on Gwen. "Even if whatever we shared wasn't real, you never even gave it a chance. This entire time you were cozying up to management.

Is that why Bastian's really here? Because you paid him off with your—"

"You'd best not finish that sentence." Gwen's voice was dangerously quiet. "And not just because you know it's not true. Bastian risked his life for yours countless times. And how did you repay him?"

By betraying all of them.

"Gwen," Rora began, "I didn't mean to tell Abrecan, I swear—"

"Stop lying!" Gwen screamed. "I saw Abrecan's note. He told us what you did. You betrayed us." Tears spilled down her cheeks. "If you were heartless enough to use me for a new hand, then you'd sure as fuck be heartless enough to reveal our plan to Abrecan—just because it got in the way of what you wanted. Fucking patronage." She spat the last word from her mouth as though it were filth.

"No," Rora said. "I—"

"Get out," Gwen said. "Right fucking now."

"This is my room—"

"Are you sure you don't want to talk about this?" Marzanna interjected.

Slowly, Gwen removed her pistol from its holster at her belt. She didn't aim it at Rora, but the implication was clear. "She's only going to reveal our plan to Abrecan a second time." She looked directly at Rora. "You've proven that you can't put me or any of the people you've claimed to care about first. You only care about yourself, your stupid hand, and performing for the emperor. So, you can fend for yourself, just as you wanted. But I won't let you put these people at risk anymore."

This time, no one objected.

Rora glanced at her friends, eyes pleading. Despite the conflict in their faces—warring between loyalty and betrayal—they looked away. Only one person spoke up.

"This isn't right," Marzanna said. She turned to Rora.

"Shame on you." Then she eyed Gwen. "Shame on both of you."

Without another word, Rora left the room, closing the door behind her. The chatter from performers in nearby rooms filled the hallway.

When Gwen looked at Marzanna, it felt as though her blood was on fire. "What would you have me do?"

"I don't know," Marzanna admitted. "But this doesn't feel right. None of this does."

No, indeed.

"Living feels right." Gwen roughly shoved her pistol into its holster and ran a hand over her face. There would be time to process this later. Now, she had to focus on keeping these people alive.

Mind reeling, she ran through all of the possibilities remaining to them for the final competition and made a decision.

"We'll still sabotage their props, but we'll need to do it differently," Gwen said. "We'll play off their knowledge of our former plans. But there's something else."

She looked at all of them. Despite the guilt marring their features, there was also determination. It was in the straightening of their shoulders, the clenching of fists. They were angry. More than that, they were ready to fight to live.

Taking a deep breath, she said, "You guys aren't going to be the ones to mess with the props. I am."

Surprise streaked across everyone's faces.

"Ideally, I'll fuck with all of the props during the opening group number," she continued. "If anything goes wrong, I want you guys to keep Abrecan and the others occupied."

Bastian's eyes widened, and she thought she saw him shaking his head.

As they discussed the plans late into the night, eventually relocating to another room, she couldn't help but notice the strange way Bastian looked at her. Rather than seeing pride on his face for her doing everything she could to save these performers—the very people he had shown her were worth fighting for when he prevented her from boarding the flesh trader vessel—the look on his face said one thing.

He didn't think they'd win.

CHAPTER 28

G wen leaned on the ship's railing, watching the stars soar by as they traveled along the powerful current of the solar wind.

It was strange not to be running back and forth in the engine room, making sure everything hadn't combusted during flight, as she once had on the *Crusty Tulip* and countless ships before. She'd never really had a chance to simply sit and watch the passing stars and planets beyond the gravity and oxygen fields.

The main deck of *Obedient*, which was partially open to space, was filled with noises of the crew at work as they patched up parts of the sails or tended to the rigging. All of the performers had been permitted above deck after takeoff, and most milled about and studied the skies.

To anyone on nearby planets, their ship would look like a shooting star.

Footsteps sounded behind Gwen, and she turned.

Rora walked past on the opposite side of the open deck, taking a seat atop a barrel. Alone.

The sympathetic part of Gwen wanted to go over and talk to her, but the more prominent part wanted to kick the acrobat in the shins. She had betrayed her and used her to get a new implant. Ultimately, she had chosen herself—her career aspirations—over Gwen. It stung like a thousand meteor shards breaking through the gravity field and pelting her skin. She had had a few fucking good cries in the past few days.

As to Rora's accusation, it was true Gwen had started to spend more time with Bastian, but it had been out of necessity at first—to go to the library and intervene in the second competition. But now... Well, after he risked his life to rescue her from the flesh traders, she'd discovered what a loyal person he was. She saw the man behind the beastly demeanor more and more every day.

As though her thoughts had summoned him, Bastian appeared from the captain's quarters along with several members of the show management team—or what should be the captain's quarters and were instead the Mistress's suite. The show management team saw themselves out before closing the door and dispersing across the ship, most going below deck.

When Bastian saw her, his gaunt face lit up with what she could only describe as sheer joy. He strode over to her, leaning on the railing beside her.

"Any news?" she asked.

He shrugged. "The usual departing procedures and cautionary steps upon arrival. Nothing I hadn't expected."

They watched the passing stars in silence for a time.

"Are you sure about this plan?" he said, eyes still on the wonders of the Crescent Star System. "After what happened with Rora, I think it might be too risky. Abrecan and the others will be ready for us. Destroying one prop versus another or changing the timing isn't going to make that much of a difference. Besides, what if he tells the Mistress?"

She nearly rolled her eyes. This had to have been the thousandth time he'd asked since they'd reformed their plan. "I appreciate your concern, but I'm positive. This is going to work." Holding up her fingers, she ticked off each in turn. "I'll crack the supporting beams on Abrecan's target, run a rough sander over Thaniel's wooden juggling pins... I'll do it during the first group number while Abrecan and the others are on stage. They won't even see me coming. Piece of cake."

"We need you as the cyborg tinkerer," he persisted, and she could feel him turning toward her. "The discovery you made the other day has so many implications. We need to dig into that further and see what it has to do with the Forgetting. And we can't do that if you get caught."

And brought in for implant extraction, he didn't need to voice.

"Trust me. This will give the others the edge they need. Besides, Abrecan tried to fuck with me, so it's past time someone fucked with him."

Frowning, Bastian turned fully toward her, no longer pretending to watch the passing celestial orbs. "I *do* trust you —perhaps more than I should—but I think you're letting your feelings over what happened with Rora cloud your judgment."

She stiffened. "This has nothing to do with her."

"Doesn't it? You want to prove her wrong. To show that her betrayal was all for nothing. That she should have picked you. Am I wrong?"

"There's nothing between Rora and I anymore."

"That doesn't answer the question."

Slowly, she ran a hand over her face.

She had mixed feelings where Rora was concerned. The woman was selfish and ruthless and had proven as much. If she continued down this path, she'd have only her trophies to keep her warm.

The truth of it was, even as she was falling for Rora, Bastian had come along. She hadn't expected it, hadn't planned it, yet he'd somehow found his way into her heart. The instinct to protect him had overwhelmed her at the docks, and she realized she couldn't leave him behind.

From where he stood beside her, heat radiated off him.

She saw past the hollowed cheeks to the kind eyes that always found hers.

"You know I can't sit idle and wait with my butcher's knife on the sidelines anymore," she said at last. "I want to help, and I think I can do that."

She turned back toward the stars, and some time passed before Bastian spoke again.

"Thank you."

Brows drawing together, she turned to him. "For what?"

"For reminding me why I wanted to be in a place of power," he said, his voice soft as he studied the sky.

"And why is that?"

"To protect those who can't protect themselves."

She blinked, wondering at the weight behind those words.

Abruptly, he turned to her. Hesitating, he spared a glance for the crew mulling about the deck before his gaze settled back on her. Unlike his powerful strides in the theater, when he closed the distance between them, his steps toward her were cautious. Quite different from the confident ringleader she'd come to know.

Suddenly, he was before her, a mere breath away. Their eyes locked. In those brown irises, hope and fear warred for dominance. Above them both, there was a flicker of admiration.

For a moment, it felt as though he stared right through her, down to the core of who she was. Past the girl who'd crumpled in the operating room or fled to the docks in search of a ship, and right to the woman who stood before him— doing everything in her power to help the people she cared about.

The woman who would no longer run away from something, but toward it.

Slowly, he raised a hand, cupping her cheek. Calloused palms scratched her skin. The way he touched her… it was as though he held the single red rose in the palace's garden between his fingers.

"What are you doing?" Even to her ears, her voice was breathless.

If she was being honest with herself, she hadn't stopped thinking about how he'd touched her in the inn, how she'd been moved by instinct to protect him when he'd been shot, and how he'd kissed her outside his room to protect her from the Mistress.

She realized then she wanted him to be happy, to learn to see himself the way she did—as a strong, capable man.

Unbidden, her thoughts slid to Rora and all she'd done to save the woman she'd grown to love so quickly. The woman who'd betrayed her. The woman her heart still longed for.

Damn her. She cared for them both.

A question budded in Bastian's eyes.

"There's something I wanted to ask." As he spoke, his eyes swept over her face, taking in her every feature. "I hope you know this has nothing to do with Rora. The timing isn't ideal, but… after what happened the other day on the docks, I realized certain things cannot wait. Our lives are at risk every day, and…" He trailed off.

Looking up at him, she leaned into his touch. "Why, Mr. Kabir. Am I making you nervous?"

"Of course, you are." He sounded exasperated. "You're brazen, infuriating, more stubborn than a bull, and always mildly offensive when you speak."

"You sure know how to make a girl want to spread her legs."

"But you're loyal and thoughtful and kind, and I haven't been able to get you out of my mind since the day we went to the library." He sighed. "And please… call me Bastian."

"Good. I was only going to call you Mr. Kabir when you were being irritating anyway." She smiled. "What's your question?"

"Can I kiss you?" When he spoke, his voice cracked. It was the sound of a broken man who dared to hope—who dared to let himself want.

Her eyes, both flesh and machine, flickered back and forth between his dark, satin ones. "You know you sound like a character from one of your romance novels, don't you?"

His face brightened. "You've read them, then? The skeptic has been converted."

"I had to see what this obsession was all about."

She'd read four of them, in fact. They were a delightful mix of smut and humor—humor at the sheer idiocy of some of the characters. But she'd been curious about the man behind the beast. Quite a lot could be learned from knowing what a person liked to read.

She had discovered what a kind, sensitive person Bastian Kabir could be.

Despite all the darkness they had shared in the operating room, they had come out stronger. She'd thought she'd break, and she might still. But he'd shown her she had things to fight for. He had been her shining light in that darkness, her compass, and she realized she very much wanted to hold on to that light and never let it go.

Smiling, she nodded. "I'd like that very much."

Beaming, he leaned in. Neither of them could stop smiling as their lips met. He tasted of peppermint, and she breathed in his smells of sage, shoe polish, and sweat. His lips were soft, and his thin body warm. For several long moments, she forgot everything but the feel of his arms around her as his lips melded into hers.

All too soon, he broke the kiss, pulling back.

"Nice of you to ask me this time," she said, thinking of their first kiss outside his room.

He snorted. "I didn't think you would say yes."

"Is that reason not to ask?"

"Of course not. The first time… well, that was a necessary precaution."

"Which failed spectacularly."

A knowing smile brightened his face. "Or did it? We may not have fooled the watchmen or the Mistress, but it gave me an excuse to kiss you."

She shoved him playfully before grabbing his jacket and pulling him in to kiss her again.

Even with the sadness weighing on her heart over how things had ended with Rora, she couldn't stop the hope fluttering inside her stomach along with some very agile butterflies.

"Stars," he gasped. "I forgot how wonderful that felt."

She frowned. "When was the last time you kissed a woman… or a man?"

Clearing his throat, he said, "For the record, I'm only attracted to women. As for how long it's been…? Ten years. I haven't been with anyone since I was betrayed by my family and fiancée and then recruited for the circus. I haven't wanted to. That is, until you."

Biting her lip, she looked away, trying to disguise the blush creeping up her cheeks. Then she cleared her throat, gathering the courage to ask an uncomfortable question, one she knew he didn't want to answer. But if anything was going to happen between them, she had to know more about the man who didn't want his memories back—and why.

"What was your family like?"

Slowly, he pulled away from their embrace and leaned on the railing. "They weren't good people. My family is from Harvest, a planet in the Smoke Ring Solar System, where they ruled over the city of Rift and lived like celestial gods. There is royalty, but the biggest currency is power. And in Rift, power can only be gained through alliances and trade."

Stars. He really *could* remember more of his past than most. She couldn't recall the name of the planet her family was from, let alone any details about them. How had his memories remained this intact?

"You told me you had been sentenced to death by hanging," she began. "That your family forced you to work in their illegal business to get the money you needed for a medical procedure. What was that illegal business?"

"Gwendolyn——"

Suddenly, it clicked.

"The captain of the flesh trader vessel... she recognized you." The words spilled from her mouth. "What was the illegal operation you were involved in? Were you a *flesh trader?*"

He stiffened, not turning to look at her. For what felt like an eternity, he studied the stars before eventually shaking his head.

"No, I was a smuggler. I smuggled weapons——swords, pistols, explosive arrows, guns, cannons——and sold them to the highest bidder. My family kept quite a few of the weapons for themselves, but most of what I smuggled between planets or cities was sold to drug lords, paid assassins, mercenaries, gang leaders, underground rebels, terrorists... People who would eventually harm others.

"I questioned my family's smuggling business, but I never did anything to stop it. In fact, I sold more weapons in the auctions when I was desperate for the procedure. I'm ashamed of what I've done. I... I don't want to remember the horrors I committed."

Bastian was a smuggler.

The realization should have horrified her. Instead, she was numb, unable to do anything but stare in shock at the passing stars, listening as the sounds of the crew faded to silence.

Not now. Not him, too.

The thought of Bastian lying to her——hiding things about his past——so soon after Rora's betrayal had her head swimming so fast, she thought she'd be sick.

"I-I have to go."

"Gwendolyn, please—" He started to reach for her but stopped himself.

"I need some time to process all of this."

Hurt flashed across his eyes, but he didn't say another word.

She fled to her quarters below deck.

Unlike most of the performers, she was given a private room.

It was far more spacious accommodations than her quarters on the *Crusty Tulip* and every other vessel she'd worked on as a ship tinkerer. Cirque du Borge's ship, *Obedient*, was also far larger. Still, there was only enough room for her bed, a mirror, and a table with a washing basin.

Closing the door, she sank onto her bed. Leaning forward with elbows on her knees, she ran a hand over her face.

What have I gotten myself into?

CHAPTER 29

S omewhere above them, a crowd roared. The thunder of voices was punctuated by the sound of gunfire.

Gwen peered around the frayed black-and-white curtain at the base of the underground ramp leading up to the stage. "Goody. A friendly audience."

The circus had set up portable stages and props in an archaic outdoor amphitheater on Jinx. It was similar to what Gwen had seen on Anchorage but without the signature white-and-silver-striped tent. Pirates, thieves, and lowlifes firing off guns into the air—and at each other—filled hundreds of crumbling stone benches that surrounded the round stage.

"This is a fucking shitshow." Her tits were sweating so badly that her shirt was damp.

Beside her, Marzanna and Akio peered past the curtain and up the ramp.

Any minute now, the performers were going to run onto the centermost stage for the group number... and Gwen was going to fuck with some props. Hopefully without drawing the attention of the show management team, watchmen, or performers.

"It's a miracle they didn't shoot our ship down." Marzanna's voice lacked its usual confidence as she stared up at the group of pirates drunk on power as much as the finer spirits.

"Or loot it after we docked," Gwen muttered.

Marzanna sniffed. "They might still if they haven't already."

Upon arrival, it had been announced that all the citizens of Jinx were invited to come, watch the show, and there was no need to withhold themselves from anything—violence included.

An arm bumped into Gwen as another performer pressed in beside her. Dozens of performers huddled together, trying to peer up at the amphitheater above.

According to the Mistress's earlier instructions, after they'd arrived at the amphitheater and were ushered below ground, all of the performers were to remain in the rooms below ground before and between acts. After the group number in the beginning, each act would perform once, and then everyone would return to the stage for the finale. After which time, the audience would decide which acts they'd enjoyed the best.

Meaning, the acts they don't shoot.

Pushing her way through the crowd of performers lingering at the frayed black-and-white curtain, Gwen made her way to the back of the room.

Nestled beneath the amphitheater, the room felt more like a cave with its walls hollowed into the ground. Eventually, she found herself an open space and tried to relax. She'd need to be calm and collected for what she was about to do. But she was as tight as a bowstring.

At least she was ready. She had her tools slung casually in her tinkerer's belt at her waist, which included hammers and a metal file.

She could do this.

"Don't slump your shoulders, Ms. Lockwood."

Gwen tried not to flinch at the sound of Bastian's voice, infused with his usual ringleader authority. They hadn't spoken during the remaining trip on the ship or since arriving on Jinx.

But as Bastian lectured Rora and the other performers, she couldn't help the way her heart lurched. Her thoughts slid easily to their shared kiss on the deck. And stars, she wanted to kiss him again. Fuck, she wanted to do so much more than just kiss him.

But could she trust him?

If anything, Rora had proven Gwen wasn't the best judge of character. And damn it, she couldn't be hurt again. Not this soon.

She averted her eyes as Bastian walked past her. For a moment, it seemed as though he lingered, and his steps were hesitant. Then the moment faded, and he walked past her.

"It's showtime!" one watchman called. "Performers, line up."

The cyborgs rose to their feet at once and stood in organized lines. Akio and Marzanna spared Gwen a worried look before they ran up the ramp and onto the center-most portable stage at the base of the amphitheater.

Good luck.

As the remaining circus staff busied themselves cleaning up or moving props, Gwen ducked around the curtain and strode partway up the ramp. She turned down a nearby hallway that was beneath the audience's benches.

Countless props were all neatly organized according to the order of performances.

Glancing around, she didn't see a staff member in sight.

As quietly as she could, she strode through the maze and found Abrecan's target for his archery and knife-throwing act. Again, she looked around and saw no one.

Taking a deep breath, she removed the hammer from her belt and raised her hand to strike the supporting beams.

"Ms. Grimm. I had hoped I wouldn't see you here."

Fuck.

Lowering her hammer, she spun on a heel.

"Mistress." It was an effort to keep her voice neutral as Celeste emerged from a dark hallway she hadn't seen before along with a dozen watchmen. "I was just coming to check on some of the props. One of the performers had asked me to—"

"I'm not in the mood for games." Celeste gestured to her hammer. "Drop the weapon, if you please."

Gwen looked at the watchmen, who were slowly circling her. At that moment, it felt startlingly similar to the night she'd been surrounded by flesh traders. "I don't think so."

Like then, she wasn't going down without a fight.

"I feel I have been very fair with you," the Mistress said with a sigh. "I've given you several warnings, yet... I must admit, I wasn't surprised when Mr. Karlight told me of your intentions for the third competition. I had hoped it wasn't true, but..." She shrugged. "I did tell you what would happen if you didn't comply with our policies at Cirque du Borge."

"You mean, when I don't willingly murder innocent people?" Gwen thought about reaching down to the knife sheathed in her boot but didn't dare. Not with the watchmen closing in. "Excuse me for having a fucking conscience."

Celeste merely dipped her chin as though acknowledging an old acquaintance blathering at a dinner party.

"Take her."

The watchmen moved in.

Gwen had a split second to decide whether she would run or fight. But she knew at once she didn't stand a chance against twelve guards. Turning, she dashed toward a nearby bike ramp, narrowly missing the arms of reaching watchmen. Leaping, she bounced on several trampolines before her feet slammed into the ground. Ignoring the pain in her knees, she ran.

But before she could reach the ramp leading to the amphitheater—and freedom beyond in the crowds of pirates —a hand grabbed her jacket and a watchman hauled her backward. Her screams were drowned out by the sounds of cheering above.

Arms wrapped around her, and she was dragged back into the shadows. Kicking and clawing, she fought with everything she had. But there were too many of them.

Watchmen pinned her hands and feet to the floor while more pulled free their wooden batons. In the process, someone had torn the hammer from her grasp.

"Break her legs," Celeste said from somewhere behind her.

Panic tore through her chest. She screamed, struggling to get free.

She had a single thought as she watched the wooden baton swing toward her right shin in an impossibly slow arc.

Bastian was right.

Pain rattled through her as bone cracked. Tears streamed down her cheek as she shrieked in pain. But she didn't beg, didn't ask the Mistress for mercy. After what she'd seen in the competitions, she knew she'd have none.

The Mistress came into view.

Celeste Beckett was a goddess of death, red as the dawn, as she approached Gwen. As was her custom, the Mistress was garbed in scarlet, from her hair to her gown, to her cape, to her nails. As she came to kneel before Gwen, she raised her hands.

Fear paralyzed Gwen, and she forgot to move—to fight.

Celeste's perfectly manicured scarlet nails were no longer nails but ten massive talons. The metal was sharpened to an impossibly fine point.

"I warned you what would happen if you crossed me," the

Mistress hissed. "And don't think I didn't notice a certain acrobat's new implant. Despite your growing talent, I'm far too close to let your delicate disposition get in the way."

She raised a hand toward Gwen's eye, directing a talon at where the base of her implant connected to flesh.

She's going to cut me open right here.

Screaming, Gwen flailed her arms and legs, trying to break free. But it was no use. The watchmen held on fast.

"I don't need your eye," Celeste continued, hand raised. "But I won't let you keep it either. You will walk the streets of Jinx as a worthless human. That is, if you live long enough after I—"

"Celeste!" a voice roared. "What's going on here?"

Glancing past the talon above her eye, Gwen realized for the first time that the opening act had ended. Bastian and the performers descended the ramp and moved toward their private quarters below ground.

Many of the performers lingered in the doorway, but they hurried toward safety at the sound of more gunshots. Only Bastian stood his ground. After a moment, he strode toward them until he was mere steps away from where Gwen was held down.

The Mistress turned her gaze back to Gwen's cyborg eye. She tapped it gently with a metallic fingernail. "I caught Ms. Grimm about to destroy some of our performers' props, so I am carrying out her punishment." She turned to Bastian. "You know as well as I do the price for disobedience. The contract states I can terminate any contract at any time for any reason. Now, run along, little ringleader. Unless you have something you'd like to say?"

"Take me instead." Bastian's voice was raw as though he'd been the one screaming. "You want me as your apprentice again? Fine. I will do whatever you say. Just… spare her. Allow her to remain with Cirque du Borge."

His eyes were round with fear as he glanced at Gwen's broken leg, twisted at an unnatural angle.

"I'm quite certain she has learned her lesson." His pleading eyes fell on Gwen. "She won't step out of line ever again."

Once, Gwen had wondered if Bastian would stand up to the Mistress for her. After the second competition, she'd seen him hesitate as the watchmen beat her in the middle of the theater. But he didn't hesitate now.

At that moment, she wished for nothing more than a few minutes alone with him. To apologize for being a complete and utter fool. His past didn't define who he was—not when he was trying so hard to be a better man. To protect her and the others. How could she not see that? Stars, she wished for the nights on the ship back just so she could kiss him again and tell him how sorry she was.

Instead, only a grunt of pain escaped her lips as Celeste spoke.

"An interesting proposal."

As the Mistress rose to her feet, relief swelled in Gwen's chest.

"I accept." Celeste extended her clawed red hand toward Bastian. Slowly, he took it, his hands visibly shaking. "You will come to my quarters immediately upon departure. For the remainder of this competition, you will continue your role as the ringleader. Understood?"

Bastian nodded.

"Good." The Mistress moved toward their rooms below ground and crooked a finger over her shoulder. "See to it that this mess is cleaned up."

Just like that, Celeste and the watchmen disappeared.

Bastian ran over to Gwen, falling to his knees beside her. Reaching toward her, he stopped, eyeing her broken leg. "Oh, stars. Gwendolyn…"

"I'm fine," she lied. "Just… help me to my feet."

Slowly, he slipped an arm under her, pulling her upright.

"Oh, fuck." She hissed as more obscenities flew from her mouth. "I can't put any weight on my leg."

He nodded, still holding on to her. "Let's get you to the healer. He will put your shin in a cast—"

"No." She shook her head. "Not yet. First… I need to apologize. I should have listened to you. You were right. And what you shared with me the other night…"

"Now isn't the time." Slowly, he moved toward the main room, Gwen hobbling with him. "First, I need to get you help. And then I have to return to the competition."

"Right."

As the healer realigned her broken leg and wrapped it in a cast, she watched the competition from a private balcony above the circus's quarters. Interestingly, the Mistress had insisted that she "bear witness to the feats of Cirque du Borge."

One act after another came across the various stages.

She tried to still her heart as Bastian spun in a circle on center stage, his cane raised in the air as the cyborg beasts strode in circles around him. Marzanna and Akio flipped back and forth far above the crowd in their trapeze act. Abrecan never missed the target, and Thaniel juggled more absurdly large objects to the applause of the audience.

Other acts weren't as fortunate.

Gunshots rang loudly as audience members directed guns at the performers. Blood spurted dark across the stages as the crowd jeered. In some cases, the performer was able to finish their performance injured. In other cases, performers collapsed onto the stage, never to rise again. Watchmen dragged their bodies away to the booing of the crowd.

It was after the audience had shot the firebreather that Rora appeared.

Jogging up the ramp, Rora smiled brightly. When the yellowed artificial light hit her, it was as though the entire world slowed. Gwen didn't hear the skeptical murmurs from the crowd or notice how the spotlights creaked as they turned, following her. All she could see was the beautiful acrobat.

The slackline had been secured to a portable stage, which was rolled to the center.

When Rora was a few feet away from the center of the rope, she turned to the audience, arched her back, and shimmied into a deep belly roll.

Gwen tried to ignore the fact that her body found that particular move very erotic.

Soft drums pattered in the background as Rora slowly dipped backward until her hands touched the ground behind her. Flipping her feet into the air, she walked on her hands until she was beneath the rope. She pushed herself off the ground, catching the rope with her legs and swinging up into a seated position.

As she rose to her feet, the rope swayed beneath her. To Gwen, it seemed as though it was trying to buck her off. But Rora walked forward, leaning into each step as the slackline swayed back and forth. When she reached the end, she turned, waiting for the rope to still. When it did, she launched herself forward.

Flipping, she caught the rope in both hands before spinning once more and landing nimbly at the other end of the slackline. The rope swayed gently, and the audience gasped, clapping louder.

Again, Rora moved her hips as the wave passed up her stomach to her chest and neck.

Gwen was thankful for the distraction of pain in her leg.

Far slower this time, Rora flipped forward. Her legs arced through the air before sliding apart into a deep split. She wrapped her feet along the rope at either end. Then, she flipped herself down toward the ground, spinning in endless circles with only her feet securing her to the rope. As she spun, she moved her outstretched hands to the center of the rope, stopping herself from spinning before slowly lowering her feet to the ground.

Several gunshots fired off into the air as she air-walked her toes along the ground.

Gwen's heart nearly stopped as she waited for Rora's body to drop, as lifeless as the last performer.

Instead, Rora flipped over the rope and onto the ground.

More gunshots fired off into the air, and Rora bowed deeply. The audience clapped, yelling unflattering, sexist praises. Turning, she descended the ramp back to the performers' quarters below ground.

Even after Rora broke her heart, Gwen found herself exhaling in relief.

Rora wasn't safe from extraction yet, but she was safe from the audience—for now.

"That is all I can do for you, Ms. Grimm."

Looking up to the healer, Gwen nodded her thanks. Barbosa disappeared far too quickly for a man of his age— probably eager to be away from the woman who kept pissing off the Mistress.

Then it was time for the finale.

Her mind was blurry from pain, so the final act seemed to move far quicker than the others. Once they were done, Bastian strode forward, flipping his cane into the air.

"Did you have a good show?" he called, earning a roar from the audience. "It's time to pick your favorite acts."

How could I do this to him? The thought swept across her mind even as guilt tightened her chest. *He loves being the ringleader, and he's good at it, too. And now it's my fault he will be forced to work for a woman he hates more than himself.*

The performers split from the final pose of the finale and moved to stand beside their respective acts at different spots around the stage. One by one, those acts came to stand beside Bastian, and the audience cheered or booed each performance.

Holding her breath, she prayed no one would be shot. The audience cheered for Abrecan while Thaniel was met with heartier praise.

When it was Rora's turn to come forward, she flipped forward and fell into a split at Bastian's side. He held an outstretched arm toward her as she rose to stand. The audience clapped wildly, far louder than any response Gwen had heard yet.

Smiling broadly, Rora waved at them before returning to her spot farther back on the stage.

When Bastian called Marzanna and Akio forward, the audience stilled before a deafening roar consumed the amphitheater. The sound was a rolling wave, booming across the rows of benches. The two trapeze artists bowed together.

Before they could move back, a gunshot split the air.

Flinching, Gwen froze for several moments. Looking around, she scanned the performers to see if any of them were hurt. They clutched unbloodied stomachs, breathing sighs of relief when they realized their innards were securely behind fleshy walls.

Then Akio staggered forward.

Jerking forward in her seat, Gwen clasped the railing of the balcony before her.

"No!" Rora cried, dashing to center stage.

Marzanna and Rora caught Akio before he could topple over, somehow keeping him upright. He held a hand to his shoulder. Pulling it back, it was covered in dark scarlet. More blood seeped from the wound, pooling on the stage below him.

Several boos erupted from the audience.

"Someone help him!" Gwen shouted from her private balcony, but the sound was lost to the crowd.

Marzanna and Rora did what they could to stop the bleeding. Although the injury shouldn't be serious, the implication behind it was.

Some of the audience didn't like the performance.

"It seems the audience is undecided on this act," Bastian said, eyeing the watchmen at the base of the ramp.

"I'll ask again," Bastian boomed. "What did you think of this act?"

Gwen held her breath.

Please let them be safe.

As the audience cheered loudly for a second time, no more shots were fired. Bastian nodded toward Akio and Marzanna, indicating they should move back. There were more acts who'd yet to face their fate.

Act after act was brought before the audience. The next ones to be booed were shot without hesitation. Blood splattered the stage as performers dropped. Some were lucky enough to only get hit in the shoulder or leg. Others weren't— bleeding out or dying instantly.

Once the final acts had been given a chance before the audience, they were left with fifteen acts who weren't shot... and a pile of bodies.

Gwen didn't hear when Bastian announced the ten winning acts. All she could see was the endless carnage. Blood spilled over the sides of the center stage.

Watchmen ushered the winning acts off the stage and to the rooms below ground—away from the trigger-happy audience.

They had done it.

Her friends had survived the final competition.

She should feel relieved. Instead, all she felt was dread.

Soon, they would be performing for the emperor, a man who had helped create and instate the Cyborg Prohibition Law. Although there was a chance to reverse the law by convincing the Union Council cyborgs weren't a threat to society, the fact remained—the Union wasn't currently safe for Gwen or her friends. But that wasn't the worst of it. Bastian would be at the beck and call of a woman he feared. And for what? Nothing Gwen had tried to do had made a difference.

Again.

But they wouldn't see the emperor just yet. First, she had to harvest the parts of the losing acts. She prayed she could save most of the cyborgs from death. But she knew she would be too weak from her own injuries and dizzy with pain to do more than what Celeste demanded of her.

With the aid of a crutch, she limped back down to the room where the performers were, a question playing through her mind.

Why does the Mistress want these implants?

That night, when she resumed her role as the Grimm Reaper, she harvested the implants alone.

And this time, it was far worse than ever before.

When she didn't work fast enough to harvest the implants, courtesy of the pain in her broken leg, the watchmen stepped in. They wielded axes, hacking apart both the dead and living cyborgs to retrieve their implants.

Where the implants from the dead cyborgs had gone to, she had no idea. She didn't even know if a secret arrangement with a flesh trader to pick up the former performers on Jinx had been made. Who knew which was the worse fate—to remain on Jinx or to be sold as a slave.

Soaked in scarlet, the watchmen hauled Gwen back to the ship.

As *Obedient* departed the planet of pirates and thieves, she wept on the main deck, clutching the railing with bloodied hands.

Once again, she had failed the cyborgs. Meanwhile, more memories slipped from her mind like the blood of the people she'd tried to protect slipped from her hands.

The Mistress had won.

And now she had Bastian in her clutches, too.

CHAPTER 30

V ictory wasn't always sweet. But no one said victory
was paired with death.

As Cirque du Borge's massive ship, *Obedient*,
soared toward the emperor's home planet, all Gwen could see
were the images of the broken cyborgs when she'd extracted
implants—alone.

It had been weeks since the last competition. Her chest felt
hollow, and she shook as though from a chill even though the
weather in the capital city of Allegiant would be warm this
time of year.

Larger than all thirteen of the other planets in the Union,
Covenant boasted its own lush lands and oceans teeming with
wildlife as well as several continents with massive cities and
booming industries. The ship's artificial gravity and oxygen
fields flickered before shutting off as they entered into the
planet's natural gravity field.

Descending from the sky, they followed the line of lights
toward the great city of Allegiant. The emperor's capital was a
massive peninsula surrounded by a lake on three sides. On the
water, hundreds of docking stations were set up for ships.

They landed softly in the water before the engines were

turned off. The sail billowed in the gusting breeze that pulled them toward the city. The emperor's palace sat atop a hill, looming over incoming and outgoing vessels.

"Bastian!" Gwen called out.

The former ringleader appeared above deck, heading straight for the quarterdeck where the Mistress and show management team had assembled for their final address to the performers before their arrival.

"There's something I need to speak with you about—"

Turning on a heel, Bastian looked at her, expression cold as a tomb. "I'm sorry, Ms. Grimm. But I can't speak just now."

Without another word, he left.

Sighing, she closed her mouth, unspoken words still on her tongue.

Ever since the third competition ended and they set sail for Covenant, Bastian hadn't been the same.

During the long flight to the emperor's planet, she'd done everything she knew to do, but she hadn't been able to get him alone for even a moment. She'd asked to speak to him in private, mentioning there was a high-level tinkering concern that required his attention at once. When she managed to intercept him on the main deck, it was as though she spoke to the shell of the man she'd met months ago and not the Bastian she'd come to know and care for in recent weeks.

Something's wrong with him.

Desperate, she tried spying on him. She didn't have to go far to learn where he spent most of his time. He'd disappeared into Celeste's room for hours during the voyage and followed the Mistress as though he were her personal hound. But with Gwen's broken leg making it difficult to get around, she couldn't learn much more than that.

Now, the show management team—and Bastian—stood at attention behind the Mistress on the quarterdeck. Celeste droned on about how they would descend the ship in their ridiculous finery, how they must carry themselves through the crowd, how it was important they present themselves with dignity since no one will expect such things of cyborgs. Everyone was to use their show names, and no one was to reveal any personal information about themselves or the inner workings of the circus.

Scratching at the silly hat the watchmen insisted she wear during their trek to the emperor's palace, Gwen pulled the attached veil lower over her face, determined to keep her eyes on anyone but the man at the Mistress's side. Irritably, she strapped her welding goggles atop her leather top hat before putting it back on. If she was going to have to wear this stupid thing, then she wasn't going to pretend to be anything she wasn't.

She was the cyborg tinkerer. And the Grimm fucking Reaper.

And she hated herself more than any of the performers possibly could.

As she had every day since the third competition, she tried to push back the fog clouding her thoughts—the loss of lives on Jinx, the guilt of having not been able to save the cyborgs, and the gaping hole in her chest from losing both Rora and Bastian.

She had to focus.

They were about to enter the viper's den.

Eventually, *Obedient* was secured into place at the docks. Descending the gangplank, she struggled to keep pace with the other performers as she hobbled with her crutch.

The humans standing at the edges of the docks and along the streets ahead were dressed in clean, colorful garments rather than the grease-stained browns and beiges Gwen was accustomed to seeing on the manufacturing planets and moons.

But it wasn't the apparent wealth of the onlookers that

had her gut turning. As the performers walked past in their boisterous costumes, people spat at their feet.

"Filthy cyborgs," person after person hissed.

Individuals of all genders and identities spread out on either side of what must be the main thoroughfare to the palace. The citizens of Allegiant stood for blocks along the cobblestone streets, scowling at the performers marching in a parade toward the palace.

Naturally, the feds standing guard at every paved street corner did nothing to stop the hostility. Even as the people threw rotten produce and animal dung into the street or at the performers, the feds stood at attention.

For once, Gwen was thankful for the silent, masked watchmen surrounding the performers in their march toward the emperor's grand palace. They pushed back reaching hands and kept the crowds along the sides of the streets. They also cleared the way for the show management team, who rode atop Celeste's cyborg horses. All of the performers' gear and equipment trundled along behind them in cyborg horse-drawn carriages and carts.

As they walked, Gwen noted hot air balloons in the emperor's colors of jade, violet, and gold rising into the sky. Men with top hats and feathers and ladies with laced gloves leaned out of the basket with golden binoculars held to their eyes.

Tourists who'd come to watch the spectacle, no doubt. It was the first time in ten years since the rise of the emperor that Cirque du Borge had entered the capital of the Union.

Gwen couldn't help but wonder if they knew about the emperor's plan to convince the Union Council to revoke the Cyborg Prohibition Law.

Men and women hung out of second- and third-story windows overlooking the street. When they started throwing stones, Bastian barked an order for the performers to open their umbrellas, which they had been given for this very purpose.

Scowling, Gwen opened hers, struggling to hold both the umbrella and her crutch as rocks pinged off the top. She glared at the people on the streets ahead, those she could see from where she strode in the middle of the group of performers. They leaned out of massive stone balconies with intricate wrought-iron railings. When one larger woman pulled her top down, flashing her breasts at the performers, she had just about had it.

Dropping her umbrella, she started to push through the watchmen. A rock pinged against her hat, knocking it askew and pushing back the veil that covered her eye.

The crowd jeered. "Cyborg eye!"

The woman had yet to put her drooping tits away, and Gwen growled. She'd bloody climb the side of the several-story building with a broken leg if she had to. Before she took two hobbling steps, someone caught her wrist. Turning, she was surprised to see Marzanna holding on to her, pressing her umbrella back into her hand.

"Don't," she warned.

Something sharp hit the side of Gwen's head, and she gasped. Grumbling, she shoved her hat back on and took the umbrella, raising it above her head before another stone could hit her. As she did, two stones pinged off the canopy. Thank the stars the things were made out of rubber.

Gwen took a step closer to Marzanna as they walked, allowing the other performers to filter around them. Beside them, Akio's shoulder was bandaged, and his eyes were drawn.

No one was the same after the third competition—not Bastian and definitely not her friends. The gowns, coattails, top hats, and makeup couldn't disguise the apparent lack of hope in their eyes or the slowness to their steps.

Rather than the relief Gwen had thought they would all

feel by winning the competition and claiming one of the top ten spots, Akio and Marzanna had retreated into themselves— likely replaying the horrors of the carnage on Jinx.

Unlike Gwen, they hadn't seen the blood of their fellow cyborgs spilled. Perhaps they had been in denial about what the Mistress would or wouldn't allow. Maybe they had once thought that remaining a part of Cirque du Borge was still the best option for cyborgs in the Union. But now? Hell, even Gwen didn't know.

"We have to keep our shit together," Gwen whispered. "If we don't, then all of this will have been for nothing."

Marzanna's eyes were distant, clouded with memory. Eventually, she shrugged. "What will happen will happen."

A thought occurred to Gwen.

"Rora had mentioned that the emperor has the power to purchase contracts, even from Cirque du Borge."

Marzanna frowned. "So?"

"*So*," Gwen began. "First, we convince the emperor and the Union Council that cyborgs are perfectly respectable citizens and no threat to innocents. Then… well, perhaps we can convince him to bring us on to his court and to be our patron. Anything is safer than returning to Apparatus with Mistress Morbid."

She gestured to her fucked-up leg.

Slowly, Marzanna sighed. But before she could respond, a large rock smacked into her umbrella and bounced off Gwen's and several others.

"If the emperor revokes the Cyborg Prohibition Law, it will change everything for us," Gwen continued. "It might mean the assholes throwing rocks at us might think we're scientific marvels a year from now. Cyborg implants would once again be manufactured and accessible. You could finally have a new foot that's installed properly. Hell, I bet the emperor would pay us a salary in marks rather than false promises."

"It's worth a shot," Marzanna said. "I'll talk to Akio."

Now, if she could only get a moment alone with Bastian to tell him of their latest plan. Would he be willing to leave the circus behind?

She couldn't ignore the irony of this most recent turn of events.

Rora—the woman who'd betrayed them to win the competition all for the opportunity to perform for the emperor —wouldn't be the only one vying for the emperor's patronage.

Eventually, they made their way to the palace gates, which were opened wide for them. The watchmen entered the inner city first, and the wary performers followed closely behind.

Gwen stuck to the middle of the crowd of performers, slowly lowering her umbrella to look around. Unlike the streets, there weren't citizens hanging outside of upper-story windows or crowds gathered along the sides. The inner city was nearly empty of merchants or hawkers. Instead, a few horse-drawn carriages clopped across the immaculate cobblestone streets. There was no garbage or dirt on street corners. Men and women stood near shops, laughing and passing gold coins between hands for a scrap of silk or a velvet top hat.

Blood rushed to Gwen's cheeks.

There were people dying from starvation in the manufacturing districts, and these people were paying *gold* coins for a *hat?* Depending on the planet, gold was worth hundreds—sometimes thousands—of paper marks.

Eventually, they made their way to the castle proper where a troop of guards met them. Unlike the watchmen, who had two pistols strapped to their back, a sword sheathed at one hip, and a wooden baton on the other, the emperor's soldiers wore traditional steel armor and helmets. Swords were sheathed at their sides along with several guns. Their uniforms were far fancier than the average fed officer.

By the time Gwen trundled into the courtyard, her leg was screaming with pain.

They were led through the palace's main doors and down countless hallways and passageways until they were brought before two massive oak doors. The palace guard stopped, turning to the show management team at the front and the performers behind them. The watchmen stood at mute attention.

A soldier with red tassels attached to his shoulder armor said, "There are to be no weapons past this point." He gestured to the tables on either side of the door. "Place your weapons here. You will be searched before you're permitted to speak with the emperor."

Stepping forward, Gwen dropped her umbrella onto the table. The thing weighed nearly as much as a copper bathtub, and the table shook from the weight. She exhaled heavily before removing her pistol and knives from hidden pockets, holsters, and sheaths in her tinkerer's leathers and dropping them onto the table beside her umbrella.

The remaining performers did likewise, though most didn't carry weapons. However, the watchmen didn't remove their weapons. When the palace guard didn't allow them entry into what must be the throne room, Celeste spoke up.

"Do as he says."

Celeste didn't bother to turn around. Instead, she stood directly before the door with hands folded demurely in front of her. The other members of the show management team stood beside her, waxed mustaches twitching and hands smoothing already immaculate skirts.

As if there was one whit of reluctance or humility about her.

As usual, Bastian stood at Celeste's side with his eyes focused ahead.

Please just look at me. I need you.

Nothing happened, of course.

Once everyone placed weapons, umbrellas, and a number of questionable accessories onto the table, the guards patted them down, and then the doors opened. They swung inward, revealing a throne room as massive and ornate as the castle itself. The floor was covered with furs and rugs, and beneath that were tiles flecked with gold. On the opposite side of the room was a massive, empty stone chair set atop a raised platform with stairs leading up to it. In front of that was a table with thirteen chairs.

Thirteen chairs for the leaders of the thirteen planets of the Union.

The emperor ruled over Covenant while the governors and governesses were representatives from the thirteen planets, respectively. Though none possessed power over the physical territories. There were more planets and moons in the Union, but those thirteen were the largest.

At the end of the long table was a man in his mid-forties.

Titus Valerius, emperor of the Union—the largest intergalactic alliance in the surrounding solar systems—was a man still in his prime, though silver lined his raven hair and beard. Around his eyes were laugh lines, but deep caverns bracketed either side of his lips. Atop his head was the gilded crown of the emperor. If that wasn't enough to identify him, he wore a violet, jade, and gold cape with fur lining.

Seeing them enter, he rose from his seat of honor at the end of the table, smiling.

"Welcome!" Titus's voice echoed between the pillars, booming far louder than the gurgling fountains in the four corners of the room. "I have been expecting you."

Celeste strode forward, making a sweeping bow. "I am Celeste Beckett, the Mistress of Cirque du Borge. We are here upon your request."

Servants pulled the emperor's chair back, and he strode around the table to meet them.

Guards and servants lined the room, and the governors

and governesses turned to watch them. None bothered to stand, but some watched with a slight interest in their eyes. The circus's soldier escort parted, but they didn't leave. Instead, they surrounded the cyborgs with their hands on the guns or swords at their belts.

The emperor took Celeste's hand, placing a kiss on her fingers.

If only he knew about those talons.

"It is an honor to meet you, Your Imperial Highness." Celeste raised her eyes to his.

Gwen blinked.

It was odd seeing any measure of modesty—fake as it likely was—from this woman. The very same woman who ordered the murder of dozens of cyborgs and the sale of those who remained to flesh traders.

"The pleasure is mine."

Titus turned to the circus. "Tomorrow at sundown, you will perform for myself and the Union Council."

The performers around Gwen whispered excitedly.

Although anyone with at least Abrecan's intelligence could have guessed this was the reason they were here, it was as though it clicked for the first time. Most of the performers smiled, shifting in skirts and straightening jackets.

"After the performances, I would request a meeting with the representatives from the circus," Titus continued. "It's my hope that you might answer a few of the Council's delicate questions about the technology behind cyborgs.

"For now, I invite you to take the east wing. Rooms have been prepared for all as well as a feast in your honor. Eat, drink, and rest tonight. See the sights if you wish, but do not stray outside of the palace grounds. My city is safe for its citizens, but they do harbor unfortunate feelings toward cyborgs."

And whose fault is that?

"Welcome to Allegiant," Titus said.

Knowing a dismissal when she saw one, Gwen turned to leave, following the shuffling performers out of the throne room.

Collecting her things, she re-sheathed her knives in the hidden pockets of her dress and returned her pistol to its holster.

When they arrived in the east wing, dozens of rooms were open and prepared. The beds were made with clean sheets smelling of lavender, vanilla, and rose petals. Curtains had been pulled back to reveal windows several stories up.

It appeared the emperor wished to store his cyborg guests in a massive tower—away from his human citizens. How kind.

Still, he was arranging a meeting between the Union Council and the show management team—one that would hopefully end in the social and legal acceptance of cyborgs.

As everyone got ready for the emperor's dinner, picking rooms, unpacking their bags, and redressing, Gwen chose a room near the stairs and tossed her pack onto the bed and placed her skimmer in the closet. She immediately left in search of Marzanna and Akio. They had picked the vacant rooms next door.

As she entered, hearing their conversations, her heart immediately dropped.

"Most of the circus is dead," Akio said. "They're just going to keep picking us off one by one no matter where we go. What's the point?"

Sighing, she limped into the room and closed the door. The others turned to her. "Oh, good. I was hoping I'd catch you guys." She turned to Marzanna. "Did you share my plan with Akio?"

Marzanna nodded.

"What's the point?" Akio repeated. "We're cyborgs. The emperor might say some pretty words now, but nothing is going to change. The Council will turn their backs on us *again*.

There are no safe places for cyborgs—especially not Allegiant. Hell, even Bastian left us."

They were just words, yet it felt as though a knife had plunged between Gwen's ribs.

"Something's wrong with him." Even as Gwen spoke, her heart dropped to her feet. "He's refusing to speak with me. Something must have happened to him. Maybe we can follow him tonight, see if we can get him alone and figure out what's really going on."

"Get it through your head, Gwen," Akio said. "He's decided to throw in his lot with the show management team, after all. He won't help us anymore."

"That's not true," Gwen persisted. "He wouldn't just abandon—"

Me.

Would he?

Marzanna strode over, placing a hand on Gwen's shoulder. "I'm sorry. I don't know why he left us, but he did."

Swallowing back the lump in her throat, Gwen shook her head. This wasn't happening. Something was wrong. It had to be.

Slowly, an idea formed in her mind.

If they wouldn't help her, she knew someone who would.

"Please rehearse tonight," she said. "You did great on Jinx, but that's no reason to stop practicing. We still have a chance to secure patronage. Go easy on your shoulder, Akio. I'll join you guys when I can."

Akio threw his hands up in the air. "Are you leaving us now, too?"

"I'm going to get to the bottom of this."

Marzanna squeezed Gwen's shoulder before dropping her hand. "Just let him go. He isn't worth it."

"Yes, he is."

Running down the hall, she ducked her head into room after room. Several doors were slightly ajar. Knocking, she pushed the door open, only to find several of the performers getting their jitters out.

One man leaned against the wall, his cock free of his trousers. A second man kneeled before him, his mouth on the other man's cock and a hand working the base.

When the door swung open, the man on his knees looked up from his work, his lips red.

"Get the fuck out," said the man whose hardened cock stood proudly above unzipped trousers.

Clearing her throat, Gwen said, "If you want privacy, close the fucking door next time."

She kept going, hoping to find the one person she'd avoided for weeks. The one person she swore she'd never speak to again.

When she finally found the room she sought, she knocked.

Rora opened the door a few seconds later, arms crossed. "What do you want?"

"I need a favor," Gwen said.

"Why should I do anything for you?" Rora demanded. "You wouldn't listen to me before."

"Because I can give you what you want most in the world."

"Oh? And what's that?"

Gwen exhaled heavily. "Me."

CHAPTER 31

Rora laughed. "You flatter yourself." But she didn't close the door.

Looking over her shoulder, Gwen glanced around. Countless performers roamed the hall, moving from room to room. Some held bottles of champagne and glasses in their hands while others were in various stages of undress, bringing accessories and makeup trays back and forth between rooms.

Drowning out the memories of what happened on Jinx.

"I need your help to figure out what's going on with Bastian," Gwen said, keeping her voice low. "Something's wrong with him. It's like he's a different person."

Rora rolled her eyes. "I'm not going to get mixed up in a lover's quarrel with my ex-girlfriend's ex."

"In exchange," Gwen continued, bringing her hand up to hold the door before Rora could close it, "I'll tinker your hand to make sure it's up to snuff before tomorrow's performance. And if the emperor does offer you patronage... I will come with you."

And be your cyborg tinkerer.

Rora hesitated, and Gwen saw what she sought in the

woman's eyes—greed, eagerness, the desire to win. The acrobat knew as well as Gwen that, at some point, her refurbished hand would sputter out. She'd need a new one or regular tinkering at the very least.

Gwen pressed on, knowing she had Rora right where she wanted her. "You want to win patronage and stay on with the emperor or one of the members of his court, right? I can help you. I can be the very thing that gives your performance an edge."

Leaning against the doorframe, Rora crossed her arms. "You know what that means, right? If I get patronage, you'll leave the circus and everyone in it behind. You'll remain here in court with me."

Gwen swallowed back the tightness forming in her throat.

For weeks, she'd tried spying on Bastian without success, courtesy of her damned leg. The others wouldn't help her. They could hardly help themselves. Not to mention, they believed Bastian had left her. But in her gut, she knew he wouldn't do that. He just wouldn't. With no one else to turn to, that left the last person in the world she'd thought she'd team up with again—and at a great cost.

If she was going to save Bastian, she might have to give him up.

If she couldn't convince him to attempt to secure patronage alongside Rora, Akio, and Marzanna, he would continue with Cirque du Borge. At best, if she did somehow convince him to vie for patronage, there was still the chance that the emperor would only choose one or two acts. But if all went according to plan and Gwen could somehow get him out of the Mistress's clutches, at least he'd have a chance to live a happy life.

Without Gwen.

"I know," she managed.

Rora raised her eyebrows. "What do you need me to do?"

"To start, I'd like a date for tonight's dinner," Gwen said.

"Help getting ready, too, I suppose." She gestured to her unruly hair. "And a nimble person who can help me spy on Mr. Bastian Kabir."

Slowly, Rora opened her door. "Alright, then. Let's do this."

When they got ready in Rora's room, it was entirely different from the first time. Neither of them spoke more than strictly necessary, nor was there the tangible excitement that had been there before the masquerade ball on Apparatus. Both women elected to wear black gowns the color of a moonless sky. The gowns were slim-fitting to the waist with narrow skirts—easier to sneak around, should that be necessary.

As they did the finishing touches to their hair and makeup, Gwen explained her plan to Rora.

"I'll approach Bastian at the ball," Gwen said, ignoring the softness of Rora's hands as she fixed her hair. "If I still can't get anything out of him, we'll follow him and see what he's up to and learn anything we can. He's been attached to Celeste ever since the third competition."

"I'd been wondering about that," Rora said. "He's always hated her. She treated him like garbage when he was her apprentice, or so I've been told. It's strange he'd be spending so much time with her."

"He made a bargain with her," Gwen said. "During the third competition, when the Mistress threatened to extract my implant and leave me on Jinx, he offered to become her apprentice again to save me. But he wouldn't blindly follow her like this. Something's wrong. I just know it."

Rora's fingers stopped moving in her hair as she looked directly at Gwen through the mirror. "You didn't... try to go through with your plan, did you?"

"Of course, I did," Gwen snapped. "With minor alterations. And thanks to you—and the Mistress—I have a broken leg to show for it, and Bastian is... well, something is wrong." Her eyes darkened. "If you hadn't told Abrecan, none of this would have happened."

"I didn't mean to!" Rora said, voice raised. "I would never want to hurt you, Akio, or Marzanna. Even Bastian. You're my friends! I just... When Abrecan threatened my arm, I panicked. What would you have done if he'd threatened to rip out your eye?"

"Fought like hell."

"And when that wasn't enough?"

"Well, I suppose I'd have one less eye."

Rora threw her hands up. "You'll never understand what it's like to want something so bad you'd do anything to get it."

"I wanted you!" Gwen yelled, face heated from rage. "I wanted you," she said in a quieter voice. "Why else do you think I'd break the rules against making and installing new implants? I wanted what was best for you. I wanted you to be happy." A barking laugh escaped her. "And you played me like a fool."

"I'm sorry," Rora said. "Despite what you might think, what we shared wasn't entirely a lie. I didn't mean for it to get that far, but it wasn't all an act."

Gwen didn't bother responding, not believing a damned word. Rora finished Gwen's hair in silence before moving to her own.

When they were finished, they walked down countless hallways to the massive ballroom. Unfortunately, Gwen needed both her crutch and Rora's assistance to move down the halls in her gown. Other performers strode in front and behind them, alongside friends or dates. Gwen couldn't help but notice how far fewer performers there were since the last ball she'd gone to with Rora. She'd been hopeful then, excited to get to know this beautiful, dark acrobat.

Now, she held the arm of the woman she'd thought of as her enemy only hours ago—the woman who'd betrayed Gwen and her friends to Abrecan. The woman Gwen had been willing to give up everything for in her moment of despair when she'd tried to run away on a flesh trader vessel.

But Gwen was a different woman now, too.

She realized she had to fight for the things she wanted most. Once, it had been her life—she had to be willing to give up her freedoms as a human and become one of the most hated people of the Union to survive her brain tumor. Then it had been fighting for the performers of Cirque du Borge as they were picked off one by one in the competition. Now, it was for the man she loved.

It hadn't been until the absence of the stoic ringleader during their trip Covenant that she'd fully realized how hard she'd fallen for Bastian Kabir. His absence weighed on her heart like a physical pain. She longed for his companionship, counsel, steadfast attitude, and approach to conflict. And every moment she'd seen him with Celeste was like a kick to the tits.

On the main level of the emperor's castle, massive doors three stories tall were open. Gwen and Rora followed the line of performers walking toward the music and the warm, yellow light spilling out from the ballroom. Human soldiers stood on either side of the door, but as they walked in, she noticed there were also plenty of armed watchmen patrolling as well.

The room was even larger than the ballroom on Grandstand.

At the back were stained glass windows expanding the length of a wall taller than most inns. A buffet had been set up on opposite sides of the room—long tables with countless delicacies, smelling of roasted duck, baked apple, and soft cheeses. Directly in front of the door was the dance floor, and beyond it were round tables with cushioned armchairs. Many of the performers had already started dancing to the upbeat melody the band played. But Gwen couldn't help but notice their hesitancy.

It would seem the memory of another dance floor

surrounded by watchmen with bloodied batons couldn't be wiped from their memories so easily.

Some performers sat at tables, but more stood throughout the room in small clusters, speaking with one another. Because that's all there were at this dinner party—cyborgs.

"It appears no one was able to attend the ball in our honor," Gwen said. "How surprising."

Why would the emperor go to such lengths to host a dinner party… only to have no one but the "guests of honor" attend? Why not forego the farce altogether and save his resources for the day he intended to speak with the Union Council about the Cyborg Prohibition Law?

Rora strode into the room, and Gwen barely kept pace with her before they situated themselves before a punch bowl. Bastian wasn't there, not yet anyway.

Not long after, Marzanna and Akio arrived, wearing various looks of surprise to see Gwen and Rora together. Crossing the room, they stopped in front of them.

"Ladies." Marzanna nodded to them, an eyebrow raised in Gwen's direction.

Gwen cleared her throat. "I have a plan."

"I'm sorry," Rora blurted.

Starting, Gwen turned to look at her, as did all their friends. A look of relief spread across Marzanna's face, while Akio had an air of skeptical interest.

"I never meant to reveal the plan," Rora said. "I panicked when Abrecan threatened my hand, and I'm so sorry for everything it cost you. But he lied in his note. I would never, ever betray you. You're my best friends."

Marzanna crossed her arms. "Whatever you intended to do, Abrecan learned of our plan and told the Mistress. The watchmen broke Gwen's leg in retribution, and Akio was shot. Things might have gone better, don't you think?"

"*I'm sorry*. How many times do you want me to say it? Ten times? A thousand? I'll do it. But I didn't mean for any of this to happen." Rora's eyes filled with tears. "If I was as heartless as you think, I wouldn't have stepped into the line of fire when Akio was shot. I would've stayed safely at the back of the stage. But I didn't, and I wouldn't abandon you." She turned to Gwen. "Any of you."

Gwen's lips pressed together.

"I wish I could take it all back," Rora said.

Glancing back and forth between them, Marzanna sighed. "It's life or death, Rora. Either we fight to live, or we can die like the Union wants us to. But we do not hurt our own. We are all each other has in this world." When she looked at Gwen, a spark of hope returned to her eyes. "And I'm not ready to roll over just yet."

Gwen smiled, nodding.

Welcome back, Marzanna.

"Do whatever you feel you must," Marzanna said. "Tomorrow, I plan on being fucking spectacular and gaining the emperor's patronage to get out of this hellhole we call a circus. I have no intention of returning to Apparatus after tomorrow's performance."

Rora opened and closed her mouth, studying Marzanna and Akio before finally nodding. "I hope we can all acquire patronage together." A genuine smile spread across her lips. "That would be a dream come true in more ways than one."

"Not that this isn't fun, but I'm starving," Gwen said. "I need to eat something before we become spy ninjas. Catch you guys soon."

Marzanna spared a less than confident glance toward Gwen's leg, but she said nothing as Gwen took Rora's arm and they hobbled over to the buffet tables.

As Gwen shoved several dumplings down her throat, she glanced toward the entrance, and her heart nearly stopped.

Dressed in trim black pants, a vest, and matching jacket, Bastian strode into the room. His top hat was tipped slightly forward, and he wore a vacant smile. He held his cane in one hand and Celeste's arm in the other. Matching her vibrant nails and hair, Celeste wore yet another scarlet gown; only this one had red beading throughout and a neckline that fell off her shoulders.

Gwen had never stopped to look at the woman before, but now she could see just how beautiful Celeste was. Her curly, red hair shined in the artificial light of the ballroom, and her gray eyes swept the room, taking in everything at once.

They strode toward the dance floor and were immediately swept into the dance. Their steps were so synchronized that it was as though they were made for each other, for this very moment.

Gwen clenched her fists so hard that her short nails dug into her palms, breaking the skin.

"Chill out, tinkerer," Rora said, taking her arm. "If I recall correctly, in this dance, you're supposed to switch partners during the song. Let's see if we can get you close to him." Pausing, she eyed Gwen with suspicion. "You didn't wear your boots again, did you?"

"Of course, I did."

Rolling her eyes, Rora towed her onto the dance floor.

Gwen limped behind her, crutch in tow. "Is this really a good idea? I'm not exactly in the best dancing condition."

"How else do you expect to get close to him?"

With nothing to say in response, Gwen allowed Rora to lead the dance. Like most dances, it was one Gwen didn't know, so she stomped around the dance floor with as much grace as an elephant in a tutu.

Rora glared at Gwen when she accidentally stepped on her foot, and she mumbled an apology. When it was nearly time to switch partners, something Gwen only knew because Rora whispered it into her ear, they moved as close as they could to Celeste and Bastian, neither of whom spoke during the dance. It was odd since most of the couples chatted as they flitted across the dance floor.

When the music changed keys and everyone started swapping partners, Rora practically shoved Gwen into Bastian's arms. As Gwen stumbled forward, her leg screamed in protest. She reached a hand out to catch herself, which he caught automatically. Despite the warmth of his hands, they felt cold. His eyes connected with hers, and no recognition sparked in them. It was as though he stared at a complete stranger.

Celeste narrowed her eyes, but she, too, found another partner, as did Rora.

Clearing her throat, Gwen straightened. Without a word, Bastian took her right hand in his and placed his other on her lower back as they moved throughout the song. She did her best to follow Bastian and the other dancers, but she was far slower thanks to the crutch under her left arm. As she struggled to keep pace, all she could think about was the softness of his skin and how he'd kissed her on the deck of *Obedient*.

Get your head in the game. Say something to him.

When she cleared her throat, rather than a delicate, ladylike interruption, she sounded like she was choking on her supper.

"How's your evening going?" As soon as she spoke the words, she nearly winced.

What the hell was that?

"Fine, thank you," Bastian replied.

When he didn't say anything further, she tried again. "You look nice. Is this a new suit?"

"Yes, it is."

Oh, for the love of—

"Did Celeste pick it out for you?"

"Yes."

"You've been spending a lot of time with her recently."

"Shouldn't we all spend more time with our Mistress?"

"I've been meaning to talk to you." Her crutch bumped

into Bastian's shoe, and she started to apologize, but his face held no recognition of anything having happened. Did he not feel pain? "It's about what you told me on *Obedient* before the third competition."

His eyes scanned the dancers beyond them. "I don't recall us speaking."

She started. Could he be lying? But she pressed on.

"You'd told me about your family and what they made you do…"

"Cirque du Borge is my family," he said. "The people I knew before don't matter any longer. Performers don't need their memories to heed their calling. All that matters is that our Mistress is pleased."

The music changed, and the performers once again changed partners.

"Good evening, Ms. Grimm." Bastian took the hand of a woman in a bright blue gown. But Gwen couldn't see her face through her tears.

Turning, she pushed through the dancers and off the dance floor. Leaning over, she stood beside one of the food tables, pretending to reach for one of the delicacies. Meanwhile, angry tears streamed down her cheeks.

Rora appeared a few moments later.

"Well?"

Gwen turned, ready to snap at her. She wanted to snap at anyone, but Rora especially. All she could feel was the anger and despair threading through her veins. "He doesn't remember anything. It's like he's a completely different person. Sound familiar?"

Rora froze. "Are you crying?"

"What the hell does it look like?" Pushing past her, Gwen limped toward the massive windows at the back of the room and walked out the door. She shuffled down the terrace, seating herself on a stone bench. Not far off, she could hear the laughter and chatting of lovers in the gardens.

For the first time in years, she allowed herself to feel defeated. Gwendolyn Grimm, the Union's best tinkerer, had found a problem she couldn't fix. And she felt utterly useless.

Tears tumbled down her face, and her whole body shook with sobs. She placed her head in her hands.

Skirts rustled nearby, but she didn't bother to look up. A moment later, a hand was on her back.

"You really do love him." It was Rora's voice, which held a hint of surprised amazement.

Gwen didn't bother to reply.

Slowly, Rora lowered herself onto the bench beside Gwen. "I thought your relationship with him was just a rebound. You getting back at me. But now I can see that what you have is real."

They listened to whistling crickets and the croaking of frogs for a time—the sounds broken only by the rhythmic thumping of lovemaking somewhere in the boxwood hedges.

"You can't give up now," Rora said at last. "He needs you now more than ever."

Gwen wiped her face with the back of her hand. "Nothing I do matters. I tried to help the performers, but all I've done is butcher half of them to death."

"And the rest are alive," Rora added. "You discovered something isn't right with the chips."

Gwen sniffed. "Some good that did. We still can't remember our pasts. People are *dying*, and I've lost the person I wanted to save the most."

"Without you, I'd be in a coma or dead, as would Marzanna." Rora's jaw set with determination. "If we can be saved, so can Bastian."

"I can't reach him," Gwen said. "I tried, but it's like he's not there."

"The Mistress must have done something to him," Rora said. "Why else would he be following her around? He hates the woman, for goodness' sake. Not to mention, if they can take our memories, who's to say they can't do other things to us?" Rora took her shoulders, forcing Gwen to meet her eye. "It's time to buckle up, buttercup. If you want to save your man, you're going to have to fight."

Slowly, Gwen nodded.

Rora was right. She couldn't give up now. She couldn't let the Mistress win.

Bastian needed her. It was time to fight back.

CHAPTER 32

Rora stood and extended her cyborg hand toward
Gwen. The very same hand that Gwen had made
for her; the hand that started this mess in the first
place.

Against all odds and common sense, she took it.

Rora guided Gwen back into the ballroom. "Let's see what
we can learn about your man tonight."

Looking around, Gwen couldn't see Bastian or Celeste
anywhere.

They hurried over to where Marzanna and Akio had
seated themselves at a table with several other cyborgs.

"Have you seen Bastian?" Gwen asked.

Brows furrowed, Marzanna pointed toward the main door.
"He just left with Celeste."

With a murmured thanks, Gwen and Rora hurried out of
the ballroom. To the right, she saw a flash of red disappearing
around a corner.

"That way!" Gwen grabbed Rora's arm, speed-hobbling
down the halls.

"Where are they going?" Rora asked as they turned down

hall after hall in the opposite direction of the bedrooms in the east wing.

"They must be heading to the courtyard," Gwen said.

Turning down several more hallways, they eventually entered the main foyer. Celeste and Bastian exited the entrance to the palace, which several guards held open. Rora grabbed Gwen's arm, and they crouched behind a column. Leaning forward, they peered around it, trying to listen.

"Don't stay out after dark," one of the guards said. "Even the palace grounds aren't safe for your kind at night."

Celeste nodded, smiling. "We won't be long. We want to check on our beasts, make sure they're settling in."

They disappeared beyond the main palace door, which was bolted behind them.

Gwen frowned. "They're going to the stables? Now?"

Shrugging, Rora pulled her toward the door. "Come on!"

They strode forward, hands clasped. Rora leaned into Gwen, a bright, random smile on her face as though Gwen had just said something hilarious.

"Flirt with me."

Gwen blinked, not understanding, but then she looked at the guards and realization dawned.

Slinging her free arm over Rora's shoulders, she leaned close and nibbled Rora's earlobe before whispering sweet nothings into her ear. Laughing, Rora swatted at her playfully, a sway to her step. Gwen followed her lead.

When they came up to the guards, one said, "What's your business?"

"I want to show my darling the town," Gwen said. "We've never been to Allegiant before."

Although she couldn't see the man's face beneath his helmet, she could have sworn she saw him lifting an eyebrow.

He doesn't believe us.

Without pausing to think about the stupidity of her actions, she leaned in and pressed her lips to Rora's. Just as she had all those weeks ago, Rora yielded easily to Gwen. The acrobat smelled of her usual rose and peach blossom perfume, which plumed into Gwen's nose as Rora's breasts press against her abdomen.

Parting Rora's lips, she slipped her tongue into the shorter woman's mouth, kissing her for a moment longer before letting go. When she did, Rora breathed heavily, her lips reddened and eyes glazed.

The soldier harrumphed. "I'll tell you the same as I've told every cyborg who's approached this door. Be back before dark. Otherwise, things will end badly for your kind."

Gwen winked at him with her human eye. "You're a doll."

Unbolting the door, he opened it, and they strode out.

On the other side of the door, several guards stood with long guns tipped with spearpoints. Gwen paused to smile at them before staggering down the street with Rora, the two of them laughing at nothing at all.

When they were out of sight of the main door, Gwen removed her arm from Rora's neck. "Where are the stables?"

Rora ran a finger over her lips absently. Clearing her throat, she lowered her hand and pointed down an immaculate cobblestone street. "I think I saw it this way when we were walking in."

A few minutes later, they were met with the smell of manure.

As they turned down the end of a street, she spotted the entrance to the stables, where a stable boy stood guard.

"That's it?" Gwen gestured to the lack of guards. "Are they not afraid of thieves?"

Rora shrugged. "I guess the emperor is confident within his own walls. Maybe the punishment for crimes here is much steeper than it is on other planets."

The stables consisted of a massive stone building two stories tall, nestled between stone buildings on either side and separated by narrow alleys. From where they stood in the shadows across the street, Gwen thought she could see windows on the side of the stables. She pointed at them.

"Think you can get up there?"

Pulling up her skirt, Rora revealed a rope and small grappling hook.

"How the hell did you hide that in there?" Gwen asked. "I would have stabbed myself in the crotch."

"Eloquent, as always, Gwen." She gestured to the stable boy. "Distract him, would you?"

Gwen scratched her head. How the hell was she supposed to do that? But it was now or never.

Striding from the shadows, she ambled toward the stable's front entrance. The boy looked up from where he sat on a wooden stool behind a counter. When he saw Gwen's cyborg eye, his face went from polite attention to obvious disgust.

Nostrils flaring, he said, "Can I help you?"

"I hope so." Moving slowly on her crutch, she stopped and leaned on the counter. She ran her tongue over her teeth, blinking slowly. "Can you tell me where the nearest tavern is? It seems I've lost my way."

From the corner of her eye, she caught a flash of movement as Rora crossed the street and disappeared down the alley beside the stable.

"There are no taverns in the palace proper," the boy said. "You'll have to return to the main city." In a softer voice, he added, "Or whatever dark hell you came from."

There was a sudden clank of what must be the grappling hook against the stone before a louder clattering on the cobblestones.

The boy stood. "What was—"

"When I was your age, I thought cyborgs were abominations, too," Gwen lied, slurring her speech. The boy hesitated, uncertain whether to leave this deranged cyborg alone—to possibly enter the stables and eat the animals—or check on the sound. "Unnatural, with the technology. No one should have that kind of power." She tapped her cyborg eye. "That was, until I got this. I'd always been good at figuring out what a person really wants when I was human. But it wasn't until they installed this eye that I went from discerning men's desires to seeing into their minds."

The boy's eyes widened.

Stars, he couldn't be older than fourteen.

Gwen shrugged. "I never thought such a thing was possible. Now that I have this ability, I realize it isn't a gift but a curse. I'd always thought people had pure intentions overall. Only the few vile ones locked up were the dark of heart. But do you know the nasty, vile thoughts men have? It isn't the machine that makes cyborgs monsters. It's us, our human nature. The machine only amplifies what's already there."

"Th-that's not true," the boy stammered, looking around. "The machine makes you evil."

She allowed her eyes to flicker to the desk, where she spotted oils behind the counter and grease stains around the crotch of his pants.

Thank the stars I'm not a teenager anymore.

Cyborg eye whirring, she looked hard at the boy, pretending to read his thoughts. "Ah, I see. You're one of them."

"One of who?"

"You're one of the folks driven by lust. Shouldn't you be keeping guard? It seems you've been quite distracted by other activities this evening."

His eyes widened in horror. "How could you know that?"

"I told you already." She pointed at her eye. "Cyborg powers."

She hadn't heard the sound of the grappling hook in a few minutes, but she wasn't sure if Rora had gotten into the upper-story window yet. Racking her brain, she tried to think of something else to keep the boy occupied.

"You saw someone not long ago." She pretended to look

deeply into him. "A tall fellow with olive skin and a woman with bright red hair."

The boy's eyes widened further, if that was possible. Slowly, he nodded, glancing over his shoulder. But there was only a massive wood wall, behind which horses whinnied. At the side of the wall was a doorway with a half-gate.

"They came around here a few minutes before you." He paused, looking her up and down. "I thought you said you were looking for a tavern."

There was a loud crashing outside.

Flinching, she glanced backward. The boy was on his feet at once, pausing long enough to give her a look that said, *"Don't touch anything!"* before he disappeared around the corner of the building.

"Fuck." Turning, she started to shuffle after him.

"Gwen!"

It was Rora. She was in the alley on the opposite side of the building the boy had run off to. Gwen hurried over and hid beside her. Even in the shadows, Rora seemed pale, her dark features having lost some of their usual warmth.

"What did you find?" Gwen demanded, surprised to find her hands gripping Rora's shoulders.

"You should probably see this for yourself." She gestured to the rope and grappling hook, which dangled from the window one story above them.

"I'm in no shape to climb. That's why you're here. Just tell me what you saw."

Rora shook her head. "You really should see this. Now."

There was an edge of urgency to Rora's voice that froze the words she'd been about to speak.

"There's a stack of crates around back," Rora said. "You should be able to climb up to see through another window. Come on."

Nodding, she followed Rora behind the building. Hiking up her dress and tucking her skirts into the belt at her waist, she dropped her crutch on the ground before climbing up the crate. With Rora's help, she eventually made it.

She peered down through the glassless window, which overlooked dozens of stalls two stories below. Nearly fifty watchmen were stationed throughout the stable. One stood at each animal stall, as well as two at every entrance and exit, and more walked the length of the building. The cyborg animals, including the red dragon, were within their cages. At the stall in the back corner was no animal at all, but a man.

Bastian kneeled at the center of the stall, utterly motionless. A table had been set up next to a wall beside him where Celeste had an open tool kit and several portable mainframes with screens where green text flowed upward. She held something small in her hand that Gwen couldn't see. Looking back at Bastian, she realized what she'd missed before.

His port was open on the back of his neck.

She turned to Rora, eyes wide. Recognition filled both of their eyes.

Celeste was tinkering with his chip. Had that been why Bastian hadn't seemed to remember Gwen or their conversations? Could Celeste have changed his memories?

Or deleted them?

Standing, Celeste went over to Bastian, running a nail along the side of his cheek. "I appreciate your assistance, my pet." She walked behind him, placing a chip into his head. "Can't be too careful with everything so close to unfolding. I want to be certain you understand your orders for tomorrow, and what to do if things don't go according to the plan."

She held something between her fingers, which she slipped into a hidden pocket of her scarlet gown.

"I doubt you'll ever need this chip again. Once you kill the emperor tomorrow, you'll likely be tried and executed. There will be no point in returning your memories or personality to you. As charming as you once were, I don't need the old Bastian Kabir. I need my little soldier."

As she spoke, Bastian didn't move. He simply stared ahead at the wall.

"I didn't bother to seek out most of my performers. I didn't care what their background was. But Carlisle? I sent him to find you. I needed someone with combat experience who was forgettable. And you, my darling, are most certainly forgettable."

She waved her hand dismissively in the air as though Bastian had spoken.

"Sure, Abrecan knows his way around a bow, but a gun is far more subtle and far harder to detect. Besides, the man is as wide as a mountain. The minute he walks into the room, everyone will be watching him, wondering just what violence he's capable of. No one will be looking at the thin, dark ringleader.

"But my, were you resistant in becoming my apprentice again. I needed a way to get you away from the others and test my new coding. I suppose I should be thanking the little tinkerer for being so predictable. Though, she has been quite the nuisance."

She patted his cheek. "Rise, darling. Go back to your rooms, speak to no one, and prepare yourself for tomorrow. We won't meet again until the show."

Rising from where he kneeled in the stall, he brushed his knees off and left without a word. Even from here, Gwen could see the vacant look in his eyes.

Rage coursed through her, as powerful and engulfing as a black hole in deep space.

Turning, she slid down on her ass, moving clumsily from one crate to the next, ignoring the screaming pain in her leg. When her feet touched the ground, she scooped up her crutch, already moving toward the front of the stable. She was going to *kill* Celeste.

Before she cleared the end of the alley, a wrist caught her. She slowed to a stop, trying to pull her arm free.

"Gwen! Don't!" Rora hissed.

"Let go! Didn't you see what happened? Celeste messed with his chip. She's going to force Bastian to kill the emperor!"

And for what?

Gwen's mind raced, her heart along with it. "We have to help him."

"We will!" Rora hauled Gwen back into the shadows of the alley. "But not like this. Didn't you see all the watchmen in there? We'll become mindless zombies just like Bastian if we go charging in there."

Stopping, she turned toward Rora. Her face was flushed, and anger still coursed through her, but she knew Rora was right.

"We'll help him, but not like this," Rora said. "We have to be smart."

Damn you. Why do you have to be so levelheaded right now?

Gwen wanted to shoot something—or someone.

"Fine," she bit out. "Let me go."

As Rora released her wrist, she heard footsteps outside and watched as Bastian walked up the street, back toward the castle.

You are anything but forgettable.

Tears filled her eyes.

"What has she done to you?"

Rora grabbed Gwen's hands and turned her to face her. "I'll bet you my new hand that Celeste has Bastian's chip with his memories. That's what she slipped into her dress."

Gwen nodded, remembering. "We have to get it back from her tomorrow somehow. During the performance, maybe. And stop Bastian from…"

Killing the emperor.

Exhaling heavily, Rora looped her arm through Gwen's and pulled her back toward the palace. "What I want to know is, why does she want to kill the emperor in the first place? He's trying to help change the law. He's on our side!"

Gwen's fists clenched as the palace came into view. "And why not do it herself?"

"Should we tell him?"

For a moment, Gwen considered whether or not they should reveal Celeste's plans to the emperor, but she eventually shook her head. "He won't believe us. At best, he would turn us over to Celeste. At worst, we would be tossed into the dungeon. Either way, we wouldn't be able to help anyone."

As they passed back through the palace's main gates and into the castle, Rora said, "Time to make one of your master plans."

Indeed, it was. But how the hell was she supposed to get close enough to Celeste tomorrow to swipe Bastian's chip while still keeping an eye on the man programmed to assassinate the emperor?

Somehow, she'd have to manage it. Otherwise, none of them would make it off the planet alive. With the emperor and all order gone, the humans would slaughter the cyborgs. Celeste didn't know it yet, but she was about to spark civil unrest—and with the cyborgs at the center. She was about to make them into the very monsters people believed them to be.

Monsters that everyone wanted dead.

CHAPTER 33

Heart heavier than a large woman's tits, Gwen limped back into the emperor's palace.

"Go. Hang with the others." She turned toward their rooms. "I'm going to turn in for the night."

Rather than going to the ballroom, Rora followed Gwen, offering her an arm. "I'm not much in the mood for a party, so I'll walk you upstairs."

Slowly, Gwen took her arm, and the two of them made their way back to Rora's room.

Eager to return to her tinkerer's leathers once in Rora's room, Gwen gestured to the back of her black gown. "Would you mind helping me with this? I wasn't good with dresses without a broken leg. And my ability right now is downright atrocious."

A faint smile touched Rora's lips. "Sure."

Immediately, Gwen regretted her decision.

When hands lightly grazed her hips, she became all too aware of Rora's touch. Fire skirted down her chest, and she swallowed instinctively. Slowly, Rora unlaced the back of Gwen's gown. The sudden lack of pressure against her chest had nothing to do with the gasping breaths escaping her.

Get a hold of yourself. This is the woman who betrayed you, who used you.

But Gwen's body paid no mind to such things.

As Rora reached for each button, undoing them individually, her fingers traced the skin on Gwen's back, sending gooseflesh down her arms.

Eventually, the dress hung loose, and Gwen had no option but to turn to Rora.

Rora's dark eyes flickered back and forth between Gwen's. The deep neckline of Rora's dress did nothing to hide the rapid rising and falling of her chest as she breathed.

It took every ounce of control not to reach out and run her fingers along where Rora's breasts stopped and her dress began.

Slowly, Rora turned her back to Gwen. "Undo mine?"

This is a very bad idea.

Even as the need for Bastian coursed through her veins, a very different need for Rora settled between Gwen's thighs.

Nodding, she reached up, fumbling with the intricate laces at the back of Rora's gown as she balanced with a crutch under her arm. Pain shot down her leg at the lack of support, but she ignored it. Her nerve endings felt like they were on fire. As one lace loosened, then another, Rora's gown slowly slipped off her shoulders... and then onto the ground.

Quite suddenly, Gwen forgot to breathe.

Beneath her black gown, Rora was completely naked.

How had *that* detail escaped her when they were getting ready?

Gwen took in the sight of Rora.

Her light brown skin shone warmly in the faint artificial light of the room. She was lean and strong, her arms and legs corded with fine muscles. Legs sculpted of granite turned slowly as Rora spun to face Gwen. Her ass and breasts were round and full, carrying the weight of Gwen's gaze and desire.

Rora looked at Gwen, her eyes holding a question.

She only wants you now that she got what she wants—a new hand and a chance to perform for the emperor. She used you, for fuck's sake. With the scraps of her remaining self-control, Gwen clutched her gown to her chest and cleared her throat. "We should get dressed. Then I'll see to that hand of yours, as promised."

Slowly, Rora nodded before grabbing clothes and heading to the washroom. When she closed the door behind her, Gwen breathed a sigh of relief before changing into her leathers. But as she did so, all she wanted was some time alone in her bedroom with some lubricants and candlelight to work off some... tension. Alas, she'd have no such relief anytime soon.

When Rora emerged from the washroom, she wore a nighttime dress that did nothing to hide her figure—or her nakedness underneath.

In silence, Gwen saw to Rora's hand. Some things needed tinkering, but for the most part, it had held up well since its installation.

As she finished, Rora said, "Did you see anyone in the hallway when we were walking back?"

Slowly, Gwen shook her head. "They must still be at the party."

"Maybe."

When Gwen rose to leave, Rora caught her hand.

"I know I have no right to ask this but..." Rora trailed off before taking a deep breath and pressing on. "Would you stay here tonight? I hate the idea of being alone—especially with what the Mistress has planned for tomorrow."

On the outside, such a request *might* make sense.

If the Mistress intended to attempt to assassinate the emperor tomorrow, having your sort-of-not-really allies close to you in case of an emergency was logical. Hell, it could even be considered an extra level of precaution should the Mistress and her watchmen come in search of Gwen to finish what they started with her legs. They wouldn't know where to find her.

But this was Rora.

A woman who had betrayed Gwen. A woman who could evoke an immediate reaction from Gwen's body even now. A woman who was helping her rescue Bastian, the man she loved.

"I shouldn't," Gwen said. "Stars, I want to, but I don't trust myself around you. And, well, I don't trust you."

Rora nodded. "I earned that. Still, if you stay, you could take the bed. I'll sleep on the sofa, and it will be perfectly respectable. Besides, shouldn't we stay close in case we need to move quickly tomorrow to find Bastian?"

For Bastian, Gwen would do anything.

Exhaling heavily, she said, "Fine. But I snore."

Gwen awoke the next morning with sunshine in her eyes and a clit in desperate need of attention. Blinking, she pulled herself to a seated position. Just as she had said, Rora slept on the small sofa near the door, giving Gwen the bed. What an interesting turn of events from the night Rora had slept in her bed after Gwen had installed her new hand.

Despite dreams that would have had a priest doing penance for months, Gwen hadn't slept better in weeks.

As she got ready, Rora stirred before waking fully. She cleaned herself and dressed before helping Gwen don clean pants with her damned cast.

Once they were ready, they left their room in search of breakfast. Only, when they were in the hallway, it was deathly quiet.

"Where is everyone?" Rora asked.

Gwen didn't move for several long moments as she listened. Nothing. Not a single servant scurried in the hallway, and the chatter of excitable performers behind doors was notably absent.

Limping toward the door across the hall, Gwen grabbed the handle. It was unlocked, and she pushed it inward. Empty. She did the same with several more rooms. There wasn't a single cyborg in sight.

Fear gripped her chest.

Had the Mistress proceeded with her plan during the night? Had Bastian killed the emperor? Was she too late yet again?

As quickly as she could, she shuffled down the hallway on her crutch.

Rora's footsteps sounded softly behind her. "Where do you think they are?"

"I don't know. But I intend to find out."

They made their way downstairs and back toward the ballroom from the night before. As they neared the closed doors leading to the ballroom, raised voices rumbled down the hallway. She couldn't distinguish the words.

Gwen tried the handle.

Locked.

"Let's try the back entrance through the gardens."

It took longer than she'd like for them to make their way into the gardens and find the box hedges from the night before. Slowly, they retraced their steps up to the doors leading into the ballroom. The entire time, there was no guard or servant to be seen.

Although the door into the ballroom from the gardens was closed and appeared to be locked, Gwen could see clearly through the massive windows at the back of the room.

She pulled Rora to crouch beside her behind a section of stone wall near the massive window. Heart drumming in her ears, she leaned over and peered through.

The cyborgs were dressed in their finery from the night before. But that wasn't all of it. They were bound at the hands and sat in rows against the walls. Most were gagged. The emperor's soldiers stood before them with guns pointing.

Rora gasped.

"What the hell is going on?" Gwen whispered. "Where are the watchmen? Where's the Mistress?"

Both were noticeably absent.

But she couldn't miss the dark figure tied at the center of the room, isolated from the others and hands tied before him. *Bastian.*

Her heart sank as she realized the emperor never intended to have them perform. This entire thing—the performance, meeting with the Union Council to change the law—had been a lie to get them here. But why?

"Where is your Mistress?"

It took Gwen several moments to locate the emperor. He emerged from behind a pillar near the dance floor, his voice sounding as if it had been through the furnace and then doused in water. Quite unlike the composed man they had met the previous day.

The performers shifted, pressing their backs farther into the wall. None spoke up.

"She was supposed to attend the ball last night." Titus continued, prowling the room. "And where is your cyborg tinkerer?"

"We don't have one."

It was Marzanna. She sat toward the back of the ballroom beside Akio.

"Do you expect me to believe that a cyborg establishment of this size operates without a tinkerer?" Titus nodded to one of his soldiers, who cocked his gun and aimed it at Marzanna. "I'll ask one last time. Where is your tinkerer?"

"Hide," Gwen whispered to Rora.

In an instant, she was on her feet. She wouldn't let her friends get hurt. Not if there was something she could do about it. She moved toward the nearby door and banged her fist on the frame. Through the glass, she could see the guards turning in surprise. One ran toward her, unlocking the door.

"Someone called for a tinkerer?" Rather than her usual saunter, Gwen leaned heavily on her crutch as she walked into the room. "I'm not big on parties. And you'll imagine my surprise when I woke up this morning... and no one was around."

She leveled her gaze on the emperor. The man who'd made her life—and the life of every cyborg in the Crescent Star System—fucking miserable.

Eyebrows raised, she gestured to the performers tied up around the room. "Tell me this isn't a bondage party. Because if it is... I'm going to be really bummed I missed it."

The emperor frowned. As he strode toward her, the sun from the windows behind her caught the gray at his temples. He stopped in front of her, taking in her leather boots, pants, and jacket and toolbelt at her hips, his gaze lingering on her crutch and cast. His nostrils flared in revulsion as he studied her cyborg eye.

"A broken tinkerer is better than none, I suppose." He sniffed. "What's your name?"

"Offended." Gwen bowed. "At your service."

"Your name, cyborg."

As the emperor spoke, there was a flash of movement behind him. On the floor at the center of the room where he sat, Bastian worked at his bonds with a small blade concealed between his hands.

Gwen's heart plodded a merry tune in her chest. Was this the moment? Was he about to attempt to kill the emperor?

Seeing her gaze, the emperor started to turn, but she blurted, "Gwendolyn Grimm." The emperor turned fully back to her. "My name is Gwendolyn Grimm."

Realization crashed into her, and her heart sank into her gut.

She'd just revealed her real name. If the emperor put

everything together—and the fact that she hadn't been a cyborg before the Cyborg Prohibition Law—he now had the legal right to execute her.

She was as good as dead.

His next words confirmed the fear icing her chest.

"The ship tinkerer?" His eyes settled on her cyborg implant. "I'd thought to recruit you for my navy. But I hadn't heard you were... one of them."

Ignoring the disgust in his voice, she said, "It's a part of my reputation I like to keep quiet. Easier to get jobs that way."

Behind the emperor, Bastian stared glassy-eyed at the window, his hands working steadily at his bonds.

Nearby, one of the soldiers shook his head, and Titus nodded in return.

"You lie, Ms. Grimm," the emperor of the Star Crescent System hissed.

"All good women do."

"Do you know what happens to humans who break the law?" Titus took a step closer until their noses were practically touching. "New cyborgs—and their accomplices—are either executed or put in jail for life. At the discretion of the judge, of course."

Swallowing, she was unable to find words to defend herself. Her life was forfeit, and perhaps everyone in the circus as well. Would the emperor go after her family?

Stars, why couldn't I have made up a name?

"Unless you're under the emperor's protection."

Before she could fully register his words, there was a flash of movement from farther back in the ballroom.

Bastian's bonds fell to the ground, and he scooped up the cane beside him.

Her eyes never left Bastian as she unsheathed the daggers hidden up her sleeves.

The emperor might have the ability—and legal right—to

kill Gwen. But she wouldn't let Bastian be sentenced to death beside her.

Perhaps everything she'd gone through to become a cyborg had led to this very moment. She'd been on borrowed time just so she could live long enough to save a man who had so much yet to do in this world.

With impossible slowness, Bastian raised his cane. It was only then she realized what it actually was—or what it hid. The ringleader clicked a button on the cane's handle, which released a cover at the end. At the base of the cane was the barrel of a long gun, which Bastian pointed at the emperor.

Gwen pushed His Imperial Highness aside and raised her knives into the air as she yelled. "Titus, DUCK!"

Then she threw both knives at the man she loved.

CHAPTER 34

G wen held her breath as her knives soared through
the air.

She'd thrown knives in deep space at pirates
boarding her vessel and with gravity far more finicky than
Covenant's natural gravity. Hell, she'd trained under countless
sailors since she began working as a tinkerer.

But as she watched her knives fly toward Bastian, it was as
though they moved slowly, hanging in the air, destined to kill
the man she was trying to save.

Then time returned to normal speed, and she heard the
crack of metal on metal.

Smoke plumed as a shot was fired. Screams filled the room
from cyborgs and humans alike.

The smoke cleared, and Gwen sighed.

Bastian's cane, the one he never parted with, clattered
onto the ground, along with the knife that had redirected the
gun's aim. The second knife was embedded in Bastian's chest.

Gwen staggered forward, nearly losing her footing.

Did I just kill Bastian?

She noticed the slight wobble to the knife, as though it
were a flagpole swaying in the breeze, and she recalled his

second implant. Sighing, she watched as he pulled the knife free, seemingly unharmed. The tip of the blade was bent— likely from the metal plating beneath his chest.

Soldiers rushed toward Bastian, disarming and forcing him to his knees. As they did, the emperor raised his hand. To her surprise, silence descended over the room. The performers stared at Bastian with unmasked shock.

More soldiers emerged from the wings of the room, leaving their posts at each of the exits. Every single one directed a gun at the performers, many of which swiveled to point at Bastian... and Gwen.

She realized quite suddenly that the human soldiers outnumbered the cyborgs four to one. Perhaps more.

"I should have expected a display of violence." Titus rose from where Gwen had pushed him onto the ground. His hair was slightly disheveled, but he was completely unharmed. "That's what technology does to the human brain. It rattles the mind and makes us more prone to act on basic barbaric instincts."

Says the man who tied up his honored guests.

The emperor turned to study Bastian.

The ringleader's left eye was surrounded by a ring of purple. When had he been hit? Several soldiers held his arms and neck while others stood around him with unsheathed swords and guns.

Even from across the room, the emperor's presence seemed to loom over Bastian, unbridled authority pooling around him. "Why?"

Why did you try to kill me?

Gwen bit her lip so hard that she tasted blood.

But Bastian didn't respond. Instead, he looked at the far wall with eyes devoid of emotion.

"What was your motive? Did someone put you up to this?" Titus persisted. When Bastian still didn't look him in the eye, a soldier grabbed his chin, forcing him to look at the emperor. "Answer me!"

Still, the ringleader didn't meet Titus's gaze. Instead, his eyelids lazily blinked as he stared sightlessly.

"I did it of my own volition," Bastian said at last, his voice strangely monotone. "I've hated what you've done to our society with the Cyborg Prohibition Law. I saw an opening, and I took it."

"Bullshit." Gwen stepped toward him.

Soldiers directed more guns at her, but she ignored them.

The emperor raised an eyebrow at her. "Don't think I've forgotten your involvement in this. I saw your knives."

"In that case, you're welcome," she said, before adding, "Your Imperial Highness. I was trying to save your life and his."

The emperor turned to face her.

"You think I won't kill an assassin in my midst?"

"Not if he's innocent."

When Titus laughed, it was a throaty chuckle—like the sound a dog makes just before it throws up. "A man who's attempted murder is hardly innocent."

"I'm the cyborg tinkerer," she said. "I know his cyborg technology has been tampered with and by someone on the show management team. They have programmed him to do it. He would never have raised a hand to you otherwise."

"Who programmed him?" Titus demanded.

"Celeste Beckett, the Mistress of Cirque du Borge and Keeper of Beasts," she replied. "I saw her tampering with his chip last night."

"Why did you say nothing before?"

"Would you have believed a cyborg?"

Titus didn't reply but gestured to the soldiers around the room. "Find Ms. Beckett at once. Tear this palace apart if you have to."

"I'm here, Titus."

Before the soldiers could move, Celeste strode from the

garden door and into the center of the ballroom. Several watchmen followed her, one of which had a hand clamped on Rora's arm and directed a pistol at her head.

The emperor's eyes narrowed as he looked at Celeste.

"You don't recognize me?" Celeste asked. "I suppose you wouldn't. It's been ten long years, and quite a few things have changed."

Nearby soldiers shifted the barrels of their guns from Bastian and the performers to Celeste and her small group of watchmen.

"Allow me to introduce myself," Celeste continued. "My name is Emmeline Bellemore."

Titus's eyes widened. "It's not possible. The Bellemore estate was burned to the ground. There were no survivors."

Gwen's blood grew cold.

Could it be true? Celeste was Emmeline Bellemore, one of the scientists who'd founded cyborg technology? How had she survived?

"We had hidden underground laboratories where we performed secret experiments," Emmeline said. "I was there the day the bombs came. The bombs that destroyed my technology, my research, and family. But you didn't just kill them. You murdered hundreds of my employees and their families, all of whom had nearby residences."

Gwen looked at Rora, whose eyes were also wide.

"According to your own laws," Emmeline said, "you should be tried and executed for murdering hundreds of people."

"Lies." Titus waved his hand in casual dismissal. But despite the neutral expression on his face, his back grew rigid. "That fire was an accident. The investigators who brought in the evidence said as much."

"And how much did you pay them to say that?" Emmeline demanded.

Some of the soldiers shared glances while others held an air of disinterest. None lowered their weapons.

Titus merely smiled. "Are you here for revenge, Ms. Bellemore? Is that it?"

"Three, four, and seven," Emmeline said. "That's how old my children were when you murdered them."

Titus sniffed. "Do you deny Ms. Grimm's accusation? Or did you program this cyborg to attempt to assassinate me?"

A slow, dangerous smile crept across Emmeline's lips. "I did."

"I must say, you've made this far too easy for me," Titus said. "You've admitted in front of everyone here your involvement in my attempted murder. You've also given me the very thing I needed."

For the first time, Celeste—or Emmeline—seemed uncertain of herself. The angry blush faded from her cheeks as doubt flashed across her eyes.

"Not only is the entirety of Cirque du Borge mine now, thanks to the law and your attempted crime, but I had been looking for someone who could create a weapon. And now I have the last two people in the Crescent Star System with the ability to do so."

Gwen's brows drew together.

"I've waited ten years for the Union's temperament to grow unfriendly toward cyborgs," Titus continued. "They are monsters, and now my people agree. It's time cyborgs were wiped out from the Union for our own safety. As we've seen today, cyborgs are violent creatures and can't be trusted not to give in to their barbaric instincts—whether or not they were programmed to do so."

He spared a passing glance at Gwen.

"You're crazy if you think I'll help you," Emmeline said. "I'll die first."

"You will. But I don't need you. Not anymore." Titus looked fully at Gwen now. "I need a cyborg tinkerer *and* a ship tinkerer to make a weapon powerful enough to destroy cyborgs. I didn't expect to get both in one."

Gwen could feel the eyes of the performers on her like a physical weight.

It was then she noticed the watchmen slowly emerging from the shadows and stationing themselves in a perfect circle around the room. None moved. None made a sound. All the while, the emperor's soldiers fixed weapons on Emmeline, Bastian, and Gwen.

"We will use the technology from a ship's cannon to summon enough power that we can destroy a cyborg's mainframe with a single blast from a distance," the emperor said. "We have tried to build smaller weapons over the years, but none worked. I intend to wipe cyborgs from the Union as I sit safely on my ship. When it is over, there will be nothing more to fear. The cyborg threat will have finally passed. And in the meantime, we will use the circus performers as test subjects until the technology is perfected."

Her mind reeled with this information. She thought of her friends and what this weapon could mean.

An end to life as they knew it.

Thoughts raced through her mind, one clashing with the next.

She made a decision.

"I'll help you." Gasps echoed from performers around the stage as she spoke. "Only if you agree not to harm or experiment on Bastian or my friends."

"I won't leave any cyborgs alive," Titus said through gritted teeth.

Gwen shrugged. "Good luck finding another cyborg/ship tinkerer hybrid." She gestured to Bastian. "He searched all of the Crescent Star System for me."

Well, it had been a happy accident on Anchorage, but the emperor didn't need to know that.

As he studied her, Titus's dark eyes flickered back and

forth.

She couldn't help but wonder how desperate the emperor was. Had he really frightened off or killed as many cyborg tinkerers as people said? There certainly weren't any she knew of—hence Bastian's recruiting her in the first place.

After what seemed like an eternity, Titus said, "Agreed. Anything else?"

"As a matter of fact, yes." She turned and pointed at Emmeline. "I'd like the pleasure of killing the woman who fucked with my boyfriend's brain."

"No," he said. "I'd like to keep her around for insurance purposes, should you prove unable to create this weapon."

Emmeline opened her mouth to speak, but Gwen spoke first. "Then you'd have an unwilling tinkerer *and* an unwilling scientist. That's a gamble if I ever saw one."

Titus snickered. "I can force you to work. You've already shown you have people you care for."

"You can try, but what leverage are they if you plan to kill them anyway?"

Face pinching, the emperor drew his mouth into a thin line.

Gwen met his glare, waiting for him to make a move. She'd played her hand, and it was time to see where the cards fell. Either she'd be put to death for becoming a cyborg or she'd given herself a small chance to save her friends.

The emperor nodded to one of his soldiers near Bastian. The man picked something up before tossing it at Gwen's feet. Blinking, she smiled and grabbed her knife.

"You better be as good as you think you are," Titus said. "Or else your friends will pay for it. You have yourself a deal, Ms. Grimm."

Emmeline didn't move from where she stood a few feet away. Instead, she watched Gwen with narrowed eyes.

Held by a watchman a few paces away, Rora shook her head almost imperceptibly, eyes pleading with Gwen.

Don't do it, she seemed to say. But she knew what was at stake and did nothing to stop Gwen as she limped over to Emmeline.

When Gwen stood before the Mistress of Cirque du Borge, the murderer of hundreds of cyborg performers, and the bitch who broke her leg and stole Bastian's memories, she raised the knife to her throat. The room was silent as everyone watched, waiting for what came next.

With a wicked grin, Gwen leaned into Emmeline. Pressing her cheek against the woman's, she whispered, "Do you have it?"

Pulling back, she studied Emmeline, trying to read her expression. The Keeper of Beasts showed no emotion on her face. None other than annoyed skepticism.

Gwen was careful to keep her voice low so only Emmeline would hear. "Give me Bastian's chip, and I'll help you. We can work together to get back to the ship—"

Emmeline showed her teeth in what she likely fancied as a smile.

"I have no intention of leaving this place."

"You'll let the entire circus be used in experiments for some ridiculous revenge?"

"That man killed my husband, my children." An ember of fervor burned behind Emmeline's gaze; a fervor that had likely been locked safely away for ten years... and was now set free.

"And he intends to kill every cyborg in the Union—cyborgs you helped create," Gwen persisted. "Don't abandon them. They're your children, too."

Smiling, Emmeline removed her hand from a hidden pocket. Gwen had been so preoccupied with getting Bastian's chip back that she hadn't even noticed the Mistress's moving hands. Suddenly, Emmeline shoved Gwen backward. Stumbling, she couldn't catch herself with her bad leg and crashed to the floor.

Emmeline held a device with a large red button. Slowly, she pressed down. The watchmen, who had stood silent and unmoving around the room, jolted as though they were awakening machines. Slowly, each of them moved a hand toward their masks—masks Gwen had never seen them without. Removing the hat and mask, they tossed both to the ground.

Horror frosted her veins.

Beneath the helmets were cyborg faces melded haphazardly with flesh. Some had cyborg eyes, like Gwen's, that whirred with an angry red light while others had cheekless jaws of steel with unnaturally pointed canines. Yet others bore steel plating extending upward from machine-enforced chests to necks seeming to lack any flesh at all. Most of the watchmen bore bruising and unhealed flesh around implants—new implants.

All at once, she realized.

The cyborg implants Gwen had been removing for weeks... Emmeline had been using them on the watchmen. The Mistress hadn't just been reclaiming valuable circus property. She'd had a plan this whole time. Hacking off the watchmen's body parts, the Mistress had replaced them with machinery to make the ultimate soldier.

And the watchmen had had no choice at all because Emmeline had tampered with their chips and removed both their memories and free will—just as she had to Bastian.

A dangerous fervor swelled in Emmeline's eyes. "This is what you feared, Titus. Humans who are as strong as machines and lack empathy. I've made it so."

As the watchmen strode forward, closing in on the soldiers, glass shattered inward. Cyborg animals crashed through the garden windows, bellowing.

Gwen looked at Rora, whose eyes were round with fear.

We are so fucked.

CHAPTER 35

The watchmen moved like a horde of the dead, flesh hanging from machine. Some wielded weapons—swords, guns, knives, batons—while others used hands of gears, wires, and plating, tearing the armored royal guards in two.

The cyborg restraining Rora dropped her as though he'd entirely forgotten her existence and ran toward an oncoming soldier.

Reaching for her crutch, Gwen scrambled to her feet and hurried over to Rora. "Come on!"

Rora wrapped an arm under Gwen, and the two narrowly missed an arctic bear as it barreled over the ground where they'd just been. Screams erupted as the creature sank its teeth into the nearest soldier, tearing his arm from his body with its cyborg jaws.

But it wasn't just the watchmen and the animals.

Around them, the performers fell on top of the soldiers. They didn't flinch as the bladed end of the guns stabbed through flesh and machine. Clawing at each other as much as the soldiers, one by one, the performers took the soldiers down.

Bodies sodden with blood littered the floor like discarded set props.

Mouth agape, Gwen and Rora stared at each other. The performers, watchmen, and animals had turned into mindless zombies, throwing themselves into danger to kill the emperor's soldiers. Yet… Gwen and Rora were unaffected.

Before Gwen could think more about it, she spotted movement.

Emmeline moved across the ballroom toward the emperor. Bears, lions, tigers, and every other cyborg animal moved around her as though programmed not to touch her.

Bastian's chip.

Lunging, Gwen caught Emmeline's ankle, and they both tumbled to the ground and into the middle of the roaring beasts.

"Get off me!" Emmeline screamed as she clawed at Gwen with her metal fingernails.

Managing to dodge a few of Emmeline's swipes, Gwen scrambled on top of the Mistress. As she did, Emmeline became more frantic, her talons biting into Gwen's neck, face —whatever she could reach.

"I know why you are unchanged," Emmeline gasped, eyes fearful. "But why are they? No one else should be able to move on their own right now."

They?

Looking up, Gwen spotted Marzanna, still bound at the wrists, as she retreated into a corner, away from an approaching soldier. Rora had picked up one of the watchmen's wooden batons and hurried after her.

Gasping, Gwen realized what she meant.

The only cyborgs in the ballroom not under Emmeline's control were the two Gwen had tinkered. Somehow, tinkering with their chips using the portable mainframe a few weeks ago had saved them from this fate.

The coding.

Gwen must have overridden the Mistress's coding. Either that, or rebooting their system had. But why wasn't Gwen a mindless zombie? She couldn't tinker her own chip.

Emmeline landed a blow to Gwen's jaw, and she toppled sideways. The Mistress pushed to her feet, screaming as she watched the emperor and a troop of his soldiers disappear through a doorway.

Groaning, Gwen struggled to get up. Where had her crutch gone?

"I'll finish you later," Emmeline hissed before watchmen surrounded her and marched in pursuit of the emperor.

Crawling over to where her crutch had fallen a short distance away, Gwen grabbed it before hurrying after her friends.

Screaming, Marzanna held up bound hands as the soldier aimed his gun. At the same time, Rora swung the wooden baton against his breastplate, which rang loudly. Spinning, he turned and prepared to fire his gun at Rora.

Raising her pistol, Gwen aimed and fired.

The bullet landed neatly between the soldier's eyes. He swayed for a moment before collapsing.

Hearing the gunshot, nearby soldiers turned. Within moments, countless soldiers descended upon them. Far more than Gwen could have fought off on a good day, and there wasn't time to reload her pistol.

"We have to get out of here!" Rora grabbed Gwen, hauling her toward the ballroom doors.

Marzanna ran behind them with the soldiers at her heels.

With trembling hands, Rora unbolted the ballroom door, and they narrowly missed several gunshots.

Not knowing where they were going, they turned down countless hallways, desperate to get away from the madness. But the voices of soldiers were never far behind.

"In here!" Marzanna opened what could only be a storage

closet before the three pushed inside and closed the door after them.

The three women breathed heavily, trying to suppress their gasping breaths as the soldiers trundled past the closed door. When the sounds of their footsteps faded, air whooshed out of Gwen's lungs.

Looking around, she noticed a handful of cleaning supplies and a small window in the corner of the room, which let in enough sunlight to see.

"What happened?" Rora whispered. "Why is everyone acting like that?"

"And why aren't we mindless soldiers?" Marzanna added.

Quickly, Gwen explained her revelation.

"I have to go back," Marzanna said. "I have to find Akio."

Removing a knife from her boot, Gwen cut the bonds on Marzanna's wrists. "We will. But we need a plan if we have any hope of saving everyone and getting off this planet alive. Because we can't stay here. If the Mistress doesn't kill the emperor, the man will hunt us down after today. If not as retribution for what Emmeline did, he will search for us in his crazy plan to make a weapon to destroy all cyborgs."

Rora paled.

"As if our lives weren't complicated enough." Marzanna sighed heavily. "What do you have in mind?"

Gwen scratched the shaved side of her head. "My last plan failed spectacularly."

"Well," Rora began, "there are only three of us and a lot more of them. We'll need a distraction."

Nodding, Gwen said, "Did either of you see the dragon when the cyborg animals appeared?"

Slowly, they both shook their heads.

"You want to free it." Understanding dawned in Rora's piercing brown eyes. "I'll bet it's still in the stable. The Mistress probably wasn't able to turn it into a cyborg she could control in time, so she would've left it behind."

Thank the stars for small mercies. The damage a dragon under Emmeline's control could have done would have been earth-shattering.

"I'll release the dragon," Rora said. "I can move the fastest and climb through the stable window, if need be."

Gwen turned to Marzanna. "That leaves rescuing Bastian and Akio to us. We'll also need to find Emmeline to get Bastian's chip back and convince her to set the cyborgs free. If we don't, all of the performers and watchmen will die in her crazy plan for revenge."

"If we don't," Marzanna said, "she's going to start a war."

She probably already has.

"More reason not to fuck up," Gwen said. "Rora, once you free the dragon, meet us in the palace gardens. We'll regroup with as many people as we can and head for the docks. Hopefully, we can get *Obedient* up and running before the city is on high alert and its friendly citizens are upon us."

Adjusting the crutch under an arm, Gwen reached for the door.

"Wait."

Stopping, Gwen turned to Rora. "What is it?"

Shifting past the cleaning supplies, Rora came closer to Gwen. "Before we go, there's something I need to say." Pausing, she bit her lip. "I'm sorry. For my part in using you, I'm so sorry. But I care about you, Gwen. And I'm going to prove it. You'll see."

Marzanna cleared her throat.

Not knowing what to say, Gwen simply nodded. "Alright then. Let's go save the cyborgs. Shall we?"

With a racing heart, Gwen watched Rora disappear down a hallway, headed for the courtyard and the stable beyond.

Checking the hall a second time, Gwen and Marzanna

headed back toward the ballroom. As they did, they encountered countless bodies lying in the hallways, both cyborg and human. Reaching down, Gwen picked up a gun and passed it to Marzanna. She then reloaded her pistol and took several knives off the bodies and stuck them in her empty sheaths.

As they neared the ballroom, raised voices echoed down the hall.

"Titus! Come out and face me, you coward!"

Emmeline.

Gwen and Marzanna hurried toward the sound.

Down several more hallways, Emmeline and a group of fifty watchmen stood before a massive oak door with metal embellishments. The watchmen had somehow acquired a table and were ramming it into the door. Splinters of wood flew in every direction while the door appeared unchanged.

As Gwen approached Emmeline, the sound of bells in the city proper sounded through the windows. The city knew something was amiss.

They were running out of time.

If they didn't get the hell out of the palace and soon, there would be soldiers and mobs of angry humans. Neither of which Gwen fancied seeing today.

"Emmeline! Stop!" Hobbling over to the Mistress, Gwen had to shout to be heard above the city's tolling bells and the banging of the table against the door. "Look around you!" She gestured to the countless bodies, both human and cyborg, that littered the hallways. "How many good people are you going to kill for your vendetta? If we don't leave now, we're all dead."

"I'm almost there." Emmeline spoke as though talking to herself. Sweat beaded on her temples, and her normally immaculate red hair was in disarray.

"There's no way you're making it through that door anytime soon," Gwen said. "And the longer we wait, the closer the city guard is to filling the palace. The feds will be here soon if they aren't already."

Even though her eyes were trained on the door as the watchmen pounded the table against it, doubt flickered in Emmeline's gaze.

"What the emperor did to you and your family is unspeakable." Gwen leaned closer to the Mistress. "I'm sorry about what happened. But these cyborgs"—she pointed at the watchmen—"are relying on you. They are your creations and your new family. They need you to protect them now. Protect them like you wish you could have protected your other family."

Gwen thought of the family she couldn't remember, her memories of them completely gone.

Slowly, she dropped her hand to the pistol at her hip. She didn't reach for it, though. Instead, she waited, watching Emmeline.

If the Mistress wasn't going to protect the cyborgs, then she had to be taken down. Gwen prayed she could figure out that damned remote control quickly enough to get the cyborgs to head toward the docks.

When Emmeline sighed, it was as though the eye of the storm settled over them. Despite the bells in the distance, there was quiet as the group of watchmen stopped and held the splintered table between them, sensing their Mistress.

Removing a device from her pocket, Emmeline clicked several buttons. Suddenly, the remaining watchmen and performers turned from the door and moved to surround Emmeline, Gwen, and Marzanna.

Gwen nodded. "Are the performers programmed to know where to go? Or can you return their free will?"

Emmeline shook her head. "I need to manually work on each chip to remove my override. For now, all of the cyborgs know to retreat to the ship."

That would have to be good enough for now.

"Have them meet us in the gardens."

In the ballroom, Marzanna ran to Akio, who sported a number of superficial injuries but nothing fatal.

Scanning the room, Gwen looked for the one person she longed for most in the world.

She spotted Bastian at the back of the ballroom, standing at the door leading to the gardens. Hurrying over, she ran a hand over his face, which was smeared with blood. She looked over him before sighing in relief. Thank the stars, he didn't appear to have any major injuries either.

"I can't wait to have you back," she whispered.

His gaze was fixed on a far wall, his eyes vacant.

As the cyborgs filtered into the gardens, Gwen waited beside Bastian at the door.

Emmeline appeared with the last of the watchmen. Even now, their unmasked faces were startling. Flesh and machine layered over each other as though the Mistress had tried to fit as much of the technology as she possibly could into each person.

Before Emmeline could walk past her, Gwen caught her arm. Allowing her crutch to clatter to the floor, she removed the pistol from its holster and cocked it. She didn't point it at the Mistress, but the implication was clear. "I'll ask nicely only once. Before we go any farther, give me Bastian's chip. Right fucking now."

Emmeline's eyes narrowed as something primal flickered across her gaze. Slowly, she reached into a hidden pocket on her dress before passing a small object to Gwen. Glancing down, she held a small chip with the strange marbling.

Slowly, she raised the pistol to Emmeline. "Fuck with Bastian's brain or memories again, and you're a dead woman." Turning from the Mistress, she glanced around at the crowd of unmoving cyborgs. "What the fuck are you all waiting for? Let's go!"

As Gwen tucked Bastian's chip into a pocket, she breathed

a sigh of relief. But she didn't dare to hope. Not yet. They still had to make it out of Allegiant alive. And there was no telling what awaited them outside of the palace gates.

Skidding to a halt, Gwen looked around as the cyborgs marched through the gardens and toward the main gates.

Turning to Marzanna, Gwen said, "Where's Rora?"

CHAPTER 36

Retracing their steps from the night before, Rora ran with everything she had.

As she hurried through the palace, she stopped many times to duck behind piles of bodies when soldiers stormed by in pursuit of cyborgs.

Eventually, she made it to the front doors and slipped quietly out.

The city was eerily quiet as she ran.

No one stood guard in front of the stables, so she hurried inside. The building was empty of animals and people. Only the empty cages—and the dragon—remained.

The dragon flashed its teeth in a snarl, clearly agitated. Shaking its head as though trying to shake off flies, it flicked its long tail back and forth. The bars of the cage rang as its scales smacked against it, again and again.

Swallowing, Rora tried not to think of what happened to her last hand.

Taking a deep breath, she strode toward the stall at the back of the room where the dragon's cage was stashed.

Its claws appeared and retracted again and again as it watched her approach.

As she neared it, she realized the fireproof cage was locked with a massive chain and padlock. Looking around, she couldn't see any keys nearby.

She spotted a pile of tools neatly packed in a massive box. *The circus crew's tools.*

Grabbing what appeared to be oversized crimping pliers, she hurried back to the dragon.

"H-hi," she began as she approached. "It's me again. Long time no see."

The dragon's lips peeled back in a snarl.

I shouldn't have expected a warm welcome.

Slowly, she extended the pliers toward the padlock. Before she could get anywhere close to it, the dragon swiped its cyborg talons at her. It couldn't fit its entire claw between the bars. But several talons swiped so close she could feel air whooshing past her hand. Heart racing, she jumped backward.

"Quit it! I'm trying to help."

The dragon merely snarled.

Somewhere in the city beyond, bells rang.

Again, she approached the dragon. Only, as she came forward this time, she tried to soothe it as she once did in the caves. "I'm sorry for what happened to you. None of this is right. And I'm sorry for my part in it. But I want to help you now. We can help each other."

The dragon looked rather inclined to swipe at her through the cage's bars again. But it must have realized its own potential for escape. She latched the pliers onto the padlock and pressed as hard as she could, but nothing happened. The lock didn't even have an indent. After several more tries, her human palm was slick with sweat.

Again, and again, she tried, but the damned lock was too big. Or she was just too small. Too insignificant, as always.

She'd made it to Covenant, but nothing came of it. Nothing at all. She hadn't even had a chance to perform.

The emperor hadn't been the person she'd thought he'd be—a nobleman and consumer of the arts, someone who wanted to change the Cyborg Prohibition Law. Instead, he was a mass murderer aspiring to complete some long-awaited genocide. All he wanted was to use the performers as part of his experiments to kill cyborgs.

She thought of everything she'd done, everything she'd sacrificed to get here. Leaving her parents, chopping off her hand, joining Cirque du Borge, traveling the Crescent Star System, performing, fighting for every inch during the competition, using Gwen, betraying her friends... It had all been for nothing. It had all been in search of a career, a dream that left her with the same ache in her chest as before.

Her parents had taught her that her value was in her performance, in being the best. But what good was being the best if it meant standing on the backs of those you loved?

Tears streamed down her cheeks as she thought of the deaths of countless cyborgs in this asinine competition. She thought of the bodies she'd seen during the obstacle course of the first competition, of the performers toppling off the cliff during the second competition in pursuit of the dragon, and all those who had been shot by the pirates on Jinx during the final competition. So many dead.

She pushed the pliers until her human hand was raw, but she didn't stop. They needed a distraction if she and her friends had any hope of escaping. A burning city would be more preoccupied with a loose dragon than a few escaping cyborgs.

The pliers clacked against the lock's thick metal.

Gwen had been right. Rora was wrong, so very wrong. Achieving a dream wasn't worth it if it meant hurting her friends. She had risked losing everyone she loved by trying to protect herself and her hand. Why couldn't she see that before?

Rora's cyborg hand whirred as she pressed harder and harder. Sparks skittered across her skin and down her clothes, singeing the edges of the fabric. Still, she didn't stop. Somewhere in the distance, the dragon growled. Letting loose a cry, she pressed down on the pliers with everything she had. The pliers clacked together as the broken lock fell to the ground.

Before she could get out of the way, the dragon hurled itself into the cage door, and the door slammed into her chest. Flying across the stable, she crashed into the wall of a nearby stall. She fell to the ground, bouncing twice. Gasping, she couldn't get more than a shallow breath.

As the room around her spun and her thoughts blurred, she finally managed to take a deep breath. She almost wished she hadn't. Pain rocketed through her side. Slowly, she brought her hand up to her forehead.

When she held her hand before her face, it wasn't the blood on her cyborg fingers that surprised her. It was her limp hand.

Once again, her cyborg hand was useless.

Only, this time, it wasn't quite so devastating. She'd sacrificed everything—her friends, her relationship with Gwen —to get this new hand. Now, she sacrificed her hand to save her friends.

Heat pricked Rora's cheeks. Even her legs felt warm.

Blinking, she looked around. The entire room was alight with bright orange flames as the dragon soared around the stable, wreaking havoc.

Sharp pain glanced across her chest as she forced herself to her feet.

There was a strange popping sound. Looking up, a piece of the ceiling crashed down, and she dived out of the way just in time.

The dragon clawed at the window too small for it to fly

through with its cyborg talons. More sections of the walls fell away before it bellowed a deafening roar and flew off into the skies—toward the city.

Guilt mingled with the relief swelling in her chest.

What have I done?

CHAPTER 37

"We can't leave yet!" Gwen shouted at the backs of the cyborgs as they trotted through the gardens toward the main gate. "We have to wait for Rora—"

But even as she spoke, the sound of a dragon's roar pierced the sky.

She did it. She fucking did it.

"Marzanna!" Gwen turned on a heel, heading for the palace. "Go to the stables. Find Rora. Make sure she's okay."

"Just what the hell do you think you're doing?" Marzanna shouted after her.

"I have an idea," she called back. "Head for the ship once you have Rora. I'll meet you there."

She hoped they could get through the city. But with the tolling of the bells, she wasn't sure. If the city was even remotely organized—and she didn't doubt the capital would be—there would be feds awaiting them at the main gate. They wouldn't be able to make it to the docks.

Moving as quickly as she could, she leaned on her crutch as she hurried back to her room. It took what felt like an eternity before she got to her door. Hurrying inside, she found what she sought.

Grabbing her skimmer, she moved toward the door but hesitated. Turning, she snatched her pack, pushing the portable mainframe into it along with her tool kit. She didn't trust Emmeline farther than she could throw her. And thanks to Gwen's broken leg—courtesy of the woman in question— she wasn't throwing anyone anytime soon.

Sparing a glance for her crutch, she dropped it and donned her magnetic boots. Stepping onto her skimmer, she groaned at the pain from the weight on her leg. There would be time to deal with that later.

Kicking the board on, she flew out of her room, through the palace, into the ballroom, and out into open air.

Flying high, she saw exactly what she'd been afraid of.

Hundreds of feds formed lines in front of the palace gates. Her friends stood on the other side, attempting to lower it, unaware of their impending doom.

Where is the dragon?

Spotting the creature where it perched on a rooftop, sunning like a housecat, Gwen flew over to it.

"Hey!" she shouted. "Remember me?"

As the scaled creature turned its feline gaze on her, she grabbed her pistol and aimed.

Sorry, little buddy.

Then she fired.

The dragon roared as the bullet pinged harmlessly off its scaly hide. Reloading, she shot a second time. That got its attention. Scraping its claws against the shingled rooftop, it pushed into the air, wings flapping furiously as it flew toward her.

Yanking on her board, she turned around and headed back toward the palace gates.

Gwen felt the fire before she saw it.

Shifting the gears on her skimmer, she dived down,

narrowly avoiding a plume of flames. Behind her, the dragon snarled.

As she flew back toward the palace, she noted more soldiers pouring down the city streets, eager to hunt the cyborgs.

The soldiers would never let them leave this planet. They wouldn't believe the cyborgs had nothing to do with the attack on their emperor or that one woman had turned them all into mindless zombies. To the prejudiced humans, all of the cyborgs would be guilty and either executed or used in experiments.

Seeing Gwen and her scaled companion, the soldiers and feds in front of the palace gates turned. Eyes wide, they aimed guns and crossbows skyward. She flew toward them, revving the engine, the ground flying by beneath her. Arrows thunked into the base of Gwen's board, but none hit the engine. The dragon wasn't so lucky. Countless bullets bounced off its underbelly. When a crossbow bolt wedged into one of its legs, the creature roared.

The dragon spewed fire over the city, cooking soldiers inside their metal armor. Men screamed, and the smell of roasting flesh filled the air. Those untouched by the dragon's first bout of flames reloaded their guns and crossbows and fired again. Temporarily unconcerned with Gwen, the dragon turned its full attention toward the soldiers.

Quickly, she circled back to her friends.

They'd slipped out of the main gates while the soldiers had their backs turned and were running through the city streets. Rora had an arm slung over Marzanna's shoulders, but they kept pace with the other cyborgs.

Gwen flew down to them, shouting over the screams of dying men and the crackling flames. "We need to get to the ship before the forcefield goes up!"

She knew as well as any tinkerer of safety protocols on important planets, such as Covenant. Those who could afford it installed massive forcefields over a city or location, which prevented ships from returning to space by erecting a massive, impenetrable forcefield in the shape of a dome over a location.

Her friends nodded, and she took to the air.

The dragon had made quick work of the soldiers. Most of them were dead or far too injured to raise a weapon toward the cyborgs running past them.

Once more, Gwen reached for her favorite pistol and reloaded it.

Sending a quiet apology into the ethos, she flew toward the scarlet dragon and fired. This time, the bullet didn't just bounce off its hide; it pinged off its head.

"Oops."

Turning, the dragon belched flame.

Revving her engine, Gwen flew toward the city where squadrons of feds stormed toward the smoking palace.

Civilians ducked inside buildings, slamming doors and pulling shutters closed. Seeing them, she tried to shove her guilt down.

These people would kill you, given a chance.

She weaved between the buildings, dragon fire at her heels. It didn't catch at first since most of the buildings were made of stone with slate roofs, rather than the wood common in rural areas. But when she ducked around an automated carriage, the dragon's hot breath behind her, wood, wheels, and other debris flew into the air as the flames met the fuel tank, and the carriage exploded.

Flying off her skimmer, she skidded across the ground. The cobblestone streets bit into her skin, slicing through her clothes. She tumbled beneath an alcove. As her skimmer skidded down the street, the soldiers' arrows on the base of the board snapped off.

Another roar split the sky, which was quickly followed by gunfire and the zipping of arrows.

Ignoring the pain from countless cuts and her broken leg in its torn cast, she clambered to her feet and hobbled toward her skimmer. As she emerged from beneath the alcove, a plume of flames erupted down a nearby street. She rolled forward, grabbing her board and landing feetfirst. Then she took to the sky.

The dragon was once again thoroughly occupied by the dozens of soldiers in the streets below and on rooftops. Its cyborg talons ripped through slate roofs as it clawed at balconies where soldiers aimed massive crossbows, trying to bring the scarlet dragon down.

As she'd hoped, with a dragon on the loose, the city should be less inclined to host execution parties for the escaping cyborgs.

Silently praying the dragon would survive the day and apologizing for antagonizing it, she turned, looking for her friends. It took her a few minutes to find them, but they were nearing the docks. She flew down to them.

"How much farther?" Rora asked, gasping.

"Two blocks." Sweat poured down Gwen's face, and she ignored the throbbing pain in her leg.

At the docks, people scurried to their ships, land-bound or ready for space travel. Men and women pushed each other aside in their haste, and some even shoved people into the waters far below. Gwen hovered low on her skimmer, her empty pistol in one hand.

When one man tried to push their group aside, she held her pistol to his head. "I wouldn't do that if I were you." He didn't need to know the damned thing was empty.

Eyes wide, he scurried around them.

When they neared *Obedient*, watchmen guarded the gangway and were stationed across the ship's main deck.

"You aren't supposed to have returned yet," the watchman at the base of the gangway said.

"We got back early," Gwen said from where she hovered

on her skimmer. "Step aside. There's been a change of plans." When the guard didn't move, she looked around. "Where the hell is Emmeline?"

Rora ambled forward. "I know that voice." Raising her hands slowly, she removed the watchman's mask. The woman didn't move at her touch.

The mask and helmet clattered onto the dock as Rora gasped. "Philippa? I thought you were dead."

Philippa had a fair complexion, and she might have once been blond. But like every watchman Gwen had seen today without their mask, her head was shaved. She had large brown eyes and a soft jaw that suggested she had once been beautiful.

"There isn't time for this." Without warning, Gwen struck Philippa over the side of the head with her pistol. Rora managed to catch her before she fell to the ground. "Bring her on board. We'll tinker with her chip later if we're still alive by the end of this."

Emmeline appeared before the gangway.

"Timely as always," Gwen muttered. "Have the cyborgs prepare the ship for takeoff. We leave yesterday."

"Who put you in charge?" Emmeline bit back, but she had already pulled out the strange device she'd used earlier to control the cyborgs.

"I did when you tried to get us all killed."

The watchmen and performers hurried onto the ship in a strange silence before standing utterly still on the main deck.

After a minute of working on her device, Emmeline pocketed the machine once more. "Done."

All at once, everyone started moving. The watchmen who'd remained with the ship as well as all the remaining watchmen and performers who'd come from the city readied the engines and lowered the sails.

To Gwen's annoyance, Abrecan had somehow been one of the few to survive.

With the deaths of the watchmen and performers, there were fewer than one hundred cyborgs now.

"Marzanna!" Gwen shouted, uncertain where she'd gone off to. "Get Bastian's chip back into his head. He has some experience flying, so we need him up and running."

Unlike the rest of the cyborgs, Bastian's chip hadn't been tampered with by uploading malicious coding. Instead, he'd been given a completely new one. Therefore, they should be able to bring him back to help in their escape without the need to update his coding in a portable mainframe.

From the little Bastian had told her of his past, he'd overseen some of the trading vessels for his family's business. She prayed Emmeline hadn't done anything to his original chip.

Come back to me. I need you.

Marzanna appeared before her, and Gwen passed Bastian's chip to her.

The forcefield still hadn't been put up, and Gwen breathed a sigh of relief. They were going to make it. They were—

Suddenly, a rippling boom shook the city. Waves tossed the docked vessels, and they all clung to the sides of the ship.

A shimmering wave of air rose from the edges of the city and surrounding land and water. Several ships were already skyborne, hoping to flee the burning city and its dragon. They throttled the engines to get out of the range of the forcefield. But it caught one ship, slicing the back clean off. Without its engines, it fell, splashing into the lake below. The second ship bounced off the forcefield, careening backward, but it managed to remain airborne.

Too soon, the forcefield closed, forming a massive shimmering dome around the city.

They were trapped.

CHAPTER 38

R ora looked at Gwen. "What now?"

Gwen thought frantically.

The forcefield was made of energy, plasma, or particles and was likely tied to a doctored-up reverse gravitational machine of sorts. No smaller generator would be able to support a forcefield of this size. A narrow slip of energy from the very top of the forcefield trickled down to the palace at the center of the city. That had to be where the machine was. If she could disable it, even temporarily, they should be able to slip into space and, ideally, before the shield came back up.

"The plan remains the same." Gwen grabbed her pack, which contained the portable mainframe and a small tool kit. She removed the mainframe and passed it to Rora. "Put this somewhere safe. Have Bastian get this ship in the sky. Hover as high as you can, but don't get near that forcefield until I get it down."

Once, she'd been willing to leave these people, to abandon the circus and those she'd come to know. She'd thought she had nothing left to fight for. But these cyborgs had become her new family and in some ways had replaced the family she could no longer remember. And she'd proven to herself that she was capable. If she could solve Rora and Marzanna's sleeping curse, she could sure as hell figure out how to bring down a forcefield.

Glancing to Bastian, whose eyes shone with a strange vacancy, she wished more than anything she could say goodbye. But there wasn't time to wait for Marzanna to remove Emmeline's chip and replace it with his. The longer they waited, the more time they gave the feds and emperor's soldiers a chance to catch up with them. There was also no way of knowing how long it would take for her Bastian to return. Lingering, she studied his features, wondering if it would be the final time. His olive skin was pale, and dried blood was crusted on his face.

The once irritable ringleader, who'd clung to power for a sense of purpose, was not the beast he'd pretended to be. He cared deeply for the performers and for her.

It's my turn to save you.

Swallowing back the tightness in her throat, Gwen turned from him as she reloaded her pistol. Marzanna and Rora studied her with knowing eyes.

You plan to sacrifice yourself, their expressions seemed to say.

Emmeline eyed Gwen with a stiff set to her jaw.

"I'm the only one who has a chance of getting that forcefield down. Not too long ago, I was no cyborg tinkerer. I figured that out. Now, it's time to tinker with a generator. I'll get back as soon as I can." Gwen limped onto her board and kicked her skimmer's engine on. "As soon as the forcefield goes down, set a course straight for space. Don't wait for me."

Without another word, she set off into the sky, heading straight for the narrow slip of energy connecting the forcefield to the center of the city. She prayed she wouldn't capitally fuck this up.

But she wasn't the same tinkerer who'd signed a circus contract for a chance at life. She'd learned more about coding, engineering, and tinkering. In so doing, she'd learned to be more confident in herself. She hoped she'd hold on to that confidence when she came face-to-face with a forcefield technology she didn't understand.

The dragon, still holding visiting hours with the city guard, didn't notice her flying over houses and buildings a short distance away. She soared over the palace's gates. A strange buzzing filled her ears as she neared the slip of energy. The closer she flew, the louder it became.

To her surprise, the energy didn't come from an outdoor courtyard, as she'd expected. Instead, it came from what she'd once thought was an enclosed room within the castle itself. Now that she was in the sky, she could see a massive opening in the roof.

A shimmering white-blue energy crackled and sparked.

Flying down, she groaned before removing her pistol and a knife. Half a dozen guards in steel armor surrounded a massive generator. She fired her pistol, shooting a man in the head. At the same time, a knife flew from her other hand. It connected with a second guard's neck. Both fell to the ground.

The remaining soldiers spun toward her.

Turning her board, she grabbed two more knives from the sheaths on her good leg, moving to cut down the next guard. She struck out, managing to knock his helmet free. A hand latched on to the back of her skimmer, and she tumbled to the ground. Rolling, she sliced upward with her knives, catching a soldier in the armpit.

The final three soldiers surrounded her.

She moved on instinct, courtesy of years of experience out in open space. Even with the adrenaline coursing through her veins, she was far too slow. Dangerously slow with her leg dragging.

When the first soldier charged with his sword, she slipped within his defenses and ran her knife over his exposed throat.

Pain tore through her senses, and tears welled in her eyes from the movement.

Over the roar of the forcefield, she heard the telltale click of a gun being loaded. Unable to move fast enough, a zing of pain shot through her as a bullet punctured her shoulder. Dropping her knives, she grabbed the soldier she'd just killed. She yanked with all of her might, using his body as a shield and narrowly deflecting a second bullet.

Something clattered to the floor, and she moved on instinct, dropping the body.

Two others dived for her at once. She rolled backward, cringing as pain rocketed through her shoulder and leg. Fingers scrabbling, she found a discarded gun, praying it was loaded. Aiming, she fired. One of the soldiers fell. But the last guard was on her, body crushing her into the ground.

Hands wrapped around her throat, and she gasped for air.

Somehow, the gun had slipped free from her grasp. Desperate, she felt along the ground for a knife, a weapon, anything. As blackness filled her vision, she knew she had mere moments before she lost consciousness.

Her fingers touched a cool metal surface, and she grabbed it, slamming it into the soldier's helmet. The two helmets slammed together, metal clanging. With a grunt, he fell off her, and his helmet clattered to the floor. Seeing her knife a few feet away, she lunged for it before the man was on her again. She sliced upward, and he reeled back, clutching his eye. Blood flowed from the wound, blinding him in one eye. Swinging, she thumped him in the temple with the hilt of her knife. His body went limp before he collapsed onto the marble floor.

Rising to her feet, she limped to the massive machine at the center of the room. She pulled her pack off her shoulders, grimacing at the pain. But she removed her tool kit and lay it out on the ground.

As she'd guessed, the machine was set up similarly to a

ship's artificial gravity generator. There was the very obvious off switch—a red handle at the corner—but it would only be a matter of time before more soldiers arrived and turned the machine back on. She couldn't risk alerting the palace to her presence yet. The noise of the forcefield may have covered up the gunshots, but a lowering forcefield would certainly raise suspicions.

She moved around the machine, skidding on the fallen soldiers' blood.

Removing the metal plating from behind the forcefield's off switch, she saw massive wheels and gears, along with complex wiring, ducts, and rotor system spinning on a circular track.

As she watched the machine work for a moment, an idea formed.

She thought of how she'd swapped Marzanna's wiring to fix her foot, and how it had short-circuited, sending her into a coma for weeks.

Could it really be that easy?

Donning rubber gloves from her pack and reaching into the machine, she replaced several of the wires, moving them to different outlets. Some of the wires sparked as she worked. The machine made a strange coughing noise, the gears clinking as the generator worked harder to maintain the forcefield.

Still, the forcefield remained functional.

Damn it. She knew plenty about ships, but—like cyborgs—forcefields were outside of her area of expertise.

Before she could brainstorm further, she heard a roar over the hum of the forcefield's plasma energy. When she looked up, her heart dropped. The dragon hovered above the opening in the ceiling.

Not now.

It slipped around the forcefield's energy, flying into the domed room. She rolled, narrowly missing a plume of white-orange flames. Behind her, her tool kit melted into useless liquid metal.

Looking around, it took her a moment to spot her skimmer. It lay several paces away, partially buried beneath soldiers' bodies. The dragon turned in the room, circling back. Ignoring the piercing pain in her leg and shoulder, she staggered forward and shoved the bodies off. She grabbed the board and dodged behind a nearby column as another spout of fire filled the room where she'd just stood.

Mounting her board and kicking the engine on, she left the safety of the column to face the dragon, her feet sliding on the blood oozing from her shoulder. Flame erupted from the beast, and she flew around the room, dodging between pillars.

The generator towered before her, a beacon. That was the answer.

Her heart pounded as she waited in front of the machine, the dragon flapping massive wings and turning to face her. In those agonizing moments, she wondered if she would see Bastian, Rora, or her friends again. The roaring of the forcefield became a distant humming in her ears over the roaring of her pulse.

Wait... Wait...

The dragon faced her and arched its back, breathing in deeply. Then it loosed flames.

Now!

She kicked the skimmer, willing the board to move faster than it ever had before. But she wasn't nearly fast enough. As she flew upward, the flames chased her, dancing up her board. As her leather jacket caught fire, she could feel the skin on her arms instantly bubble with blisters. But she couldn't risk taking the jacket off or even letting go of her board. Biting her cheek, she held back a scream, clutching her board with all her remaining strength. Below her, the fire melted the generator, and the machine sputtered.

As she zipped out of the room and into the open sky, the

forcefield shimmered before descending back toward the ground.

The entire peninsula shook as the shield collapsed. An explosion like a wave of air boomed across the city.

In the room below, the dragon roared, the sound like metal scraping metal, as a part of the castle exploded. Fire and electricity and a searing heat blasted up from the generator. It was all she could do to keep out of the range of the sparking flames. Debris flew in every direction, peppering her with shards of stone, glass, and metal.

Tears filled the corners of her eyes. Damn it, she didn't have time to be injured.

As she flew back over the city and toward the docks, she noted where cobblestone streets and house foundations had cracked from the impact of the explosion. The city fell silent for several long moments before the screaming started. Soldiers rallied, and arrows zipped up toward her board, slamming into the base. One managed to poke through, splintering the wood.

As the ships came into sight, the dragon bellowed once more. It was the sound of fury taking flight.

Looking back, she saw the unmistakable shape of the scarlet dragon rising out of the castle's depths. Smoke fizzled up from holes in the beast's wings, and it was covered in ash. But it flew straight for her.

That was one resilient fucker.

Squatting lower, she zipped toward the water. She breathed a sigh of relief as *Obedient* rose into the sky. With any luck, that meant Bastian was awake and guiding the ship toward space.

Rather than setting a course for *Obedient*, she flew toward the docks where soldiers yelled. As she feared, some were in the midst of preparing ships in pursuit. Seeing her and the pursuing dragon, the soldiers aimed guns and crossbows. More arrows stuck to the bottom of her board, but she didn't turn back. Instead, she flew closer to them. Another bullet connected with her wounded shoulder, and she cried out, blinking back more tears. Somehow, she managed to stay on her board, but her vision grew fuzzy, and she became lightheaded.

I'm losing too much blood.

She clutched her board with her injured arm before she sliced off the first ship's docking lines with her free hand. She nearly lost her footing as the pain in her leg throbbed nearly unbearably.

Soon, the dragon's flames descended over the docks, and the soldiers turned toward it. She made quick work of the remaining docking lines.

Turning, she looked back at *Obedient*, which was growing smaller as it neared space.

Arrows zipped past her as she soared straight upward. Behind her, the dragon bellowed. Wings flapped furiously as it closed in.

As the ship grew larger, getting closer, Gwen struggled to remain conscious. The air grew thin and cold, and her head swam as blood streamed down her arm from the bullet wounds and countless cuts, making her board slick. Behind her, the dragon no longer belched flames, but it didn't stop either. Too close, she heard the gnashing of teeth and a clicking as its talons appeared and retracted.

The ship was close enough now that she could see the faces of her friends, waving and calling to her. Some grabbed lines and moved frantically about the ship. Bastian stood at the helm with his eyes fixed on her. Eyes filled with fear.

Suddenly, Gwen's skimmer sputtered. The engine coughed, and the board shook. Her feet slipped on blood, and she clutched the skimmer with both hands. She was so close. She could see Rora, Marzanna, Akio, and the others crying out.

I'm not going to make it.

She tried to capture the image of Bastian's face in her mind—his disheveled hair, angular chin, and his brown eyes alight with life—but her vision blurred. She couldn't even muster the energy to wave in farewell. Suddenly, the effort to keep her eyes open was too much.

The board sputtered for a final time as the engine died. Slowly, she started to descend toward the ground.

Back toward the scarlet dragon.

CHAPTER 39

A booming rumble of sheer energy shook the city as the forcefield dropped.

Rora clutched the railing while the ship rocked, nearly capsizing. Splashes of bodies tumbling into the water surrounded her, and she prayed they were passengers aboard another vessel and not one of the cyborgs.

Leaning on the ship's railing, she held her breath as flames erupted from the building across the city Gwen had disappeared into.

Get out of there.

She studied the horizon, waiting for any sign of a skimmer.

"Get us up!" Emmeline barked somewhere nearby.

"Not yet!" Bastian called from the helm, though he guided the ship out onto open water and turned the vessel so their course was set directly for space. "We have to wait for Gwendolyn."

"She'll make it," Rora said. "She can do this."

"None of us will make it if we wait until that angry lizard is upon us," Emmeline said.

She was right.

The moment Gwen got to the ship, so would the dragon. *Obedient* was fast, but not fast enough to outpace a dragon during takeoff from the water. Even if they were airborne and preparing to enter space, engaging the oxygen and gravity fields took time. They might not be able to lower it for Gwen and put the fields back up if the dragon was mere moments behind her.

Suddenly, a form appeared above the city, and Rora gasped in relief.

"Yes!" Marzanna screamed beside her. "Go, Gwen!"

As Gwen flew over the waters, Bastian slowly raised the ship toward space, instructing Marzanna on how to turn on the artificial gravity and oxygen generators. Countless watchmen and performers scurried about the deck, wordlessly doing tasks to ready the ship for space. Soon, the ship hovered at the edge of Covenant's natural gravity.

Below them, both Gwen and the dragon drew nearer.

The beast arched its back. Instead of spewing fire, it shook its head, wings flapping.

It can't breathe. Let alone breathe fire.

When Gwen neared the ship, Rora's heart hammered as she made out more details. By the looks of Gwen's shoulder, she'd been shot at least once. Her body, cast, and tinkerer's clothes were tattered and covered in blood. She clung weakly to her skimmer. Like the dragon, she swayed as she neared them.

"Come on, Gwen!" Rora called. "You're almost there!"

Bastian shouted to Marzanna, "Get ready to bring down the oxygen and gravity field."

Marzanna nodded and rushed back to the main control panel in the room beneath the quarterdeck.

"Everyone, grab a line and secure it to your waist!" Bastian called from where he stood at the helm, holding the ship steady.

The crew did as instructed, including the emotionless watchmen and performers.

When everyone had a line secured to their waist, Bastian shouted at Marzanna, "Lower it now!"

Rora took a deep breath before the shimmering fields went down, and the air grew thinner. Immediately, her thoughts blurred. Through the haze, she could see Gwen's board start to sputter out. Still, the dragon pressed forward, beating its wings. But it, too, moved far slower.

Gwen's eyes found Bastian's for the briefest moment, and Rora looked back and forth between them. Beyond the jealousy swelling in her chest was another feeling entirely—acceptance. They were good for one another.

A strange look flickered across Gwen's face before her eyelids fluttered. At that moment, Rora realized Gwen was saying goodbye to Bastian.

Oh no, you don't.

As fast as she could, Rora dashed up the stairs to the quarterdeck. But as she ran, her feet started to lift off the deck, and she stumbled, clinging with her human hand to the railing.

Bastian held up a sword, about to jam it into the helm.

Chest heaving, Rora struggled to breathe. "I can keep the ship steady."

Nodding, Bastian pulled on his mooring line. "Throttle the engines in reverse. When I have Gwendolyn, shift the thrusters. Get us into space. Make sure the others pull us in as fast as they can."

Grabbing the helm in her human hand, her cyborg hand hanging uselessly, Rora nodded. "Aye, aye, Captain. Go save our girl."

Bastian looked at her for a long moment before he nodded and ran toward the railing, shouting, "Put us in reverse, now!"

Slowly, the ship flew backward—toward Gwen and the scarlet dragon.

As Gwen's eyes closed, her board completely dead, the dragon closed the distance between them.

Pulling on his mooring line once more, Bastian dived off the side of the ship with his sword in hand. He half fell, half floated toward Gwen, arms outstretched.

Holding her breath, Rora watched him draw nearer.

Gwen was fifty paces away, thirty paces, then twenty.

Then he had her. Wrapping an arm around Gwen's waist, he brought the sword up, daring the approaching dragon to come closer. The beast was nearly on them. From where Rora stood, she could make out the colors of its scales. They weren't entirely scarlet, but a mixture of red, black, gold, and violet.

"Pull them, now!" Rora shouted. "And get us moving forward!"

The watchmen hauled Bastian's mooring line in as the ship jerked before moving steadily toward space.

When the dragon snapped its jaws, Rora held her breath, sweaty palm clutching the helm. It missed narrowly. The watchmen continued to pull them back toward the ship, and the dragon beat its wings furiously. It reached toward them, swiping its talons, and Bastian sliced up with the sword. The sword clanged off the beast's scales and redirected its strike.

They were ten paces from the ship. Rora could see the blood floating from Gwen's shoulder into the frosty air.

Hurry, she wanted to call out. But her head swam, and her chest ached.

The moment the watchmen grabbed a fistful of Bastian's shirt, dragging him onto the deck, Rora shouted with the last of the oxygen in her chest, "Get those fields back up!"

There was a pause before the gravity and oxygen fields slammed into place.

The dragon collided with the shimmering field mere moments later, and its roaring pierced the air. As it did, the creature's jaw drew wide as it tried to suck in oxygen. Twisting its head back and forth, it fought to breathe. After struggling a few moments longer, it gave up the fight. The talons and massive scaled body stopped moving, its head slumping to the side as it lost consciousness and started to fall back toward the ground.

Good riddance.

"Bring the gravity and oxygen fields back down." Bastian rose to his feet, placing an unconscious Gwen onto the deck.

"Why?" Marzanna demanded.

"Because if we don't, the dragon will die."

Akio crossed his arms. "That's a bad thing because…?"

"Because it's a cyborg, just like us," Bastian replied.

"A cyborg who tried to eat us," Akio said. "And might still if given a chance."

Bastian shook his head. "It wasn't given a proper chance, nor was it shown any kindness. It was provoked out of necessity, but we shouldn't leave it here to die."

"That's a terrible idea." Marzanna reached again for the switch to the gravity field. "Hang on to your tits, ladies."

It didn't take long to tie a rope around the dragon and bring it onto the ship. It did, however, take far longer to chain its mouth closed as they dragged the unconscious dragon below deck to another fireproof cage.

A new challenge for another day.

Once in space, Rora had one of the watchmen take her place at the helm, eager to find Gwen. Several of the performers had brought the tinkerer into what had once been the Mistress's quarters, leaving a small pool of blood from where she'd lain on the main deck.

As Rora hurried down the stairs, she caught sight of the healer leaving Gwen's room. Before she reached the door, Bastian appeared beside her.

They stared at each other for several long moments.

Slowly, Rora exhaled. "I think we should talk."

CHAPTER 40

P ain ignited Gwen's senses. For a moment, she couldn't decide if she was dead.

Her leg throbbed as though it had been chopped off and sewn back on by a child, and her shoulder wasn't in much better shape. Death shouldn't be this painful.

But as her thoughts cleared, she was surprised by the feel of sheets beneath her fingertips.

Voices sounded somewhere beyond her comprehension.

Why aren't I dead?

Before she could open her eyes, she heard the voice of someone she thought she'd never hear again.

"Ms. Lockwood," Bastian began, which was followed by the click of a door closing. "I don't think now is the best time. I'd like to see to Ms. Grimm. Can we talk later...?"

Rora exhaled heavily. "This is about Gwen."

The floorboards creaked, but Bastian didn't reply. Gwen was careful to keep her eyes shut, content to listen for now.

"I really messed up with the competition, and I want to apologize," Rora said. "I *need* to apologize to her and to you. When I was freeing the dragon from the stables... everything became so clear. I've been so *stupid*. And I couldn't see it until now, but... I love her.

"I didn't mean for it to happen, didn't expect it, but she has my heart. Whatever is left of it. I should have *never* tried to use her. That was wrong, but I did *not* betray you on purpose. Abrecan tortured the information out of me. You have to believe me."

There was a long silence.

"When I recruited you, I knew what you had done," Bastian said. "It was in the angle of the blade. Only someone cutting off their own hand would do it in the way you did. I learned how ruthless you could be in the pursuit of what you want." A long pause. "Far be it from me to take Gwendolyn's choice from her, but... you don't deserve her. Neither of us does."

Slowly, painfully, Gwen leaned up in bed. "I'll be the judge of that."

Standing in the doorway, Bastian and Rora turned to her.

Were they in the Mistress's cabin?

Bastian's eyes lit up like a shooting star while a slow, tentative smile slid across Rora's face.

"Hello, Ms. Grimm," Bastian said.

A smile touched Gwen's lips. "That's Ms. Fucking Grimm to you."

Gwen took in Rora's disheveled hair and the ash on her cheeks. Her gaze settled on Rora's limp cyborg hand. The hand she'd given up to free the dragon and save them all. Without that distraction, they would have never made it out of the city alive.

"I was falling for you, Rora," Gwen said. "I faced a *dragon* for you in the second competition. When I saw you after Abrecan had hurt you, I thought it was my fault. I thought the reason you were near dead was because I had installed your implant wrong. More than that, I thought you'd betrayed us, and I suppose part of me still thinks that you're just here to use me for another new hand. But I nearly threw myself on a flesh trader vessel when I thought you were dying. If it wasn't for him"—she pointed at Bastian—"the flesh traders would have taken me."

"I'm sorry for everything," Rora began. "I know what I did to you, using you, was... unspeakable. But I did *not* willingly betray you to Abrecan. And I wish I had been stronger, that I had realized how important you were to me. Or I would have given my hand up in an instant. I'm ashamed of myself."

Gwen opened her mouth to speak, but Rora kept on.

"From the bottom of my heart, I'm sorry. I should never have made that stupid plan to use you to get a new hand." Tears slipped down Rora's cheeks. "But you should know... what was happening between us wasn't a lie. I'd set out to win your favor, but you stole my heart instead. I love you, Gwen. I'm just sorry it took me this long to realize it."

Part of Gwen didn't believe the apology, unable to wrap her mind around the fact that someone who had so blatantly used her could want her now after everything. Another part of her—the part that dared to hope—knew people were capable of change. Bastian had proven as much. And if Rora could learn to choose Gwen first, to love and care for her and not use her, well... maybe there was hope for them yet.

Slowly, Gwen said, "I forgive you. But trust needs to be earned."

"Of course."

Turning, Gwen studied Bastian, eyes roaming across his hollowed cheeks and worried eyes.

"It's my turn to apologize," she said. "I should have listened to you during the third competition. But I was stubborn and thought I could help. Because of me, Emmeline sank her claws into you, took your chip, and tried to make you kill the emperor. I hope you can forgive me."

The way Bastian nodded, it was as though he were a

soldier acknowledging the order of his captain. His eyes faded as he looked past the room and to whatever horrors Emmeline must have put him through.

"You don't have to apologize for another woman's actions —" he began, but Gwen cut him off.

"I do," she said. "And I'm sorry for being a complete and utter fool."

Slowly, she swung her feet off the side of the bed. At that moment, she realized two things. First, she wasn't wearing any pants. Second, she had a new, clean cast on her leg, and her shoulder had been bandaged. How long had she been out?

As she rose to her feet, Bastian said, "What are you doing?"

Pain seared her senses as she stumbled toward him. The irony of the role reversal—Gwen limping toward Bastian as he had limped toward her at the inn after rescuing her from the flesh traders—didn't escape her. But the pain was too much, and her legs gave out. She started to fall, and he caught her, scooping her up into his arms.

She looked deeply into his eyes. "Your past doesn't define you. You've been trying to be a better man, and I should have seen that. Instead, I ran at the first sign of conflict. Thank you for confiding in me. I'd like to continue where we left off. That is, if you still want me."

Still cradling her in his arms, he strode over to the bed and placed her gently down. As he did, his face lingered before hers, tears welling in his eyes.

"Of course, I still want you."

His mouth was on hers, warm and inviting.

She forgot the pain of her body, the pain of being separated from him, and everything they'd done to escape Covenant. At that moment, all she knew was the softness of his lips and the tenderness of his touch. His hands slipped into her hair as he sat down on the bed, and he kissed her again and again, tasting of their shared tears.

The space between them was too much. She needed him, all of him. Her touches grew hungrier as her hands roamed his chest, his back, trying to take all of him in at once. His teeth sank into her neck, her ear. He expertly avoided her injuries as his tongue traced a path down her chest and between her breasts where her loose shirt hung low. Slowly, his lips made their way back to hers, and his tongue ravished her mouth.

Gasping, he pulled away, and she was rewarded with the sight of his hardened cock beneath his pants.

He cleared his throat. "I'm sorry. You're injured. I shouldn't have… We shouldn't…"

Reaching up, Gwen wrapped an arm around Bastian's neck and pulled him back down to her.

"I'm not *that* injured," she lied, pressing her lips to his, eager for his touch.

Stars, she needed this—to know he was alive and himself again. Slowly, he wrapped his arms around her back. The way he pulled her close, it was as though he feared she might float away into space if he didn't anchor her down.

"I'll let myself out," Rora said from somewhere near the door.

"Don't." Gwen extricated herself from Bastian. "There's one more thing we should talk about."

Rora's hand hovered where she reached for the handle.

Exhaling, Gwen gathered her courage and prayed she was doing right by them both.

Gwen looked at Bastian where he sat on the bed beside her looking surprisingly unabashed by that public display of affection. "I love you for the man you are and can be. And I want to support you and stand by your side on the long road ahead." She looked away from Bastian's hopeful eyes to Rora's. "And I love you, Rora. Despite everything, my heart never got over you. And you proved to me by facing the dragon today that you can put others first." Taking a deep breath, she forged ahead. "I love you both. And I want you both in my life."

I want you both in my bed.

But she didn't dare voice that desire aloud. Not yet.

"You love me?" When Bastian spoke, his voice held such surprise that Gwen wanted to reach out and touch him. To show him how truly deserving of love he was. But she didn't. He had to decide for himself if he wanted to be with her in this way. Slowly, his expression turned inward. "Are you saying... you want to be with both of us?"

Gwen nodded. "Is that such a bad thing? Plenty of people in the galaxy are married to multiple spouses. Not that I want to get married anytime soon, mind you. But I want to be with both of you. If that's something you're both open to."

Relief flooded Rora's features, and she smiled brightly, her head bobbing up and down. "I want to be with you, Gwen. In any way you want." Her gaze touched Bastian. "I'd be open to sharing you with him."

Gwen turned to Bastian.

Before her eyes settled on him, he pressed his lips to hers.

A moan escaped her lips. "I'll take that as a yes."

Bastian pulled back, his lips red. "As long as I can have you, I'm willing to share you. However, I think we need to lay down some ground rules before I lose myself in you."

Gwen nodded, waiting.

"I want to be in a relationship with you," he said. "Occasionally, I'm willing to share a bed with you and Rora, but not always. I'm an open-minded man, but I'm a selfish one, too. And I want you to myself more often than not when we're together physically."

"That's fair," Gwen said.

"I'm open to sharing your heart with Rora, but *my* heart is yours," Bastian continued. "I need to know that what I share with you stays with you. And if Rora and I happen to become friends and the three of us decide we want to be in a relationship together, that is something else entirely, which we can address at that time. For now, I just want you, Gwen. Can you accept that?"

"I can," Gwen said. "I respect you and want to give you what you need, too."

Rora stepped toward the bed. "I echo everything Bastian said with one exception."

Gwen cocked her head to the side. "What's that?"

"I'll fuck the two of you together as often as you want."

A bolt of desire shot down to Gwen's core, so hot, so consuming that she thought she'd drown in it.

Swallowing, she said, "I want both of you right now, but only if that's something you both want."

Bastian leaned forward, cock twitching, and kissed her hungrily. Between kisses, his teeth pulling at her lips, he said, "Are you sure you're feeling up to this right now?"

Stars.

"Um, yes. Very much yes."

Bastian looked up, nodding to Rora. "I'm willing if you are."

A weight settled on the opposite side of the bed as Rora moved in beside them. Kisses trailed Gwen's ear and neck as a small hand traced the line of her curves.

Slowly, Gwen shifted until she faced Rora. The acrobat leaned on an elbow, long lashes fluttering. Behind her, Gwen felt the press of Bastian's cock between her legs.

"Lock the door and don't come back until your clothes are gone," Gwen said, her voice breathy. "I want you both right fucking now."

Bastian helped Gwen slide her long shirt over her head. The cold air of the cabin kissed her chest and her nipples pebbled. Standing up, he unbuttoned his shirt and tossed it to the floor. Just like the night at the inn, he was thin enough that she could see the outline of his second implant. But he also seemed somehow sturdier than before. He was a tall man with broad shoulders and a naturally large build. And she ravished the sight of him, her eyes sweeping down the line of hair on his chest, to his abdomen, to the faint outline of hip bones, and to…

His cock was so hard and so long that Gwen couldn't help her sudden intake of breath. A small bead of moisture formed at his tip, and fuck. She wanted that man right fucking *now*.

There was a thud as the door was bolted.

Shifting her gaze, Gwen watched as Rora hooked her thumbs into the sides of her pants and slid them slowly down. Kicking them off, she moved to her shirt, pulling it gracefully over her head. As Rora pulled the band from her hair and her tight curls fell around her face, Gwen's gaze slid down to the shaved flesh between her legs.

Gwen bit her lip. "Get over here. Now."

There would be a time for slow lovemaking with Bastian and Rora—together and separately—but today wasn't that day. She needed to feel their bodies pressed against hers. To know they were alive and well and right beside her.

When the dragon was nearly upon her, she thought she'd never see them again. She still felt the ache of that separation. It was like a physical pain, and one that could only be healed through touch.

Bastian settled in close beside her. The touch of his skin against hers sent another bolt of pleasure shooting right down to the flesh between her legs. She breathed in sharply, growing wet with desire. His fingers traced gentle swirls on her back, and she leaned back and kissed him.

As Rora's steps neared, Gwen said to Bastian, "I want you to fuck me." She turned to Rora where she stood beside the bed. "And I want you to fuck my face. Any objections?"

Rora bit her lip, shaking her head, as Bastian moved so he was above Gwen.

"None whatsoever," Bastian purred.

As Rora climbed onto the bed, Gwen reached up,

wrapping a hand around Rora's neck and pulling her down for a long kiss.

"Before we begin, I want to feel you," Gwen said. "Just for a moment."

She'd had a moment before to hold Bastian and kiss him, to feel him beside her. And she found she needed that with Rora as well. She needed to kiss her and know this was real and not the most epic wet dream she'd ever had.

Rora smiled. "I hope you like what you find."

Gwen's hands roamed the length of Rora's body, which felt like it was sculpted from fine, warm marble. There were muscles everywhere, and *stars*. Planets must be envious of that ass.

Slowly, she moved her hands up to Rora's face. Cupping her cheeks, Gwen's human and cyborg eye flickered back and forth between Rora's. True sorrow mingled with desire and hope in the acrobat's eyes. After a moment of hesitation, velvet lips crashed into Gwen's. Not needing further encouragement, she parted Rora's lips with a tongue, eager to taste her *everywhere*.

As she kissed Rora, Bastian nibbled the soft flesh where Gwen's legs ended and a softer flesh began. His hand slid down, and he hesitated before her opening. Gwen leaned into the touch, needing to feel him as much as she needed Rora. His fingers slid into her easily.

"Oh, Gwendolyn," he moaned.

Gwen moved her body, fucking Bastian's fingers. Again and again, he plunged inside her, fingers curling right where it counted, but it wasn't enough.

"What are you waiting for?" she said to him. "Fuck me."

An animalistic growl escaped his lips. He was a man hungry for more.

And she was a woman hungry for everything he could give her.

His cock slid into her wet folds.

Gasping, it took her body a moment to adjust to the size of him. He was far larger than she'd anticipated, even after seeing him. And *stars*. She wanted him down to the hilt and arched her back toward him. Above her, he bucked, his thickness sliding in and out of her.

Releasing Rora, the acrobat moved until her legs were on either side of Gwen's head.

Hands grabbing Rora's hips, Gwen pulled her down until she was a breath away. Ever so slowly, she ran her tongue over the length of her. She was sweet and salty and entirely Rora. The taste was so intoxicating, it made Gwen's mind spin. She was rewarded with Rora writhing and gasping. As her tongue moved, flicking up and down, her eyes locked with Rora's. Then she moved her hand, lingering before Rora's opening, waiting for Rora to object just as Bastian had for her.

Instead, Rora grabbed Gwen's hand, pressing her fingers into the dampness between her legs. Even as she did, Rora's hips moved against Gwen's face. Rora no longer tentatively received what Gwen had to give her. Now, she was ravenous— a woman seeking her own pleasure.

A moan escaped them both.

Gwen brought up a second finger, and then three, her tongue never stopping.

All the while, Bastian's cock slammed into her as though he couldn't get into her fast enough, hard enough. As though their parting weighed just as heavily on his heart as it did for her.

Rora came first, giving in to pleasure as it washed over her.

Still bucking, his cock sliding into Gwen's slick flesh, Bastian's breaths grew ragged. Rora moved to lie beside Gwen and brought her hand down to stroke Gwen's clit as Bastian fucked her.

Gwen moved in rhythm with them both, leaning into Rora's touch and arching toward Bastian's cock.

Leaning down, Bastian's lips melded with Gwen's, his teeth catching on her lower lip. His cock swelled inside her, impossibly hard, as his lips roamed the length of her neck. Then his gaze shifted to Rora beside her. Something unspoken passed between them. An agreement, perhaps. Then as one, they turned their full attentions back to Gwen—Bastian fucking her and Rora's fingers moving with torturous slowness.

Gwen entwined her fingers in Rora's curls as the acrobat kissed her neck. With her other hand, she squeezed Bastian's thighs, urging him on. As she did, she used Rora's hand for her own pleasure as Bastian fucked her.

Stars, she couldn't get enough of them. She would never get enough of them.

Too soon, she unraveled around them. As she cried out, both of their names on her lips, she felt the warm splash of Bastian's seed against her stomach.

Moments later, silence descended. The only sound was their heavy breathing.

After Bastian wiped her stomach, Gwen turned to them.

"Want to go again?"

CHAPTER 41

Hours later, Gwen woke to a steaming cup of tea beside her bed, cheese, and a biscuit along with a note in Bastian's handwriting.

Good morning, beautiful. Here's a little something to regain your strength. I'll be at the helm when you're ready. – Bastian

Smiling, she quickly ate.

The bastard already knew the way to her heart was through her stomach.

There was also a small wash bin in the corner of the room with fresh water along with a sponge and a second note, this one in Rora's handwriting.

Call if you need help getting dressed! (Or undressed.) Xo Rora

Wiping herself down as best as she could, Gwen cleaned the remaining smoke, ash, and blood from her skin. Next, she cleaned and redressed her shoulder. Afterward, she attempted to don a pair of leather trousers, but the pain was too much for her leg. Instead, she pulled on long socks and a loose-fitting casual dress. Expecting space's deep chill, she also wore her leather tinkerer jacket, torn and burned as it was, and kicked on her boots. Thanks to her broken leg, she couldn't tie her one boot, but she did manage to slip them on and left one shoe unlaced. Last of all, she took a deep swig of the flask on her side table before strapping her tinkerer's belt to her waist along with her pistol and knives.

For a long moment, she stared at the bed, tempted to lie back down and never get up. Everything hurt—every cut, scrape, and blister—along with her gunshot wounds. Most of all, her leg screamed for her to sit. But she wanted to see Bastian, Rora, and the others more than rest. There'd be time enough for that later. Grabbing a new crutch that had been placed beside the bed, she hobbled out of the cabin.

The deck was dark except for the faint light of the passing stars above the gravity and oxygen fields and a few humming light bulbs in electric lanterns. Only watchmen worked above deck, tending to the sails and moving about the ship. Where was the crew?

The circus staff and crew had been among those Emmeline had turned into mindless zombies, so most everyone should have made it back. Why were watchmen working on the ship and not the crew?

But Gwen couldn't keep her eyes on the Mistress's mindless soldiers for long.

Rora stood near the railing with Akio and Marzanna.

Turning around, Rora smiled broadly as Gwen approached. "Hello, beautiful."

Everyone rushed toward Gwen at once. Akio and Marzanna wrapped their arms around her, muttering friendly profanities. Grunting, Gwen tried to shrug off the pain from the physical contact.

"You fucking showed that dragon," Akio said.

"Glad you're not dead," Marzanna added.

Smiling, Gwen exchanged pleasantries, planting a soft kiss on Rora's forehead. Akio and Marzanna glanced back and forth between each other, a knowing smile on their lips.

Gwen and Rora had a long way to go before there would be true trust between them. But Gwen was willing and excited to give whatever was between them a real go.

Eventually, she turned toward the quarterdeck and strode up the stairs.

Seeing her, Bastian came forward, encompassing her in a gentle hug.

She could still feel the outline of the plating beneath his chest, but he somehow felt sturdier than before. Perhaps it was his newfound self-confidence shining through. Although he would have to face parts of his journey within himself, they would get through whatever came next together.

Slowly, she let go, pulling back to look into his eyes. "The others told me what you did—diving off the ship when my board died. Why did you come after me? You risked everyone's lives by trying to save mine."

After everything she'd gone through to save them, he'd nearly doomed them all. If the dragon had been even a little quicker, they could have been barbecued.

"I couldn't let you die," he said. "Not when I could do something to save you."

She started to cross her arms but stopped, grunting. "I don't need saving."

"Of course not."

She pursed her lips. "Sarcasm is unbecoming."

A smile spread across his lips. "You are strong, capable, smart, and—most importantly—you are kind." He stroked her hair. "I love you."

Tilting her chin up, she kissed him gently. "While I know I'm spectacular company, let me save you next time."

Bastian snorted.

"Enjoying my cabin?"

Turning, Gwen saw Emmeline stride up the stairs to the quarterdeck with several watchmen at her heels.

If only you knew.

"Thanks for your help escaping," Gwen began carefully. "But I think it's time we returned everyone's memories and get the crew running the ship."

"All in good time." Emmeline came to stand before Gwen and Bastian, the watchmen forming a circle behind her.

The way the watchmen stood, tall and menacing—and the fact that they clearly didn't possess any free will whatsoever—had Gwen's fists clenching. Did the Mistress plan to try to regain control of the ship and circus? She was crazy if she thought Gwen would stand idle now, even if it meant a second broken leg.

Which would really, really suck.

"Buying a cyborg circus, that's one elaborate scheme," Gwen said. "All to take down the emperor. Why not start a new life elsewhere? Hell, you could have even made a new cyborg implant manufacturing site outside of the Union to spite him."

"The man killed my family," Emmeline hissed.

Beside Gwen, Bastian made the faintest nod to Marzanna and Akio on the main deck, who walked off and disappeared from sight.

"So, you want to start a war you can't win?" Gwen snapped. "Congratulations. The emperor is now going to hunt down the family you made for the rest of our lives. And every other cyborg in the Union will be arrested and either killed or used as science experiments." Guilt turned her stomach for all the innocent cyborgs who had no idea what was coming for them. "Don't you have any remorse?"

Emmeline sniffed. "Don't preach to me, girl. You're the reason the emperor got away. If you hadn't tackled me, the emperor would never have fled the room or been able to quarantine himself."

Gwen was losing her patience faster than a groom's trousers on his wedding night. "If you hadn't taken my boyfriend's memories—along with everyone else's in the circus —maybe I wouldn't have had to." In a swift motion, she removed the pistol from the holster at her hip. Pointing it at Emmeline, she said, "As I said before, I think it's time we returned everyone's memories. Right fucking *now*."

A cold smile split Emmeline's face like a tomb cracking open. Or perhaps the memories of someone else's tomb.

Behind Emmeline, the watchmen, who'd assumed their usual formal attire and weapons, unstrapped the two pistols from their backs and aimed them at Bastian and Gwen.

Ignoring the pistol aimed at her nose, Emmeline said, "Stand down, tinkerer. This is my ship. And we go where I say."

"No."

Bastian shifted.

"Did you learn nothing from our encounter on Jinx?" Emmeline purred. "You must not care for your second leg all that much. Or your implant." Eyes still on Gwen, she said, "Kill them both."

Before Gwen could pull the trigger on her own pistol, Bastian shouted, "Now!"

Suddenly, her hair floated up from her shoulders, and her feet hit the tops of her magnetic boots, which stuck firmly to the ship's deck. At the same time, an armed wrapped around her waist.

The watchmen's bullets floated uselessly in the air.

Marzanna, Gwen realized. *Bastian signaled to her to be ready to turn off the gravity field. He knew this was coming.*

Celeste and the watchmen floated up toward space and

the charged oxygen field that hovered around the ship. Like the dome that hovered above Covenant, this field was made up of pure energy and would be incredibly painful to the touch. Perhaps fatal, if they were lucky.

"You have less than ten seconds to change your mind." Bastian clung to the helm with one arm, the other wrapped around Gwen's waist. Unlike Gwen, he didn't have magnetic boots, courtesy of her having worked in space for her entire adult life. But he'd been prepared for them both, that sweet, sly fucker.

"Return the performers' and watchmen's memories to them, and we will let you live," Bastian said. "Wait too much longer, and there might not be much left of you."

When Emmeline screamed, the sound was that of an enraged kraken, hungry for violence.

After a moment, the former Mistress of Cirque du Borge shouted, "Fine!"

"Now!" Bastian shouted again, and the gravity field slammed back into place.

Grabbing Gwen, he hauled her out of the way as Emmeline and the watchmen slammed back down onto the deck. Then he dashed over to the watchmen, grabbing their weapons before they could get to their feet. He tossed them over to Gwen. Picking up a second gun, she aimed it and her pistol at Emmeline.

"Let's get that portable mainframe of yours."

Rora appeared at Gwen's side with an electroshocker in her hands.

"Where did you get—?" Gwen began but stopped as Rora shot each of the watchmen in quick succession.

"It was Abrecan's. I grabbed it while you slept," Rora said, her eyes on the fallen watchmen, who were scattered and unconscious around the quarterdeck. "Can't have Emmeline changing her mind now, can we?"

As Emmeline worked on the first cyborg, Gwen said, "The

Forgetting—how did you do it?" Cocking her pistol, she added, "And give their memories back while you're in there. Aye?"

Cheeks turning a red dark enough to make her hair blush, Emmeline said, "It's a coding. During annual checkups, I set up a coding so that a section of the data pool will be moved from the accessible memories to storage. The memories are still there, just inaccessible to the host."

"*Person*," Gwen corrected.

Something had been nagging at her since the memories of her own parents had faded.

"My memories," Gwen said. "Why did they fade so quickly?"

"I used advance coding for yours," Emmeline replied, eyes fixed on the portable mainframe before her, the green text rolling. "Our last tinkerer figured out the origin of the Forgetting. Before he could tell the circus or complete his thirteen-year contract, I killed him. I didn't want your curiosity to get the better of you, too. I thought if I removed more of your memories, you'd be too preoccupied with other things to dig into it."

"That backfired," Gwen bit out. "And Bastian? Why can he remember more than most cyborgs?"

A humorless smile traced Emmeline's lips. "That man was consumed by guilt when we found him. I knew the more he remembered, the more eager he would be to throw himself at a new master's feet to escape his past. So, I gave him a different coding—one that let him keep most of his memories."

Another thought occurred to Gwen.

"Why wasn't I affected by your mind control at Covenant?"

Mouth twisting, Emmeline's eyes never moved from the screen. "In order to make cyborgs more malleable, more open to suggestion—"

"Mind control. I get it. Move on."

Sharp eyes fell on Gwen, but Emmeline continued. "Through my position as the Keeper of Beasts, I learned that by using a rare metal in a cyborg's chip, my coding was quite suddenly far more effective."

Gwen gaped. "That's why you, the Mistress of Cirque du Borge, worked a regular show management position—so you could have access to the animals and experiment on them. And for what?"

"To see how I could better control the minds of humans."

"The metal. What is it called?"

"Magilunar."

Gwen frowned. In her treks across the Crescent Star System, she'd never heard of it.

"Stupid girl," Emmeline hissed, turning back to her work. "Why do you think we went to Jinx? For some asinine competition?" Shaking her head, she scoffed.

Eyes widening, Gwen had to force herself to shut her mouth. "The metal is from Jinx?"

"I should have killed you when I had a chance," Emmeline said. "I'd gotten enough Magilunar for you and the dragon, but there wasn't enough time to implement it in both your chips. Not if I had any hope of using the dragon against the emperor. But that damned creature wouldn't submit." Fierce eyes snapped up to Gwen. "And you somehow managed to use the beast against me. The only two creatures in the whole circus not under my control."

Gwen rolled her eyes. "You're welcome. I saved your life."

Emmeline worked in silence on several more performers' chips before speaking again. "How were Marzanna and Rora immune to my 'mind control,' as you call it?"

"Chance," Gwen answered honestly. "Both of their systems were rebooted on accident. One was my fault. But I was able to restart their chips and bring them back from an endless sleep using a portable mainframe. It must have messed with your coding."

Nodding, Emmeline said, "How interesting."

Eventually, all of the performers and watchmen had their memories and cognitive functions returned to them, including Gwen, Bastian, and Rora.

As images of her family and former life on Orthodocks blossomed in her mind, relief washed over her. She might never see her family again, but at least she knew who they were and where she came from. Though the emperor may very well arrest her family now that he knew her name. She hoped he'd be too preoccupied with other things to think of the Grimm family.

With an army of very angry cyborgs behind her, Gwen said to Emmeline, "Bastian promised you'd live. But you won't be in a position of leadership anymore." She nodded to the cyborgs. "Take her below deck and lock her in the brig. Only Bastian or I will speak directly to her. No one else is to approach her, understand?"

There were murmurs of consent before the former Mistress was dragged below deck by her gorgeous red locks.

Good fucking riddance.

Sighing, Gwen listened to the screams of the woman who'd fucked with her memories, her boyfriend, and tried to kill her girlfriend in some pointless competition, all to make super soldiers in a plan for revenge.

Well, those super soldiers now had their memories back. And they wouldn't be controlled by the Mistress ever again.

CHAPTER 42

"Where to, Captain?"

Gwen stood beside Bastian at the helm, wrapping an arm around his waist. For the first time in a long while, it felt like all was right in the world.

"A fucking good question," Marzanna said as she strode up the stairs to join them on the quarterdeck with Akio at her heels.

Rora appeared from what had become Gwen, Bastian, and Rora's cabin. Coming up to join them, she placed a soft kiss on Gwen's cheek before linking their fingers together.

Bastian's eyes swept over the others before landing on Gwen's. "The stars are the limit?"

"Don't you mean *the sky is the limit*?" Akio added helpfully.

"How much fuel do we have?" Gwen asked.

"Not a lot," Bastian said. "But enough to get us to a nearby planet before we need to refuel."

"We'll need to find a way to support ourselves," Rora said. "We can't exactly go back to being performers."

Tapping her chin, Gwen said, "Not necessarily. If we go someplace outside of the Union, why not? We could launch Cirque du Borge 2.0 and call it The Circus of Cyborgs."

While everyone gaped, Rora laughed. "That could work."

"Why don't we head for the Smoke Ring?" Gwen suggested, feeling guilty for her words even as she spoke them. "Harvest is the closest planet to us—"

Bastian took a step backward as though she'd struck him. "No."

"I know you don't want to see your family, but it's our only option," Gwen said. "Besides Jinx, Harvest is the closest planet to the Union this time of year. And it's outside of the Union, which means the emperor may not have the power to arrest us—*if* he finds us."

The Smoke Ring was the nearest solar system to the Crescent Star System. Solar systems beyond that would take months or years to get to, which required ample fuel, a larger ship, and money they didn't have.

"Do you think your dad will be sympathetic to our situation?" Rora asked.

"No," Bastian said flatly. "The man is a merciless cunt."

Gwen blinked.

Did he just say cunt*?*

"Do you have a better idea?" Gwen tried. "I'm willing to go wherever we have enough fuel to get to that's outside of the Union."

Bastian shook his head. "There isn't anything else."

Frowning, Marzanna said, "Who's your dad, anyway?"

His eyes grew distant, rimmed with fear. "Kazim Kabir. Sultan of Rift."

For a moment, Gwen stared dumbly at Bastian.

First, Rora was a fucking lady. Now, Bastian was the son of a sultan?

Stars help her.

Gwen was the first to break the silence. "Didn't expect that."

When no one offered a better solution, they eventually set a course for Harvest.

Marzanna and Akio disappeared below deck with the other former performers. When they were gone, Gwen reached out and took Bastian's hand.

"I'm sorry," she said. "I wasn't trying to upset you. But I hope you know I'll be with you the whole time. Whatever your dad throws at you, he'll be throwing at us both."

"At all three of us," Rora said with a gentle squeeze to Gwen's hand.

A sad smile traced Bastian's lips, and he nodded before leaning over and pressing a kiss to Gwen's cheek.

"Not to belittle the family trauma you're processing," Rora said. "But I think the cyborgs of the Union are going to have a worse time of things than we will."

They sighed in unison.

In the coming months, the human citizens of the Crescent Star System would be informed of what happened on Allegiant and be out for blood.

But the emperor wouldn't forget about the circus, not when Gwen and the Mistress were a part of it. Two of the only people in the Crescent Star System who could make a weapon to destroy cyborgs. Even if they managed to arrive on Harvest with their limited fuel, they'd have pursuers on their tail, perhaps squadrons of feds.

The emperor would never stop looking for them.

They'd have to lie low and make new lives and names for themselves. Could they really relaunch the circus? It certainly wasn't the most subtle idea.

Somehow, they would find a way. If they could survive the competition, they could survive whatever the emperor—or Bastian's dad—threw at them.

As they sailed between shooting stars, Gwen, Bastian, and Rora tossed new potential names back and forth. They'd have to leave their former identities behind.

"What do you think of Belle?" Bastian asked.

"As my name? I like it."

"But it's nowhere near as beautiful as you are."

Rolling her eyes, she swatted him on the arm.

He tapped his chin. "I think I shall call myself Bieste for my good temperament."

"That's a terrible idea."

"What would you recommend?"

She thought for a while before she eventually said, "What about Adam?"

He kissed the tip of her nose before pressing his lips to hers. "That's a fine name."

Turning to Rora, Gwen said, "What about Aurora for you? It's different enough from your name, but close enough to remember. And I think it means dawn."

Sliding an arm around Gwen's waist, Rora said, "I love it."

Once, Gwen had thought she would spend her remaining days on Anchorage—gambling her time and money away. Then an opportunity strutted into her life dressed in a pinstripe suit. She'd feared what becoming a cyborg could do to her. More than that, she feared she couldn't be the cyborg tinkerer they needed. She thought she could only hurt the people she cared about. Somehow, she'd found a home with these cyborgs. In a universe of people who hated them for what they were, they'd become each other's family. As it turned out, she wasn't the worst cyborg tinkerer, after all.

As their ship soared atop atmospheric waves, sails blossoming in the solar winds, she realized she didn't fear what was to come. Instead, she embraced the adventures of the unknown. For, at last, she knew she had everything she needed —people who loved her and belief in herself.

Who knew? Perhaps one day, the galaxy would once again see the marvels of the cyborg circus.

GLOSSARY

Allegiant: The home city of emperor of the Union and capital of the planet Covenant.

Anchorage: A manufacturing moon in the Crescent Star System.

Apparatus: A city on the planet Grandstand and home to Cirque du Borge.

Covenant: One of thirteen planets within the Crescent Star System. It is also the emperor's home planet and where the Union's rulers reside.

Cirque du Borge: The circus of cyborgs.

Crescent Star System: The solar system that comprises the thirteen planets of the Union.

Cyborg Implants: The technology implanted into humans that makes them cyborgs. Implants can be visible, such as limbs, or literal implants under the skin. Due to their rarity and the advanced nature of the technology, they are worth millions of marks in the Union after the Cyborg Prohibition Law was put into place and the manufacturing of more implants illegalized.

Cyborg Prohibition Law: A law created by Emperor Titus Valerius and the Union Council, which made the creation of new cyborgs, the use of surgical implants, and robotic surgery illegal. Current cyborgs are allowed to remain as they are, but the creation of new cyborgs is strictly prohibited. New cyborgs and those assisting them are subject to execution or a lifetime sentence in prison.

Federates ("feds"): The local police force in the Union.

The Forgetting: A memory loss experienced by new cyborgs.

Governor/Governess: Rulers of the thirteen planets within the Crescent Star System after the Union was founded.

Grandstand: One of thirteen planets within the Crescent Star System. It is the home of Cirque du Borge and also where undesirables are often transported, including dragons.

Jinx: A moon outside of the Crescent Star System known for harboring pirates, thieves, and others who evade the law.

Marks: Paper money in the Union.

Obedient: The ship of Cirque du Borge.

Orthodocks: One of thirteen planets within the Crescent Star System.

Redwood Conservatory: An elite all-girls boarding school through college that specializes in performing arts.

Rift: A city on the planet Harvest that is ruled over by the Kabir family.

The Smoke Ring: A neighboring solar system of the Crescent Star System.

Union: An alliance between the thirteen planets of the Crescent Star System, with a leadership comprised of an emperor and an intergalactic council called the Union Council.

Union Council: The council consisting of twelve governors and governesses. They assist the emperor in ruling over the Crescent Star System.

Watchmen: Hired mercenaries at Cirque du Borge.

ACKNOWLEDGMENTS

To my husband, confidant, and partner in all things nerdy, Kevin. Thank you for encouraging me not to wait to pursue my dreams, for the endless hours you willingly gave as I blubbered over things big and small in the journey to prepare this book for publication, and for your love and support. None of this would be possible without you.

To my son, Kylan, thank you for helping me be brave enough to take chances. You have opened my eyes in so many ways. I look forward—with slight trepidation—to the day when you are old enough to read this book.

To my family of origin, thank you for encouraging me to chase my dreams with abandon.

To my grandparents, Gloria and Don, thank you for investing in my dreams and for your faith in me. I wish you were here to scold me about the contents of this book.

To my in-laws, thank you for all the times you watched Kylan so I could play pretend with my characters. This book would have taken a lot longer without you.

To my nerd squad and to Pat, thank you for always endorsing my nerdy eccentricities. Renaissance faires are a stomping ground for inspiration, and found families even more so.

To my friends, Sathya Achia Abraham and Elena McPhillips, thank you both for your friendship and for reading many of my terrible manuscripts before this one. You guys are the real heroes.

To my critique partners, Briston Brooks, Claire Winn, and Cortney Radocaj, without you this book wouldn't be what it is. Thank you for pushing me to be a better writer.

To my alpha reader and friend, M. L. Tishner, thank you for weeding through the earlier versions of this manuscript and sharing in my excitement throughout this process.

To my other beta readers, Angela Teal and Kevin, thank you for sharing your time and eyes with me.

To Jenna Moreci, Courtney (Lyra Parish/Kennedy Fox), Sacha Black, the Wander Writers group, and so many others, thank you for answering my self-publishing questions. I would be floundering without you.

To my editors, Kaitlyn Johnson (developmental editing), Jenny Sims (copyediting), and Judy Zweifel (proofreading), thank you for your hard work and diligence in editing my work and preparing it for the eyes of readers.

To Kylie Stewart, thank you for sharing your voice with me. It has been amazing to hear how you depict Gwen, Bastian, and Rora.

To Tara Spruit, thank you for bringing my characters to life in your character art.

To David Gardiner, thank you for making me feel like a steampunk goddess in your photoshoot and for the most epic author headshot.

To the fans of iWriterly, thank you for your unending support. Without you, I wouldn't be where I am today.

To all those not specifically listed in this acknowledgment, thank you for your impact on my life and this story. This was a journey I couldn't have done without the help of so many.

ABOUT THE AUTHOR

Meg LaTorre is a bestselling science fiction and fantasy author, YouTube darling and founder of iWriterly, creator of the free query critique platform, Query Hack, co-host of the Publishable show, and blogger (*Writer's Digest*, Savvy Authors, Writers Helping Writers, et al.). Formerly, she worked at a literary agency, and she has a background in magazine publishing, medical/technical writing, and journalism.

Photo Credit: David Gardiner

In her free time, Meg enjoys spending time with her husband and son, running, going to Renaissance faires and comic cons, and napping.

To learn more about Meg, subscribe to her YouTube channel (iWriterly) and newsletter, follow her on Twitter (@MegLaTorre) and Instagram (@Meg_LaTorre), support iWriterly on Patreon for insiders on upcoming books and the latest YouTube videos, or visit www.iWriterly.com.